Praise for the novels of Night's Edge

"Science fiction author Czerneda will charm fantasy readers with multidimensional characters, a vivid setting, and powerful themes of hope and renewal."   —*Locus*

"A warm and intricate fantasy opus with large themes woven into a charming story."
— Charlaine Harris, *New York Times*-bestselling author

"*A Turn of Light* is deft, beautiful storytelling."
—Ed Greenwood, bestselling creator of the Forgotten Realms

"Infused with idyllic enchantment, Julie Czerneda weaves a heart-warming bucolic tale, packed with magic both wild and strange—a top-notch fantasy read!"
—Janny Wurts, author of the Wars of Light and Shadow series

"Luminous and beguiling. With Marrowdell and its enchanting in-habitants, Julie Czerneda has conjured a world that readers can sink into and disappear. I lost myself to this tale that is, by turns, lovely, lyrical, and thrilling. This book is a feast for the mind and the heart."
— Lesley Livingston, author of *The Valiant*

"Known for her powerful and insightful sf novels, Czerneda brings the same exacting sensibility to her brilliant fantasy debut.... Fans of L. E. Modesitt Jr. and Charles de Lint will love this fantastic and magical fable."   —*Library Journal* (starred)

"There's so much magic and wonder to be discovered in this world.... Absolutely stunning, with little touches and major flourishes that really bring that magical realm to life."   —Beauty in Ruins

"An enchanting and gentle fable, ri   will Je   and cha   ou will love."   —Charles de Lint, Wor   or

T0182609

A CHANGE OF PLACE

Eldad

JULIE E. CZERNEDA

DAW BOOKS
New York

Cover illustration by Matt Stawicki
Flam's Map by Roger and Julie E. Czerneda
Other maps and sketch of Bay of Shades by Julie E. Czerneda
Author photo by Roger Czerneda
Edited by Katie Hoffman

DAW Book Collectors No. 1961

DAW Books
An imprint of Astra Publishing House
dawbooks.com
DAW Books and its logo are registered trademarks of
Astra Publishing House

Printed in the United States of America

Library of Congress Cataloging-in-Publication Data
Names: Czerneda, Julie, 1955- author.
Title: A change of place / Julie E. Czerneda.
Description: First edition. | New York : DAW Books, 2024. |
Series: Night's edge ; #3
Identifiers: LCCN 2024023571 (print) | LCCN 2024023572 (ebook) |
ISBN 9780756410698 (hardcover) | ISBN 9780698193543 (ebook)
Subjects: LCGFT: Fantasy fiction. | Novels.
Classification: LCC PR9199.3.C92 C47 2024 (print) | LCC PR9199.3.C92
(ebook) | DDC 813/.54--dc23/eng/20240604
LC record available at https://lccn.loc.gov/2024023571
LC ebook record available at https://lccn.loc.gov/2024023572

First edition: September 2024
10 9 8 7 6 5 4 3 2 1

To Betty Helena Whipp Czerneda

As I write this, Mum, you're about to celebrate your 100th birthday in the company of three generations of family, including me. You'll be ever-so-smart in your pretty spring hat and, I must say, will look not a day over a healthy, happy 80. You've still that mischievous twinkle in your eye. That smile, brimming with delight at the world and warmth for those in it. We've been official family since your 52nd birthday (celebrated at the stroke of midnight at our wedding), but I've felt like your daughter since the first night we met, when, with that twinkle and smile, looking ever-so-smart, you gave me a big squeeze before you left to go dancing.

Thank you for everything.

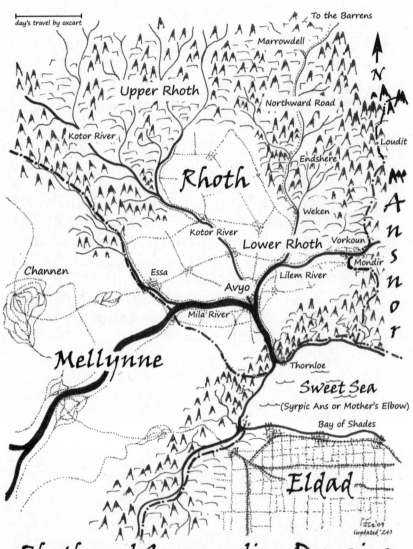

day's travel by oxcart

To the Barrens

Marrowdell

Upper Rhoth

Northward Road

Kotor River

Loudit

Rhoth

Endshere

Weken

Kotor River

Lower Rhoth

Vorkoun

Channen

Essa

Avyo

Lilem River

Mondir

Mila River

Mellynne

Thornloe

Sweet Sea

(Syrpic Ans or Mother's Elbow)

Bay of Shades

Eldad

JC₂ '09
(updated '24)

A N S N O R

Rhoth and Surrounding Domains

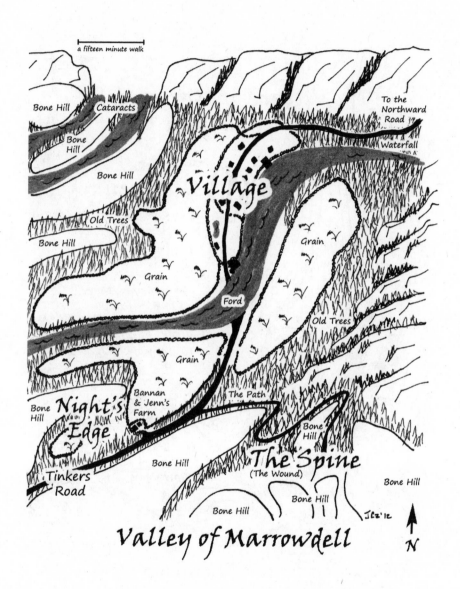

a fifteen minute walk

Bone Hill

Cataracts

Bone Hill

Bone Hill

To the Northward Road

Waterfall

Old Trees

Bone Hill

Village

Grain

Grain

Ford

Old Trees

Grain

Bone Hill

Night's Edge

Bannan & Jenn's Farm

The Path

Bone Hill

The Spine
(The Wound)

Bone Hill

Tinkers Road

Bone Hill

Bone Hill

Bone Hill

Jcz '12

Bone Hill

Valley of Marrowdell

N

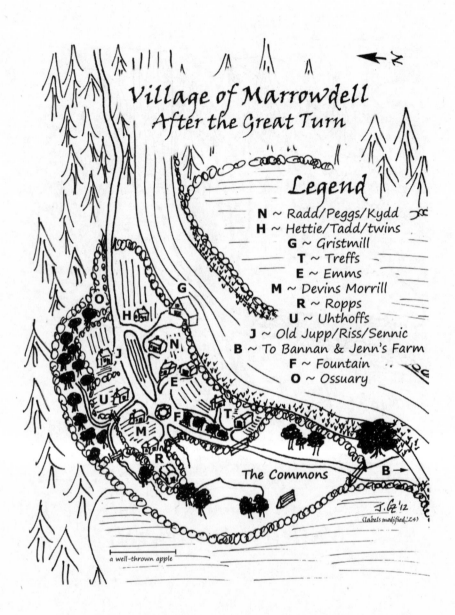

Flam's Almost Useless But Hopefully Blessed Map of The Journey to Vorkoun

This way to Rhoth ← Home (Loudit)
and the Northward
Road to Marrowdell
(Roche's home).

Stars Witness the three of us are bold and brave and worthy.

First Night.
Inn we can't afford.
Sleep in stable.

Stars protect us from falling rocks!

Stars Witness we don't catch lice.

Stars protect our friend.

Second Night.
Inn we can afford.
Take a bath.

Where we leave Ansnor.

Stars Blessed we'll be on time for class.

Stars Grace we are allowed into Rhoth. We can't afford the trip back.

This way to Avyo, capital of Rhoth and past to Eldad. ←

Vorkoun and the university.

Mondir
(Ansnan again)

Lilem River

RJCe'24

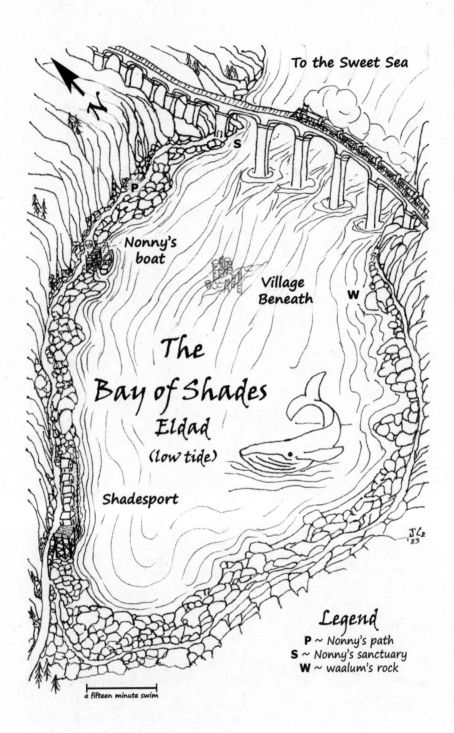

To the Sweet Sea

N

S

P

Nonny's boat

Village Beneath

W

The Bay of Shades

Eldad

(low tide)

Shadesport

JC₂
'23

a fifteen minute swim

Legend
P ~ Nonny's path
S ~ Nonny's sanctuary
W ~ waalum's rock

Prologue

THIRTEEN YEARS AGO, Within the World of Vineyards and Goats . . .
The three stood at the causeway's edge, red velvet cloaks flapping around their legs, leaning recklessly on the crumbling rail to stare out over the abyss.

Their focus was not the raging river at its base nor the immense valley it cut like a knife. Not once did they glance at the mighty bridges in the distance spanning the halves of Vorkoun, Rhoth's easternmost city, or regard the ancient stone towers that climbed the valley walls and each other. Their rapt attention was claimed by the far side of the valley, where the slope gentled alongside the river, becoming striped with vineyards nestled between fields of green and gold, pasture and barley. A cluster of large sturdy buildings stood within a copse of trees, protected from the chill north wind by the mountain rising at its back, a pastoral scene unlikely to stir any interest at all.

Or so it seemed to the small troop waiting by the carriage that had brought the three from Ansnor. The wind was heavy with damp, a storm brewing, but that wasn't what had the soldiers casting worried looks over their shoulders. In earlier, peaceful times, Ansnans had dwelt in this half of Vorkoun, calling it Mondir, full partners and friends of the Rhothans. Together, they'd carved this causeway to better connect their domains and foster trade, safely above the spring floods.

Now the flat span of pavement and rail was home to feral goats and the wild dogs that hunted them, part of a disputed border stained with the blood of soldiers like these, who knew full well they trespassed.

The three exchanged words, then the leftmost gave a curt nod. Raising a filmy scarf, she let the wind pluck it from her grasp. The soldiers watched it fly up, dance lightly in the air, then fall at their feet.

A roar shook the causeway. The horses reared and fought to run. Holding their reins, the soldiers cursed and shouted their own fear. The three stood unflinching, faced outward into a rising cloud of acrid dust.

As it settled, the soldiers saw what had happened.

The pastures and fields, vineyards and buildings were gone, buried beneath a sweeping talus of rubble. Above, the mountain bore a new and terrible scar, marking where part of it had given way.

And a young soldier named Edis Donovar reeled with the rock's anguish, it being her family's gift to hear stone. To hide her reaction, she bent to take up the scarf. It bore a crest with a fox and sunflower.

Rhothan. The enemy.

She dropped it hurriedly. Took a quick step to distance herself even as a sigh of wind caught the scarf and sent it soaring again.

It drifted across the river valley to land in the ruins.

Where no one saw the scarf be pulled, ever so slowly, beneath the ground.

Four Hundred and Seventy Years Ago, Within the World of Toads and Dragons . . .

There was magic, enough. Beings who used it, or were it, or both. There was sky and earth and seasons, of a sort, though it didn't snow. How could it? Water stayed where it was summoned, in fountains and wells, and what rained from sky to earth in its seasons was mimrol. Silver and warm, mimrol carved rivers and filled lakes, spreading magic as it flowed.

Dragons hunted the air, kruar the ground, and toads, though cousins, stayed out of sight. Terst farmed and built, bringing peace where it could flourish, and avoided dragons and kruar too. All had their place, whatever they thought of it, or if they even did.

But there were those, the sei, who thought a great deal. Sei pondered what was beyond the ken of others, being as curious as they were powerful, and one fateful day the sei wondered . . . was there more?

And one day wondered . . . could they touch it?

And all would have remained as it was, with magic enough and peace, but on a day when the light of an unseen sun dimmed, on a day when anything seemed possible, one sei reached from the world of dragons and toads, into that of vineyards and goats . . .

Tearing both worlds open.

Making both worlds bleed.

Spilling magic.

The sei mended that tear, as best it could. Used itself like thread. Held on, accepting that penance.

While dragons and toads, as well as kruar and terst, explored what the sei had wrought.

Today . . .

There's a world of vineyards and goats.

There's a world of dragons and toads.

Writhing through both is the edge where they meet, for the sei holds, still.

Magic, wild and potent, lives there.

And so does Jenn Nalynn.

ONE

*J*ENN NALYNN SAT at her ease on a chair unlike any in a Marrowdell home but every bit as comfortable, inside a many-sided building grown from living blue crystal and stone and lit by lamps that burned mimrol, not oil. The walls were cluttered with extraordinary art from far away places and the tables with ordinary tools, and she was in the company of those who were friends.

If not flesh and blood.

A seeming any turn-born could assume at will, which is how those sitting with her appeared out of courtesy. Weathered faces with ruddy cheeks and noses, deep blue eyes and bright red lips—they wore masks of magic to shield others from the blinding light of the Verge that filled them.

Being turn-born herself since last fall, Jenn wore one as well, though hers had been made by a house toad who'd first swallowed one of the sei's white moths, and the mask was now, as far as she could tell, stuck to her face for good. Thankfully she couldn't feel it nor did it show; she looked exactly as she should and remembered, and Peggs, her sister, agreed.

Light filled a turn-born because their skin had become glass and their bodies hollow, a consequence—there were always those—necessitating a stuffing, of a sort, be consumed as soon as possible after a turn-born's nature asserted itself. The material had to be from the edge, since turn-born were of that realm as well and craved it, and each chose what caught their fancy, taking their name from it. Sand. Riverstone. Clay. Tooth—filled with jagged teeth Jenn had been relieved to discover were from ancient sharks. Fieldstone. Chalk. Flint.

While Jenn herself had been tricked into swallowing a sei's pearl-like tears and was now something else again. Not that she regretted it, for by so doing she'd been able to heal the sei who held the edge and Verge together and safe, but her insides made her different and, according to the turn-born who above all valued order and restraint, unpredictable. They worried, she knew, about her being the only turn-born in the edge, with no other to disagree with her expectations and curb her power, so she did her utmost to heed their advice and not wish at all.

Mostly.

The turn-born of the Verge were terst—a people outwardly like Jenn and those of her world but of this one—born at the turn, as she'd been. Sunset, in other words, when the light of her world mingled with that from the Verge, revealing the magic of both. According to Wisp, terst mothers-to-be, aided by their healers, did all they could to avoid the tragedy of giving birth at that moment, for such children were lost to their kind, abandoned immediately after birth at the gate of the turn-born enclave or, at times, kept until located by the turn-born and taken before reaching the cusp of maturity.

Their number varied: never more than a few. Seven there were now. Five sat with Jenn, Tooth and Flint about other business. Or avoided her, having been among those who'd voted to end her life not so long ago, though turn-born weren't inclined to dwell on the past and more likely, Jenn reminded herself, the pair were busy packing their wagons. The turn-born were about to leave the Verge, being also tinkers who traded within the edge. They'd return in four days, at sunset on what was for her the spring equinox, when the light of the Verge and edge would be in exquisite Balance and the boundary between its thinnest.

In practical terms, the Balance was the easiest time to cross with other objects, such as wagons filled with goods from the edge, but it signified, Jenn believed, more than that.

She sensed its approach, as if she caught the first notes of a distant song and strained to hear more, or sniffed a hint of sun-warmed rose.

This would be her first Balance as a turn-born, why, in part, she was here, and why now, with the bundle between her feet.

Kaj, the little white dog, curled like a question mark on Mistress Sand's lap; how a dog survived in the Verge, let alone lived this long, being less a puzzle than its origin. Shortly after becoming turn-born but before gaining, as Sand told it, a proper respect for her new power, Sand had found the dog in the edge and loved it at once, having a hole where her heart had been on losing her family. She'd wished the dog to thrive and stay with her forever. And so it did and would.

Such a wish by a turn-born was called an expectation, for it would be answered whether in the Verge or along the edge, including Marrowdell. Still, if any of the existing turn-born had disagreed about the dog, the magic would have failed and the dog perish.

The Verge and all who lived in it were within the threads of every turn-born expectation woven into its magic and shape. Jenn felt them everywhere, like a complex tapestry stretched across time. It was just as well, her dragon had assured her, that it took turn-born ages to agree on anything new, for the Verge was perilous and wonderful as it was.

As for the dog, Jenn quite liked to think those other turn-born had been, in this instance if no other, sentimental.

"More, Sweetling, na?" The slight accent, that soft "na" at the end of a question, were common to them when they spoke Rhothan— a courtesy for their guest. And likely welcome practice since they'd been forced to study the languages of the edge. According to Wisp, the turn-born were unable to agree on which tongue mattered most to know—and were loath to use magic to change themselves in any way, a feeling Jenn heartily shared.

Otherwise, in the Verge the turn-born spoke as Wisp, without sound at all.

"Yes, please." She held out her cup for Master Riverstone. The beer had been brewed here from grain harvested in Marrowdell, thus of both realms, and the drink satisfied a craving they shared—though one she hadn't felt until tasting it.

Ancestors Blessed, their supply of it must be running low by now, as Marrowdell's was of almost everything—except for an abundance of sour pickles—after a long winter with summer and the next harvest months away. Jenn hastily lowered her cup before he could pour. "I've changed my mind, thank you."

Mistress Sand chuckled. "Didn't I say so, na?" she said, as if following up on an argument over before Jenn's arrival. "Our sweetling has a good heart. Thinks of us, she does, and is kind."

Jenn blushed.

"Now, what have you brought us, na?" Sand's bright eyes fixed on the bundle.

Chalk cleared a table and Jenn put her bundle on top, resting her hands on it, suddenly unsure. The turn-born came to stand around the table and, feeling their rapt attention, she cleared her throat. "As I told you—" Sand having insisted on hearing the latest gossip the instant she'd arrived "—Hettie's had her twins, and Peggs and Wen will have their babies before you come again. We—" She and Bannan, who'd thought of it. Plus the fathers—Tadd, Kydd, and Wainn, though the latter had been more puzzled than convinced—and those grandparents and relatives and friends able to keep a secret, which excluded the Treffs, most of the Ropps, and Devins.

Dizzied by names, Jenn paused to recall where she was. "We want to surprise them with special birthing day gifts," she finished in a rush. Hettie's coming slightly after the fact wouldn't bother that cheerful person one bit. "Gifts from outside Marrowdell. We collected some items to trade for them."

Her gaze strayed involuntarily to the magnificent works gracing the walls. Paintings in different styles, their frames exquisite. Sculptures and carvings. Bells and whistles. Works unique and rare and doubtless expensive, telling her a great deal about the taste and eye of those who'd brought them here, and she'd have been daunted—

Except those with her knew Marrowdell. They'd appreciate the items she'd brought were, to the villagers, unique and rare and irreplaceable in their own way. With greater confidence, Jenn set out her trove one by one.

An ornate, if dented, candlestick that had been Gallie's and before that Lorra's; a pretty wooden bead carved by Zehr, threaded on a string braided by Alyssa Ropp; a book of poetry once the Treffs'; the tapestried cushion Riss had sewn for their new home; Bannan's metal soldier's cup; and a large pine cone, oozing sap from its tip. "Wainn sent this," she explained, touching the cone with a careful finger—not that there was ever need to explain Wainn.

Last but not least, the antique leather tube that had held her map, with its gold clasp and Larmensu crest. Bannan hadn't wanted her to give it away, but that was, Jenn knew, what gifts were for—to be given as many times as possible. As had everything she'd brought.

Perhaps not the pine cone.

"What do you think?" Jenn looked at Sand, her eyes alight with hope. "Will this buy four birthing day gifts?"

Sand gave each item her close attention, especially the leather tube, which she picked up and examined, trying the clasps. Done, she gave Jenn a short businesslike nod. "Trust us to choose them, na?"

"I do," Jenn replied, for she did. Every fall the tinkers brought to Marrowdell what was needful and of use, along with treats and the toys Riverstone made the children. They'd know what would be suitable, no matter what the marketplace, for they traveled the entire edge.

"Would you like to know where we go, na?"

Sand had caught her fairly, Jenn this very day having pored over her beloved map wondering where—other than, as her dragon said, somewhere warmer and less damp than Marrowdell in spring—the turn-born would travel this time. Despite that curiosity, she found herself shaking her head. "I'd like to hear all about it once you're back."

"Meet us here at the Balance, Sweetling, and we'll give you what we've found." A wink and wave over the table. "We're very good traders. Maybe this will buy a little more, na?"

Jenn forced herself to ignore the odd tingle she felt at the word *Balance* and remember her manners. Bannan had told her the tinkers he knew would expect to be compensated for their effort. This was, however strange to think within the Verge, their vocation and livelihood. "If there's extra," she stated firmly, "please keep it for yourselves."

The five laughed at this, but not unkindly, and Sand said, "You brought us ample compensation, Sweetling."

And with that, Riverstone picked up the pine cone, bringing it to his nose and closing his eyes as he sniffed. He passed it, using both hands, to Chalk, who did the same then passed it with equal reverence to Fieldstone. Around it went, the humblest gift, until all had smelled it but Sand.

When it was her turn, she lifted the cone at Jenn, as if in toast, before bending her face over it for a long moment. When at last she raised her head, she smiled blissfully. "Marrowdell."

Wainn had known. How was an interesting question, but Jenn couldn't help but enjoy their obvious pleasure. She would make sure to tell him.

"Time to go, Sweetling," Sand announced, making a little shooing motion with her hands. "We've much to do." A wicked grin. "And your dragon will fuss if you're late."

"But I've questions—" Jenn protested even as she moved, "—about the Balance. About—" so much, her mind reeled for an instant.

Sand made her clicking sound, tongue to teeth. Dismissal. "Cross at that turn, Sweetling, and you'll learn all you need. Now, away with you."

But when Sand brought Jenn to the gate, instead of farewell, she leaned close and whispered, "You left out news of your truthseer, the handsome Bannan. Does he still please you, na?"

Thinking of her love, Jenn Nalynn's answering smile came from the bottom of her heart and lit her eyes.

Seeing it, Sand laughed and grabbed her in a hug, squeezing until Jenn let out a squeak and felt most thoroughly loved. When done, her friend cautioned, "Be turn-born, Sweetling, till you cross. The dimming is nigh."

To her the Verge looked its surreal and wondrous normal, if such a word applied to a place where the sky might be underfoot and mountains hang down, not to mention the feathery purple fronds on what seemed trees and the achingly rich silver of mimrol, filling the little lake in front of her, but she understood the caution. Hadn't Wisp warned her not to tarry?

Thinking of her dearest and oldest friend, Jenn smiled again. "My dragon will keep me safe," she said.

Knowing it was true.

Pointless. Perilous. Wisp lay on the seductively warm sand of the Verge by the lake of mimrol reciting all the words related to his judgement of the girl seeking out the terst turn-born on a whim.

Yes, there'd been a time he'd risked a great deal to ask Sand to teach the new turn-born what she needed to know, but this excursion was assuredly not a matter, as then, of life and death.

He'd hoped she'd miss them, but, whether by wish or chance, she'd arrived just as they'd readied to leave, in time, it now appeared, to linger close to the dimming, when the Verge roused to the hunt.

Foolish. Frivolous.

Not that the girl was either, but she did care more about others than herself. While her good heart shielded Marrowdell from the dangerous excesses others might expect from a turn-born, and a naive one at that, it also, the dragon sighed, led to actions such as this.

Going where he couldn't protect her.

Trusting those he knew to be cruel and capricious.

Were they having tea?

His claws dug in. Eyes popped open in protest and the sand beneath tried to slide away. The dragon dug in more firmly.

They'd used the turn-borns' crossing, that much at least. Hers was too close for comfort to the mad sei and his to other dragons.

She trusted his judgment.

The light of the Verge, ever-changing, ever-fretful, always magnificent, was fading. There'd be no night, as in her world, but the lessening encouraged those with fang and claw to seek unprotected throats. It was, Wisp sighed again, a glorious time. One he need no longer spend protected in his sei-built sanctuary.

Because of the girl, her great heart, and care for others. For that, but most of all for love of her, he would lie outside the turn-borns' gate until she came out or he died.

Wisp rested his long jaw on a rock, wild violet eyes aimed at the turn-borns' enclave, gloomily certain the girl had brought biscuits with her. *His!* An acquired taste, to be sure, one other dragons would mock—if they dared.

His mood improved at the thought.

Grew even lighter when figures appeared. Soured slightly when the terst turn-born called Sand took hold of the girl as if she'd the rights of, say, a sister, but soared when the girl headed straight for him, without her bundle, and he saw how happy she was.

And still-flesh, which was vulnerable, so when Jenn Nalynn came close, her every step a dance of joy, Wisp gave her a stern look. ~You're late. Now it's the dimming and hunters are out. Be turn-born, Dear Heart, and safe.~

She wrapped her arms around his neck—carefully, for most of him was hard and all of him sharp—"But I am safe, Wisp. I'm with you."

A dragon might swell with pride at that. Or take advantage.

Wisp, once lord of his kind and the girl's protector since her birth, sent a breeze to toss her hair, then said firmly. ~Turn-born, now. For me.~

And felt her softness become glass.

Only then did he launch himself into the air, to hover over her as she walked the few steps down the beach to the turn-borns' crossing, one of the spots of weakness in the boundary allowed by the sei, who hadn't been pleased by the war of dragon and kruar and set these restrictions, and punished those in charge.

Including him.

It had brought him the girl. For that—only that—he was grateful.

The girl, able to sense the crossing in either form, stopped just before it to look up at him. "Come home with me, Wisp." A dimple. "There'll be biscuits."

And damp and cold, it being Marrowdell's spring. Wisp swooped down to stand beside her. ~I'll cross here with you, Dear Heart,~ he told her.

Then spend the night in the warmth of the Verge.

Still. ~Will there be biscuits tomorrow?~

Her laugh was a promise.

TWO

*I*N MORE SOUTHERLY lands, or those warmed by a sea, spring announced itself with flowers and the appearance of sweet green shoots. In Marrowdell, high in Rhoth's northern reaches, spring's arrival brought gloomy skies, bone-chilling nights, and mud.

It could bring peril as well. Marrowdell's river, a mild, gentle flow alongside the village and its mill the rest of the year, easily forded on foot, each spring took its inevitable share of snowmelt from the hills beyond. Most years, the excess water churned and tumbled safely out of the valley, passing through the cataracts between the Bone Hills and over the waterfalls beyond the mill.

Jenn Nalynn had been twelve the spring when floes of ice dammed those falls, raising the river. The same spring a curious toddler, Cheffy Ropp, ventured on an untrustworthy shore and slipped in—his mother, Mimm, leaping after—both disappearing beneath the dark deadly flow—both up again, the mother waist deep and struggling, her son in her arms, crying for help.

Hearing, Uncle Horst hadn't hesitated. The former soldier had charged into the river after them. He reached the mother, who thrust her son into his arms as she lost her footing and sank.

They'd found Mimm's body later that spring, cradled in a mass of branches ground to shore by the flood, as if the river gave her back for burial.

A river, Ancestors Wary and Worried, with its ice breaking up late again this spring.

When Jenn had moved into Bannan's farmhouse after the Midwinter Beholding, she'd never dreamt anything would keep her and Peggs from visiting one another regularly. All winter long they'd walked over the frozen river, the ice a convenience.

But these past two days, jagged floes had made the ford too dangerous to attempt, cutting them off from the village.

Jenn shivered under her cloak. It seemed impossible that last night she'd walked in the Verge, whose only season was a summerlike warmth. No warmth here. Not yet, at least, and hearing the ice snap and snarl in the distance made it feel colder.

Wish the river safely calm again, even warm? Hurry spring on its way?

Ancestors Tempted and Tormented, she could.

And mustn't. Ice and rivers were like seasons, forces assuredly not safe to tamper with—

As if in agreement, there came a crack like thunder followed by a horrid grinding crash that set her teeth on edge.

She was not to think about it, that was all. This morning, she'd distracted herself so well imagining the turn-borns' mysterious travels and the hoped-for birthing day gifts, she'd almost burnt the biscuits. Which, as consequences went, hadn't been terrible.

Mud now. Jenn nodded, glad of something safe to fuss about. Spring meant mud on livestock and clothing. Mud coating barn floors and cart wheels. Muddy paths that sprouted spears of ice overnight, thawing by day to sticky goo liable to swallow boots. Nothing moved with any speed but returning flocks of waterfowl, and they knew better than land.

Mud, she decided—sharing responsibility for a home and barn and paths—was her proper concern.

Careful of the basket over her arm, Jenn took mincing steps along the packed rim of tired snow beside the muddy trail to the barn, determined not to add another layer of thick brown to her already coated boots, a gift from her beloved truthseer. Gifts she quite liked. Boots, however, were nowhere near as useful in spring as Bannan Larmensu believed, prone to fill up, fall off, or get irretrievably stuck in the mud.

If they did get stuck, she'd be back to bare, washable feet. Jenn stopped to give the closest mucky puddle a wistful look.

A breeze tickled her left ear. Formed words, that being how Wisp spoke in the edge. "Dry the nasty stuff, Dear Heart." A chuckle in her right ear. "You can, you know."

Being turn-born and magic, her wishes so potent Marrowdell itself would answer, regardless of consequence. Her dragon, she sighed to herself, was a little too fond of that perilous power.

A power she mustn't use. "What I know is I won't," Jenn insisted and, just in case, hurriedly thought of pots with baked-on custard bits, that being her latest difficulty in the kitchen. Heart's Blood, there was no way to know what might happen. She'd asked Bannan, who'd grown up in Vorkoun beside a river larger and more powerful than theirs, and seen his dear face go white. He'd told her the threat wasn't only the water they could see, but what was still to melt and come, and stressed that any flood risk here would be multiplied for those downstream.

Meddle, he meant, and a rush of unnatural floodwater could savage lands like Endshere, where people lived and Aunt Sybb be traveling through on her way north.

Being very much like a bird herself, tiny and frail, but with a huge heart and unyielding courage, their aunt, the Lady Mahavar, would be even now on the Northward Road, coming like the first warmth of summer to Marrowdell to be with them. A change of place, she'd say on arriving, that did such wonders for the heart, hers and theirs, and nothing must—

As Aunt Sybb would say, "Worry wears body out," a saying she'd typically follow with, "Work, not worry." Hard to imagine what she'd say to an overzealous dragon, considering their aunt did all she could to ignore Marrowdell's magical denizens, but Jenn planned to ask her advice on this and so much—

For now, she stood as straight as possible, slipping a bit on the rounded snowpack, to fix her sternest gaze on a spot midair that seemed, for an instant, to shimmer like wings. "Please stop mentioning it, Wisp." In any way, especially not to simply to avoid the inconvenience of boots, which mattered not to Wisp.

Especially not, Ancestors Besotted and Bewildered, when she wanted most to stay the woman she was and Bannan loved. Flesh and blood, not a figure of glass and pearl and light, and that wanting, she'd learned from Mistress Sand, was critical. If she let go, if she forgot what she remembered herself to be, she wouldn't be at all.

Jenn firmed her grip on herself, the basket, and the present. Wisp hated anything damp and utterly loathed mud. And flew more than walked, making this particular visit about something else. She lifted the napkin, sensing his rapt attention. Steam rose, courtesy of the hot biscuits within, sweetened with the last of their dried summerberries. Larders grew bare, another reliable sign of spring.

"I left you some in the kitchen, Wisp." Where dragon and house toad spent most of their time, keeping warm by the cookstove. "So you don't have to come with me to the barn," she added hopefully.

"Oh, but I do, do, do!" A naughty little wind plucked at the napkin. She had to grab it or see it fly. The wind spun her cloak around her and Jenn swayed. "You've no idea how much."

Oh dear.

Bannan had reminded her about today's task, one he would be in the midst of at this very moment.

"Is this about Scourge?" Jenn asked her dragon warily.

In answer, the wind gave her a playful nudge.

Bannan and the huge ugly horse glared at one another across the barrow of grooming tools. They'd been glaring long enough the barn's house toad had closed its eyes, apparently asleep, and the red mud splattered on the floor, walls, and rafters—and the man's clothes—begun to dry, looking like spots of dried blood.

He'd not, the truthseer vowed, flinch first. He threw the barn wall an anxious look. Fields and hedges separated their farm from Marrowdell's pretty little river. In summer, its sleepy murmur would be drowned out by bird song—

Impossible to miss the river's deepening roar of discontent now, a sound all too familiar to someone raised by the mighty Lilem, a river wider than this valley and plied by steamships and fishers summer through fall. In spring? The powerful river would scour its banks and do its utmost to eradicate Vorkoun, the city that dared straddle it. His mother's estate, the Larmensu family home, might have been situated a prudent distance and elevation above, but in his years there, floodwater had threatened it twice.

Rivers were dangerous. A fear Bannan had done his cautious best to share with Jenn, knowing what she—

The idiot beast abruptly shuddered his hide from cropped mane to tail, sending up clouds of loose hair except from the fresh muddy patch over his withers. "MORE!" The words came as a harsh little breeze to his ear.

This being no horse at all but Scourge, his mount these long years and, as he'd learned in Marrowdell, a magical being called a kruar.

If he looked deeper with his true sight, Bannan knew what he'd see. The glossy black hide would disappear, replaced by a lacework of dreadful scars where Scourge's natural armor had been ripped away by his own kind, the deepest wounds across the broad chest and up both shoulders. Instead of the dense short mane, a series of sharp, flat edges, like broken swords, rose along his neck, and the wonder was, the disguise carried over to the touch.

"No. You'll only roll in the mud again, idiot beast, and undo all my work." Bannan dropped the currycomb in the barrow and dusted off his hands. "I'm done."

A disdainful curl of lip, exposing fang. A red rim to the eye glaring down at him. "NOT DONE."

Bannan folded his arms across his chest, determined to win this once. Scourge testing him wasn't new. He had for years, starting that misty morning in a Larmensu paddock when the creature had got it in his thick and stubborn skull a young and terrified truthseer was his new rider.

He spared a moment's pity for his young nephew Werfol, latest with the Larmensu gift. The boy had gone home to Vorkoun with two of the beasts vying for his attention. The truthseer smiled to himself. Those kruar weren't Scourge. And Werfol had his family—

"Bannan?"

—as did he. His smile grew warm.

Scourge purred, cocking back an ear. His stance went from belligerent to a loose-hipped nonchalance, fooling no one, least of all Jenn Nalynn.

The love of Bannan's life stepped gracefully around the kruar, avoiding the clouts of mud though her boots left their own, a most welcome basket over her arm. Scourge's nostrils flared and his lips made shameless come-hither motions.

"You eat rabbits," the truthseer reminded him. And anything else the kruar could catch, which in the dark days before Marrowdell included men. He shook off the memory, gladly falling into the gaze of Jenn's deep blue eyes.

He'd hidden his worry, last sunset, as they'd walked together down the Tinker's Road, the same road that ran by their farm. They'd held hands and skipped, laughing, over puddles. Reaching where the road ended in an impenetrable mass of tree trunks, he'd given her a quick kiss and stood back, so his love could leave him.

With her dragon, to see her friends to arrange gifts he'd—Ancestors Foolish and Frivolous—suggested, and if she hadn't come back—

A breeze, now warm and soft, found his ear. "Butter is good." A sly, "Cheese is better," made them both laugh.

"I didn't bring any," Jenn admitted. "Are you hungry?"

"Only because the doddering old fool would rather get brushed than hunt." This breeze came from above, hot with mischief, and Bannan briefly closed his eyes.

Ancestors Taunted and Teased, he should have known the dragon wouldn't miss the chance to ridicule the kruar. Old enemies become reluctant companions, the pair knew exactly how to torment each other.

To Bannan's surprise, Scourge blew a contented huff. "Jealous."

A fierce little wind stole the grooming implements from the barrow, spun them in midair, then aimed them at the kruar, who reared to the rafters to bat at them with his hooves.

"Wisp!"

The implements fell, some into mud, Bannan noticed ruefully. The barn felt suddenly less crowded.

Scourge dropped his forefeet to the ground, dipping his head in satisfaction. "Jealous."

"No cheese," Jenn Nalynn declared, her cheeks flushed.

"Jenn—!" A figure stumbled into the barn with that hoarse shout, supported by his grip on the stirrup of a real horse. Both limped. "Ban—"

Before Sennic finished his name, the truthseer was at his side, easing a shoulder under the other man's arm, taking his weight. Jenn came with him, soothing Perrkin, the soldier's aged gelding, her eyes dark with worry.

Man and mount were sopping wet and battered. They'd risked the ford to reach them, and there could, Bannan knew, be only one reason. "The river."

Chilled by Sennic's grim nod.

Until this year, Wisp had managed to avoid the noxious seasonal change called spring, remaining in the warmth of the Verge, crossing only if he sensed Jenn Nalynn in their meeting place, and then with reluctance. This was when Marrowdell turned on its inhabitants, landscape and weather conspiring. The ever-damp air filled with the stench of old rot. The ground turned treacherous. Bones came out of the snow.

The present state of its river, though, proved a revelation. The dragon followed it upstream, flying above the spray, admiring the violence below. Did anything in the Verge rival the sheer malice of those plates of ice spinning and tipping in its wild current, some larger than Bannan's house, intent on destroying all in their path?

The toads' queen, perhaps.

Wisp roared, cracking ice, dismissing the comparison. Like the little cousins who revered her, trapped in the edge by the sei's meddling and abandoned by the turn-born, their wicked queen couldn't leave the Verge.

Could she?

Jenn Nalynn's house toad had accomplished the feat. Granted, carried in a bag by the truthseer into the Verge with Jenn, then out again by the girl herself, surely options not at the queen's disposal.

The girl's toad was a disturbing creature. Bannan's was occasionally helpful, if inclined to fuss. Wisp suspected hers of ambition far beyond a little cousin. A house toad to watch.

By those less than a dragon. Wisp roared again, letting his shadow flow over the traitorous ice, leaving such thoughts behind.

THREE

*A*DREADFUL DREAM IS a portent of disaster offering neither hope nor useful warning.

They come to those who carry that magic in their blood, and Roche Morrill, once of Avyo, exiled to Marrowdell, and most recently of Ansnor, has dreamed six such dreams.

Roche's seventh dreadful dream took him on the road south and he never forgot it.

> *He stood in the shallows, the little river cool on his legs and sparkling but then it wasn't and the sky grew black and the water rose and the water spun and the rock beneath his feet cracked apart—*and something terrible *reached through to grab his legs and to pull him down—he sank into the depths and couldn't breathe—*

"Wake up."

Roche gasped for air. Fought to breathe.

Someone—by the grip it'd be Disel, the former smith's apprentice—shook him, hard. "Come out of it, Roche."

He pushed away her hands, squinting at the light blazing through the now-raised curtains of the coach. "It's morning?"

"Well past, my noisy friend." Flam, the third of their group, cocked his head as if listening. "Lost my bet."

"Driver's too busy with her team to care about squawks from in here." Disel dropped back on the bench beside Flam, across from Roche, taking hold of a strap as the coach bounced and rocked. She frowned at him. "What in a comet's icy hell was that? Another of your dreams?"

How well the pair knew him, including how he'd been bespelled to always tell the truth, if not that it had been a wish by his friend since childhood, Jenn Nalynn, who'd become impatient with his lies even as she'd become magic and beyond his reach.

Loving someone else after all.

"Yes. A dreadful dream." Remembering, Roche felt short of breath. "There was water. Blood. I drowned . . ."

A moment's pause, then both spoke at once. "Won't happen," Flam stated, waving the creased little map he'd begun sketching the day they'd left Loudit. "Stars grace, the road ahead is high and dry, the spring floods spent—"

While Disel said, louder and with a frown at the musician, "Every bridge is high and stone and safe."

The building of such marvels was what Roche hoped to learn in Vorkoun—but the dream's fear filled him. "We should turn back," he gasped, and wasn't wrong.

Disel leaned forward to rap him on the forehead with a knuckle. "Anything in there?" she quipped. More seriously, "We'd lose our scholarships to Riversbend."

"Roche, I swear by the stars we'll be fine," Flam insisted. "You'll see."

Ancestors Tried and Tested, the Ansnans were so innocent. Swaying with the coach despite his own hold on a strap, Roche knew such a dream meant profound change, maybe not to him but to those close to him.

And hadn't his latest cost lives? Yes, those of murderers and villains, but the result had shamed the people of Loudit, the lensmaker's illegal trade exposed, and sent the three of them on new paths, for the scholarships Disel feared to risk had come from the townsfolk, their share of the lensmaker's ill-gotten gains.

Though the events forewarned by that dreadful dream had led to his making a friend the like of which Roche couldn't have imagined. Edis Donovar, once an Ansnan soldier, had staggered, betrayed and dying, into his life.

Leaving it healed, her body changed by magic.

She'd saved him in turn, vowing friendship and to come at his call wherever her realm of magic, the Verge, touched his world, in places like Marrowdell and the mine where they'd met. Edis had assured him there were such in Vorkoun, not that either of them knew where. It added an adventurous flair to his journey, Roche determined to find her again, however long it took.

Until now. Heart's Blood, a dreadful dream presaged danger and strife, regardless any good to follow.

Flam and Disel waiting, faces full of concern.

For their sakes, Roche let out a shaky sigh. "High bridges, you say?"

"The highest north of the Sweet Sea," Disel confirmed. "And towers like you've never seen before."

Opening his map, Flam nodded fervently and pointed to where he'd written "Vorkoun," along with several exhortations to the Stars. "The biggest and best!"

"I want to see for myself," Roche assured his friends, the truth they needed to hear.

His despair he kept to himself.

Uncle Horst was older than her father, if not as old as Lorra Treff, his gray hair in full retreat. All of the villagers had grown thinner by spring, but lean and wiry was how he'd always been, while almost as strong as Davi the smith. Still, Jenn saw differences. He'd been wounded and almost died last fall, having been attacked by nyphrit while defending her. A winter spent healing had left him with a pronounced limp, and pain had deepened the creases at the corners of his eyes and mouth.

But a winter with Riss, whom he'd loved so long in secret, had lifted a darkness from him, giving hints to how he might have been in his youth before the burdens he carried descended. When he'd a name none here knew, not even Riss, to this day.

Now Uncle Horst sat shivering in their best chair, bruised and favoring his left wrist, with a nasty graze along his jaw he'd let her cover with salve. "Perrkin—Ancestors Blessed, Jenn, I don't know how the old boy did it." At the thought of his brave horse, Uncle Horst struggled to the edge of the chair. Dropped the blanket she'd put over his shoulders as he made to get up. "I must see to him—"

Jenn put a gentle hand on his arm. "You must get something warm inside you. Bannan will take excellent care of Perrkin." The gelding was sore and exhausted, but amazingly whole. Tough as nails, she thought, like his rider. "Have some tea, Uncle Horst."

She blushed, having forgotten, again, that wasn't the name he used now.

When a tiny Jenn misspoke the surname he'd given the villagers as Horst, the former soldier had added it to his own instead of correcting her, becoming Sennic Horst. Uncle Horst, family friend and protector of Marrowdell, he'd remained until marrying Riss Nahamm this past fall, when he'd gladly chosen her name and become Sennic Nahamm.

As if, Ancestors Grim and Grieving, a sequence of new names might wipe away his past, a past that included being paid by the Semanaryas of Avyo to hunt down and retrieve their daughter Melusine at any cost, only to be there at her death and Jenn Nalynn's birth.

Ignoring your troubles, Aunt Sybb would say, only tucked them under your bed to gather dust and grow, a saying she used in particular when first arriving in Marrowdell to discover a certain lack of housekeeping, but one Jenn felt applied to their often grim friend.

Of course, Jenn and her sister Peggs, and the rest of their generation, having grown up calling him Uncle Horst, as often as not they forgot. She looked for the little smile in his eyes, the one to say he'd noticed but didn't mind, to find nothing but worry.

Uncle Horst took the warm cup she pressed into his shaking

hand, the one missing two fingertips because he was a swordsman and had fought long ago. She steadied the cup until sure he'd a good hold, then asked very quietly, "What's going to happen?"

"Ice has dammed the waterfall. The river's slowed, spreading into the fields. Ancestors Blessed, that's what made it possible for us to cross at all." He paused to take a sip, then gave her a somber look over the rim of the cup. "There's no knowing how bad it'll get, Dear Heart. We've set the rest of the horses loose, to seek what safety they can on the Northward Road. Everyone's watching the water, ready to move to higher ground."

Meaning here. Jenn gave a mute nod, numbed by the thought of the villagers abandoning their homes.

His gaze shifted to the door. "Davi came behind me with supplies, just in case." A frown. "He should be here by now."

"The road will be slow going, even for Battle and Brawl." Which was true, the Tinkers Road more mud than passage.

If the worst happened, they wouldn't be the last to face that trial. And those come after needs must wade the icy water first.

She must be ready. Jenn leapt up to refill the kettle and set it on the stove, then added porridge to thicken the soup in the pot hung above the fire. Done, she turned. "What more can we do?"

Uncle Horst gave the contents of his cup unusual attention.

Ah. Jenn sat rather quickly across from him, folding her hands in her lap. Her heart, the heart she remembered, hammered in her chest, and she was almost afraid to ask, but knew she must. "What more do you think I can do?"

His pale eyes lifted. "Nothing safe to ask, Dear Heart, according to Master Dusom and Kydd. I'm guessing you know that."

Jenn bit her lip but nodded, relieved until he went on, "Wainn, however, insists you must rescue the hives."

Puzzled, she asked faintly, "Aren't the bees asleep in them?"

"I assume that's why. They'll drown when the flood reaches the orchard."

When. Jenn shied from the word, with its urgent temptation to act, then had a better thought. Wisp played with the bees in summer, trapping them in flowers and tumbling them in air. Surely he'd be willing to save them for her. "I'll take care of the bees," she said, in better cheer as Bannan came in the door.

He looked a question.

"Wisp will move the bees to higher ground," she explained hastily, to forestall any concern.

Forgetting she'd yet to ask her dragon.

Wisp, the truthseer admitted, could be helpful. Just not, in his experience, in any way expected. But they'd more pressing problems. "Davi's team is mired on the road. The mud," he added unnecessarily.

Jenn rose to her feet. "The poor lads." Meaning, he was sure, Battle and Brawl. Not that she wouldn't sympathize with Davi Treff, but the big smith was capable of pulling out his own boots. Ancestors Mighty and Determined, he'd already slogged his way up the road to the farmyard to ask for help, only to turn around again.

"I'll come." Sennic rose only to stop, bracing himself with a hand on the chair back, lips gone white. "I'll come," he gritted out, eyes daring them to argue as he straightened.

Bannan gave a brief, respectful nod. "Davi freed the horses. He asks for our help to pull the cart the rest of the way." And a challenge that would be; the big wheels were sure to be deep in the mud, given its heavy load. The road to the farm was in no better shape than the paths they'd used in the marches where, each dreary spring, they'd been forced to abandon what couldn't be carried on their backs.

Bannan shook off his doubts.

Jenn, in the midst of donning her shawl, lifted her head as if she'd heard them, her blue eyes almost purple. "We'll take it across the field instead."

The men glanced at one another. Marrowdell's fields were, from harvest till snowmelt, the domain of hidden creatures who objected, violently, to any trespass. They'd killed Bannan's strayed ox between one step and the next. Whisperers, some in the village called them, but he knew them as efflet. "Are you certain, Dearest Heart?" Bannan asked carefully.

No mistaking the purple now, and if he dared look deeper, would he see Jenn or a figure of glass filled with pearl? "We will have help," she insisted.

Of that he suddenly had no doubt at all.

Asking Wisp for a favor was one thing, asking the shy wild denizens of Marrowdell quite another, but Jenn had to try. She led the way to the gap in the tall hedge surrounding Bannan's farm. Instead of going straight, along her path to Night's Edge and her meadow, she turned to the field and stopped, letting Bannan and Uncle Horst catch up.

Wind caught at her hair and laces, racing unimpeded the breadth of the valley. Ice growled and snapped in the distance, as if hungry. Jenn flinched and Scourge snorted a wordless comment.

Likely to do with the foolhardiness of people in general. Not even kruar crossed Marrowdell's guarded fields.

Which, according to those who'd lived outside Marrowdell, weren't like other fields. The ground in front of her should be lined with last year's stubble, its ruts mud and puddles. Instead, it stretched outward from her toes smooth and dry, as if the soil were freshly worked. In place of hay or grain, what grew here was kaliia, pushing through from the Verge and cared for by the efflet until the turnborn returned to harvest it.

The unseen creatures played in the snow and would clear it from her path. It didn't make them safe or tame. At the Great Turn, they'd died to protect her and Wisp from the nyphrit on the Spine. She'd seen what their claws did to flesh.

Now their sole task was to protect the tender shoots ready to reach for this sun's warmth.

"Stay here, please," Jenn said calmly, then took her first step.

A disturbed rustle rose from all around her, a rustle that subsided abruptly, as if efflet had arrived in number and settled, wary, to watch her.

Jenn stopped. She lifted her boot from the soft perfect soil, the impression of her foot exposing pale shoots that turned black and shriveled to naught before her eyes.

No wonder the efflet were zealous in their duty.

"I need your permission," she told them. "The road is impassable. To save Marrowdell from the river, we must cross your fields. With the greatest care," this as the rustling resumed in force, with an edge to it. She crouched and held out her hand, palm up, then moved it from side to side slowly, as if floating. "And with your help, we won't touch the ground."

A startled pause.

They were strong, in their numbers; while Jenn didn't know if they were strong enough, she'd poised the question and the efflet appeared to be considering it. She held her breath, feeling the tension in the men behind her. Even Scourge, for a wonder, was still.

Then all of them, including a now-very-vocal kruar who snapped and snarled his outrage at empty air, were lifted and sped across the empty field.

Jenn turned her head to see Bannan's face full of joy.

Even at its darkest moments, Marrowdell had the power to take his breath away. As now. After a quick deeper glance, Bannan resolutely did not look at what carried them quickly across the field. The mass of sharp hooked claws looked more likely to slice them to bits than be gentle.

But gentle they were, if abrupt. The efflet aimed them straight at one of the thorny border hedges, sweeping them up and over before what seemed an inevitable and painful collision, to dump them on the road.

What had been the road. Bannan stood, helping Sennic to his

feet, Jenn having been deposited with greater care. Mud splattered them as Scourge, the idiot, spun about trying to catch efflet in his jaws. The truthseer's "Stop that—" overlapped Jenn's soft protest. "They're only trying to help."

The latter brought the beast to a shuddering halt, eyes rimmed with red and ears flat, and the breeze was scalding hot. "I don't need *help*."

From her wince, she heard.

"We'll need all we can get," Sennic said, his voice strangled and faint. He pointed toward the village.

The shallow ford was gone. The river—a seething mass of ice chunks and debris, now coursed mere steps from where they stood by the mired cart and supplies. Having consumed the lower reach of the kaliia fields, it nibbled away the road, growing closer as they watched.

A road already sodden with meltwater from the slope leading to the Spine and its snow-filled meadow. Dozens of tiny streams worked their way through the forest, feeding the creek that now ran alongside in a hurry to join the flood.

And what wasn't water, was thick red-brown mud.

"We have to save them!" Davi shouted hoarsely. He stood with his horses among the trees, as close as he dared to the new shoreline. Some of the trees—the old ones the villagers knew not to cut—were leaning, their roots undercut here, if not in the Verge.

The big smith didn't mean the neyet.

The village was under water. Trapped between the rising river and unclimbable crags behind, its people perched on rooftops or in trees, while livestock huddled on the shrinking rise of land in the commons.

Blindly, Bannan reached for Jenn's hand.

Finding glass.

She mustn't make it worse, though what worse might be Jenn Nalynn couldn't and wouldn't imagine. She thought feverishly of scrubbing pots and muddy floors, tasks much easier than determining what she could possibly wish that wouldn't ruin more. Consequences. There were always consequences. She supposed Mistress Sand would be gratified that she hesitated.

Bannan held her hand. She remembered how that should feel, though didn't, being turn-born—probably terrifying poor Davi, who'd never seen her like this, though she trusted Uncle Horst to love her regardless her shape. The kruar pranced in the mud, ready to leap into the flood at her behest and die with honor and glory, that being his nature.

As for hers? Were Sand here, or any other turn-born, her wish—whatever it might be—would be instantly smothered, countered by theirs. Turn-born must agree. Deep inside, however much Jenn cared for them and they cared for Marrowdell, she knew they'd let everyone perish before taking such a risk. They'd grieve, she knew, but wait for the next group of settlers to come to the valley and learn the mill and become what they'd call friends.

Her thoughts raced like the river, faster than the single needless breath she made herself take, to remember being flesh as well as all else.

All else . . . One hand warmed by Bannan's, Jenn held out the other. Moths, tiny and white, bubbled from her palm. Her sei heritage. Helpless and frail.

Yet neither. Calling forth that aspect, she felt suspended in the blue of sanctuary and peace. Held inside her a mountain's shape and a world's power. Her moths became a cloud filling the valley, reaching every corner, spreading her plea.

"Save them."

And Marrowdell answered.

A moth landed on Wisp's snout. Unseasonal and unwelcome, the sei's messenger, unless—

The dragon went almost cross-eyed as the thing took dainty

steps, fragile little wings still as if his own speed through the air meant nothing to it, and this one bore no satchel—

"Save them," it whispered in her voice.

Wisp wheeled sharply, a wingtip clipping through spray, and raced to return to Jenn Nalynn.

Even as he did, the sky filled with moths giving her message until "SAVE THEM! SAVE THEM!" echoed from the Bone Hills to the Spine and the dragon honestly feared what might answer, so great and powerful was her call.

But the imprisoned sei remained quiescent, the edge it held safely intact.

Others heard. Efflet flew beneath him, glistening yling in their midst, the stout little warriors carrying slings of their silk, letting themselves be seen by the light of her sun so Jenn Nalynn would know they heard and came.

Nyphrit stirred as well, swaying the tops of what weren't trees but neyet, anchored and unable to move. Wisp bellowed a warning, well aware the foul things sought to take advantage and do harm. They cowered but stayed, snapping their yellowed teeth. Bold nuisances.

He'd eat them later.

For now, surging up through ground and flood, dropping from cloud and sky, came dragons.

Here was an answer Wisp was sure the turn-born hadn't expected, one beyond her control.

Not beyond his.

~OBEY ME YOUNGLINGS!~ he roared, harrying the nearest, biting and shoving his way to the front of a force every bit as deadly as the river.

FOUR

JENN COVERED HER ears as the dispute of dragons drowned out the river's rumble. Consequences, she thought numbly. Her moths had returned to her and she'd been so happy to see the small ones appear in answer, flying to the villagers' rescue.

Ancestors Wild and Wondrous, she'd never anticipated dragons.

Who, according to Wisp, ate anything they could catch, including one another. In the Verge, some had tried to eat Bannan and this tumult of wings and claws and very pointy teeth appeared set on eating those in Marrowdell.

Scourge reared, with rage or joy she couldn't tell and surely didn't matter at the moment. What did was the kruar attracted the attention of several dragons who dove to attack their ancient enemy.

Dragons who veered off again as Jenn raised her hand to forbid them.

If any had doubted Marrowdell was inhabited by more than people and their livestock, they'd ample proof now. Efflet and yling prudently vanished as dragons filled the sky, the beating of uncountable wings sending gusts to stagger those watching from the road and threaten the safety of those in trees.

Bannan felt a thrill of fear at the sight of hundreds of gaping, well-daggered mouths, well remembering how the tiny teeth of their young had sliced his flesh.

He muttered a prayer under his breath, sure the others did as well. "Hearts of my Ancestors, don't let the dragons be hungry."

If they attacked anyone Jenn Nalynn loved, it would be the end of dragons and likely the end of them all.

There. Jenn spotted a dragon different from the rest. Larger, aged silver instead of riotous color, and a wild, familiar, violet eye turned her way in acknowledgment before Wisp fought to the front of the rest and roared a command that shook the very ground.

Fully human again, she sagged into Bannan's arms. "Trust Wisp," she wanted to say, but couldn't catch her breath, as if so much magic crossing at once from the Verge stole the air from her lungs. Or made her forget what she was, which she wouldn't and mustn't—

So as dragons swooped down over the village and the hapless villagers understandably began screaming, Jenn Nalynn closed her eyes and reached up to kiss the one who knew her best.

Bannan returned her kiss with matching desperation, as if equally afraid and in need of courage. Done, she buried her face in his jacket to heave deep grateful breaths that sounded like sobs. Only when he gave her a gentle shake did she dare look up.

Villagers flew slowly over the floodwater toward them, clustered by household. They hung in midair as if suspended by magic.

"The dragons have them," the truthseer said, his voice filled with awe as he saw what she couldn't, the creatures once more invisible.

So they wouldn't be seen helping prey, Jenn decided, well aware of dragonish pride.

Ancestors Blessed, the result was all that mattered.

There was Lorra Treff, arms tight around a puzzling square

wrapped in a quilt. Her daughter Wen had her arms full of toad, and daughter-by-marriage Cynd bore what looked to be her sewing basket.

There were Anten and Covie Ropp, the former clenched to an invisible leg while the latter admonished the children, Alyssa and Cheffy, who were swinging from their own dragon and likely to be dropped in the river if they didn't behave.

Zehr had little Loee. Gallie Emms had hold of—Jenn squinted—yes, strings of sausage. Strings pulled taut, contested by others. She earnestly hoped Gallie would let go, sausage a small price for being saved.

Uncle Horst gasped!

Jenn tore her gaze from the sausage squabble to see Riss, holding a pair of canes, flying their way with Great Uncle Jupp, who clutched his silver horn, his long colorful scarf fluttering in the wind of their passing. As the Treffs were landing, or rather being let go above the muddy road, Hettie and Tadd, each with a baby, were being lifted into the air and carried with all the care Jenn could ask.

What had Wisp said to his fearsome kind, to tame them like this? Jenn had a sinking feeling she knew, and hoped none of the dragons tested his boasts of her turn-born and sei power, a power quite beyond her to manage at this moment, with her heart about to burst with worry and joy.

Mostly worry.

There were sufficient dragons to ferry everyone across—though why they must rather than use breezes like Wisp, who'd carried Covie that way once before, was a curiosity for later—but not room for all to arrive at once. Bannan realized this first, moving from her to help guide—and unglue from the mud—the early arrivals to make room. Davi simply picked up his mother, complete with the burden she refused to relinquish, and carried her to the side, lifting her up on Brawl. He did the same with his wife, then looked for Wen—

Who wasn't there.

Jenn blinked. She'd watched the woman, and toad, land on the road, safely on her feet. At what second had they vanished and how?

The why? Well, that was a worry, she decided. Wen had given Frann Nall her promise not to cross the river, a promise she'd never explained and no longer had to keep, Frann having died, Ancestors Dear and Departed—

"Jenn!"

Putting Wen and promises aside, for now, she whirled around in time to see her sister and father float gently to rest atop the cart's load of supplies. "Wisp," she whispered, her heart in her throat. "Thank you."

A little breeze tossed her bangs, then was gone.

Peggs and Radd had brought two baskets each. Kydd came close behind, as if he'd exhorted his dragon to catch up, arms around the Nalynns' largest stew pot. He was deposited in a puddle, but managed to hold the pot clear.

Anten and Covie arrived and stood, holding each other upright.

No, he fought to keep his wife with him!

To no avail. Covie broke away, forcing her way to the brink of the floodwater, crying out. "Devins! Devins!"

Heart's Blood, she'd fall in and drown, like Mimm! Jenn froze in horror.

Bannan got there first.

Promising to apologize later, if they'd a later, Bannan launched himself at Covie. They fell into mud quickly become silt as the floodwater found them and greedily sucked them away and down—

Teeth fastened in his coat and pulled. A wind whirled this way and that, pushing back against the current and keeping thick ice at bay, buying seconds.

His hand locked on Covie's belt, the truthseer flailed with the other, finding a leg like iron. He wrapped his arm around it, heaving Covie closer. Scourge stepped back, dragging them from danger. A step. Another.

All at once, hands seized them, half-carrying them to safety.

"Devins was—to stay with us. I went—back—for Roche's letters," Covie sobbed, clinging to him as if she'd no strength left to
stand. "I came—out—Devins was gone. Running to the pasture—
his cows. He was to stay with us—climb the roof—be safe—"

Anten took her from Bannan. "He's lost, Dearest Heart," he said,
weeping. "He's lost." Covie buried her face against his shoulder.

Bannan leaned on Scourge, looking to where the village had
been, searching for any sign of the young man. Finding none.

Refusing to give up, he looked deeper.

And saw dragons.

Get younglings to work together? To help people instead of eat them?

He was a bad influence. The thought gave Wisp pause, into which
voices, emboldened and unwelcome, intruded.

A sly, ~They have extra cows. I want one——~

A louder, ~Too many pigs. Give me two——~

A chorus, ~The pony's old and tough. That at least!!~

~HOW DARE YOU MAKE DEMANDS OF *ME*!~ With a roar,
Wisp threw violent gusts to fold wings and tumble the fools, silencing dissent with the reminder he wasn't as they, confined to claws
and teeth and toughness.

He was master of air, here and in the Verge, once and always
greatest of them all!

Which was just as well, were he honest, the turn-born's repair of
his body having healed his wings, while leaving his left side crippled
and useless.

Not that any would risk challenging him!

Other than those few dragons older and thus more powerful.
They kept to their mountaintop aerie in the Verge, hoarding their
magic, preferring their memories of ancient conquests to the least
effort toward a new one.

He'd never get *that* old. Better to let his ancient enemy bury his
poison fangs in his flesh first.

Wisp let out another roar. Not that he'd give Scourge the satisfaction—other than sharing the pleasure of watching a flock of dragons flail and collide with one another like silly little birds.

Unfortunately, they'd work to do before the floodwater rose further. The girl depended on him and he would not fail her in any regard.

Wisp let the air still, then rise beneath them. ~Do as you're told, younglings.~ This calm and almost gentle. ~Save the animals.~

The *or else* he left hanging.

One dared speak. ~Great Lord of Dragons, what of the man among them?~

Wisp curved his neck, bringing an eye to bear on the clustered animals. The youngling was correct. Devins Morrill stood on the shrinking patch of dry land, coils of rope over his shoulders and arms across the backs of his cows. He stared into the sky, unable to see the dragons.

Having learned more than any of his kind about people, if not by choice, Wisp grasped that the man stayed with the animals in his care to see them rescued or die with them. A mad courage, impossible to explain to the younglings even if he'd bother.

Wisp experienced an unexpected admiration. ~I'll fetch him. Take the beasts to the turn-born's meadow. Unharmed! Keep them there until the farmers come,~ he added, understanding the limits of efflet tolerance as well.

He plucked Devins from the herd, quelling the man's incoherent protest with a quick breeze in his ear. "We'll take them all. Hold still."

Though it didn't help when Marrowdell's animals sensibly reacted to being grabbed by invisible claws by struggling against their fate, bawing and neighing. A couple of the younglings lost their grips and had to dive to recapture their passengers.

Good practice, Wisp decided, inclined to be smug until he caught the faintest scent of fresh blood.

He whipped his head around to glare at the younglings, seeking the one who'd been careless. Too late. Obeying him, they flew in a tight mass swiftly up the valley to Night's Edge, livestock dangling midair.

Be glad it was only a trace, he told himself, and Marrowdell's beasts survived to complain.

Being smug and glad, Wisp overlooked the dragon who caught up and flew with the rest, but lacked a burden.

A dragon who twisted between wingbeats to capture drops of forbidden blood from its clawtips with its long forked tongue, bringing that back to its mouth, hissing at the taste.

Marveling at it.

While behind them all, the river erased the last of the pasture. Ice battered the giant oak that marked the ford. The rose climbing the wall of the Nalynn home withered and fell away.

Marrowdell was lost.

FIVE

"ANCESTORS STUNNED AND Stupefied," Peggs whispered. She gripped Jenn's hand as the pair joined the rest of the villagers in watching the impossible. Full-grown cows and pigs, including the great boar Himself, floated by overhead like grotesque balloons, legs dangling and more than a few voicing complaints. There were the early calves, but no piglets, Patches and Silk yet to give birth.

Which they well might, after being flown by dragons.

Someone called out, having spotted Wainn's Old Pony, who appeared to take flying in stride, but there was no sign of Devins.

There would be, Jenn told herself. While she'd believed in Wisp and knew he'd try to do as she asked, she hadn't been sure he'd convince dragons to ferry livestock. But he had and they did. By that logic and her heart, her dragon would save Devins, too.

Sure enough. "There!" Bannan shouted, pointing up. A cheer rang out, if a ragged and puzzled one, for Devins wasn't being brought here, but going with the animals.

Jenn supposed it made sense, as someone needed to calm them, but her heart went out to Covie, whose arms had reached out for her son only to drop, empty.

Then it was time for everyone to shuffle out of the way as Master Dusom arrived by dragon, books under each arm and dignity intact.

Last and not least came his younger son Wainn, hands empty. Jenn cheered with the rest.

Until Wainn's invisible dragon swept him over those below, making everyone duck, then tossed him high into a tree as if to prove dragons weren't to be taken lightly.

Not that she had or would, Jenn thought, inclined to be cross with this one.

Others rushed to the tree, only to hesitate, those of Marrowdell well aware you no more climbed an old tree than threatened it with an axe.

But the tree released Wainn unharmed, branches twisting in ways no branch should to ease him to the ground. Once there, Wainn gripped the trunk, in thanks—

No, Jenn saw with dismay, for support. His face was pale and set with pain. Covie, their healer, was the first to move, followed by Dusom, who dropped his books in the mud in his haste to reach his son.

By the time Jenn got there, she had to peer over shoulders to see Wainn now sitting against the tree, held by his father. Covie had freed one of the young man's arms from his coat, working to stanch a small but nasty-looking hole in his shoulder. "—shallow," she was saying, giving a reassuring nod. "He'll be fine."

From the prick of a claw that could easily have done much worse. Jenn gritted her teeth, determined to have a conversation about dragonish manners—

Wainn looked up and found her, his expression bleak. "Jenn. Save the hives. The hives!" The harsh gasp took the last of his strength. His eyes rolled up as he fainted.

The dragons seemed to have left Marrowdell, to everyone's relief, but efflet and yling lingered, invisible again, ferrying what they could manage up the muddy road to Bannan's farm. The emptied cart was abandoned, firmly stuck and the river still rising. Cheffy and Alyssa, who might have found being flown in a silken sling a wonderful game, were as somber and pale as any adult, seeing their home overwhelmed by water and ice.

For now, Jenn hoped. Ancestors Fated and Fraught, floods came and went. Surely they only had to wait.

It would help if they knew for how long.

Once assured Covie would stay with Wainn, Anten went ahead to find Devins and check on their stock, Jenn having told him where to find the path to her meadow, Night's Edge.

The rest of Marrowdell's inhabitants began their slow trek up the road to safety, none looking back.

There was no sign of Wen Treff. There rarely was, everyone quietly acknowledged, refusing to worry aloud, even though they did. Instead, they fussed over Wainn, who remained unconscious despite being laid over Brawl's broad withers for the trip to shelter, and who'd asked after bee hives instead of the woman he loved and their child inside her.

Which was more than strange, even for Wainn.

Bannan had gone to prepare what he could. He'd ridden Scourge, the kruar seemingly immune to mud unless rolling in the stuff, then sent him back to help.

Now Jenn smiled encouragement, looking up to where Peggs sat on the kruar, who was a much higher mount than her sister had ever sat before—and had fangs, to make matters worse—but with a little sigh, her sister put an arm around Hettie's waist as best she could, her stomach a bit round for that, her other arm looped through the handles of two baskets. Hettie carried her wee babes in their slings and had baskets as well. Both women looked pale, if resolute.

Jenn rested her hand on Scourge's great shoulder. "Don't worry. He'll keep you safe."

The kruar glanced at her, huffed, then moved off with slow cautious steps.

At some point, Jenn's boots had been swallowed by the mud.

While she regretted their loss, it was for the best. They'd slowed her down. Unfortunately, having bare feet let her feel the drop in temperature as the day settled to afternoon and the sun sank toward the Bone Hills. There'd be a freeze tonight, as if the damp wasn't sufficient discomfort to face.

She could hurry spring. Warm the air.

But if she did, more ice would melt, more quickly, increasing the flood and putting people in danger who didn't have dragons to lift them to safety or a turn-born to give them better weather—which was a trouble of its own, clearly.

The spiral of thoughts left Jenn slightly dizzy as well as downcast, and she looked around for a safer way to be of use. There. Kydd, struggling with the enormous iron pot they used for harvest stews. Hastily she slogged her way to his side and took hold of a handle.

With a grateful nod, he shifted his grip to take the other. "Peggs insisted," he panted.

Jenn wasn't surprised her sister would think of how best to feed them all. "It'll help," she replied. "How did you—"

"Enjoy my flight?" Kydd glanced at her, lips quirked to the side. "Let's say I've new sympathy for any rabbit taken by a hawk. For a moment—" he hesitated then went on, "—to be honest, I closed my eyes and put my trust in your dragon." He surprised her with a chuckle. "Dragons. Ancestors Fortunate and Fabled. Who'd have thought?"

Who indeed, Jenn thought wryly. Those of Marrowdell were used to life with house toads, helpful and rarely underfoot. But to learn they shared the valley with efflet and yling—let alone dragons?

Lorra Treff would doubtless have something to say about that.

The beekeeper's face turned serious again. "No one outside must hear of this, Jenn. I fear it would draw the worst, most perilous attention." A slow, grim nod. "I'll speak to the others."

Others being those few able to remember the magic of the edge once beyond it. Tadd and Allin said such individuals had the "light of Marrowdell" in their eyes—not that Jenn could see it for herself.

Those two and Kydd. Bannan, Lila, and Werfol. Roche Morrill, though he'd left the valley—and was, in that regard, a worry. Without meaning to, Jenn had wished him to stop lying and always tell the truth and now he must.

Of course, being in Ansnor now, where magic wasn't frowned on as in Rhoth—

She shifted her grip on the pot handle.

—maybe no one would believe him. Poor Roche.

Aunt Sybb remembered as well, which was beyond wonderful, for all the rest forgot Jenn herself once on the Northward Road. As for being rescued by dragons, they'd tell their own reasonable and ever-so-ordinary version of events over cider to friends in Endshere. Marrowdell's secrets were safe—

Perhaps not all of them. "Have you seen Wen?"

A sharper glance. "Is she missing?"

"I don't know. She came across with her mother. And a house toad," Jenn added, how the rest of the little cousins were doing with their houses underwater another worry among many she could do nothing about. "Then vanished."

Kydd gazed into the wild dark forest alongside the road, with its forbidding tangle of branches and thorns, and gave a small shudder. "We'd hoped she'd stay."

On their side of the edge, he meant, not the river, for he'd learned all Jenn could tell him about the Verge and Marrowdell, and how some moved between. Turn-born. Dragons. Kruar.

Not ordinary people, not and survive. It was how her mother, Melusine, had perished, being taken across by accident. And why Jenn herself was turn-born, Melusine giving birth at the turn of light, for that's when crossing was easiest.

Wen had an undeniable connection to Marrowdell but the Verge? She and her baby would die.

"Wen can't cross without me," Jenn assured Kydd. "So she won't cross at all."

"Are—" Whatever he might have asked, or guessed, was interrupted as those behind them caught up.

"Our turn." Tadd Emms took Jenn's place at the pot, his father Zehr the other.

Radd Nalynn joined them. "We're almost there," he said, his voice full of unfamiliar strain despite an effort to be reassuring. He raised one of the baskets he'd brought. "I've pies, Dear Heart."

Jenn smiled at him. "Good to know," she made herself say, well aware the basket held three at most, stretching with care to a slim piece for each. Still, the smallest taste of Peggs' famed baking would be welcome.

Or would it remind them what lay drowned in the village, and the challenges they faced?

Aunt Sybb would say to pay attention to the accomplishment of any moment. While usually this was to encourage patience during lengthy embroidery sessions, Jenn felt the truth of it.

"Good to hear," she repeated and, with a smile, took a basket from her father and put her arm around his waist.

Together, they helped one another slip and slide up the road.

With what little Bannan could do to prepare for those about to arrive, he was beyond grateful Marrowdell itself did more. Like its larger counterpart in the village, the farm's well was inexhaustible, its pure water flowing even during the depths of winter. Their privy, like those in the village, remained sweet and clean no matter how many used it, an incalculable improvement over the need to dig latrines in half-frozen mud.

Something he and Tir—and Sennic—appreciated more than most.

People would queue for their turn. He trusted Marrowdell to excuse those who elected to piss on a hedge.

Hurrying into the house, ignoring the mud clinging to him from head to toe, Bannan unrolled the straw mattress they kept for visitors such as Tir, to make ready for Wainn, then quickly stoked the fire in the fireplace. If his teeth were chattering, those about to arrive would be chilled to the bone.

He came out of the house and heard cows lowing in the meadow, the beginnings of distress in the sound, though they'd had an easier end to their journey. The path to Night's Edge, shaded by the hedges, was still frozen.

And not where he was needed. The efflet and yling had arrived, setting what they brought outside the barn. He'd have been amused by the tidy, if unusually slanted, stacks of bags and jars if not for how few they were.

Cheffy and Alyssa jumped from the sling held by invisible hands—yling having no feet—and turned at once to bow in the Vorkoun style they'd learned from his nephews. Who were, Ancestors Caring and Cautious, safe with their parents.

The truthseer looked deeper to see the yling dip in the air in response, spears held in their second set of hands. Having some experience with the small beings, he judged these as weary and bedraggled as the people they'd helped. "Thank you all," he told them, and gave his own bow, fingers brushing the air above the mud.

Efflet whispered menacingly from the hedges, back to fussing over their fields and once more a threat.

"Dearest Hearts!" After shouting from the entrance to the farm, Anten slipped and drove his way across the yard, falling to his knees to gather Cheffy and Alyssa in his arms. After a too-brief moment he lurched upright. "I'm to yon meadow, to find Devins and help with the animals. Bannan, do you have any—anything?" he finished, his round face creased with doubt.

Anten knew as well as any Bannan and Jenn had given up their plans for a calf or piglets, Scourge having taken the barn as his due. The truthseer shook his head ruefully. "Buckets. Some rope. I'll gather them for you."

A voice from below his elbow announced, "And we can help." It was Alyssa, Cheffy nodding beside her, tear-streaked faces determined. "What should we do first?"

Not "why can't we be in your house" or "what's happened to ours," but how to help everyone. Marrowdell's children, Bannan thought with a swell of pride.

"It's important these get inside, Dearest Hearts," their father told them soberly, waving at the supplies.

Without a word, they picked up what they could carry in their stout little arms and went into the barn, returning for more at a run.

Cheffy paused. "Perrkin is here." With relief.

Anten shook his head. "Another to go thirsty."

"Not so." The truthseer slapped him on the shoulder. "We'll work out how best to bring the animals here for water later. Right now, Perrkin is going to work."

Insisting Anten sit for a moment, Bannan filled two buckets and a water sack at the well, securing those to straps on Perrkin's saddle. The aged gelding lifted his gray head and flared his nostrils, those straps usually for swords and a spear.

"Send him back and I'll refill these," Bannan told the farmer, who rose to his feet again and took hold of a stirrup for support. Perrkin, who knew Anten well, swung his head around in greeting, then looked forward, ears pricked but waiting for a command. A soldier's mount who'd supported the wounded before this, he'd stand like a rock as long as asked.

"Good boy. Brave boy," Anten murmured, his voice catching. A rough hand patted the gelding on the shoulder. "Let's give the others a drink, shall we?"

The pair set off down the path to the meadow.

As more arrived.

The giant hooves of the draught horses churned the farmyard into red-brown soup as they made their way across. Davi hung between the pair, boots raised, the muscles of his shoulders and arms straining his coat. Lorra and Old Jupp rode Battle, the foolish woman still clinging to her unwieldy package as if the yling were thieves and not helpers. Covie and Dusom were on Brawl, supporting Wainn between them. Bannan pointed to the house.

Scourge made it there first, slipping around the team to kneel gracefully at the porch to let Peggs and Hettie, burdened with babies and baskets, descend. Once they were clear, he spun on his heels to run back the way he'd come.

He owed the beast days of grooming for this. With bacon. The declaration might not be realistic, Ancestors Strained and Stranded, but Bannan preferred hope.

It kept him moving.

Turning back, he saw Davi strip the mud-caked harness from his team, then aim them at the well with affectionate slaps on their rumps. Big heads swung around. "No mush today, lads," the smith told them, that being their reward for hard work and rightly expected.

With heavy sighs, they went to the well and began to drink. Davi rubbed his hand over his face, leaving it over his eyes for a long moment.

No mush. Nor hay, not on this side of the flood, and Bannan doubted the meadow could sustain Marrowdell's livestock until the flood broke.

His task was to help the people. Heartsick, Bannan waved the next to arrive, Cynd, Riss, and Sennic riding Scourge, to the barn. This time, as the kruar passed close on his way to bring more, the truthseer whispered, "Thank you."

In answer, a cynical lip curled to show a fang. *Don't expect this again,* that meant. Bluster. Scourge cared about the villagers, in his own way. As a source of bacon and cheese—and sausages—yes, but he'd respect for some, not that the kruar would ever admit it.

Water dribbling from thick lips, Battle raised his head, watching Davi climb up on his teammate's back.

With a sudden kick and shouted curse, the man drove the startled draught horse out of the farmyard, straight for the old trees.

"He's going after Wen," Sennic cried out. "Stop him!"

Bannan went to mount Scourge, but the kruar shied away, then sped over the mud in hot pursuit, ears flat and teeth bared. The truthseer shouted, "No biting!" and followed at a run, taking the long way around the yard to gain better footing.

Arriving at the road in time to see the kruar duck down to catch Brawl from underneath, using neck and shoulders to flip the massive horse over as if it were a rabbit, then politely prance away instead of going for the kill.

Davi flew off, sliding to a stop in the mud.

As poor Brawl struggled on his side, Davi started crawling on all fours toward the trees. Ancestors Beloved and Bereft, wouldn't he do the same for Lila? The truthseer hesitated a heartbeat before going after the smith, mud contesting every step. "Davi! Stop!"

"I must find Wen! Heart's Blood. Help or leave me be!" Words smothered by an ominous growl.

It came from the forest just ahead, from the gnarled trees— neyet—who'd endured the suffering of the Wound. Jenn had healed the injured sei, but they remained ill-tempered and perilous.

And too close. Bannan dove and grabbed a thick leg. "Wen's safe in the forest," he panted, praying it was true. "You won't be." That was. And neither would he, without Jenn.

The big smith ignored him, dragging them both forward. Branches snapped overhead in warning. Stubbornly, Bannan held on.

A shadow crossed his vision. A breeze chuckled in his ear. "This is undignified."

"Just help, will you?" the truthseer croaked.

Scourge bent down and neatly plucked Davi from the mud by the back of his coat. The man cursed and fought, but there was no escaping those jaws. A red eye glinted. "Where do you want him?"

Sitting up, Bannan pointed vaguely at the farm. "Safe. Away from here."

Neck arched, Scourge carried off Wen's brother.

Brawl regained his feet and stood shivering, eyes wide; the gentle giant as shocked, Bannan judged, by Davi's unaccustomed roughness as by being rolled by the kruar. Making his way to the horse, he cupped the hairy chin, unable to reach higher, and clucked reassurance. "Time to go home, lad."

The horse's first step took a lurching, powerful effort. The second seemed easier, a welcome sign he'd taken no lasting harm. Scourge capable of restraint? Something else to tell Tir.

Bannan looked ahead to where Davi, slump-shouldered and miserable, stood among those who'd keep him from risking himself again.

Ancestors Blessed, surely Wen knew how much her brother loved her. Her family. Her friends. Let alone Wainn.

What in Marrowdell pulled her away with such terrible force she'd risk her life, her unborn's life, and abandon them all to grief?

The final five, including Jenn Nalynn, worked their way up the road, burdened with baskets sure to be worth investigating later and a pot that was not. If she'd wished the mud to dry and the road solid again, she'd have trapped their feet. While Wisp was glad Jenn Nalynn thought of such consequences and refrained, it made watching their slow progress tedious.

And while he easily might have lifted them all, it would have spoiled the old kruar's effort to be of some use.

Not that the dragon thought of it in quite those terms.

Wisp had been mildly amused to see Scourge topple the big horse and carry off the man. What was more entertaining? Watching his enemy kneel in mud to endure people climbing on his back, only to walk unnaturally to keep them there.

This trip, after some discussion, the kruar took the girl's father and Zehr, the carpenter, each holding a pair of baskets. Zehr's son stayed well clear, as if aware Scourge was nothing so tame as a horse.

Leaving the girl, Kydd, and Tadd to slog up the muddy road. With the pot. When they stood, wasting time to debate who should continue to carry it, Wisp sent a breeze to lift the thing into the air and send it soaring to the farm.

Jenn smiled, but it was a faint and sorrowful movement of her lips and the dragon lingered, dismayed. "What else can I do, Dearest Heart?" he sent to her ear.

She pushed hair from her eyes, smearing red mud on her forehead where none had been thus far. "Wen's gone into the forest. Can you find her?"

"Does she wish to be found?" Wisp asked cautiously. The strange woman talked to toads—to him as well—and knew what she shouldn't. A being to be avoided, in his opinion.

"I don't know what Wen wants. I know I wish to find her," the girl added wistfully.

And could, with her mother's magic, but hadn't. Vindication of his own reticence, the dragon decided. "Then I suggest we let her find herself."

"Wise Wisp." Jenn gave a crisp nod. "In that case, please help me ease Wainn's worries. Where did you put the bee hives?"

Hives? He let his breeze tickle her left ear but she didn't laugh. "Why would I put them anywhere?"

"I asked you to save them."

This was unsettling. "You asked me to save the people and their animals, Dear Heart," Wisp reminded her. "I did that."

"Yes, you did," she agreed, but too quickly, as if impatient. "We're all very grateful. But you did save the hives, didn't you? Took them to higher ground?"

Wisp grew wary. "Why would I?"

"The hives are the bees' homes."

"You didn't ask me to save people's homes," the dragon responded, feeling on firmer ground.

"People were outside. The bees were inside, asleep." A note of desperation. "Wisp, they couldn't get out!"

Ice filled his veins and despair his heart.

After all this, he'd failed her.

Wisp flung himself into the air and away.

SIX

"WISP?" WHEN THERE was no answer, Jenn sighed. "He's gone. Ancestors Grumpy and Grim, I shouldn't have said anything." After all he'd done, she'd upset her dragon, who didn't deserve it and, truth be told, had a tendency to sulk. "There's no telling when he'll be back."

"It was kind of you to ask," Kydd told her. "But I shouldn't worry about the hives. I've marked two wild bee colonies up the ravines. When the time comes, I'll invite them to move in." He paused as if reflecting on the good nature of Marrowdell's bees, then went on, "While I'll be sorry to lose the ones we have, I'm surprised Wainn feels it so strongly. He hasn't before."

"You'd think he'd worry about our homes," Tadd muttered under his breath. The young father looked wan and anxious.

Desperate, Jenn was sure, to check on his family. She made her tone brisk and bright, or as close to it as she could manage. "Let's keep moving."

As they walked, or tried to, she caught a frown on Kydd's face. "What is it?"

"I'm sure it's nothing." In a tone implying quite the opposite. Did he hesitate to tell her because of Tadd?

Jenn didn't think it wise or helpful to exclude Tadd, who wasn't a boy anymore but a husband and father, as well as the miller's apprentice. Beside, secrets had consequences, some of them hurtful and none of them kind.

She gave her brother-in-law a look he'd recognize from Peggs at her most firm. "You've thought of a reason—something about the hives. Is it the books?" she hazarded.

"'Books?'" Tadd's eyes widened. "Do you mean Master Dusom's library? We can't lose those. How will Elainn and Torre learn?"

As a student, he'd not been the most attentive, easily lured into mischief by Roche. Jenn supposed Tadd's new respect came with parenthood, though any book was a treasure well-shared in Marrowdell.

"We moved them to the loft. If the house stands, they'll be safe."

"Not," Jenn pressed, "*those* books."

Kydd looked at them both, pulled his boot free, then gave in with a sigh. "Jenn means the ones I brought with me to Marrowdell. Books that in hindsight proved—unsuitable."

Being about magic. Jenn didn't interrupt, letting Tadd think whatever he chose about 'unsuitable' reading material.

"I shredded the pages," Kydd went on grimly, "and stuffed them in the walls of the hives to keep the bees warm. They've been there ever since. For years. I'm sure once soaked by the flood they'll be an unreadable mush."

He didn't sound sure. He sounded slightly desperate, like Wainn. Resolving to bring up the matter again, after they were safe at the farm, Jenn changed the subject. "Is that what will happen to Master Jupp's papers? He'll be heartbroken." Though Marrowdell might be safer, those papers full of secrets from his time as Secretary to the House of Keys in Avyo and, according to Bannan, a potential threat to those in power.

Kydd, aware, shrugged. "His trunks could float across the Sweet Sea to Eldad and their contents come to no harm."

Ancestors Blunt and Brutal, she hoped not. Those papers would stir up trouble wherever found. Jenn added Master Jupp's trunks to the hives as materials to stay in Marrowdell.

They kept moving, helping each other, making quicker progress without the pot. Just as well, for the shadows were growing and they'd much ahead to do before dark. Jenn heard the river gnawing the road behind them and shivered.

"Ancestors Witness. Look what I brought with me." Tadd dug into his pocket and held up a baby spoon.

Pocket searching became a glad little game. Jenn found she'd tucked a stray sock, one of Bannan's, in hers and put it hastily away, blushing. Kydd, their artist, had sticks of charcoal and a candle stub.

The three of them fell silent, for the Nalynn home was full of Kydd's sketches and paintings, none liable to survive the flood.

Then Tadd found a rattle in another pocket and shook it, making them laugh again.

And quick as that, they were home. Or at least she was, but Kydd gave a nod to their farm and said, "A fine welcome."

Tadd, not to be outdone, proclaimed, "The very best."

Jenn had to agree, for lanterns hung from the eaves and in the barn, sending shafts of warm yellow to counter the long afternoon shadows. Lines crisscrossed from the house to the sturdy tree beyond the well, filled with clothes hung out to dry, and Davi's team dozed slack-hipped, leaning on the barn wall.

Best of all, Bannan came toward them, arms out and smiling in relief.

Holding Jenn in his arms, Bannan let himself take an unsteady breath. They'd done it. With the help of dragons and other magical beings, granted, but having Marrowdell's families here, safely above the flood, was what mattered.

"Hettie?" Tadd asked urgently. "The twins?"

Bannan pointed to the house and the younger man was away.

Kydd looked wistfully after him then to the barn, where, through the open doors, people could be seen busy at work.

"Wainn's still unconscious but Covie hopes he'll rouse soon," the truthseer told him. "Peggs is cooking. The kitchen's—" how to put this tactfully, "—rather full at the moment."

Kydd gave a resigned chuckle. "I'll make myself useful else-where." As he made his way across the yard, his shoulders straight-ened. Another, Bannan knew, who'd do whatever it took to keep the rest going.

Jenn leaned on him. "I don't suppose Wen's come."

"No. Not yet." He put his arm around her shoulders, pressing his lips to her golden hair before saying heavily, "Davi's angry with me. I stopped his search for her. Sennic and your father took him to the meadow to cool off."

She looked up, her dear face serious. "No one should go after Wen. We must say so. I will," this firmly. "You saved Davi's life, Ban-nan. He'll be grateful, once he realizes that."

If not, he'd lost a good and valued friend. Bannan lightened his tone. "Otherwise, everyone's settling in—"

Tadd left the house quicker than he'd entered. He stood a mo-ment staring at the now-closed door, hands in his pockets, then wordlessly headed for the barn.

"Ancestors Cramped and Cranky. Peggs and Hettie in the same kitchen?" Jenn shook her head. "It's the smallest in Marrowdell."

And perfect, Bannan thought wistfully. Aloud, "Shall we see for ourselves?" He offered his arm, as if they went to dance.

She raised her hand, made a face at the red streaks on it, then shrugged and tucked it neatly into his elbow where, Ancestors Wit-ness, he was no cleaner. His coat hung on a line, sopping wet. His shirt would be next.

When they reached the porch, Jenn let go and gave him a little push. "You first," she mouthed.

The truthseer entered their home cautiously, expecting chaos, finding an unexpected calm. Lorra and Master Jupp sat companion-ably by the fire, blankets and plates on their laps, mugs of tea by each. By the angle of their heads, both had nodded off.

Bubbling pots crowded the top of the stove—the newest such

device in Marrowdell, Bannan having brought it from Endshere—
producing a smell more appetizing than anything he or Jenn had yet
made, being still new to kitchens and easily distracted by one another.

Happier thoughts to counter the grim reality of the mattress in
its corner. Wainn lay motionless beneath the quilt Lorra had brought,
of greater utility than the portrait of a young Davi in his Avyo finery
leaning against a wall she'd carried across the flood.

The gilt frame, Bannan decided then and there, would burn
nicely.

Feeling a gentle touch, he glanced down to see a small clawed
foot withdraw beneath the quilt. His house toad, staying close to
Wainn. All the creatures exhibited a special attachment to the remarkable young man.

Looking down also revealed the once-muddy floor gleamed—
had it been the dragon?

The more likely explanation came down the ladder, a baby asleep
in a sling on her back. Peggs gave Bannan a welcoming, if brief smile.
"Hettie's feeding Elainn. They'll be down soon. Is Jenn—?"

"I'm here." Jenn leaned in the door, eyes wide. "You've done
wonders already."

Peggs kissed her sister on the cheek. "Busy's best, Dear Heart."
The two held each other tight a moment, golden hair mingling with
dark. The elder sister was taller and ever-graceful, even rounded
with her own baby-to-be. According to Jenn, Peggs was the second-
most beautiful woman in Marrowdell and maybe all of Rhoth, after
Riss Nahamm, and Bannan didn't argue.

The lady he loved shone with a light all her own.

The sisters pulled apart, eyes glistening. "How's Wainn?" Jenn
asked quietly.

"We're keeping him warm." Peggs gave Wainn a troubled look.
"His face changes expression. Worried. Sometimes afraid." Her look
shifted to Bannan. "It's not like him."

The truthseer nodded. The Wainn they all knew and loved was
full of joy, with a lightness of spirit to make those around him smile.

And more. There'd been times Marrowdell itself spoke through him.
Was it now?

Not a good sign, if the valley shared their fear and worry. Bannan made himself smile. "Ancestors Industrious and Ingenious, you have been busy."

An array of bundles waited near the door—the entirety of his and Jenn's bedding, other than whatever remained upstairs on their bed for Hettie and Peggs, along with, Bannan guessed, most of their clothes. A trespass he forgave at once and gladly.

He spared an instant to be relieved no one would have stumbled across Lila's box, with its perilous stack of incriminating letters. His oft-terrifying and ever-practical sister had left them in his keeping—in case she needed to bring down a prince.

A thoroughly uncomfortable gift. With his love's consent, he'd secured it behind their headboard, hopefully forever. As for Marrowdell's other trove of political scandal, those documents belonged to Master Jupp, who kept them, and his ongoing memoirs, wrapped in oilpaper. If anything in the village survived the flood undamaged, it would be the contents of his trunks.

Better to have stored food and tools in them, Bannan thought bleakly. Better for all.

Jenn indicated the bundles. "We'll take those to the—" She stopped before saying *barn*.

"I thought we'd call it the big house," Peggs supplied quickly. She helped fill Bannan's and Jenn's arms with bundles until they had to lean to the side to see past them. "There," she said, satisfied. "Ancestors Famished and Faint, please let everyone know we'll have a hot supper ready for them soon."

"We will. Thank you," Bannan told her, inclining his head.

Peggs found a smile for him. "We'll get through this together. We always have. You'll see, Dear Heart," to Jenn. "We'll manage."

A lie.

Gallant Peggs, Bannan thought, trying to ease the burden that sat heaviest on Jenn Nalynn. To be able to do so much, yet dare do nothing at all.

Knowing her sister, she'd share his fear. That if—*when*—the first of them perished, Jenn Nalynn might lose any restraint and places beyond Marrowdell pay the price.

It wouldn't come to that, the truthseer vowed to himself, using a bundle of blankets to nudge his love out the door.

Busy was best. It sounded like something Aunt Sybb would say, Jenn thought fondly, but might just be Peggs, who'd begun to spout wise sayings of her own last year, as if one reached a certain maturity and couldn't help it. Not that she wanted Peggs to stop, not at all. Peggs was indeed wise and more experienced and—

In danger. Everyone was. Jenn didn't have to be told. Thanks to the foresight of those who'd emptied their larders onto the cart, they wouldn't need to slaughter any of the livestock. Each was vital to the future of Marrowdell's inhabitants, the calves and their mothers for milk, cheese, and butter, the sturdy little bull, to ensure more calves, the sows round with future piglets who'd become sausages, bacon, and hams to replace those eaten this winter, and their boar.

Even Wainn's Old Pony had a role to play, being Cheffy and Alyssa's mount now that everyone else had outgrown him, and beloved.

Except they might have to kill some or all for the animals' own sake, for no one had sent food for them, other than some grain tucked in pockets, and the pony alone would graze clear the dried stalks in her meadow in a couple of days unless—

"Jenn."

She started, almost losing her grip, then steadied. "I'm sorry. I didn't mean to stop. I'm all right," this when Bannan didn't budge but stood looking down at her with concern in his apple butter eyes.

His eyes glowed gold, then an eyebrow lifted in denial.

"I'm not," she conceded, looking around. The farmyard looked like a bog, save where the inexhaustible well, a turn-born gift, stood in its ring of clean blue tile. People stood on the drier ground before the barn—the big house—or lined up at the privy, and she couldn't tell who anyone was, under the mud and despair. "I'm afraid."

"You should be, Dearest Heart," Bannan said quietly. "Ancestors Witness, we all are."

Jenn stared at him, taken aback. "That's not reassuring," she half-scolded, as if he were responsible, which was hardly fair but she couldn't help it.

His eyes remained somber. "We've made it here. Now we make it through this hour. This meal. Then, and only then, do we worry about the next. Don't think about days. It's too soon and won't help."

His words did, dark as they were, for they reminded Jenn how the man before her had survived unimaginably dire and deadly events, before Marrowdell. She'd hoped he wouldn't, here, but that was foolish.

Jenn gave a little nod, unaware as her head lifted, her eyes filled with fire, and her very posture became a call to arms to send the blood pounding through Bannan's veins. She only knew he smiled strangely at her when she said, "This hour, then."

She pulled at her foot, well and truly sunk into the mud, and made a face, a weary young woman again. "Ancestors Mired and Misfortunate. I could wish for less mud."

A breeze caught her hair and stole the bundles from her arms, lifting her into the air, her foot coming free with a pop. Bannan, not the recipient of dragonish aid, nonetheless laughed, and her heart grew lighter. "Wisp, you're back!"

"I never left," her dragon assured her. "Other than to do as you asked," this as she was lowered gently to one of the few patches of hard snow, her bundles whisked to those waiting. "But I could not, Dear Heart. The hives are no longer where they were."

Jenn's head tilted. "Someone else moved them?"

The truthseer heard the dragon as well, for he shook his head. "He means they've washed away in the flood."

She sighed. "Gone, then."

The breeze slipped warm across her cheek. "No. The hives are stuck in ice where the river refuses to leave the edge."

As if the river had a mind of its own. She couldn't argue. Didn't it feel as if the gentle waters she'd loved had become malevolent and cruel, turned into a force willing to kill everyone and everything in its path?

Ancestors Wary and Worn, it would be a long time before any of them trusted it again. Some, Jenn thought sadly, never would. Cheffy had been afraid for months to go near what had taken his mother. He'd grown to love swimming and splashing—and skating—but Anten and Hettie still had as little to do with the river as possible, crossing quickly and with dislike.

The urge to act—*to fix this*—welled up until Jenn gasped with the effort to resist. She reached blindly for Bannan, who somehow freed an arm without dropping a bundle to gather her to his side.

"I mustn't. I won't." Words barely uttered, to make a promise as strong as any Jenn had made before. She felt easier then, if not at ease, and pulled free. "This hour," she declared firmly, taking his topmost bundle.

"This hour," her love repeated, eyes glowing.

Master Dusom and Cheffy took the bundles at the barn doors, passing them to those inside. "Hearts of Our Ancestors, we are Beholden to you both," Marrowdell's teacher said, as if the little they'd brought would warm and clothe the entire village. "Might any of this be canvas?"

Cheffy nodded vigorously. "For us," he said, puffing out his little chest. "Who'll sleep outside with the animals all night."

Though he doubted Anten and Covie would let their young son take that duty in the coldest hours, shelter was vital. About to shake his head, Bannan stopped, then grinned. Ancestors Amazed and Ambitious, he'd something better.

Or might. "Jenn, can you open the tinkers' chests?" Tinkers were what the turn-born called themselves when they arrived from the Verge for Marrowdell's harvest. They stayed in tents and bedding better than any he'd seen in the marches, equipment they stored for the winter in his barn. "I'm sure they'd understand, given the circumstances."

She gave him a doubtful look. He returned a hopeful one. *High time the nillystones fell their way.* "I'll try."

They went inside, an excited Cheffy leading the way. The chests in question were already out in the open, taken from the storeroom to use as seats and tables. At Bannan's explanation, they were pulled into the middle, each needing two or three to shift it. The villagers stood waiting, puzzled but willing.

They saw boxes of the same rough wood as the barn, of well-fitted planks with rounded edges. The lids were held in place by black metal locks, two per side, dented as if a hammer was as needful to open them as a key.

When Bannan looked deeper, using his gift, the wood became palm-sized pieces of stone, smooth and pale yellow, fused together. The lids, shimmering blue, seemed made of crystal, somehow melted into fingers to grip the stone.

The truthseer glanced at Jenn, standing beside him.

"They're like Aunt Sybb's trunks," she whispered, unable to see what he did. "We need the keys."

"Not for these. Trust me."

With another, even more doubt-filled look, Jenn nodded and went to the nearest.

Bannan tried not to hold his breath.

Everyone was watching. To make matters worse, just as Jenn bent down to examine the chest she'd picked for her attempt, her house toad hopped on top of it, adding its sober regard. ~Elder sister. Is this wise?~

Trust the creature to complicate matters. Still awkwardly bent over, Jenn whispered, "If Mistress Sand were here, I'd ask her permission. I'm sure she'd give it." It was certainly likely, she decided, Mistress Sand caring for the villagers.

The toad didn't budge.

Well, that wasn't helpful. Jenn tried another tack. "We need what's inside. Unless you have a better idea?" The little cousins were resourceful—

Large brown eyes gave a slow blink.

—and ever reluctant to put themselves forward. Jenn sighed and put her hands on the chest.

~OURS!~

The word and denial struck with such force, she found herself some distance away and on her backside.

Catching her breath, she waved a vague reassurance at everyone, including Bannan, who'd rushed to her side. She let him help her to her feet. "I can't open them," she said, disappointed, then stared at her house toad, still squatting on the trunk. It *had* warned her.

And she'd answered. Out loud.

As far as those gathered in the barn knew, only Wen Treff conversed with toads. Ancestors Perplexed and Peculiar, Jenn had earnestly hoped not to be caught herself at the practice, there being sufficient strangeness about her as there was.

Though she supposed the villagers might have become immune after being aided by efflet and yling, not to forget dragons—

Regardless, it was churlish not to give the toads their due. They'd been waiting for a chance to help. Hadn't Scourge?

Jenn walked back to the chest and crouched to address the house toad, choosing her words with greater care. "Little cousin, the flood has put us all at risk. We need your help."

It came to attention, rising smartly on its front legs. ~These past three days, I have laid twelve eggs, elder sister, and eaten twenty-one foul nyphrit. I matter to Marrowdell.~

"You do indeed." Jenn paused. Honesty was best. "What we need now, however, is hay for the animals and shelter for those caring for them and warmth for those here—" Along with so much more, but she stopped there, having run out of nerve.

It blinked. ~I regret I cannot provide any of those things, elder sister.~

Her heart sank.

~You might ask the others. The neyet, for instance.~

Who'd provided the wood for this barn, their home, and all other buildings in Marrowdell. "Thank you, little cousin." She wanted to hug the house toad but didn't, aware of its pricklish dignity and her curious watchers.

She straightened and looked around, meeting their eyes. They weren't, she suddenly realized, curious. They were sad, exhausted, and afraid. Cynd leaned on Covie, who had her hands on Alyssa's shoulders, their menfolk in the meadow and Wen lost. Dusom and Kydd stood together but a little apart, as if they left space for Wainn, while Gallie, Tadd and Zehr nearby, rocked little Loee. Riss held a bundle of clothes as if she'd forgotten their purpose, apart from Sennic who'd gone with Radd. Marrowdell, stunned and grieving.

Worse, forced to stay here, where all knew the disturbing dreams came, for most, too close to be endured. Hadn't Roche bolted for home after only a few hours?

At the thought, Jenn Nalynn wished, with care but firmly, that her people should sleep here as easily they had in the village, feeling the expectation settle as an easing of her heart. But it wasn't enough—

What would Peggs do?

Of that, Jenn was in no doubt at all.

"Supper's ready," she announced.

Peggs and Hettie set their pots of hastily assembled soup and Jenn's porridge on the bench Bannan had made, alongside precisely divided slivers of pie. Every plate, bowl, and cup in the house was in use, and every utensil; Bannan left Jenn to retrieve his battered soldier's cup before remembering he'd traded it to the turn-born, what seemed a year ago, not yesterday.

The villagers patiently took their turn, some families saying a quiet Beholding over their repast, others silent.

Going last, Bannan and Jenn leaned against the barn wall to eat theirs. She lifted her spoon and let it drop in the bowl. "Hearts of My Ancestors, I'd be Beholden for an appetite. I'm too tired to eat."

A feeling he shared, Ancestors Weary and Worn, but one Bannan knew they could ill afford. "Every mouthful, whether you want it or not," he ordered. "We'll need our strength to be of any use."

She braced herself with a nod.

Relenting, the truthseer gave her a gentle nudge. "And I'd be Beholden if you don't tell Tir I just quoted him. Keep Us Close."

A glance up. Mud streaked her forehead and exhaustion paled her cheeks, but her eyes were as clear a blue as a sunlit pool and her lips curved. "Keep Us Close. And I promise."

He bent to collect a tender kiss that tasted of love and Peggs' cooking.

They ate steadily until they were done, Jenn adding her bowl and spoon to the tray Radd brought around, collecting dishes to be returned and cleaned. He smiled bravely. "A fine meal."

Bannan spotted Tadd, carrying two baskets from the house, a share for those in the meadow. Meaning Anten and Devins, Sennic and Radd having returned with Davi Treff. The big smith had shot Bannan a burning look before studiously ignoring his presence.

A kindness, to be out of his. "I'll take them," Bannan offered, waving Tadd over.

"I'll help," Jenn offered. "I have to talk to a tree."

He raised an eyebrow.

She looked charmingly flustered. "I'll explain later."

He looked forward to it.

The sun was lower, almost at the turn; icicles no longer dripped, the air turned cold. Done their meal, people were in the barn to arrange beds, families keeping close.

Few would sleep this night, despite—for Jenn had told him—her kind and potent wish. Shock would set in, Bannan knew, once they ran out of tasks to distract themselves. There was no help for it.

Taking the baskets, they started for the meadow.

"Bannan. Jenn. A moment."

It was Zehr, coming from the barn, Kydd in tow. "With your permission," the former said quickly, "we'll dismantle the stalls and storeroom walls while there's still some light. We can use them to bridge the yard. Make life easier."

It wasn't the truth Bannan saw in the carpenter's face, yet not a lie. Zehr needed to believe the lumber, a rare treasure in Marrowdell, could be put to use and later reclaimed for the barn. Not split and rationed to feed fires, to cook and keep them from freezing to death, a fate clear to read in Kydd's apologetic expression.

"Take down anything you can," the truthseer told them, then put his hand on Zehr's shoulder, adding solemnly, "Though we'd be grateful if you leave the roof."

He surprised the other into a short laugh. "We'll do that."

"Keep the doors closed when you're done," Bannan advised Kydd, who nodded. It would keep out some of the chill. They'd have brought in the draught horses, their big bodies a source of warmth, but there wasn't room.

Finally, they were free to go. Bannan followed Jenn, who kept to the frozen part of the path, gliding from shadow to thin beams of sunlight. She glanced over her shoulder at the barn, and he guessed why. "Don't worry about the turn-borns' chests, Dearest Heart. Everyone's warm enough tonight. Their gear would have been welcome, but like Peggs said, we'll manage."

She slowed. "And those in the meadow?"

"The animals must come to the well regularly. Everyone will take a turn going back to the meadow with them. No one will stay out in the cold too long."

A strategy workable if those already chilled had warmth and ease waiting for them, which they didn't, but Bannan didn't bother to add what she'd know.

She stopped to face him. "How long before some are lost?"

And it wasn't coincidence the turn arrived as he hesitated to answer, the sun setting and the light of this world fading in favor of that from the Verge. Efflet were exposed lurking beneath the hedges, yling in branches above.

Turning the woman he loved to glass and pearl, and his answer dare not offer false reassurance or in any way mislead the awe-inspiring wonder before him.

Who deserved his utter trust.

Bannan bowed his head, then looked into what only appeared to be her dear face, the mask over the coruscating beams of every color that filled her. "Cold and shock will set in," he said bluntly. "It won't matter we've food to last till the flood subsides and the road's passable, people will sicken before that. Some may die. The livestock won't survive." He shook his head, the truth bitter in his mouth. "That's not the worst. If the river keeps rising—" Scourge kept watch; they'd have some warning. "—we'll be forced from the farm."

With nowhere safe left to go.

Silence, cold and fraught.

The turn passed. Efflet and yling winked out of sight.

Jenn Nalynn, again a woman, gazed at him, her face still, her eyes purpled with the remnants of magic. "I can't let the flood reach here," she said quietly. Everything around them stopped moving; held its breath. "I'll have to choose."

Between Marrowdell and those downstream, including her beloved Aunt Sybb and Tir, who'd be with her. There were no words to ease the horror of that, so Bannan didn't try. He merely nodded at the path. "It'll cheer everyone up if the cows haven't lost their milk."

A quirk of her lips. "We'll make a farmer of you yet."

The truthseer silently thanked Devins, who'd talk for hours on the topic.

They got moving again, having a warm supper in their baskets and those waiting ahead.

And nothing more to say.

Wisp had come to the meadow to confirm a suspicion. None of the animals were injured, though they moved uneasily as he passed among them, even the big lazy sows, having learned what a dragon could do and no longer so trusting.

Wise to fear the younglings; foolish not to know he wasn't one. If granted time and opportunity—and the help of the girl—he might reveal himself as their guardian.

Or not.

Wisp snarled silently. If the blood he'd sensed in flight wasn't theirs, it was Wainn's, who'd arrived wounded. Whether by careless accident or malicious intent, a youngling had hidden its betrayal and fled retribution. All knew the people of Marrowdell were his, their safety the girl's need and his duty.

He would hunt down the traitor and eat its living—

The girl had come.

The dragon swooped to land at her feet. She stood with her arms crossed and head lowered. "I am here, Dearest Heart. Why are you?" It being thoroughly unpleasant in their meadow at the moment, between the stink of cow and chill.

"I—" Her head lifted. "We're running out of time. What if I ask the neyet for their help?"

Wisp was aghast. "You can't mean that."

Those come to Marrowdell had found homes waiting, stout log cabins, barns, and a mill with shutters and doors—crudely done but welcome shelter. The first arrivals, led by the foul Crumlin the wizard, had brought with them stoves and window panes, as well as the tools to shape the mill stones and forge metal.

The wood for those buildings came from neyet, who'd had no choice in it. The turn-born wanted people to live in the valley for their own purpose. At their wish, neyet died and fell, shed skins and leaves, split into lumber and log. Yling died as their homes tumbled, easy prey for waiting nyphrit. Those who survived learned to stand guard with poison spears, no longer trustful.

The neyet who'd been spared remembered their kind's unwilling sacrifice. Turn-born being untouchable, they aimed their hate at the reason for it, those on two legs, of this world. To live in Marrowdell was to avoid the old trees, and that, a dragon knew, most prudent.

The girl knew all this. Wisp had told her, so she might know the cruelty of the terst turn-born. How could she think to repeat their crime?

"Do not ask the neyet," he urged. "They cannot refuse you." And come to hate her, too, who'd done them no harm.

"Even if I didn't ask for much, Wisp? A few dry branches to burn—for warmth and food?"

The dragon quite enjoyed fires, both their heat and what people cooked on them. He did not enjoy this conversation. "If you need warmth, wish for summer. Enough neyet died to make Marrowdell. The flood is taking more." They'd have driftwood aplenty by summer. "Do not ask, Dearest Heart."

"To save—" Her lips pressed together in a thin line, her eyes wild, then Jenn crumpled to her knees, sagging against him. "Oh, Wisp. I don't want this."

"Then fix it." It seemed simple enough to the dragon.

He felt her sigh and waited. Knew she looked out over their abused little meadow, invaded by cattle, pigs, a horse, and the unhappy pony who continually begged from the equally unhappy men sat by the hedge nearest the farm.

All avoided this side of the meadow, bound by old trees and dark. Trickery, of a sort, for mere steps beyond wasn't forest but the smaller meadow Wisp called home, holding his preferred crossing into the Verge, overlooked by the massive heave of white stone the villagers called a Bone Hill. Apt name for what wasn't stone but part of the mad sei who bound the edge in place.

"The animals will starve," she said next. "I thought to ask—" A hesitation.

Her house toad was behind this, bold and filled with strange notions. Wisp kept the growl from his voice, abruptly unsure if he was offended because the little cousin had thought of possible solutions—

Or because it had done so first.

"There are none to ask, Dear Heart. The yling are busy moving their homes." And battling with nyphrit in the process.

"If efflet could coax the kaliia to grow sooner—"

"They are also—preoccupied." Ice on the distant river cracked and snapped. Louder, to a dragon, the keening of efflet. Those in the lowermost fields fought to keep the flood at bay, as if water were snow to be pushed back by their claws. They drowned in their hundreds, bodies drifting away to be seized by waiting nyphrit. If the river continued to rise, those here would do the same and die.

Efflet were as they were. They could no more stop trying to save their kaliia than succeed in the effort. The moment when only the river's snarl filled the silence, who, Wisp wondered, would mourn them?

Jenn Nalynn.

If he told her, which he would not. "The efflet cannot help you."

Nor could he. The ravines along the far side of the valley, where Tadd and Allin took the animals to graze in spring, were deep and shadowed, full of snow and frozen.

As for flying the beasts from Marrowdell, beyond the edge? Wisp shuddered inwardly. Better to drop them in the Verge and have a quick death.

The girl didn't move or speak. Stars came out. Wisp felt the chill sink into his flesh, slowing his blood except where she touched him. He wouldn't move before she did, there being no greater comfort in his life.

Still, being flesh, she shouldn't linger. The dragon struggled with his conscience.

All at once she spoke, her voice low and petal soft. "Then we must stop the flood. Wisp, where does the river come from? Where exactly," she qualified before he answered.

Meaning he had to envision the valley as it looked when he flew over it. A valley where the interesting parts were along the road the turn-born had made from their crossing to Bannan's farm, the ford, and the village—as well as the forested crag above the village that might contain bears—and the not-safe for dragons or anyone parts where the Bone Hills stretched like enormous claws dug into the ground.

"I don't know," the dragon admitted.

"In the morning, once you're warm, please find the river's source and tell me all you can. There might be an answer there, one that won't take a wish or—perhaps a small and harmless one."

"I will." Not that Wisp believed there were harmless wishes or answers to be seen from the sky, but he would do anything to please her. He used a little breeze to flip her bangs. "And you shouldn't sit on the cold ground."

"Or you," she said, being kind. "There's room for you in the house, Wisp. Though it might be a little noisy. There are," a sigh, "babies."

"Then I will cross tonight and return tomorrow. Unless you need me, Dearest Heart?"

"Tomorrow will be fine, dear Wisp." She stood. "Thank you for saving us." Her arm swept out to include the beasts in her gratitude.

The other dragons having long since left, Wisp replied proudly, "I did."

Rewarded by her glorious smile.

Hearing efflet die.

SEVEN

*H*AVING SHARED A bed with Peggs most of her life, sleeping with her sister would have been easy. Sleeping with her sister and Hettie, while keeping the twins—whose sturdy little beds had drowned in their house—safe between them, kept Jenn awake and hanging on to scraps of blanket so as not to fall from a bed she'd considered generous indeed this morning.

Still, being together was a comfort and the loft blissfully warm. Warmer than anywhere else in Marrowdell tonight, a thought that brought a tear sliding down Jenn's cheek and shook her breath.

And didn't Peggs stir and wrap her arms around her sister, and then Hettie snuggle close, and Jenn felt everything crumble inside, which was exactly when she realized one of the babies was awake and nuzzling her breast hopefully, while its twin wailed in protest.

A giggle worked its way out of her throat. Another. Another and another—

"Shhhhh. You'll wake—"

"Too late."

~Elder sister?~

Jenn choked on a laugh become a sob. Another. Another. She couldn't stop. Couldn't breathe.

Someone fumbled after the lamp. She heard the striker fall on the floor and the someone let out a frustrated mutter and it only made her cry harder.

Someone else pinched Jenn's arm, hard. "Here now!" The scolding voice was Hettie's, making the person after the striker Peggs.

Jenn hiccuped and stopped.

"Here," Hettie said, more gently, filling her arms with a warm, decidedly damp baby. Then two. Juggling the squirming mass, Jenn managed to sit up as Peggs lit the lamp.

To discover her house toad had joined them on the bed, eyes bulging with alarm. "I—I'm fine," she assured it.

And hiccuped, being nothing of the sort.

Peggs climbed back into bed, putting a shawl and her arm around Jenn's shoulders. "You'd be the only one," she countered with a brusque tenderness and squeeze. "Come on. Let's help Hettie settle the wee ones, then get what sleep we can before dawn."

When they'd be up to serve breakfast to the entire village. The enormous pot Kydd had carried was full of porridge, left to cook overnight, but the tea alone—

"Ancestors Soggy and Stinky." Hettie wrinkled her nose at her tiny twins. "Good thing you're cute. We'll be doing laundry today." She relieved Jenn of the babies, took her place on the bed, and set one to each round breast with enviable ease. "Among other things."

Jenn tucked pillows behind Hettie's shoulders. "I'll help."

Hettie gave a meaningful look at the toad, still on the bed.

"Starting with that," she said hastily and went to pick up the creature. Before she could, it hopped neatly from the bed, resuming its post at the top of the ladder with an offended air.

Having been referred to as "that."

"Sorry," she apologized under her breath and got back to bed. They dimmed but left on the lamp, the babies needing to be changed once fed. Peace descended, Hettie crooned a quiet lullaby, and Jenn's bout of what Aunt Sybb would doubtless call an excess of excitability stole her final reserves.

Her eyelids closed of their own accord, the bed spinning beneath her as she fell sound asleep.

~Elder sister. Wake up!~

Unfair.

Jenn cracked open an eyelid to darkness relieved solely by the light of the banked fire below. Heard snores from beside her. Not time yet. Relieved, she threw her arm over her face and sighed peacefully.

~Elder sister. The Wise One calls for you.~

Wise One? Jenn's eyes shot open again. Who would the toads refer to as—"Wainn's awake," she whispered, slipping out of the bed, her heart pounding with relief. She groped for the shawl and tied it around her waist. A sleepy voice murmured.

"I'll go," Jenn replied. "You're coming," this to the toad, who permitted itself to be tucked firmly under her arm, legs dangling.

Peggs sat up to watch Jenn ease down the ladder. "Call us if you need help."

"You do the same."

She could hear the smile in her sister's voice. "I'm not the one with a toad."

Jenn took the first two steps quickly, in a rush to duck her head and see. To her disappointment, Wainn looked as if he hadn't moved at all.

She took the final steps and set her toad on the floor. "Are you sure?" she whispered to it.

~He calls, elder sister. Loudly.~

Well, then, nothing for it but to tiptoe to Wainn's side. Once there, Jenn hesitated. His breathing was slow and steady. Clearly he slept, but the toad seemed certain. She leaned close—

His hand shot up to grip her shoulder, pulling her down until her face almost touched his. A face that slumbered, with lips that didn't move, above which a very different face appeared, Bannan's house toad squatting on Wainn's head, a foot using an ear for purchase. ~Elder sister, if you wish, I can tell you what he says.~

"Please."

~THE HIVES MUST STAY IN MARROWDELL, JENN NALYNN! YOU MUST KEEP THEM HERE!~ Rendered with the anguish and hopelessness of a someone trapped in a nightmare.

Instead of concern for Wen or their baby. Heart's Blood, what did Wainn know the rest of them didn't?

Maybe it wasn't about knowing, but trust. If Wainn trusted Wen to be safe, Jenn thought, relief sparking tears in her eyes, she would. Though she'd keep them in her prayers to the Ancestors.

Leaving the hives. "It's all right. The hives aren't going anywhere," she whispered soothingly. At least not soon, being stuck in the ice dam, a detail she felt unnecessary at the moment. "Why don't you wake up, Wainn?" She stroked the hair from his fevered brow, in no way expecting an answer.

Getting one regardless, courtesy of the toad.

~He must heed Marrowdell, elder sister.~

Bannan lay awake, staring up at the rafters. Hopeless. Months in his own good bed, most crucially a bed now shared with his love, had ruined him. He'd lost the soldier's useful knack of sleeping any-where, anyhow. Tir would be ashamed.

Yawning, the truthseer gave up the struggle. He tucked his blan-ket over the form nearest him. Tadd Emms. The young father had wanted to sleep on the porch, to be as near as could be to his family, but his father and mother had insisted he stay where it was warm.

Warmer. Bannan saw his breath in the moonlight as he quietly rose to his feet and collected his boots. He eased out the barn door, making sure it was closed behind him.

A shadow stirred. He froze, then frowned. "How's the river?"

"Rising. The greater threat was already here." The answering breeze purred with grim satisfaction. "Some thought to take advantage."

Nyphrit. He should have known. The squirrel-like things hunted the helpless and ran in packs, tearing prey apart with their claws. Using his deeper sight, the truthseer looked around worriedly. In-stead of nyphrit, he caught the glint of chain mail and eyes like silver coins. Marrowdell's house toads, on guard as well. He let out a re-lieved breath. "Are they gone?"

"For tonight."

He took the warning. Ancestors Bloodied and Bent, what if Tadd had slept on the porch? They'd all have to be indoors at night. "The meadow?"

"Protected." With an amused huff.

Bannan reached out his hand. Found a sturdy shoulder and gave it a grateful rub. "What would I do without you, Old Friend?" he murmured.

"Die horribly," Scourge replied cheerfully, smug as ever.

A man had to laugh.

Moved by his heart, Bannan looked to the house. A light gleamed in the loft window. Before he could take a step, to see why and who was awake, it was extinguished.

Ah, yes. The babies. He'd spent enough time with Lila and hers to know parents didn't sleep long or often at first. No one would thank him for disturbing such fragile peace.

Lila wouldn't thank him for dying here, beyond reach or knowing. She'd no current fodder for her true-dreaming, a process requiring a trance-like sleep, a potion, and paper he'd touched. His last letters had gone with her. No, his peerless sister would have to learn his fate and that of Marrowdell from the confusion of flotsam carried south by the rivers. A barrel that once held fish from the Sweet Sea. Any of Master Jupp's trunks of scandalous papers—Ancestors Secret and Sly, wouldn't those cause a stir? Kydd's hives. The bench from the porch, lovingly carved with the initials of Jenn Nalynn.

Downstream adding jugs of cider from Palma's inn. Barn roofs . . .

Corpses, bloated, nameless, and lost—

Bannan shook off his grim tally. They weren't there yet. "It would help to be some use," he muttered.

The breeze found his ear again, light now and expectant. "I heard the turn-born task the dragon to follow the river to its source." A sly note crept in. "We can beat him to it."

The moon sat full and bright in the cloudless sky, pulling shadows from buildings and trees.

Shadows that hid danger and obscured footing—he'd never

dare it alone. But on Scourge? The most sure-footed mount imagin-able?

Bannan found the knub of Scourge's mane. Clucked his tongue and jumped, letting the kruar's answering lunge swing him up and aloft, barely settled before the beast broke into a run over uneven frozen ground that would break lesser legs.

As eager as his rider to take action.

The truthseer bent low over Scourge's big neck and held on, re-fusing to doubt his choice.

They wouldn't be long.

Jenn laid her cheek on Wainn's arm, his hand in hers. As Mar-rowdell suffered, so did he, in some way more deeply than anyone else. An unfair burden even if, in better times, Wainn was a perfect reflection of the valley's peace and content. After all, he held within him so much. Wainn, who couldn't read, remembered to perfection every word on every page he'd seen. Every book, for starters, includ-ing those of magic Kydd had hidden in the hives.

And magic, in Marrowdell especially, was real and perilous. For a piece of Peggs' pie, Wainn had shared with Jenn the Rhothan wishing to change Wisp, a dragon, into Wyll, a man she'd thought to marry.

Which hadn't gone well at all, Ancestors Startled and Shaken, Bannan arriving in Marrowdell the same day—another sort of magic, she supposed, feeling warm—the point being that although Jenn knew Wisp had forgiven her, if a single verse from one book caused such trouble, what might more do, in the wrong hands?

And there were wrong hands, outside Marrowdell.

Hands belonging to people who paid no heed to harm or conse-quence in their desire for power. The mad wizard Crumlin Tralee had been one. Before him, others had come from Ansnor. Ancestors Tried and Terrible, this past winter hadn't a horrid man named Glammis Lurgan sent an evil wishing to bind Bannan's power and will?

Sitting up, Jenn thought desperately of dirty diapers, those being innocent and safer—

A cane lightly bumped her knee. "How's the lad?"

In no natural sleep, if Old Jupp's raspy bellow didn't wake him. "Resting." Jenn stood, tucking the hand that reached for her from a dream back under the quilt, then turned to the elderly man with a smile. "Sorry I woke you."

"You didn't," came another voice. "It's past time to get the kettle boiling." Jenn blinked, startled to see Lorra Treff not only up, but at work in the kitchen, gray hair up in a twist. The matriarch must have added charcoal to the stove, for the Nalynns' big pot of porridge was bubbling. She'd let the fire in the fireplace cool to embers now they were stirring, well aware they'd no fuel to waste.

Having thought to help Marrowdell's oldest residents, Jenn Nalynn found herself trying to keep up. She drew Old Jupp with her, away from Wainn's side. "Shall I fetch more water, Lorra?" she asked diffidently.

A brisk nod. "Once you do, fill the cups halfway before we add tea from the pot." A ferocious scowl. "Ancestors Destitute and Deprived, tepid will feel warm to those—" Her voice cracked, then settled. "—those outside. Jupp, get back here and stir the porridge before it sticks."

"Yes, Lorra." He clumped over to the stove, leaning one cane against the wall. Instead of taking the spoon, he put his hand on Lorra's shoulder.

Because those outside including her missing daughter.

Lorra closed her eyes and pressed her cheek to his hand, accepting the comfort.

And Jenn wondered, for the first time in her life, about the history between these two, who'd always seemed so different—other than hating the prince and being elderly.

They even lived at opposite ends of the village—

Lorra raised her head with a snap and gave him a push. "To work with you."

"Yes, Lorra." Old Jupp took the spoon, wielding it with gusto and the occasional wheeze.

Jenn felt glued in place. "But—wouldn't you rather sit and—"

"We're old, not useless." Lorra's glare pierced her like a knife.

"I didn't mean—" She stopped, because she had.

What would Aunt Sybb say? Everyone deserved a chance to help. Jenn gave a short nod and rested her hand over her heart. "Thank you."

Lorra's look softened. "We've been tossed from our homes before this, child. Let us do what we can. Go. Get the water. Get extra." She wrinkled her nose. "There'll be laundry today, by the smell from upstairs. Babies." Said as if they were pests, like flies in summer, though surely babies, regardless their smell, made Lorra think of her future grandchild.

Of how it seemed there was every chance, now, they'd never meet.

Ancestors Callous and Cruel. It wasn't kind of Wen, Jenn thought, to leave them. It wasn't kind at all.

Busy was best, she reminded herself, before she became angry over what she couldn't help or understand.

She dipped a respectful curtsy to Lorra Treff, who helped others when she couldn't help her own, then turned to get her coat and boots, not noticing the white moth perched on the frame of Davi's portrait, busy scribbling notes.

He'd yet to fall off, if come close a terrifying time or two. Scourge's doing more than his, Bannan knew. He planned to be properly grateful once he stood on the ground and could catch a full breath.

On safe ground, which wasn't here. Any spot free of icy puddles held its cohort of snarling nyphrit, who dodged Scourge's deadly hooves only to close in again. The forests must have emptied of the creatures in their rush to profit from Marrowdell's misery.

Was Wen Treff safer because they had? Or already dead?

Bannan pushed such dire thoughts aside. Wen had chosen her path, however much grief her loss would bring, and he'd a more immediate concern. The kruar took the Tinker's Road away from the river they were to investigate and ever closer to the turn-borns' crossing into the Verge.

Where the truthseer most assuredly did not want to go, nor could Scourge take him.

And not, Ancestors Testy and Tense, why he'd come in the first place. Bannan pounded on the kruar's shoulder. *Explain yourself,* that meant. Or *stop.* He'd settle for either.

He got both, the beast coming to an abrupt halt. Bannan found himself draped over Scourge's neck, staring down at glowing hungry nyphrit eyes that thankfully scattered at the low, loud growl emanating from the body beneath him.

"What's wrong?" a breeze snapped in his ear.

"Where's the river?"

Scourge lifted his head, absently shaking the truthseer from his neck down to his proper seat. He aimed his long nose at the forest beside the road.

Not even the moonlight penetrated the mass of crisscrossing limbs.

They weren't going to the Verge, was Bannan's first thought. His second? "How do we get through that?"

"I can. You," with an amused pause, "wouldn't enjoy the journey. So we go this way." Scourge's big head swung around again, then abruptly dipped. *Crunch.*

"Without lingering for snacks," Bannan suggested icily.

"Agreed." The kruar set out again, this time with long easy strides. "We must find the river's source before the old fool wakes and does it first."

A competition. If it found answers of use, he didn't care who won.

Though if they were first, surely he'd earn one of Jenn's wondrous smiles—

"Hurry up!" he urged, digging in his heels. With a kick, Scourge responded, and Bannan belatedly realized the kruar hadn't been running full out before.

Catching breath became an impossibility, holding on unlikely, and the truthseer prayed to his ancestors for strength.

Fortunately, they reached their destination before Bannan lost consciousness. As he slipped from Scourge's back, holding on a moment to gather his wits, he suddenly realized it was brighter. Sunrise?

No. Moonlight—reflected from the white flanks of the Bone Hill rising in front of them. The flesh of the mad sei was as stone this side of the edge, sheer and unclimbable, and, according to the villagers and great good sense, not to be approached.

About to protest, Bannan noticed the forest was thinner where the valley floor met the hill, an undergrowth of shrubs and small thin trees as if the neyet towering overhead knew better than touch the sei and let ordinary plants take their place.

Thinner and passable. He drew himself back atop Scourge, paused an uneasy moment to consider the immense mass looming beside them, then shrugged.

Ancestors Daring and Dauntless, they were here. He had to try.

"Let's find the river."

The welcome heat of the Verge had burned the chill from his bones, if not his heart, by the time Wisp left his sanctuary. Danger to those the girl loved? Her restraint thus far was admirable.

A restraint sure to shatter if he failed, unleashing a turn-born's unbridled anguish. Flooding beyond Marrowdell? The dragon feared it was the least of the damage Jenn Nalynn could cause in her despair.

The Verge wouldn't notice. The Verge never did. But in her world, if the mad sei so much as twitched in reaction, it would send earthquakes to rip the entire edge.

She could break the world.

Thoughts that stole any chance of sleep and sent Wisp out into the dimming. When kruar and others thought to hunt dragons.

Let them try.

Still, prudence to fly high, avoiding shadows and what lurked within them.

Hunting, himself.

There existed no helpful correspondence between the girl's world and his, where the sky might be above or below mountains and mimrol flowed silver-bright. His crossing led to his sanctuary, a convenience Wisp fully expected the sei to shift on him without warning or heed. For now, it worked.

The mad sei who stitched the edge and Verge together—penance or purpose, only its confusing kind knew—showed itself in Marrowdell as the Fingers and Spine of the Bone Hills. Here it had been the Wound, a lump fed on by nyphrit, with a haunting eye filled with stars, sending futile calls to turn-born for their aid.

Answered and healed, in the Verge and edge, by Jenn Nalynn, who'd repaired damage caused seventy years ago by those with more magic than sense.

Not that sei understood gratitude or any other emotion. This one did, however, experience curiosity, exhibiting a terrifying tendency to poke itself into the business of lesser beings where it most certainly did not belong and wasn't welcome.

Beyond a dragon's place, to trouble such a being. He discovered a certain empathy for the little cousins who must deal with him.

Wisp's quarry was a dragon of bizarre green, the sei's seeming when it bothered with him. The result of their encounters? Confusing words and broken bones—his, sei incapable of grasping the fragility of other life, yet hunt it he did.

He permitted himself an anxious snarl but refused to change course.

This sei had given part of itself to Jenn Nalynn; a claiming or gift, none could say, but by so doing, a dragon might reason, it had forged a new connection with Marrowdell.

One that, a dragon might hope, gave this sei an interest in saving it.

And Jenn Nalynn.

It was at this moment Wisp knew himself watched. He felt the

unwelcome focus as an itch between his wings, an instinct to fly
higher or seek the earth, kruar prone to attack from ambush. Better
yet, be ready to launch a counterstrike—

Wisp gave a small shake.

He was always watched. By other dragons, at a prudent distance, curious what he did. By the little cousins of Marrowdell, anxious to help or poised to flee depending on their nature and his
mood. By prey.

By the toad queen. Wisp dismissed a shiver of dread. Habit, nothing more. The last time she'd stirred from her palace of white stone—
an edifice stood alone and isolated at the outermost limit of the
Verge, avoided by all—had been during his war with the kruar, taking
full advantage of the chaos, for she was, above all, a mimrol thief.

Glutton was more like it, even if the Verge's magic was inexhaustible, and if those in the Verge were fortunate, she'd gorged herself into
a thousand-year torpor.

No, what watched him would be something else again.

The sei?

His jaws opened in anticipation, dragonsfire filling his mouth.

EIGHT

WITH LORRA AND Jupp working the kitchen, and Wainn unconscious, they let Peggs and Hettie rest as long as the twins slept.

Babies in charge of such matters. A revelation Jenn might have come to sooner had Hettie and Tadd not seemed to manage ably on their own. Granted, in a house where they had comforts like extra diapers and soft cuddly toys, plus Gallie and Zehr, who'd bring little Loee and mind all three with practiced ease whenever called upon—but even under those ideal circumstances, she now realized the babies ruled, as they should, being helpless.

Thoughts to make her smile as she walked to the well. Moonbeams lit the way. The mud being frozen, at first she didn't bother to use the boards put down last night. After twisting her ankle, she hopped on the wood, finding it so much easier she resolved then and there to ask Bannan if they might keep the boards to use next spring.

~Elder sister. You should not be out in the dark.~

There was light enough to show Jenn the house toads waiting beside the well, not that she'd argue the point. She lifted her pails. "I'm just getting water."

~Then do not be flesh, elder sister.~ With such grimness, Jenn started and almost toppled.

Whatever leapt at her missed.

The pouncing house toad did not. Seeing black clawed feet flail wildly as they disappeared inside the toad's maw, Jenn let herself be glass and pearl and safe from—"Nyphrit."

Ancestors Haunted and Horrified, she immediately pictured the path to the Spine as it had been at the Great Turn, spilling hordes of the nasty creatures who, as far as she knew, had no redeeming qualities whatsoever beyond feeding house toads.

They'd almost killed Uncle Horst.

~They are made foolish by bloodlust, elder sister, and forget their fear of you. Do not worry. Come daylight, the nyphrit will retreat. Until they do, we protect Marrowdell.~ Words that came from more than these two.

She lifted her arms, letting the light from her bared hands illuminate the farmyard, and gasped. There were more house toads here than she'd ever seen before, even at the battle to the Spine. Their huge eyes flashed, returning her light, then disappeared, hidden once more.

"Hearts of my Ancestors," Jenn said, her voice husky with emotion, "we are Beholden for the courage of our friends. Keep Us Close."

She stayed turn-born to dip a finger in the well's water in thanks, then fill the pails, and on the return journey to the porch. There, moved by her heart, Jenn looked over at the barn. Battle and Brawl dozed head to tail, guarded by valiant creatures smaller than their hooves. The doors were closed and no lamplight showed.

She kissed the pre-dawn air and blew softly. Let Bannan and the rest sleep as long as they could.

Ancestors Determined and Dutiful. Today, with what Wisp learned of the river, maybe they'd start to fight back against the flood and reclaim their homes.

Heart lifting, Jenn went inside to make tepid tea.

Bannan drew his trusty spoon, holding it at the ready as Scourge entered the shadows beside the Bone Hill. Nyphrit clambered alongside, spitting their hate, yellow eyes aglow. They came no nearer than the limit of the neyet.

Knew better, did they? Putting the spoon away, he declined the temptation to look deeper at the pale stone so close at hand, focused on avoiding the branches whipped his way as Scourge smashed through the forest.

"Ow!" Most of them. Bannan wiped blood from his eyes and ducked lower. "Be careful!"

The kruar rumbled his disdain.

This Bone Hill sloped toward the center of the valley, plunging into the ground like the tip of a giant's finger into the last field behind his farm. Sure enough, when he shot a quick glance up, the wall of white had decreased by half its height.

The shadows grew, black strokes against the stone. They seemed to bend and move, reaching for them. A disquieting illusion.

He hoped.

By hope or good fortune, they reached the tip of the Bone Hill without being attacked. Another day, Bannan might have been tempted to jump down and explore the perfect white line where the stone dove beneath the soil.

Instead, he stayed on Scourge as the kruar turned to follow the other side back the way they'd come, away from the river. Again.

He should never have let the bloody beast talk him into this—this escapade. Clearly the best way to look for the river's source would be from the air, not crashing through brush.

Meaning Wisp.

The rivalry between kruar and dragon was ancient and bloodstained. They'd led their kind to war against one another only to be punished and exiled by the sei for disturbing the peace of the Verge.

Not that the Verge he'd experienced was peaceful—

Bannan pressed his face to the kruar's neck. Ancestors Witness, they were committed now, for the sake of Scourge's considerable pride if nothing else, and he'd not abandon his partner.

However saner the other choice be.

W

Spring arrived in the lowlands and valleys, but the mountain's ridge behind the Westietas' country estate held greedily to its lips of snow, and curls of snow, and wonderful twisty slopes of snow.

Inspiring deep sighs and longing looks from both Semyn and Werfol Westietas, the boys now forbidden to play in the snow, for in late spring any part was prone to collapse without warning and bury them.

If it didn't conspire and combine with more snow to roar down the mountainside, a force able to wipe away trees and buildings. Even their father, the Baron Emon Westietas, had paused his visits to the family ossuary at the lowermost end of the ridge rather than risk triggering an avalanche, though troubled enough to wish to consult his Ancestors on a regular basis. As for their mother—

Baroness Lila Marerrym Larmensu Westietas wasn't home. She hadn't been home for some time, having business elsewhere they weren't to speak of or imagine, but was, her sons and husband knew, likely dangerous and possibly deadly.

Not for Lila but for her prey, for she hunted a man called Glammis Lurgan who'd tried to use the foulest sort of spell to ensnare her brother, their Uncle Bannan, who was a truthseer. Those with such gifts were of interest to Lurgan's customers, and Lila intended to acquire a full list of their names and whereabouts.

And possibly some heads.

All being the sort of things ordinary children would not be told, but as Semyn would be eight this fall and thus officially proclaimed heir and have to know this and more, he might as well, their mother'd said, start knowing now.

And no one in the household lied anymore to Werfol, whose own gifts as truedreamer and truthseer had arrived this winter past and still caused him difficulties.

Not, Werfol reminded himself quickly, that he'd been truedreaming, or even tempted, since the episode with a dragon who'd turned out to be a little too real for comfort.

Seeing he'd drawn the start of a little dragon on the corner of his workbook, he quickly drew in grapes and leaves on vines and beetles until it was almost impossible to tell what anything was and he'd wasted most of the page.

Ancestors Problematic and Perplexed. He sighed a deep, long sigh. Deeply.

Semyn glanced up at him. "What's wrong, Weed?"

"I'm tired of being inside. I want to go out. I want to go to our special place," he elaborated, that being the magical edge, a part of the estate a bit like Marrowdell he'd discovered with the help of a house toad, and shown his family. Unlike their mother and father, Semyn couldn't remember on his own, but he'd sworn to believe Werfol no matter what. So Werfol firmed his voice as he continued. "The special and important place I remember for you. That place."

Semyn put a pencil in the book in front of him on the study table they shared—another about barons and the House of Keys, no doubt—and closed it, indicating his complete attention. "Is our place safely free of snow?"

Was it? Probably, Werfol decided, snow melting first away from rocks and the slope past the abandoned forester's hut covered with them. With song stones, not just rocks. At the turn, they showed themselves to be people-ish sorts named scree, who laughed and knocked into each other to make songs and very much appreciated the little hammers he brought whenever he could.

Not that there were any left in the house to give them, but a new shipment, their father promised—and he'd seen the truth in his face—would be on its way once the Lilem River calmed to where boats could travel it.

"It's been a very long time since we were there." Ages and ages and ages, come to think of it, between snowstorms then rainstorms and winds—and their studies. Werfol thought of their special place more and more each day.

Not that he wondered why.

Semyn, having waited with admirable patience, began to drum his fingers on the book, as if promising it his attention shortly. "Weed, you know the rule. This late in spring, we keep clear of the mountain's snow. So is this special place safe or not?"

"How can I know without going there?" Sensing this might not be the right answer, Semyn having a new and disturbingly adult tendency to fuss over the slightest risk, Werfol hurried on, "We can check from a distance. If there's any snow, I swear we'll come right back home." Though they would surely have to stop at the coop to see the pigeons and JoJo, his goose, then by the barn to say hello to the horses and maybe Semyn would want to go for a ride—

His brother looked unconvinced.

"Wouldn't you like to go outside?" Werfol insisted, certain he was right, the sun shining in the windows and it having been a long morning over books, their tutor, Namron Setac, busy helping their father translate some trickier than usual correspondence from Ansnor, likely about the train because everything was lately.

Semyn's hands slowly but surely left his book. His eyes brightened. "Momma says fresh air is good for the mind."

A most excellent reason. Werfol wished he'd thought of it first. "Then you'll come?"

Semyn cast a distracted look at the book, as if it argued with him, then sighed his own sigh. "I can't. I'm sorry, Werfol. Master Setac expects me to review the section on the original boundaries of the Rhothan districts before lunch." He pressed his hand almost tenderly on the cover. "We're to discuss Vorkoun's with Poppa there."

As if that were a special treat.

While he enjoyed their father's company, when they had it, Werfol couldn't imagine any topic more boring, unless it was genealogy and nomenclature, and if their tutor were there, he'd be called upon to contribute, he just knew it.

If the baron and tutor were there, with Semyn, so would Dutton Omemee, to stand guard behind the heir. At least he would so long as Dutton believed Werfol somewhere else and safe.

His longing to go to the edge blossomed into a plan, then and there.

"I don't want to sit and listen to a lesson all through lunch," Werfol said, letting his disappointment show because otherwise Semyn—who was almost as smart as their mother—would notice and suspect something. He turned the page in his workbook, managing to look as woeful as possible. "I'll stay here and be hungry and think about going out one day." And sighed. Deeply.

Sure enough, his brother looked upset. "We'll go after lunch, Weed. I promise."

It was the truth, but wasn't, not all of it, and that always riled him. "Liar!" Eyes glimmering gold, Werfol shot back, "You can't promise. What if Master Setac or Poppa want you to do something else more important than be with me? Then what?"

"Heart's Blood. See if I care what you do." Snatching up his precious book, Semyn left the studyroom to find somewhere else to be. Somewhere not with him.

Well, two could play that game.

Dutton, in his chair by the door, rose to follow. He stopped to give Werfol a doubt-filled look. "This where you'll stay, then?"

"No. I'm going to finish this, then I'm going outside to visit the birds and horses and get fresh air." With a stop at the edge to check on its snow in between, he thought but didn't say. "*They'll* be happy to see me."

"Your brother has—"

"Responsibilities," Werfol interrupted, which wasn't rude with Dutton, who sincerely cared about him and his brother and had sworn his life to their service, but wasn't polite either. "I know." He let some sadness into his voice. "It'll be worse, once he's heir, won't it? I'll hardly see Semyn—ever."

Dutton coughed lightly. "I'll make sure your brother keeps his promise to go exploring with you this afternoon, Werfol. As will I," added as if there were no possibility of argument. "While you finish your studies."

Werfol gave the guard a happy smile.

If not a promise in return.

The sun had yet to crest the valley walls when Jenn Nalynn discovered to her dismay that Bannan Larmensu was not, as she'd believed, safe in the barn with the others.

Nor, according to Cheffy who'd gone looking with Kydd and Dusom, was the truthseer in the privy or taking a turn with the livestock in the meadow. "Bannan's vanished!" concluded the breathless boy. "Maybe he was ate by the bad things!"

Jenn froze, her heart like stone.

"The word is *eaten*, he wasn't, now take your breakfast, Cheffy, and thank you," Peggs said, preemptively tucking a bowl of porridge into the boy's hands and pushing him gently on his way. Her dark eyes regarded Jenn. "Dear Heart, don't listen to him. Scourge isn't here either. I'd have heard him by now."

The kruar having, these past months, come to realize begging at kitchen doors worked best with a voice. He now spoke, in his way, to any in Marrowdell willing to share bacon or cheese. The exceptions were the Treffs, Old Jupp, Tadd Emms, and the children. Uncle Horst was immune to his posturing, but for him Scourge made an exception; whenever the two traded war stories, Riss, having the softer heart, slipped them both treats.

Scourge most assuredly would have encouraged Peggs or Hettie to feed him this morning. If he was gone as well? Jenn shook her head. "Bannan wouldn't take Scourge and sneak away in the night."

They passed out more bowls, then Peggs whispered, "Kydd thinks Bannan might have gone for help. And to warn the people of Endshere. He would, you know."

It warmed her heart to hear the pair thought Bannan willing, which he would be, being the most courageous person imaginable, but Jenn shook her head again, more vigorously. "They'd have to cross the flood. It'd be too great a risk, even for Scourge."

Peggs, undaunted, tried again. "I heard someone say we should set a watch at the river bank. Maybe Bannan's gone to do that."

Hadn't he told her Scourge was watching?

"You're right," Jenn told her sister, to stop more guesses or worse, a suggestion to use their mother's gift to find Bannan. An uncertain process at best, as likely to draw home a stray calf as her missing love. "He'll come back for breakfast."

The dairy cows appeared, first to the well in the pre-dawn. The usually placid beasts uttered low complaints. Between futile lips at the mud of the farmyard, the leader pushed fretfully at Devins, who walked at their heads carrying empty milk buckets. They needed more than water. Feeding the livestock was imperative.

Ancestors Daring and Devoted, mightn't Bannan have taken Scourge to search for forage?

Cheered by the thought, Jenn took a tray of emptied bowls and cups from Cynd and went into the house to refill them, Lorra having stopped the washing of dishes between such use. People waiting their turn at breakfast weren't going to care, she'd stated firmly.

It did move the line much faster.

Covie was doling out porridge, while Hettie refilled cups. "Is it true, Jenn?" the healer asked in a low voice. "Bannan's gone and left us?"

So much for being cheered. "He hasn't left," Jenn protested. She hurriedly provided her own thought on the matter. "I imagine he went looking for hay."

"At night?" Covie frowned.

"With a full moon, bright as could be," Hettie offered stoutly. "You could read by it."

Not bright enough to daunt the nyphrit, giving Jenn a new and far scarier thought. What if Bannan had gone to fight them? Ancestors Bruised and Bloody—had he been dragged away—Scourge follow for revenge?

"Jenn!"

Someone was shaking her. Peggs. Jenn stared up at her, shivering. Why was she shivering? Why were Hettie and Covie covered in—snow?

As was the rest of the room, what she could see past Peggs, including the quilt covering Wainn and the chairs. Her sad little blizzard had smothered the fire, if not the stove, and filled poor Master Jupp's hearing pipe—

Jenn hastily wished to be warmer—

The stove flared up, making Covie leap to save the porridge, crying out as flames singed her eyebrows and hair—

"Easy, Dear Heart." Her sister gathered her close, pressing Jenn's face against her shoulder. For comfort or to hide her from Hettie and Covie's horrified looks?

Likely both, Jenn sighed miserably to herself.

"Shhh. He'll be all right," Peggs said. "You'll see. Bannan will be back and soon. You know he wouldn't want you worrying."

Jenn made herself hear the words. Tried to believe them but, Ancestors Witness, Peggs was right about one thing.

It wasn't safe for her to worry. Not safe at all. With that, Jenn squirmed free and fled the kitchen.

Outside, she followed the dairy cows back to her meadow, then went through the line of neyet to the dome of crystal her dragon called home. In summer at least, when warmed by the sun. Now it stood frozen and empty.

Jenn crawled inside and sat, arms wrapped around her knees. She took slow, deep, and deliberate breaths. The first couple trailed off in ragged sobs but she refused to move or stop until she felt calmer and ever-so-slightly in control.

Resting her forehead on her knees, she whispered, "Wisp."

Knowing he'd hear.

They'd lost the moonlight and shortly afterwards their way, if Scourge's meandering was any indication. The forest on this side of the Bone Hill should be little more than a narrow strip. If not as dark as Prince Ordo's heart, by now they should see the rock outcrop where the river came together before reaching the kaliia fields, features Bannan remembered seeing clearly from the heights of the Spine last fall.

Should. Alas, the forest had other ideas, continuing without end in every direction the kruar tried until Bannan, frustrated, gave the kruar a swat to stop the great beast. "Admit it. You're lost."

"I am not lost." Testily. "This place is well defended."

The truthseer sat straighter, hands flat on Scourge's sweating hide. "How? Why?"

"The path changes with every step." A note of irony. "Why? To make me angry." A violent shudder. "You try."

Bannan slipped down. Unable to see the hand he held in front of his face, he kept the other on Scourge.

He tried his gift, staring at the ground.

To his surprise, a thin line of little white pebbles glowed at his feet, leading into the distance. They marked a narrow path snaking away to the left, pressed into a deep hollow track by long and frequent use, and only one thing of Bannan's acquaintance in Marrowdell would fit inside.

A house toad.

"I can see a way," Bannan said, choosing not to mention the little cousins just yet, the kruar's attitude toward them a perplexed and chancy tolerance. "It may not lead to the river," he cautioned.

Scourge huffed. "There's nowhere else to go."

The truthseer wasn't so sure. If this was where the toads brought their hard-earned treasures, they had a reason. Were they truly using the pebbles to build a throne for their missing queen, or was that just the dragon's whimsy?

Whatever they built would be at the end of this path—and might be by the river, after all.

The kruar growled impatiently, a timely reminder. Ancestors Languishing and Lost, there was no gain in waiting for sunrise or more courage from the nyphrit, who continued to follow.

Bannan set a boot in the track before them, the other awkwardly on the higher ground beside it. "Follow me. Keep a foot in the track," he added, for this was no ordinary path. They'd no idea its rules.

Sure enough, with each step, the truthseer felt himself slipping into some other world. One where the forest spread apart so his outstretched hands no longer met branches that, to his deeper sight, became amorphous and gray. Sound muffled until all he heard were Scourge's deep huffs and his own breathing. Nothing from the nyphrit, as if they were forbidden this place.

The track doubled back on itself over and over, at times so sharply Scourge had to bend nimbly or clip his own heels. The kruar stayed silent. Perhaps he, being of a magical realm, sensed the strangeness, too.

All at once, Bannan realized he walked *in* the track with both feet and had room to spare. The little pebbles were now head-high columns, casting a pale light. A relief, to stop using his gift, but what was happening? He twisted to look at Scourge. "Have we crossed?" In the Verge, perspectives changed without warning or sense.

A mystified snarl. *No*, that meant. The kruar's hooves fit within the toads' track as well.

As they'd walked, they'd either shrunk or their surroundings grown around them. Ancestors Dazzled and Dazed, it could be both, Bannan thought, more curious than afraid. Yet the pebbles weren't boulders. They almost appeared carved—

Scourge lowered his head to sniff the ground, lips rippling in threat. Raised it, eyes red with fury. "This is their meddling. The little cousins. Where have you brought us?"

To what might be the point of it all. Bannan spoke aloud. "I think this is what the house toads make with their pebbles. A safe passage, hidden from sight." Having crossed to the Verge and left the edge for the less-magical world outside Marrowdell, the truthseer could appreciate the value, if not as much being trapped inside. "Have you seen anything like it in the Verge?"

A snort dismissed any suggestion a kruar might pay attention to anything lesser beings did or constructed. Scourge swung his head around. "There's no way back."

Behind the kruar's wide haunch, the track faded to a disturbing nothingness, even when Bannan tried his gift. He shrugged. "Then let's see where it goes."

"You first," Scourge grumbled.

Bannan set off, the kruar close behind, relieved beyond measure when their surroundings stayed the same relative size. What if they'd continued to shrink?

What if this was a trap—an endless maze from which they'd never escape?

No. House toads were honorable creatures. More than that, they understood the turn-born, fully aware of the danger posed by Jenn's grief. His breath caught. Started again. They might have come up missing by now. What would she think? That he'd abandoned Marrowdell? Never—

His boot splashed in a puddle, icy cold. Bannan stopped. Scourge's huge head came over his shoulder. "What now?"

Not a puddle. A series of them, reflecting the pale glow from the pillars, linked by an ominous trickle down the center growing wider before his eyes. "We've found the flood," he declared, mounting in haste. "We have to get out."

No need to say the rest, that if they didn't, they'd drown.

Scourge leapt forward, hooves splashing.

Wisp . . .

The dragon stalled midair and wheeled about, wings straining as he flew with all haste to his crossing, his pursuit of the sei abandoned. The girl called him and there was pain in her heart. He shared it, feared it.

Would fix it, no matter the cause, and on that vow, he found he could fly faster still.

His shadow flowed along the Verge, skimming lakes of silver mimrol, dropping into canyons of blue crystal before rising to darken peaks.

Followed by a second.

NINE

AUNT SYBB'S LATEST letter—chock-full of sage advice, if little news—had been written and received after the weddings of Hettie, Peggs, and Riss, which she'd attended with great joy, but well before Marrowdell's Midwinter Beholding. She'd yet to learn about Jenn living with Bannan, but her advice had proved helpful to her younger niece. Listen to each other. Don't go to bed on an ill feeling. Laugh to greet the day. Be kind. He can darn his own socks.

She should have added "don't lose him."

A whimper caught in Jenn's throat.

Aunt Sybb wrote knowing she'd meet the earliest response on her way north again. A surprise, surely pleasant, then, for her to receive several long letters on the heels of her own Midwinter Beholding, delivered by Tir Half-face when he returned from his adventures in Marrowdell with Bannan's nephews.

Letters, as Bannan had cautioned, short of certain details best delivered in Tir's personal report to the Lady Mahavar and not committed to paper, there being politics and his sister, the Baroness Westietas, involved.

Jenn rocked back and forth, her eyes closed. She'd promised Lila she'd take care of her beloved younger brother. She'd promised and she'd lost him.

Why had she thought to keep her own news secret? Aunt Sybb

highly approved of Bannan; so much so, she'd told Radd she no longer planned to bring Hane's "promising nephew" to meet Jenn this
spring. She'd have shared their dreams and hopes all these months.
More than likely, that wise lady would guess the outcome and be
eager to see the home they'd made together. No longer theirs at all.

In Aunt Sybb's latest letter there could be, therefore, no mention
of her certain joy at the news Peggs was pregnant, for she hadn't
then known. Nor mention of the delivery of twins to Hettie, whom
she'd known was pregnant, just not how much, nor that Wen was
expecting Wainn's child, sooner, it turned out, than later.

Nor that her youngest niece, having become turn-born, was incapable of bringing new life to the world, her body having no memory of it. She'd not even that of Bannan Larmensu, if he was truly
gone.

A tear froze on Jenn's cheek.

Like her letters, Aunt Sybb took the Northward Road to reach
them, bringing Uncle Hane's barely worn boots for her brother, fabric for her nieces, and as much food as she could cram into her carriage, knowing winters here were hard. She'd somehow find space
for new books and paper, as well as ribbons and lace, and it wasn't
right her heartfelt generosity in perennially overloading her carriage
would trap its wheels in mud and floodwater and cause it to tip
over—

Jenn stuffed her fist into her mouth to stifle a scream. Dirty diapers, she told herself. Pots with burnt-on flakes of porridge. Huge and
dirty pots full of baked-on diapered babies—

A breeze, warm and concerned, caressed her cheeks. It couldn't
melt the tear. "Dear Heart. I'm here. What's wrong?"

"Bannan's gone—" she hiccupped. "He took Scourge—maybe
Scourge took him—maybe it was—I think they—" She couldn't
say it.

Her gaze was caught by wild violet eyes, for her dragon showed
himself, as he rarely did.

Tendrils of steam curled from elegant nostrils borne on a long
snout, the jaws lined with fangs longer than her fingers. A hide of

silver scales as delicate as the finest linen and claws like ancient bone. The limbs on Wisp's right side were withered and useless, those of his left healed and whole, and his magnificent wings spread to wrap around and draw her under his feathered chin. With exquisite care, for his fangs were razor sharp, and he wouldn't risk scratching her.

He was warm. Hot, really, being fresh from the Verge, and only when his shared heat stopped her shivers did Jenn realize she'd come close to freezing in his home. "W-w-wouldn't have happened if I'd b-b-become turn-born," she muttered peevishly, yet stayed as she was, suddenly loathing that other self.

Wisp, who knew her best, didn't comment. Instead, his little breeze whispered, "You asked me to search for the river's beginnings, Dear Heart. It would be like the old fool to have spied on us then seek Bannan's aid to do it first. Not that they could," this with asperity, "lacking wings."

It wasn't at all sensible. It did make sense, and Jenn felt her heart resume beating as if she'd forgotten it. Which she mustn't but clearly had for a time. She pushed, gently, and the dragon released her. "Please look for them, Wisp. Please go now."

"If first you go home, Dear Heart." Sternly.

She'd worried him, Jenn knew. Hadn't she worried herself? And terrified poor Lorra and Old Jupp, though Hettie was unflappable and Peggs would have understood and tried to explain—she caught a sudden cold breath and steadied. "I promise."

"And take your foolish toad."

Her toad? Jenn looked where Wisp aimed his snout, dismayed to spot the ball of a thoroughly frozen house toad, legs outstretched, its skin blue and open eyes frosted white. "Oh dear."

The dragon opened his jaws slightly, freeing a suggestive lick of flame. Before he charred the toad, Jenn swept it up, tucking what felt like a lump of ice in the bodice of her dress, straining her buttons. "I'll take him with m-me," she said, shivering again.

Wisp backed out of her way, letting her crawl from his crystal home. Neither noticed the moth slip betwixt and be gone, satchel full. The dragon, having recklessly sought the mad sei's attention, would have been alarmed to learn he'd never lost it.

Jenn emerged to find the stars faded, the edge of the sky turning blue, and no Wisp, but he hadn't left, she knew.

She rose to her feet, holding her cloak tight around her and the toad. "I'll go straight home, Wisp. Find Bannan. And Scourge," she added firmly, Wisp less than trustworthy when it came to his old foe.

"I will!" Snow crystals swirled up and away, her dragon marking his exit, and Jenn sagged with relief.

With an effort, she turned her face to the farm and headed back as quickly as her numbed feet would allow, needing to thaw as much as her overly devoted house toad.

At first, Werfol enjoyed his excursion—a word he'd lately discovered in a book and decided meant a worthy adventure—very much. The cobble path went through the small forest sheltering the house and its outbuildings, lit by sunbeams and warm. Fat green buds tipped every branch that didn't have a red flower or yellow catkin, and tweets and trills filled the air, for the songbirds had come back ten days ago, as predicted by their cook, who knew many surprising things and was Werfol's friend.

The squirrels here were friends or at least harmless.

The ones who replaced them once he passed the discreet markers he'd helped their father place, larger and with yellowed teeth, who bent to snarl at him, were not. When one came too close Werfol brought out the house toad from under his arm—being hardly so foolish as to go adventuring alone—to let it glare at the false squirrel.

Who turned tail and vanished.

"Thank you," he told the house toad. It came from Marrowdell, as had the little toy under his shirt. He'd carried Goosie next to his skin ever since their mother left on *her* excursion, not that he worried or doubted, just to feel better about it. Which made him think how brave Araben Sethe, the Ansnan engineer, had been to come here last winter, alone.

The ground was warm and soft, with little green shoots everywhere and leaves popping open and uncurling. Most importantly, there was no sign of snow at all, not even in the shade, making Werfol happier and happier by the moment—and also less guilty, not that he should be, but his excursion might be considered sneaking and a good outcome made it more like scouting, which Dutton might approve.

The long hill of song stones came in view, free of snow—though the stones themselves, being white and round, resembled balls of it, which made Werfol giggle. When he squinted—the sun very bright— at the very top he could make out a thin line of white, surely not a worry. Above and beyond that loomed the mountain, mostly white, meaning mostly snow still, but safely distant and nowhere near.

The house toad squirmed, pushing a foot into Werfol's stomach; busy making even more and better plans, the young truthseer put it down without asking why. He'd come back this afternoon with Semyn—and Dutton—and they'd arrive just in time for the turn, he decided, full of joy. When they could see and enjoy the wonders hiding here for themselves—wonders he could see anytime he tried.

Werfol's brown eyes turned gold.

The song stones became little people shaped like balls. But instead of looking glad to see him, the scree made faces, scared ones, and rolled away from him as fast as they could, sounding little chimes of dismay as they clicked into one another.

"Stop!" he warned, keeping it a whisper. You didn't make loud noises beneath a mountain with snow. Everyone knew that, just not, it appeared, the scree. Werfol held out his hands, trying to get their attention before any crashed—

A loud CRACK as several did just that—

A huge sigh of sound answered, as if the mountain gave breath, and then ROARED—

Werfol bent to snatch up the house toad and run. Snow and chunks began to rain down from above, shattering around him. Despite himself, not meaning to, as his hands touched the toad the young truthseer looked deeper and beyond—

—to meet the regard of *other* eyes, green and dreadful eyes, eyes full of malice and triumph and a terrible greed—

—the avalanche hit! He staggered and dropped the house toad or it squirted free. Gasped, sure he was about to die and very sorry, he was so very sorry—

The rock beneath his feet cracked open.

And Werfol Westietas was pulled into the earth, as the rage of the mountain tumbled over where he'd been, smothering all.

Scourge hadn't run far before Bannan realized their surroundings were no longer featureless. The light of the pebble columns dimmed, letting more show beyond them. Impressions of shapes passed in a blur.

Suddenly a shadow paced them, overhead as if the track they were in had a ceiling. For all he knew, it did. An enormous unpleasant shadow. "What is that?"

The kruar snapped his jaws. "A nyphrit."

The *something* passed again, making the truthseer flinch and duck. Not before he glimpsed—were those claws? If so, they were longer than his body. "It can't be."

"Yet is. Be glad it's not in here with us."

A sentiment Bannan heartily shared. If a nyphrit, this was a monster of its kind—

Unless it was normal size, and they, small—

The consequence would be equally regrettable. "Maybe it's alone."

Another appeared, a vast shadow lurching alongside.

"They're never alone." Scourge snarled.

A claw plunged through the gray to snag a pebble column, flipping it over. The action tore a jagged gap through which Bannan glimpsed a huge and twisted root before the claw returned, poking as if to stab and pull them out.

If they didn't return to normal size before the magic of this passageway failed completely, the monster nyphrit would swallow them whole.

The kruar lunged forward, impossibly faster. Behind them, a frustrated chitter and wail. Ahead—

The passage was blocked!

Scourge plunged to a stop.

"It's all right," Bannan gasped. Not, he thought, that he'd reason to believe they were any safer, for what blocked the passage, filling it with its body, was a giant house toad, to his true sight glittering in its mail and gauds, eyes huge and dark.

It didn't move, glaring at them as if offended.

Or indignant. Surely they'd trespassed where they shouldn't have and Bannan opened his mouth to explain, only to snap it closed as Wen Treff walked around the toad.

She stood between its front legs, each the size of a tree trunk. Lifted a languid hand to point to where the monster nyphrit behind them continued to pry away pebbles in its hunt.

The giant toad leapt through her, *through them*—Bannan heard Scourge grunt in rare astonishment—landing behind on the path. He twisted to watch but it was over and done, the house toad peacefully pushing the pebble columns back in place with a toe, with no sign of the monster nyphrit.

Except in how the belly of the toad bulged here, then there, as its latest meal protested.

He turned back to look at Wen. To his deeper sight, her wild hair was shot through with purples and golds, no longer light gray—or were the locks glittering silver—or might some be green? It seemed the changeable light of the Verge shone through her.

Her hair, that light, framed her face and billowed past her knees like a robe, parted over her rounded belly. Accident—no, a message, he judged, heart in his throat. Wen Treff wore Marrowdell's magic. The baby inside her did not. Ancestors Dire and Dreadful, what did that bode for its future?

Eyes stinging, he let go of his gift, willing himself to see the tall pregnant woman cloaked in brown wool, the hem stained with mud—a version of Wen making it possible, if no easier, to ask what he must. "If you stay, what becomes of your baby?"

Her eyes flashed silver as she spoke—or did she sing? ~She doesn't belong here. Neither do you.~

He couldn't tell how he heard her; the words passed through his skin or did they sink into his flesh like raindrops, as if her transformation advanced—

Or Wen chose to no longer conceal herself.

Sliding from Scourge, Bannan landed with his boots deep in water. "We'll leave," he assured this magical being, letting the *for now* go unsaid. Ancestors Blessed and Bountiful, they owed it to both to return, to bring her newborn daughter to safety. Wen, the truthseer thought with sudden conviction, might well count on it.

He needn't have kept silent. The corners of her lips deepened and curved upward. ~Word will be brought.~

Bannan took a step toward Wen, impulsively offering his hands.

The huge toad rumbled, a vibration felt in his bones. Heeding the warning, he let his hands drop to his side and came no closer. "Wen. Are you—"

Safe . . . certain . . . willing? What could he ask, with this Wen as impossibly remote from her mother's parlor or Wainn's loving arms as if she'd become a Blessed Ancestor and bones in the earth?

"—happy?" Bannan chose, it being the answer those who'd loved her most needed.

~I am free,~ she replied, lifting her arms like wings. With the words came a searing rush of joy, burning around and through him, filling his every sense until the truthseer almost glimpsed, almost saw—

The moment shattered on her cold, stern words. ~Now go.~

Leaving him bereft—of what wasn't for him, Bannan knew. What Wen had found might be wondrous and fulfilling for her, but he needed more than magic. He needed people, family, and life. Love.

Most of all, Jenn Nalynn. All outside the house toads' unusual realm. Eager to return, the truthseer nodded, then confessed.

"We'd be beholden if you'd show us how."

W

He wasn't dead. He was happy about that, if surprised, for Werfol remembered most of what had happened and thought he should be.

The scree. They'd made a sudden loud noise, which you didn't do near snow ready to collapse but they hadn't meant any harm and he hoped they were fine. Being stone, they should be—

—not being stone, why wasn't he dead? The avalanche had swept right over him, blinding him with white. He remembered hard chunks of snow and ice. Some had hit him. He touched his cheek and winced.

"Welcome, little one."

Werfol went very still, all at once remembering how the ground beneath him had opened up. The eyes he'd seen. How it had felt like a giant mouth sucked him down and inside like something in a straw—*inside what?*

"Aren't you going to talk?"

Not to that voice, he wasn't. Not to something able to reach into where he'd been and bring him here, wherever this was.

"I saved your life."

Had it really?

And even if it had, *why had it?*

Questions Momma taught them to ask themselves before admitting anything, even gratitude.

He needed to know more about where he was—and with who.

It didn't help there wasn't any light at all. In case his eyes were glued shut, Werfol blinked several times, proving they weren't. Next he thought to look beyond, as Master Setac taught, but in time something warned him he might not like what he saw, so he didn't.

He reached out, discovering he was inside something soft, like a bag. Sniffed. It smelled familiar.

"Swallowed you whole, little one. What do you think of that?"

Werfol ignored the voice, now out to scare instead of trick, busy finding out more about his prison.

His fingers found a knot of rope, no, four knots connected in a square. He moved along and quickly found a second group. Filled with a sudden terrible thought, Werfol reached into his shirt.

Goosie was gone!

Goosie, with two buttons for eyes, sewn on nice and tight. Goosie, who smelled like clean boy and laundry soap, having been washed recently after an accident with a bowl of stew.

There would be knots down her side as well, where she'd been lovingly repaired.

Werfol found one. Stood with his hands clenched around what should be thread, not rope, unable to know if he'd been made small— or the toy large—but he knew where he was.

Inside his toy.

It had to be a dream. A truedream. He had to wake up. "I have to wake up!" he shouted.

"There you are," said the voice, then laughed and laughed.

Werfol feared this wasn't a dream at all.

Feeling a coward, Jenn took the Tinker's Road from Wisp's meadow so as not to witness the suffering of the animals in hers. Alas, Ancestors Miserable and Mired, there was no escaping the sound of their misery. Loved and cared for all their lives, Marrowdell's beasts couldn't understand being left hungry. Tears stung her eyes and she hugged the frozen toad. To avoid meeting any accusing or hopeful eyes, Jenn kept hers down, taking the shortest path across the farmyard to the house, the mud stiff and cold underfoot.

She slipped inside, almost gasping at the heat from the kitchen. Hands shaking, she hung her cloak then showed her sister the frozen house toad. In the light, it looked ghastly, like a hunk of old gray meat.

Peggs, to her credit, didn't flinch. "Poor thing. Is it still alive?"

"Yes. And will be fine, once warm," Jenn said, mostly to reassure herself. But where best to thaw the toad? Her gaze traveled the room. The stove was too hot, the fireplace too exposed—

"Put him in here." Peggs went to the mattress, where Wainn

continued what wasn't sleep, and lifted the edge of the quilt. "Ancestors Lost and Languid," she added pragmatically, "maybe it'll wake Wainn."

Despite her sister's avowed wish, Jenn took care not to let the block of frozen toad actually touch Wainn. She covered it with the quilt, giving the hard lump an encouraging pat.

"Dear Heart. You're shivering. Take this." She was handed a well-wrapped baby. "Any news?"

Jenn hesitated, hugging the warm bundle. Torre or Elainn? Impossible to tell without waking the baby and hardly important. Bending her head, she inhaled its scent of peace and baby breath, with a hint of soured milk. Stalling.

Aunt Sybb would say the sooner one started, the sooner a task was done, usually regarding laundry. Remembering that, Jenn looked up to met her sister's searching gaze. "No news. I've sent Wisp to look for—"

"Did you tell her?" Hettie, the other twin in its sling, appeared beside Peggs. Her usually rosy cheeks were pale.

"Tell me what?"

"The river's rising. Tadd scouted at first light and saw," as if Jenn wouldn't believe her. "The water's coming!" Her voice cracked with fear.

"Ancestors Tried and Troubled, it's not here yet, fool girl. There's work to do." Lorra delivered the admonishment without looking up from the wizened potatoes she chopped then slipped into the largest pot. She waved the knife. "No onions. That's the immediate crisis."

Making stew. Covered loaves rising by the fireplace. Old Jupp and Riss washing dishes in the tub. She'd missed breakfast.

The thought of food made her ill. Jenn passed her armful of young Emms to Hettie. "Lorra's right," she agreed. "Time to work. I'll be off." Hers wasn't here.

It was with the flood. With Bannan. With livestock starved enough to bite chunks from the thorny hedges, and it made her knees feel weak, the struggle to think of ways to help them all without harm to any. She would, somehow. She must. Soon.

"Be—" Peggs twisted her apron and fell silent, her eyes dark with worry. Hettie sighed and nuzzled her baby. Wainn muttered, possibly feeling the chill of the toad frozen trying to help her, and Old Jupp chuckled at something his great-niece said, oblivious to talk of toads, floods, and onions.

Jenn felt such a rush of affection for them, her smile came without warning.

Relaxing, her sister smiled back. Hettie half grinned, showing the adorable gap in her teeth, and the baby who wasn't asleep blinked in surprise like a tiny owl, while the one who slumbered gave a tiny coo.

Jenn kissed Peggs' cheek, then Hettie's. "I'll be back, Dear Hearts."

Lorra's firm, "Onions!" chased her out the door.

The sun was up, giving light if no warmth this early. From here, she couldn't see the rising floodwater, only hear the river's endless grumble.

To Jenn's dismay, the farmyard looked worse, if possible. Only the well remained pristine and clear—for now. It was maddening—

She caught her breath and nodded. Wisp. Her dragon would return any moment with Bannan, who knew about floods and danger—and her. Together, they'd find a way to make things better, to save Marrowdell. Didn't Aunt Sybb always say two heads held more ideas than one?

Though she also said decisions were best made in one head at a time, which—

Jenn's attention was caught by the group of villagers in front of the barn. She joined them at Kydd's beckoning wave. As she came close, she saw they'd gathered around a large pile of wood.

Thankfully, it wasn't from their barn, which surely couldn't spare this much, but consisted of the bed from Davi's cart, recovered from the road, and—her eyes widened—the door from their admittedly now-emptied larder, along with most of the shelves.

"We thought to start a fire for those come from the meadow. They're chilled through," Kydd told her in a low voice, nodding to the five who shivered uncontrollably despite extra wraps. He continued in a whisper she strained to catch, "We can't get it to burn, Dear Heart. I hate to ask, but . . ."

Of course it wouldn't burn; the wood was sopping wet and cold.

With a swallow, Jenn nodded. Stepping up to the pile, she gestured for those nearest to move back, having to repeat her request when some stayed too close for her comfort.

She eyed the immovable barn with some misgiving. Marrowdell would respond to her wish. The problem was in how little or much. Her father, who'd shifted to stand beside her, caught her look. "Should we get everyone out first?"

Should they? Order those who were dry and moderately comfortable, full of tepid tea and hot porridge, out into the damp chill of the farmyard again, on the hopefully slim chance her wish set fire to every piece of wood in range?

Put that way, Jenn thought worriedly, it was a terrible risk. "Yes, please. I'll wait."

Before anyone could move, a gout of flame swept across the woodpile, first this way then that, whiter and hotter than the utterly normal fire it spawned in its wake.

Everyone looked at her. Someone cheered and Jenn held up her hand. "It wasn't me."

It had been Wisp. Who'd arrived in time to be a great help and she'd have been ever so grateful.

Except he'd arrived alone.

A moth joined them as they followed the giant house toad, perching between Scourge's restless ears. It wasn't one of Jenn's, for it carried a satchel secured by a gem from which it pulled a slip of tiny parchment, proceeding to write on it.

A scribe, one he and Jenn believed informed the sei who held the edge together. Would the vast being wonder to find a man and kruar in the realm of toads? Or simply note their unusual size as some bizarre reference. Safer not to have attracted its interest in the first place. Whatever thoughts such a thing had, or questions, none, Bannan feared, were without risk to those of flesh and blood—a point of complete agreement between Wisp and Scourge and toads, which said all he needed to know.

It wasn't as if he could—or dared—shoo the thing away. What it learned, it learned. As for the reactions of the sei to that knowledge? He circled his fingers above his heart, whispering a quick prayer. "Hearts of my Ancestors, hear my heart's plea. I'd be beholden if you'd let us be boring. Numbingly so."

A prayer failing at once as huge black bodies were flung backwards beyond the path, followed by chunks of dimly seen ice and what had to be water!

Ancestors Fraught and Fragile. There were puddles underfoot but surely they were safe here—

Wishful thinking. The house toad began to shrink or did they grow? Scourge let out an anxious whine, the most alarming sound he'd ever heard the bloody beast make, and all at once pillars became pebbles to tumble away, and the flood rushed in—

They were in the river!

The house toad gave a mighty kick and swam out of sight. Wen had disappeared. Bannan scarcely noticed, torn from Scourge and desperately holding the last breath he'd taken before the plunge into icy cold darkness.

Currents spun, disorienting and violent. His shoulders hit stone— the bottom of the river. Ancestors Drowning and Doomed, he was at the bottom!

Teeth caught his leg, drove bone-deep. Lungs bursting, Bannan would gladly sacrifice the limb and an arm if the kruar saved them both.

But no matter how hard—and painfully—Scourge pulled, Bannan stayed stuck to the bottom. He wasn't floating. What was this? He was—he was being sucked down—

Down—

—and through.

He arched his back in a final gasp, expecting to inhale water and die.

Instead, his lungs filled with hot dry air. Dazed, Bannan rolled on his side, wincing at the shot of agony from his leg that reminded him of—"Scourge!"

~Here.~ Words, not a breeze, but *words*.

Bannan opened his eyes, confounded by wave after wave of surreal shapes and light. The Verge! He fought weakness, strove with his true sight to make sense of the place.

Finding none.

Oh, Scourge stood nearby, blood—his, no doubt—dripping from his muzzle. Lines of tension carved his big body, but his head was up, ears moving, as if puzzled. Or wary.

Heart's Blood. The truthseer rose on his elbow to look around.

The sky was overhead as a sky should be but almost never was, here. The colors were familiar, like Wen's hair but writhing with added unnameable hues. After enduring it long enough to feel safe from dragons, or whatever other dangers flew this air, Bannan lowered his eyes.

They were on a featureless plain that stretched to the horizon in every direction, unlike any part of the Verge he'd experienced before. Admittedly those were few, but this—this was unsettling different. Beneath his hands was fine sand, the texture like that deposited along a river bank. It took color from the sky but, in his shadow, appeared gray. Was this the Verge? Or more of the house toads' hidden realm—

He got to his knees. Knee. Hissing with pain, he froze in place, almost afraid to look at his other leg.

Scourge gave a dismissive huff. ~A flesh wound.~ Then added as if a mild consideration, hardly worth the mention, ~Unless there's venom.~

"'Venom'?" Bannan twisted to ease apart the blood-soaked remnants of his pant leg. Blood oozed out sluggishly from several locations; no arteries punctured, part of him deduced with cool detachment, and the skin looked normal. The rest, far from calm, glared up at Scourge. "Bloody Beast! You never said you were poisonous!"

~It didn't come up.~ The kruar's lips curled back to reveal what wasn't remotely the dentition of a proper horse. The forked tongue lifted and long fangs erupted from their hiding place. Drips of vile yellow appeared at their tips, a liquid Scourge slurped back into his mouth as if a treat. ~It's how we kill dragons.~

Ancestors Witness, he had wondered—Bannan shook himself. Anything able to harm a dragon would have killed him by now. Grimly reassured, he took off his soaking-wet coat and shirt. The coat he laid on the sand. The shirt he held up with a sigh.

On it, Jenn had embroidered the Larmensu crest to rest over his heart. His love had charmingly confessed to avoiding fine stitchwork whenever possible, and in truth her fox resembled a piglet more than a little and her sunflower, a daisy, but Bannan loved it.

Loving life more, methodically he ripped the garment into strips, wrapping those tightly around his mangled calf until sure he'd stopped the bleeding. For now at least. He'd saved the piece with Jenn's crest to tie on last, hoping it would stay clean.

Scourge lowered his head to inspect the result. ~Better than nothing,~ he judged. ~Hunters will stir once the dimming comes.~

The Verge's version of night. He'd been through it. "If this is the Verge."

The kruar snorted, his head high again, and took deep heavy breaths, nostrils flared. ~This is the Verge,~ he insisted, then looked at Bannan. ~A part unknown to me. We cannot trust it.~

The truthseer hid a smile. "Is there a part we can?"

Red eyes gleamed. ~No. But I mistrust this more. Why were we brought here?~

As if a man from outside might know. "So that wasn't a—normal—crossing?"

~No,~ with a growl beneath the word. ~We were drawn.~

"By what?"

Scourge shook his head, ears back.

Ancestors Tried and Tested. If the kruar didn't want to say, or guess, the answer wasn't good. Not good at all. "We shouldn't stay here. Help me up."

Perhaps feeling a pinch of guilt over Bannan's 'flesh wound,' Scourge knelt in the sand to offer his back. ~Don't bleed on me,~ a snap as the truthseer eased his good leg over.

Sentimental creature. Bannan slapped the kruar on the neck, grateful for the company in this strange forbidding place as well as the valiant effort to keep him from drowning.

Taking it for a signal, the kruar strode forward across the sand.

Having distracted the villagers with fire, Wisp sent urgent little breezes to tug Jenn Nalynn away from them. She came quickly, her dear face troubled. The news he brought was unlikely to change that, but he'd promised and would report. He'd flown fast and hard, scouring the heights as well as the sullen onslaught of the river, without sign of truthseer or kruar.

Only to spot what was new and alarming.

The dragon stopped chivvying her along once out of sight behind the house, near the hedge. Its branches were empty of efflet, but the little cousins weren't his concern. "I may have found where they went, Dear Heart. I need to show you. You can't be this," he added, flipping her bangs with the gentlest of breezes.

She understood at once, becoming turn-born and glass, and held out her arm.

Wisp grasped it gingerly with his good front foot. As turn-born, she would be safe from his claws and, presumably, from falling—not that he'd drop her—but it was highly unpleasant, touching this version of Jenn Nalynn. His flesh wanted to crawl away and hide.

Perhaps that was why he didn't notice the one who'd followed.

Pushing aside the feeling, the dragon surged into the air, Jenn dangling. She weighed nothing at all, yet dragged like ten kruars, her nature resisting any outside will. Wisp grumbled to himself and worked harder.

They'd not far to go.

His first beat lifted them above the forest, his second and third put them over the spreading floodwater. She cried out and no wonder. The river was about to consume the entire valley floor, newly sprouted arms beginning to surround the farm, and all were in peril.

It wasn't what he'd brought her to see. "Look to the Bone Hills."

TEN

*F*ROM THE OVERLOOK of the Spine, Jenn had admired the tapestry that was Marrowdell. The golden fields bound by green hedges, the light brown of roads and paths, the homely village itself with its colorful gardens, the deep shadows of the forests—girded by the sweep of the Bone Hills, like fingers braiding the river that gently flowed between.

Now—she fought to remember to breathe—now that river spread everywhere, fouled and deadly. Catastrophe happened beneath her and how could she tear her gaze from it?

To find Bannan. Jenn looked where her dragon bade her.

Where the river entered the flatlands, between the nearer Bone Hills, it split around a high rise of ordinary stone to merge at its base.

Now—her needless "Hurry, Wisp!" shredded in the wind of his passing. Her brave strong dragon flew as quickly as he could.

Blessed Ancestors, let it be fast enough.

Where the river once peacefully merged was a maelstrom, like those in Master Dusom's books. A whirling circle of water about the size of Davi's big cart. It shouldn't be here. It didn't belong here. Jenn felt it, knew it.

This was magic.

Wisp took her overhead. Looking down, inside she could see the smooth massive rocks lining the river bottom, cupped within the churning wall of water and ice. If Bannan had fallen into that—

Abruptly she had a heart nigh to breaking as well as an arm caught and bleeding in dragon claws, which wasn't helpful but hardly her fault.

"Let me go!" she shouted, kicking and wriggling with all her might.

"I won't! You'll die!"

As a woman, she might. Not inclined to test her dragon's wisdom, Jenn became turn-born. "Now, Wisp. Trust me."

With a groan of despair, he released her.

As she fell, Jenn wished the water out of her way.

And Marrowdell answered.

The floor of the valley shook like a horse shedding. The ice dam shattered, sending cracked floes and forgotten hives downstream to the world beyond, and Wainn Uhthoff awoke with a wild cry, startling those around him.

Upstream the rock ridge crumbled, boulders and pebbles falling into the river, damming it, directing its waters elsewhere, and Jenn didn't care where. Only that the whirlpool, cut off, sagged into itself with a defeated splash, its waters spreading outward.

By the time her feet struck the surface, it was no deeper than the trout pond where they swam each summer.

Where was Bannan?

Jenn sank. She'd no idea if it was because she was careful to stay turn-born—even the remnants of the flood dangerous—or if the water lowered with her. She didn't breathe, though she should soon. To her dismay, it was impossible to see. She held out her arms. Hoped to feel Bannan or Scourge—

Her feet touched bottom.

And went right through. This—this was where they'd gone and how! She was sure of it.

If not at all what to do next.

Wearying, to continue using his gift. The truthseer thought to rest, relying on Scourge to find the way, when all at once the sand began to change and he dared not.

For the grains grew larger—or they smaller—with every step, becoming white pebbles, then head-sized stones, then boulders. The kruar passed over each with ease, his steps becoming strides, strides lengthening into a bounding run.

Bannan crouched low, sharing his mount's patent desire to escape this place.

This wasn't the path of the house toads, secret and safe.

This was a trap.

The plain tilted. Lifted, boulders rolling down as twin hills erupted. With a sharp whine, Scourge spun to avoid them.

To face the same two hills.

The kruar turned again.

The hills reappeared and Bannan leaned forward, shouting. "You can't outrun it."

Scourge shuddered violently from head to tail, not slowing. ~We can't fight it.~

"What? What is it?"

The twin hills confronting them suddenly heaved up, joined by a lumpy ridge. Surged higher still to loom impossibly large in front of them and Scourge finally stumbled to a halt, sides heaving in defeat.

Bannan struggled to comprehend what the ground spewed forth. It resembled—it couldn't be—a house toad?

A toad like a mountain, filling the sky from horizon to horizon. White skin like shimmering silk, crusted with gems that hoarded light, a closed mouth like a jagged canyon—

Each eye the size of the sun.

Their lids opened.

Uncasing a glory like gazing into a furnace, and Bannan cringed in vain but there was no evading an assessment that stripped him to less than dust. Worthless. Useless. A failure in every sense from birth—undeserving of love—

~RESIST!~ Scourge roared.

The roar hammered his palms through the kruar's hot, living hide. Jarred his wounded leg, sending a wave of pain to cleanse his mind, and Bannan straightened. Stared back.

Fought back, for if the creature's weapon lay in lies, was he not a seer of truth?

The toad queen, for it could be nothing else, altered. Her skin became desolation, cracked and sere. Her eyes turned sickly green, centered by fathomless black. What paraded as magnificent gems became hideous pus-filled warts, studded with horrors.

Skulls. Teeth. Bone. Scraps of hide, some glinting with dragon-scale, others feathered or withered skin. Cloaks from yling and claws of efflet. Shells of nyim and nameless creatures. Things he didn't recognize but, Ancestors Malevolent and Mired, some he knew that shouldn't *be* here.

Cracked timbers. The mast from a sailing ship. Barrels and bricks. Torn and bulging bags. Stuffed toys missing eyes.

A cradle.

He refuse to believe the noble house toads of Marrowdell had anything to do with such a wicked creature, coated in heartless tro-phies, and cruel.

A limb burst from the ground close to them. Lifted into the air to hide the sky, clawed toes, one missing, spreading in threat. They'd be crushed beneath it—there was no way to escape—

The kruar gave a blood-curdling howl. Bannan shouted his de-fiance! They waited, panting, to die.

The foot didn't move.

Why didn't it move?

Hope was almost painful. He gazed up, puzzled.

A toe wiggled, waving a tiny bit of fabric caught by the claw. A rag.

A flag? Was it surrendering? Bannan swallowed a manic giggle and grabbed after his badly scattered wits. "What do you want from us?"

The foot came down, smothering everything, death incarnate—

Scourge, courageous to the end, stood proudly under it, refusing to move. Meaning Bannan couldn't cower or scream—

The foot stopped short of his head. A toe slowly bent, bringing a claw larger than them both in reach of his outstretched hand.

The rag was a scarf. Pale blue, with a crest of yellow, green, and brown, the original for the one on the strip tied around his leg. *Larmensu!*

Bannan snatched it from the claw before thinking such theft might see them squashed after all. Pressed the scarf to his face, eyes closed. Breathed in its impossible *familiar* scent and for a heartbeat he was a child again and safe, for the scarf was his mother's.

In the next, he looked up at the toad queen. "How do you have this?"

Eyelids lowered to half cover those glittering eyes. A disturbing consideration and he felt his heart stutter under its weight. He refused to look away. "This is from my home! Why is it here?"

Wide jagged lips separated, sighing out a cloud of black rot. Scourge flinched. Bannan tightened his legs to ask the kruar to hold fast, an arm over his mouth and nose.

Her voice froze both in place. Shockingly calm and soft, like a mother soothing a babe, almost sweet.

It made what she said worse.

"I collect such trinkets. I find them where darkness leaks from the edge into the Verge. The taste of ill-meant magic. The fear its use brings. The consequence and pain. Oh yes. These are exquisite." Her eyelids lowered to show mere slits. "If brief."

A sudden landslide had destroyed their childhood home outside Vorkoun, sweeping away the magnificent Marerrym estate, killing his parents, their unlucky guests, and any staff inside. By merest chance, he and Lila had gone north to visit their widowed aunt at the small and rustic Larmensu holding—Scourge had arrived without a rider, bloodied and covered in filth—they should have known what it meant, but who could? When word finally came, he and Lila had been taken straight back, too late for anything but funerals—

Hadn't he, new to his gift, sensed lies everywhere? So many they'd made him sick and Lila had taken him away—

Or had he known, somehow, even then, that something wasn't right—that it hadn't been an accident—

Bannan clenched his hand over his mother's scarf. "Who?" He didn't recognize his own voice. "Who used magic against my family? I'll know if you lie."

Scourge abruptly lifted his head, ears up and pointed. ~I hear—~

"I don't lie," crooned the mountainous creature. "I grant favors. Would you like to go home, truthseer?"

Her mouth cracked open to swallow the entire world and them.

Bannan tumbled in whorls of shadow and light, losing Scourge, losing himself. Home meant Jenn Nalynn and Marrowdell. Home meant Jenn Nalynn and Marrowdell.

It had to . . .

Didn't it?

A new voice—a wonderful and familiar one—filled the dark and Werfol scrambled to his feet. "HELP!" he shouted. "HELP!"

"Who used magic against my family? I'll know if you lie."

"BANNAN!! UNCLE! Un—cle—" Werfol's voice cracked, his throat raw from shouting so hard. He stopped once more to listen, ear pressed to Goosie's side. His shout had been his very loudest, louder than any shout ever. Why didn't his uncle hear him?

Because the voice wouldn't let him—he hated it. Hated it!

"I don't lie," said the voice that held him, talking to Uncle Bannan. Who would know it lied, Werfol thought fiercely, just as he did. "I grant favors. Would you like to go home, truthseer?"

No. No, he couldn't go. Mustn't! "DON'T LEAVE ME, UNCLE! PLEASE!"

His prison moved without warning. Werfol shook and bounced

against the walls, then everything went still and he knew what that meant.

His uncle was gone. His hope.

"I'm here, little one. I won't leave you."

Curling into a ball, Werfol covered his ears with his hands but nothing stopped that voice.

"You can talk to me. We're going to be great friends. You'll see."

Jenn's first thought, finding herself quite alone on a vast plain of sand, was of Mistress Sand and the other terst turn-born. After all, only turn-born could cross from the edge to the Verge and back with someone or something else, making it seem certain they were responsible. Except they were supposed to be shopping for birthing day gifts and not in the Verge at all—

Assuming this *was* the Verge.

Lacking Bannan's true sight, how would she know?

Jenn let herself feel the turn-borns' expectations for this place, as she had for others. In the Verge—and Channen and Marrowdell— they'd woven everywhere—through everything—overlapping expectations for water from wells and solid walls, for peace and privacy.

To her dismay, here was but one, wrapped around her like a too-tight blanket.

STAY WHERE YOU ARE!

The command throbbed with power, as if made by all turn-born who'd ever been, except her.

An expectation locking what was here, *here*—or, Jenn corrected, that was the turn-borns' intention.

Turn-born had to agree.

What if she didn't?

And if she didn't—the cautious whisper of a thought—if she expressed her disagreement as a wish, would the blanket open to let her out—or the sky crack and fall on her head?

Ancestors Baffled and Bewildered. There was, in her experience, no telling how wishes might be answered.

Except there were always consequences. Like her wish to move the river out of her way. She'd only wanted to reach Bannan and Scourge. Marrowdell's answer, redirecting the river into the cataracts, changed the valley from having too much water to none—other than their wells and the remnants of the flood, at least until the ice dam finished melting to let it drain away.

Still, Jenn brightened, it wasn't as dire an outcome as the entire valley flooding or flushing the entirety of the floodwater downstream to trouble Endshere. All in all, her wish might have been helpful.

As for her present quandary?

What mattered most, Jenn decided firmly, was why this expectation had been set here in the first place. She should find out before tampering with it—if even she could.

Her arm distracted her and she shrugged off her wet coat. Wisp's claws had left five jagged tears in its sleeve and that of her dress beneath, but only lightly scored her skin.

He'd be upset. Though her dragon had felt her become turn-born in time to keep his claws from going deeper, the scratches stung and one bled.

They could wait. She put her coat back on, leaving the hood on her shoulders, then kicked at the sand with her muddy boot. The stuff didn't flow away, sparkle, or produce eyes to glare.

Ancestors Peculiar and Perplexed. Just sand, then.

Sand and her.

A new and unpleasant feeling, being this alone. No Wisp, not that she'd asked him to follow, though it was odd he hadn't and she missed him.

No Scourge, who could hide in a shadow but surely would show in this flat dish of a place.

She sighed again, a little catch to it. No Bannan.

Spotting a blotch of differently colored sand a few steps away, Jenn walked to it and knelt.

Then brought her fist to her mouth in horror. It was blood! Fresh blood and, yes, there were more blotches.

As if in proof, a drop from her clawed arm fell to join them.

Jumping to her feet, she shouted desperately, "Bannan! Scourge!" Drew on her turn-born aspect and wished them *here*, as noisily and magically as she'd ever wished before.

Which, in hindsight, was less than prudent, for *something* answered, rising from beneath. Jenn slipped down a slope that hadn't existed an instant ago, a slope growing longer and longer as she slid, carried on a torrent of sand.

Sand that grew into pebbles, which hurt, then swelled to boulders, which were a serious hazard. Growing annoyed, Jenn Nalynn wished the grains to *stop* their nonsense at once!

Sand again. Much better.

Reaching the bottom, she scrambled quickly away from the mound, not bothering to get to her feet.

Silence. She rolled over and sat, leaning back on her hands to stare up. And up. As she stared, grains continued to pour like little rivers from what was, beyond doubt, an extraordinarily large house toad.

A toad larger than the Ropps' barn, in fact, and Jenn remembered, with a twinge of guilt and growing concern, how she'd once wished, on behalf of a Marrowdell house toad, to find their kind in the Verge. She hadn't, till now. Then again, her wishes were prone to unlooked-for results and this, she concluded, was certainly that.

On the good side, in her experience toads were unfailingly helpful and this one clearly belonged here. It must be the guardian of this place, perhaps helping enforce the turn-borns' STAY WHERE YOU ARE command—or, even better, to help those who'd strayed here by mistake.

Having thought all this before the sand finished running from the toad, Jenn stood and bowed. "I'm glad to see you, honored little cousin," she greeted. "Have you seen my friends?"

The giant toad settled its bloated girth with a shake Jenn felt through the ground, aiming golden eyes the size of—she ran out of comparisons. They were big and aimed at her, their expression disapproving. "Turn-born are not welcome here."

She had meddled with its sand. And shouted her wish, which Mistress Sand would find offensive.

"My sincere apologies, little cousin. I won't stay," she promised, determined to improve her manners. "I seek a man named Bannan Larmensu—he's tall, with dark hair and apple butter eyes, and very handsome—" likely unimportant to a toad, "—and his companion, Scourge. A kruar who's my friend." Best to get everyone sorted, she judged, and make it clear both were dear to her.

"You won't find them."

Jenn frowned. Perhaps this toad wasn't like the others. "Why?"

"Because I swallowed them."

Its creamy stomach did have a bulge. Hadn't she found blood on the sand?

Was this—this monster what the turn-born locked in here?

In a flash, Jenn became pearl and glass and fury. Shouted, "What have you done?!" and the ground shuddered.

The toad blinked down at her, unperturbed. "I sent them home."

Ancestors Confounded and Consoled, the creature might have started with that.

Settling, she found herself a woman again and somewhat at a loss. Manners, she thought. "Then I thank you. That was most kind."

Jenn looked around, unable to sense a crossing, only the smothering press of the turn-borns' command. Far from rescuing Bannan and Scourge, she'd managed to get stuck herself.

She considered the toad.

The toad considered her.

Turn-born weren't, Jenn reminded herself, beyond making mistakes. Nor did they act for the betterment of others, it being their nature to be selfish and sometimes cruel. They'd tormented Wisp when he was helpless. Might have killed him, if not for her intervention and yes, she called those who came to Marrowdell friends, but it wasn't a thoroughly trustworthy friendship, like hers with Hettie or Devins, though she believed Mistress Sand truly cared for her and the villagers.

In a sense, they'd a treaty, she thought, feeling the rightness of it. Like Prince Ordo's, ceding half of Vorkoun and all the land of the contested marches to Ansnor in return for the construction of a train from Eldad. Turn-born must agree, so in Marrowdell, the terst agreed with Jenn to do things that were helpful and friendly, like the harvest.

Not so elsewhere along the edge or in the Verge.

Making it possible and perhaps likely they'd imprisoned the giant toad for spite or because it threatened one of their plans. She could, Jenn decided, empathize, but dare she trust this creature? Ask to be sent home, too?

Ancestors Blessed, she'd no choice. "My name is Jenn Nalynn, esteemed little cousin. I'm from Marrowdell, a place on the edge, and would very much like to return there. Would you help me, please?"

"I am not a little cousin," with distinct irritation.

"My apologies," Jenn said hastily. "What should I call you then?"

"YOUR MAJESTY!" The shout knocked Jenn back a step.

And changed her thinking. Wisp had told her Marrowdell's house toads collected white pebbles to build a throne for the arrival of their queen, hinting it was a futile, if laudable pursuit. While Jenn had pictured their queen as only slightly larger and most probably green—though she'd no idea why, other than the large frogs in the river being green, though they were smaller than a house toad and unlike in every way—what loomed in front of her did have pretty golden eyes if confusingly smooth pale skin—

"You taste of light and goodness," the toad queen pronounced in a strangely grim tone. "You would prevent bad things happening wherever you are, wouldn't you?"

It sounded like one of Aunt Sybb's more difficult questions, the sort she didn't actually want answered and might be taken as a compliment—or point to a flaw. Unsure which, Jenn made a quick, if clumsy—sand being awkward—curtsy to show her respect on be- half of Marrowdell's little cousins and, instead of risking a direct answer, looked up beseechingly. "Would your majesty please send me home?"

"I don't feel like it." With a petulant pout.

"Why not?" Jenn blurted, which she probably shouldn't have, but in no sense could she reconcile what she knew of Marrowdell's house toads, their dignity and honor, their urgent helpfulness, with this—this arrogant *creature*.

Then the toad queen changed.

Warts erupted from smooth skin. Those pretty golden eyes became a wicked green and black. Dreadful things appeared, dangling from the warts like ornaments. Bones and timbers. Skulls and hides.

Including what must have come from some poor dragon.

Wisp mustn't follow her here. No one should.

All at once, as if the toad queen twisted to flaunt them, Jenn saw what was even worse.

Children's toys, the kind that should be clean and stuffed and cuddled.

These were stuffed but covered in filth and whatever was inside looked hard and lumpy and not cuddly at all.

Overcome by revulsion, now glad of the turn-borns' command and refusing to think of her devoted house toad, Jenn flicked her fingers derisively at their empty surroundings. "Over what do you rule, now?" she taunted. "Sand?"

The toad queen swelled, doubling in size. "I WILL RULE EVERYTHING THERE IS!"

Jenn put her fists on her hips and tilted her head, eyes flashing; her aunt's posture when that dear lady's vast patience had been exhausted, not that she realized. "You won't, you know," she told the queen calmly. "Greedy never gets anything but a comeuppance."

The creature stared down at her. Gave a low amused rumble. "Bold little turn-born. Who are you to deny me?"

"More than you think." Jenn became turn-born and held out her hand, releasing a single white moth to perch at the tip of her finger. "For I am sei as well."

In that instant, a flicker of reassuring blue danced over the sand and across the sky, encasing her in sanctuary.

No—she was inside a prison. The sei of the Verge, one or more of them, must have helped the turn-born confine this creature here, where she could do no—or less—harm. Though oblivious to the doings of lesser beings, from the trials of Wisp and Scourge, Jenn knew sei punished those who disrupted their peace.

Ancestors Despicable and Dire, queen or not—this foul creature was more than capable of that.

The giant toad quivered and crouched, pulling her feet over her eyes as if to hide.

Good-hearted above all else, Jenn was struck with remorse. Taking back her moth, she opened her mouth to say so—

The toes of one foot parted, revealing a spiteful eye. "None can touch me."

As it shifted and came erect again, Jenn had a clearer look at one of the toys and realized with horror she recognized it. Goosie! Larger than it had been in Marrowdell, too large, here, for little Loee to hug.

Stuffed with what wasn't soft or hard but *moved!*

"Jenn Nalynn!!" Her name, muffled and faint as if from a distance. "Save me! Please save me!"

Heart's blood, it was Werfol!

Without hesitation or thought, Jenn leapt for the toy—

The monster's front feet slammed into the sand, the percussion making her stagger back and almost fall. "HE STAYS WITH ME!" She loomed, pus dripping, foul ornaments rattling, the stench of her breath a blow.

Jenn glared up, shaking with fury. "Werfol comes with me!"

And what of the other toys? What might be inside—or who, though they didn't move or call out? Her rage grew, her magic swelling inside her, and the sky began to crack. And she didn't care if she broke the Verge and everything in it, so long as she stopped this—

A claw-tipped toe freed something from a wart. Flung it.

Before Jenn could dodge the *something* landed around her neck, cold and soggy. Frantically she tried to take it off but her fingers couldn't get a grip—

"I will send you where none will find you!"

A piteous, desperate, "Jenn!"

"Werfol!" Jenn tried to dodge around the monster, keeping her eyes on the boy's prison.

Sand gave way beneath her feet, swept her back. Horrified, she glanced over her shoulder to see a black gaping maw sucking everything into it. Sand. Air.

Her.

Swallowed by the toad queen, Jenn tumbled in whorls of shadow and light, unable to grasp anything, unable to scream or wish.

"JENN—"

Leaving Werfol behind.

The girl was GONE!

He held on to sanity, sensing her still, but detected nothing of how she was, nothing of direction. She might have been a cloud in this plain sky—a star above it—

He had to reach her. The dragon rose into the sky to try again. The ways of the earth were his to fly. HIS! He would not be denied!

He dove.

Crashed into that deception of mud-caked rock instead of passing through, breaking more bones. Bounced and tumbled to the side, dazed.

A house toad appeared, prudently distant. ~Elder brother. Please desist. You cannot pass. You only injure yourself.~ Another came beside it. More, until Wisp was surrounded by determined little cousins.

He sat up. Snarled. ~I must follow the girl. Save her!~

Wen Treff stepped up, toads easing aside to let her join them. "Desist, dragon. This door has closed."

She meant the irregular oval of rock, outlined in cracks. An oval the shape of a mouth and size of a monster, and the presence of so many house toads told him whose.

Jaw broken, he blew the words out in a gale to toss the toads, push Wen back. "YOUR QUEEN!"

~She is not permitted here.~ A fervent chorus as every little cousin scrambled back in place. ~She is not.~

Echoed by the woman. "She is not."

The words were nonsense.

Until Wisp watched in stunned horror as the house toads leapt onto the oval of false rock, each disgorging a mouthful of their precious white pebbles, the pebbles *melting* until they formed a new and solid lid, sealing him from Jenn Nalynn.

Abandoning the girl to a force of chaos and destruction even dragons feared.

The toads, wisely, left.

Too long quiet. Too long concealed. He should have seen this coming, Wisp railed to himself. Should have known the toad queen merely lurked in ambush, a nightmare waiting her moment to strike. What good was he here?

~I MUST SAVE HER!~ Wisp roared, near mad with anguish.

Knowing he could do nothing at all.

The woman lingered.

Finally, she came close and crouched, ignoring his warning snarl. She angled her head, as a dragon might, to regard him with one fell eye, the other hidden by hair. "If any can prevail against great darkness, dragon lord, it is our Jenn. What remains of Marrowdell to greet her return? That is up to you."

She offered him hope, granted him duty as if she'd the right, and he wanted to eat her heart.

Instead, Wisp lowered his head slightly. Acknowledgment, not acquiescence, never that. He would do as he chose.

Lacking a way to the girl, why, he might choose this, but to please *her*—not this strange woman who preferred to live with little cousins.

A nod. Wen turned and left.

A dragon healed—or a dragon died. His wings were undamaged,

the pain of broken bones in his jaw, shoulder, and leg tediously familiar and insignificant. About to rise into the air, Wisp paused. Flared a nostril. Caught a scent.

A youngling.

To dare to follow him suggested *the* youngling.

To hover above? His injuries must offer such a fool temptation.

He'd no time for trivialities. Turning his head down, Wisp slipped into the real and normal earth, flying the deep ways to the villagers.

Follow that.

ELEVEN

WERFOL—SOBBING, JENN FOUND herself suspended in the dark. Finding herself helped. If she continued to exist, wherever this was lay within the edge. Or the Verge.

Implying the toad queen had limits like hers.

Ancestors Dreaded and Dire, the monster had Werfol. How or why didn't matter, Jenn had to get back there. Had to save him.

But was she free to act?

Once more Jenn let herself feel for turn-born expectations, glad to sense no trace of the STAY WHERE YOU ARE blanket, but rapidly puzzled. There were expectations, yes, but they were faint, almost flimsy, as if she glimpsed the tattered remnants of an ancient tapestry, too worn to reveal what it once depicted. A small heedless wish, she feared, might dissolve its threads for good.

Or several careful ones strengthen and preserve the original intentions, not that she'd any idea what those might be. Best, Jenn decided, not wish at all.

It wasn't, come to think of it, truly dark. She glowed, or the pearl within her did, creating a nimbus around her. She reached out. Trails of new light followed her fingers.

Looked up, unsurprised to find light above, for by now Jenn comprehended she was suspended in water, or rather steadily sinking through it. She looked down to find even more lights far below, those organized and purposeful, as if she hung over a busy village the size of Endshere or larger. Under water? Who could live there?

The lights were like Werfol's eyes. Glints of gold within warm darkness.

Could those below help her save him?

Questions, however urgent, that had to wait. Ancestors Forgetful and Flighty, she'd gone without breathing much too long as it was. Jenn kicked off her boots—with a silent apology to whomever they fell upon, even if living at the bottom made it more likely than not they'd be rained on by objects, perhaps other boots—then stroked for the surface as quickly as she could.

Her head broke into air as she made herself flesh again, drawing in deep, unexpectedly warm breaths as she puzzled at her surroundings.

It happened again, almost at once. A familiar, wonderful voice in the dark, talking to the voice, but this time, when Werfol shouted "Jenn Nalynn!! Save me! Please save me!"

He was heard!

He knew it because the voice who'd stuffed him in his toy shouted even louder, "HE STAYS WITH ME!"

And because what Jenn said next was, "Werfol comes with me!" in a tone Werfol thought no one and nothing would dare argue with—

But the voice came back, grim and satisfied. "I will send you where none will find you!"

It was the truth! "Jenn!" he shouted, this time in warning.

"Werfol!" Breathless, as if she ran.

"JENN—" He stopped, knowing she was gone, just like Uncle Bannan, and Werfol banged his fists against the inside of Goosie and shouted, "YOU'RE IN TROUBLE NOW!" For Jenn Nalynn had heard him and Jenn Nalynn had magic—was magic—and would never abandon him.

His prison shook, dropping him on his back. "Turn-born. Sei." Dismissive, that acknowledgment, the way he'd say peas or carrots. "I am more powerful than either or both."

A lie. He felt it, even if he couldn't see what imprisoned him. The sort of boastful lie used, according to Momma, when you weren't what you claimed at all.

Oh, it was powerful and magic—and, in his firm opinion, evil and stupid and fully deserving of the comeuppance he'd heard Jenn Nalynn promise and would deliver—but it had, he judged coolly, the weakness common to any bully.

It loved the sound of its own voice.

A vulnerability to someone trained to listen for secrets.

Sitting up, Werfol crossed his legs and made himself comfortable. Which was easier than it should have been for he didn't have to pee and wasn't thirsty or tired. He added those mysteries to his list of questions, to ask later if there was one. They weren't as important as the rest he needed to know.

The youngest son of Lila Westietas smiled her smile in the dark and commenced his interrogation.

"What are you?"

The water was calm and, Jenn licked her lips, salty. Morning still, though low gray clouds obscured the sky and she couldn't make out the sun. Fortunately the creature hadn't dropped her into the middle of the Sweet Sea. This was a bay—or inlet or cove, she wasn't sure the difference—bordered by steep rock in front and beside her, narrowing to a blunt end. To her left, a narrow footpath wove between spare shrubs, following the water's edge.

To her right, a wonder. A real fishing village—she'd seen pictures—complete with pilings and wharfs, though oddly lacking in boats. Still, the small buildings raised on the pilings were painted bright red, whites, and yellows. Despite the ache in her heart, Jenn thought it the most wonderful thing she'd ever seen.

Until she turned around.

Dwarfing the steep rock, turning the village to a set of children's blocks, was a great bridge of stone. It strode across the bay in three immense arches, those building it undaunted by water, curving as it went. She couldn't see the top for the clouds.

Jenn swallowed, moving her hands slowly in the water. There was nothing like this in Rhoth or Ansnor or Mellynne, their neighbor to the west.

Putting her in Eldad, the furthest domain on her map, on any map. The one where people refused to believe in magic at all—according to the Eld who'd come to Marrowdell last fall, Urcet a Hac Sa Od y Dom, who'd sought proof, found her, and left without either.

The monster had done what she vowed.

No one would find her here.

She'd have to save herself, that was all.

Then save Bannan's dear nephew.

Landing—wherever he landed—knocked the breath out of him. For the first desperate moments, Bannan concentrated on getting it back, though passing out would have been fine as well. His leg burned, his stomach complained of the journey through the toad queen—not that he wanted to think in detail about *that*—and there was at least one rock beneath his spine.

Rock meant place.

The truthseer opened his eyes. There was light, albeit it disappointingly little, coming through a small opening high above. Enough to show the mass of collapsed stone wall, timber, and raw boulders forming a chancy chimney.

Enough to tell exactly where the toad queen had meant by "home."

He was inside the ruin of Marerrym House, buried beneath a mountain.

Ancestors Witness, if the mass above him hadn't fallen in twenty years, it wouldn't fall now. Bannan sat up. "Scourge?" It came out a hoarse whisper, but the bloody beast would hear him.

"Here." A familiar shape formed a deeper shadow. "What is this place?"

He started, badly, at the breeze in his ear. "You—can talk?"

"Of course I can. This is the edge."

The world tilted—or he did. "Ancestors Bloodied and Blind." It was impossible. "I lived here," Bannan blurted. "How could our home be inside the edge and I never *saw*?"

"You didn't *see* me." Dark amusement. "Till you looked."

The kruar had roamed the fields, or hunted the stables. Giving Bannan some sense of where the edge wasn't, for hadn't it taken entering Marrowdell for him to see the truth beneath the guise of a big ugly horse? And a terrifying revelation the kruar had been.

He gathered scattered wits. "Just as well. I'd never have dared ride you."

"You barely did, in those days."

He deserved that. "What about now? Can you cross from here? Get back to Marrowdell?"

"No." Flat and forbidding. "Even should I find a crossing, I won't leave you." A soft nostril found his ear, hot breath tickling. "Not until you die, that is, and I take your final breath. It will be my honor."

A kruar peculiarity, to honor a respected fallen by inhaling that breath to use later in battle. Something Scourge had done once before, most unexpectedly, for Frann Nall.

There'd be no winning this argument. "When we were with the queen—you said you heard something. What?"

"A single cry for help, called from a great distance. No other," more typical pride, "could have heard."

No idle boast. On patrols, Scourge would detect the heartbeats of those waiting in ambush. *A cry for help?* Hope had Bannan rise; dread held him still. "Ancestors Blessed—was it Jenn?"

"No. But the word was Rhothan, the voice high-pitched—perhaps with fear or pain. Or—" dryly "—the queen called out herself. A ploy. I saw no sign of a captive."

"Nor did I." Only grisly trophies. They were far from the first the monster had taken, then spat aside.

A fractured table in reach provided a leg Bannan used as a crutch. He got to his feet, testing his balance. "We find a way out." The Westietas' estate was within a ride. The Northward Road from Vorkoun. A gallop up the Hilip Valley then the foothills.

To Lila. Her dear brave boys. And Emon, never to be discounted. Resources in plenty. His pulse quickened.

Slowed. They had to escape first.

Thinking of his living family, Bannan loosened his fist. He'd kept the scarf through the tumultuous journey. He raised it to the meager light. "The toad queen called this a trinket. To mark an act of dark magic."

A snort. "Believe nothing she said."

"I don't—but why else would she have my mother's scarf?"

"To trick you. Has it worked?"

Maybe. "Lila was never satisfied," the truthseer persisted. He marshalled the arguments she'd made to their elders, standing tall and defiant while he huddled miserably in a chair. "Generations of Marerryms lived here, planting trees and grapes to stabilize the slope. There'd been no heavy rain, yet it gives way just when everyone—" His breath caught; he coughed to hide it. "—everyone was inside?"

A damp chill day too early in spring for much field work. His parents, hosting a few guests, most staff indoors. If he and Lila hadn't been away, they'd have died, too. Had that been the goal? To end the Marerrym and Larmensu? Or to leave their children orphans—

Why? He waved the scarf at the shadows. "The answer could be here."

"What if it is?"

He'd buried the rage with his grief, thought it gone. Now it flared through him, dark and deadly. The child he'd been hadn't wept at the news. He'd found a pitchfork and looked for someone to stab with

it. Lila'd stopped him. Calmed him. Taught him to hide those feelings. What had she said?

Save your hate, little brother. Nurture it. Our day will come.

"Then it will be our turn."

The saltwater helped keep her afloat, but Jenn quickly realized she'd
have to shed as much clothing as possible to stay that way, starting
with the hooded winter coat. Her treasured wool petticoat, once
Peggs' and formerly Aunt Sybb's, went next, then her long stockings.
Sputtering as water got in her mouth and stung her scratches, she
wriggled out of her outer dress with its long sleeves, leaving her in
her sleeveless underdress and simples.

Much better. Her bare feet and limbs delighted in the warm water, moving easily. She swam after her escaping clothes before they
sank out of sight, producing a bundle she could tow with a stocking.
Now, Ancestors Sly and Sneaky, to examine what the creature had
put around her neck.

A necklace, dirty and made up of hard lumps covered in slime.

About to toss it away and be done, Jenn recalled Crumlin's mirror, that had let the wizard spy on Marrowdell from the Verge. Magical objects were not to be trifled with—most importantly, this was
her only connection to the toad queen—and Werfol.

Treading water, Jenn did her best to rub the slime from one of
the lumps. It proved to be a golden shell, thumb-sized, the like of
which she'd never seen. If all the lumps were the same, the necklace
would be pretty, despite the shells being crudely holed and braided
together with coarse brown string.

The necklace, or shells, had meaning here, a troubling one; the
creature wouldn't have inflicted it upon her otherwise. A meaning
she couldn't guess but others might. Reason enough to tuck it as
deeply into her bundle as she could before setting out.

Ancestors Blessed, if the thing never touched her skin again,
she'd be grateful.

Ready to swim, Jenn bobbed in the water to pick a direction. The rocks lining the shore were coated to the waterline in slippery-looking green and sharp-edged brown shells. Below that, ropy weeds made a moving barrier she didn't care to force. The village it was. Despite a strange absence of people in view, welcoming ladders hung down the sides of its piers. Maybe everyone was inside for lunch.

Jenn put her head down, swimming strongly. It shouldn't take long.

But when she next looked up, confident she'd be close, the village had receded and she was closer to the bridge.

Ancestors Beset and Beleaguered, she'd forgotten Master Dusom's teachings of currents and tides, a fascination to a child living along a small river, where water flowed politely in one direction.

Unlike here, where a tide must be going out. It would take her with it, and it wasn't the Sweet Sea a turn-born had to fear, but passing beyond the edge!

She'd cease to exist.

Jenn fought for calm. What would Aunt Sybb say? Dwelling on the end only slows the beginning, and without a beginning, nothing gets done.

Which was mostly about darning socks but might, Jenn firmly believed, be about everything.

She stopped her futile effort to swim against the tide and let go of her bundle. It stayed by her for a sad little while, unraveling, her clothes sinking. More surprises for the village beneath the water.

A flash of gold.

Jenn grabbed the necklace before it could disappear. Ancestor Witness, she'd almost lost it! Panic-stricken, not that she knew why, she pulled its string over her head and shoved the mass of slimy shells between her breasts.

Where it felt horrible and heavy and wrong.

Werfol, Jenn reminded herself.

Past the village, shadowed by the first stone leg of the bridge on land, sat a lone house with its pier and, Ancestors Blessed, a boat. Taking a deep breath, she swam for it, staying with the current, angling as best she could toward shore.

A small comfort to think she'd either win the race or never know she'd lost.

Bannan's ability to explore hampered by the leg Scourge had, in fact, chewed—though having seen the horrific remains of the kruar's quarry in the marches, he supposed his lacerations qualified as a tender nibble—it was left to his companion to hunt a way out.

Scourge had had him move away from where the toad queen spat them—his interpretation, disliking the kruar's, which had them exit elsewhere—in case she tried to get at him again. Not a worry he shared, convinced the creature sent them—him—*here* for a reason of her own. Other than spite, or that as well. No, they'd be safe from her until finding or doing what she wanted and whatever it was wouldn't be good. Not at all.

Dark magic was his guess: what was needful for it or the act itself. Why? The toad queen posed as a collector, like the misguided but relatively harmless clients of Glammis Lurgan, but her intentions were far more inimical. What if she sought magic to spread her reach—maybe into the edge itself?

Ancestors Blind and Blighted, it meant he had to doubt everything. *What else was new?* Bannan's lip quirked, imagining Tir's vigorous nod.

While Scourge used his kruar ability to sneak where his bulk shouldn't fit but did, he wouldn't sit idle. The truthseer set himself to study his immediate surroundings, drawing on memories—those of a child, granted—to pull sense from the ruin.

This—this had been the main floor. The second must have been shoved over it; the small broken table next to him belonged upstairs, on the wide balcony leading to their sleeping quarters, where he'd sit, reading by the light from—

Bannan squinted, trying to see up. Tall windows had lined the river side of the second floor.

Gone now. In their place, a daunting confusion of rubble.

The vaulted ceiling, a Marerrym pride, had been supported by entire tree trunks, of a size no longer found in these mountains, left with their major limbs intact as if still alive. They'd made it feel as if nature itself chose to live with them, caring, protective, to keep his family safe.

Now horribly askew, limbs shattered or buried, the immense main trunks had held back the landslide, preserving this hollow beneath and perhaps more. If any had survived, if only briefly, it was their doing and he was grateful.

Yet wasn't this the edge?

Gripped by a sudden dire suspicion, he used his gift and gasped.

These hadn't been trees at all. They were neyet—or rather their corpses—having bone and shape and form of their own. He hadn't seen this in Marrowdell's much smaller buildings, but there, the turnborn had ordered the magical creatures to become logs and planks.

He doubted these had been any more willing to die. Feeling sick inside, Bannan circled his fingers over his heart. "Ancestors Dear and Departed, there is no excuse for our ignor—"

A faint scuffling sound from behind made him stop. Scourge, curse his bloody nature, wouldn't give such notice, loving nothing so much as to scare his rider half to death by sneaking up from behind.

He picked up the table leg, heart starting to pound.

Another scuffle. A puff of dust. The truthseer turned, using his deeper sight.

Red eyes glowed within every nook and cranny of the ruin surrounding him.

Nyphrit!

Bannan hurriedly pulled himself back into the small pool of light. Nothing to be done about the red trail he left in the dust, though his blood scent answered the question of why so many this fast. Sunlight would slow them. While it lasted. He'd best hope for no passing clouds.

Pulling his lips from his teeth, he raised his makeshift club.

There. Again. Something nudged her foot.

She wasn't alone in the water.

If not pouring all her strength into each stroke and kick, Jenn would have laughed at herself. Ancestors Fecund and Fresh, there wouldn't be a fishing village without a plenitude of fish to catch, would there?

She quite liked trout. Hadn't, to be honest and she was, enjoyed the dried oompah Lila had sent in a barrel, leaving those for Master Jupp, who'd been delighted and overate. The emptied barrel—with its labels of far-off places—stood by their bedside as a table, a reminder of the wider world like the glorious map Bannan had asked his sister to find for her.

His first gift.

Stroke, kick. The water grew rougher, the closer she came to shore, and she'd quickly learned to keep her mouth closed as much as possible.

Jenn entered the shadow of the bridge. Eld construction, it had to be. The work wasn't like Rhoth's or Ansnor's, cunningly fitted, no two stones alike. Here, the rock had been cut to fit, producing a uniform surface more like pavement than wall. Unclimbable. Not even moss could find a niche.

Her map, long since memorized, told her where she was, in the sense of as far as possible from where she'd been. The Verge, Jenn supposed, didn't count, being outside everything else.

Bannan must be beside himself with worry, having heard Werfol's cries—unless he hadn't for some reason, including the toad queen's wicked whim—

Wherever she'd sent him—

Jenn's rhythm faltered and she sank, then rose again, striking out with determination.

Home, the thing had said.

Well, it wouldn't be Marrowdell. The toad queen was too malicious, in her opinion, to do anything helpful. Bannan's ancestral home had been destroyed, so it wouldn't be there. To the marches between Rhoth and Ansnor where he'd soldiered those many years?

She hoped not.

Home could, Jenn reminded herself quickly, be a person. Wasn't Bannan the home of her heart as she, most assuredly, was his? Before her, she knew he'd have said home was Lila and his nephews and Emon, their father. The sum of his family, who lived in Vorkoun, the Rhothan part of it, and if the monster sent him there, he'd be safe and loved—

Ancestors Desperate and Grieving. A home surely shattered, with Werfol taken where none of them could follow—

A gentle bump from below.

Jenn slowed to kick her feet in that direction, to discourage whatever it was. A swell tossed her lightly back where she'd just laboriously come, and she felt a shiver of fear. As turn-born, she wouldn't drown, but she would, Jenn thought wearily, sink. Putting her no closer to shore.

Something nipped her arm, near the scratches! She cried out, swallowed an ocean, and sank anyway.

Turn-born it was.

The glow shining through her skin of glass revealed an unexpected underscape. Above, the surface churned, full of shadows and froth. Below loomed great rounded shapes—rocks bigger than houses, dressed in leggy weeds and clumps of what seemed like flowers, with long petals bending back and forth with the waves. Things crawled among them, or formed flocks like birds.

Another contact with her arm. Jenn turned her attention to what descended with her.

Fish. Long and knife-shaped, with huge cold eyes rimmed in silver and thin pointed teeth jutting past the tops of their jaws. They snapped and swirled around her, crowding for a chance to bite, clearly frustrated by her changed form.

Ancestors Tormented and Tried, they'd eat her alive if she changed back.

~Elder sister, do you require aid?~

Jenn looked around wildly, hunting the source of the voice, which wasn't, she realized belatedly, a voice at all, but a meaning in her head. It was how house toads spoke in the edge. Were they here? The words sounded—heavier.

It didn't matter. She'd either sink and disappear among the rocks below, perhaps to be stuck in a crevice forever—or at least until she grew weary of it and forgot to be at all—or be eaten if she became flesh to swim up again. "Oh yes. Please!" Bubbles followed the words, a reminder she'd only the air inside she recalled from her last gasp above and mustn't waste it.

The biting fish scattered and disappeared with annoyed flicks of their forked tails.

Something large and dark appeared below, drifting above the underwater garden, its shadow trailing. It rose in slow sinuous motion, even as Jenn continued to sink, until they came face to face.

Her reflection caught in huge dark eyes, eyes wincing closed at the light from inside her, and Jenn would have apologized—but all she noticed were the dreadful size of *its* teeth.

~You must be flesh, elder sister, for me to lift you to the surface.~

Oh. Closing her eyes, summoning her courage, Jenn Nalynn became a woman again.

What breath she'd left whomped out of her as she was rammed from below.

Bannan had been right to worry about clouds. The smallest dimming of sunlight emboldened the nyphrit. They dashed from crack to shadow, chittering excitedly to themselves, slipping nearer.

Hadn't eaten in a while, he supposed. Unless these had a way to hunt outside. Which, Ancestors Fortunate and Famed, might mean a way Scourge had found—and where was the bloody beast?

Bannan clamped down the urge to shout. The kruar wouldn't be ambushed by such as these.

Might miss the chance to take his last breath, the macabre

thought almost worth a chuckle. The truthseer eased his weight on his hip then brandished the table leg.

Chased two of the things back, that did.

For a second. They stared at him. Smelling blood, sensing weakness. Straightforward little evils, the nyphrit. Doubtless responsible for the lack of corpses, a most unhelpful thought, under the circumstances.

The light dimmed. Darkened. The nyphrit poured from their hiding places and Bannan rose to his good knee, determined to smash as many skulls as possible before they took him.

Something jumped on his lap. He flinched and went to strike it. Stopped just in time.

A house toad!

The little cousin sprang away from him, seizing a nyphrit midleap. Others appeared like the magic they were, pouncing to swallow their enemy whole. Much tidier than Scourge, who'd leave gore everywhere, and very thorough.

Bannan leaned on the table leg, using his deeper sight to enjoy what wasn't a battle but a rout, too worn to cheer but smiling, oh yes.

These differed from Marrowdell's toads, being smaller. Armored, when revealed to him, but in small cunningly worked plates, not chain mail. Not gems but some bore purple and gray—Marerrym house colors—in ribbon, yarn, and bits of cloth tucked between those plates, implying they'd been here from the beginning.

The first Marerrym had set hand to stone to build here three hundred years ago. The edge itself, according to the dragon, was almost five hundred years old, that being when the mad sei caused the first rupture—and what did it say, that Wisp remembered the event?

Ancestors Wild and Wondrous, he'd been born and raised in the care of house toads and never guessed.

Bannan's mind whirled with questions. Was this part of the edge like Marrowdell, where dreams tested your worth? Or like Channen, where anyone could live but, as the valley, only some remembered its magic when they left?

Wait till he told Lila.

Who'd insist they scour what family records existed for hints of magical gifts in past Marerryms and Larmensus and possibly others—and not to forget the staff and their ancestors who'd lived here. Though how it mattered now—

Bannan returned his attention to the toads.

Finished with the nyphrit, the bulk of whom wisely fled, the house toads settled in a line in front of the truthseer. A couple pushed black legs back inside their mouths then grew still again.

Waiting.

"Thank you for saving my life." He bowed. Their heads dipped. "Do you know me?" he asked wistfully. Without Scourge to interpret— and where *WAS* the bloody beast—they couldn't answer him.

Yet did. One hopped forward to briefly press a foot to his.

Then another did the same.

And a third.

Belatedly he realized the house toads were trying to push him, very gently and politely, out of their way. "You want me to move? All right." He got up and used his crutch to hobble from the spot. The sun had come out from the cloud, beams angling further to the side anyway. He followed it and sat on a chunk of stone.

The toads formed a squat circle, facing one another.

Then calmly proceeded to vomit white pebbles.

"Let me show you my magnificence, little one."

The repaired seam on Goosie's side split open and Werfol fell out. Remembering his lessons, he tucked in his arms and legs, rolling when he hit—ground?

A beach. There were beaches and sandbanks exposed along the Lilem during summer, a favorite place to visit in summer's heat, but Werfol didn't mistake this sand for anywhere pleasant. Bracing himself, he opened his eyes, dazzled by a light of colors he didn't know.

The Verge. Uncle Bannan had told them stories of his trip into it—not many and most cautionary in that way adults had of trying to make sure you didn't want to go somewhere but really made you want to more than anything—

The colors made him sick, but he knew how to fix that. Werfol looked beyond them, using his gift and expecting wonders—or at least answers.

Only to be disappointed. He was alone on a vast plain, with nothing but sand, sand, sand. Where was the voice?

Hiding. It liked games and trickery.

Patience was a weapon. Waiting, as Momma explained it, scraped the nerves of the guilty, true and highly inconvenient when he'd been in trouble and the one waiting.

Werfol got to his feet and brushed any sand from his clothes and hair. Tugged his coat straight, then stood, hands clasped behind his back and composed. He could, he thought proudly, wait a very long time, having outlasted Semyn many times when they'd played this game.

That wasn't a game. He'd learned that, in Marrowdell. How much of what their mother taught her sons had a serious purpose, meant to keep them safe from harm and make them powerful. He was, Werfol decided then and there, going to thank her for it.

When he saw her.

If—

His chin wanted to tremble and he firmed it. Ancestors Witness, Momma would never believe he'd been buried beneath that avalanche. She'd never give up hope. If anything, she'd expect him to find his way home.

He would, Werfol vowed.

Time passed. Uncle Bannan had said using his gift in the Verge drained him, so the young truthseer closed his eyes to conserve his strength. To keep from thinking about scary things or worries, he went through the lists he'd memorized. Names, things, verbs, customs, whatever might be useful someday, if completely useless here. He and Semyn competed to see who'd get everything right first, and sometimes he won, but mostly Semyn did, being the smartest—not that he'd ever say so.

His brother, Werfol thought with fierce new fear, mustn't ever come here, not for anything. The Verge drove those without gifts mad, their uncle warned, and that wasn't to happen, and he felt his hands, still behind his back, become fists.

Forced them to relax. Took a peek and saw the endless, empty sand.

Closed his eyes.

Lists.

The powerful had no business meddling in the lives of others, which, in the dragon's long experience, didn't stop them. When Wisp led his kind to ultimate victory over the kruar—a sure outcome disputed by his counterpart, Scourge, who led his—he was the one to pay for what the sei referred to as "needless chaos." He supposed their defi-nition of *needful* chaos was what came next. He allowed himself to be crippled by other dragons, zealous to distance themselves from his goals and former leadership, for that was at least a noble, appropri-ate end.

But that hadn't, he'd learned to his utter dismay, been the end at all. The sei rescued him at the brink of death, let him heal suffi-ciently to survive, then gave him to the terst turn-born as their slave, to live beneath their enclave and serve as drudge. His mind dulled. His spirit faded. Much longer and he'd have forgotten what he was.

Oh, but then the sei found him a new duty, a baby having been born to a woman of Marrowdell at the turn. A child who, on attaining her turn-born power, would threaten the stability of the edge and the Verge. He was to watch her, guard her, and tear out her throat before she caused harm.

Inflicted him with a sense of her, deeper than instinct. A con-nection he'd loathed at first.

But later? However inconceivable to the sei and Wisp himself, he'd come to love Jenn Nalynn with all his fierce, unbroken heart. And her love had restored him.

Making it ironic—or another kind of healing—that the work he'd loathed when slaving for the terst turn-born would be all he could do for her now.

Wisp flung himself from the earth in the midst of the farmyard, visible and causing consternation to the villagers present he'd have enjoyed under other circumstances.

Spotting Kydd Uhthoff, he sent a sharp chill breeze. "Jenn Nalynn has stopped the river and tasked me with helping you home. Prepare yourselves. This time you'll be walking."

They'd no need nor right to know more, so with that, the dragon snapped his wings and rolled, flying straight for the village.

To his surprise, the water was gone here as well, except for isolated pools. Rising higher, he saw why. Jenn's wish had opened the gate of ice, releasing the flood from the valley and completely draining the river.

A useful outcome, the dragon judged, if briefly inconvenient for those downstream. Efflet—for some survived—were already busy, plucking debris from their fields, shifting the bodies of fallen neyet. They'd much to do before the kaliia would be free to grow.

~Hear me!~

They stopped, aiming their gaze up at him, claws knuckled at their chests.

About to order them to take the larger pieces of wood to the village, the dragon paused, conscious of their sacrifice and pride. On impulse, he sent breezes to collect the dead neyet. Others to swirl the debris aside into piles. As efflet bowed in thanks, he wheeled hastily and left.

The girl's fault, he grumbled to himself, this new softness. Next they'd be expecting him to help groom and protect their fields. Where would it end?

Mud smothered the village, making it impossible to discern path from pasture from fallow garden plots. The old oak, growing through to the Verge, had flexed its knuckled roots and lowered its branches to fend off ice and the logs, the effort leaving fresh scars, but flotsam piled high against walls and hedges.

The only place untouched was the well, its water sparkling, its stone and tile surround clean and dry.

Turn-born magic. They might have spared some for the rest.

Wisp got to work. His breezes became shovels, clearing the road and pathways. He focused on the buildings next. Dry the mud, blow it clear. Open doors and windows.

Water had entered the first floors, soaking everything. Between stains and river stink, no one would want to go inside.

So he pulled everything out, to dry on the cleared road heedless if it were a book or bed or set of plates. Soft things were the worst and Wisp left them in piles. The villagers would know how to clean them. Or not.

About to move to the next house, he heard a commotion behind him and whirled—having never forgotten the youngling.

But it wasn't the other dragon, wisely scarce or too puzzled to attack.

But yling.

They flitted about, disguised as wind-tossed leaves, light glinting from their spikes of hair, stretching lines of their silk from roof to tree. Others swept up socks and blankets, pants and pillows, for yling were master weavers and knew about cloth. They dipped each item in the well, wringing it out, then hanging it. In no time at all, the village stood beneath a canopy of rescued and important things.

A yling appeared in front of his nose, pointing impatiently to the next house.

Choosing not to be offended, Wisp resumed his task.

The villagers would be coming.

Once the girl had tried, in their meadow, to explain her strange notion that work was better than worry. Wisp had countered with the joy of dismembering a winter bear or, even better, being slothful on a warm ledge of rock, and she'd laughed her wonderful laugh, conceding his point. Rabbits had danced.

She'd never felt so far away—

Lacking a bear or ledge, the desolate dragon supposed work would have to do.

TWELVE

JENN NALYNN WRAPPED her arm over the ladder's slimy rung and lifted her free hand to wave her thanks, but her rescuer was gone beneath the waves.

An odd sort of rescue, trying not to be drowned while being plowed through the water with such force her body made waves of its own and she'd—Jenn pulled up the shoulder of her dress—almost lost her clothes.

Not the unpleasant necklace, which she supposed was to the good.

But a rescue nonetheless, by something akin, in her thinking, to a house toad or perhaps more like a well-intentioned dragon, from its size and power, yet not, there being just one with such good manners in the entire edge.

According to Wisp, who would know.

She hung on, bobbing up and down in the restless crunch of water to shore, thinking of her dragon. No doubt Wisp would be thinking of her and worrying excessively.

Jenn eyed the rungs left to climb.

Maybe not excessively.

One at a time, she decided, much as she longed to be dry again. Using her toes for some cautious searching, having seen things with spines on the rock behind the ladder, she found a rung below water to support her foot and pushed up.

The rung snapped. She barely kept hold of the ladder. Clung to it, now thoroughly alarmed. How weak was the rest?

The wood was wet most of the time, at a guess, as were the thick posts woven like an open basket around the rock supporting it. Wet and rotten. She should trust only wood above the highest waves.

Jenn cast a longing look at the boat nearby but it moved with the water, pirouetting like a nervous pony from the end of hanging ropes. While it didn't crash into the pier, those ropes being a clever arrangement to prevent damage, there appeared no safe way to approach it, much less climb on board.

The ladder it was. Gritting her teeth, Jenn waited for the next upward shove from a wave, using the lift to grab for the next rung. Got it! The water then tried to suck her down and away with it, but she held on. Next wave, she was able to reach up with her left hand and take hold. A knee on the lower rung, a foot, and all at once, she was climbing.

To her dismay, a stout wooden railing blocked the top, making no sense at all. Did no one expect the ladder to be used? Unless those living here knew the ladder to be rotten and unsafe—

Sitting on the top rung, Jenn wrapped her shaking arms around the post, hands clasped around her elbows, and considered her predicament. Until she stopped shaking, climbing up and over the railing was out of the question. She'd wind up in the water again.

Glancing over her shoulder, the drop looked further and was, rocks starting to show, framed by pretty white froth that didn't mislead her for an instant. Heart's Blood, she mustn't fall.

Leaving the pier. Jenn rested her chin on her arm.

Holes gaped where planks had fallen through, a token few patched, the rest abandoned. A tipped barrel rocked back and forth in the breeze, lidless and empty. The house—it was more a shed—had an ill-fitting door and boarded-up windows.

A white bird landed atop her post. It was large as a goose, if thinner, with a wicked eye; she wasn't at all sure its intentions. Stretching back its head, it opened its orange beak and proceeded to make a deafening racket, cawing over and over.

Ancestors Loud and Ludicrous. "Shh!" Hushing it merely drew an amused look from that eye.

If it called others of its kind to mock her, fine and deserved, but Jenn did not like the sharp hook at the end of that beak, made for rending flesh.

Nothing for it but to move.

She worked her way from sitting to standing on the ladder with some difficulty, her legs thoroughly cramped and feet numb. Once up, she eased her arms up the post.

The bird chuckled deep in its throat.

"I'll have—you—know—" Jenn puffed, "this is—progress." There. She'd a grip on the railing. Now to climb up and get her leg over it.

A second white bird, identical to the first, landed exactly where she'd aimed to go. Its feet, she noted absently, were webbed like a goose's, if also bright orange. The two chuckled at one another, then bent to regard her.

"Out of the way. Shoo!" She brought up her foot and kicked at it.

It hopped aside, then back again, clearly entertained.

The first, seizing its opportunity, dove to the railing and grabbed for the necklace around her neck, taking hold and giving a sharp pull. Startled, Jenn lost her grip and started to fall.

Strong hands grabbed her arm and leg, hauling her unceremoniously over the rail and dumping her on the pier.

Jenn fought to catch her breath. "Than—thank you."

She couldn't tell who or what had saved her. The figure standing over her was shadow and rags, and smelled quite strongly of fish. And something else.

"What ye d'ng 'ere?" A woman's voice, deep and rough.

Speaking Eldani, or a version of it. Jenn was grateful for the wish she'd made last fall, however inadvertent, to understand and be understood. "Trying not to drown."

The head lifted as if to check there might, indeed, truly be water involved. Lowered again. This time Jenn caught the white of eyes and teeth under the hood. "Shoulda gonna Shadesport. Nah 'ere."

The village had a name.

Well, here was where she was. Gingerly, Jenn sat up. When the figure stepped back, her layers of rags disguising any shape, she took the chance to stand, if shakily, wary of the gaps near her feet. While she understood the language, the words made less sense than she'd expected. "This was where I was brought," she said, being the truth.

"By what? Naught good. Naught w'that!" A hand like a black claw reached out, pointing at her.

No, not at her, the necklace.

Jenn flattened her hand over it, raising her head, eyes flashing. "It's not mine by choice. This was put on me by an evil creature. She sent me here—I believe to die." She lowered her hand, sweeping it out over the sparkling bay. "What saved me lives there."

The other moved in little darts, like a bird or fish. She shifted abruptly close, crouched to peer up at Jenn, shoulders hunched. "The waalum tossed ye m'way, did they? Whyfor?"

Waalum? "I hope so you would help me. Please." She fought a shiver. "I'm very far from home."

The black hand reappeared from the bundle of cloth. Jenn brought her pale one to meet it. "Far you are," with almost reluctant concession. "Well, don' stand out 'ere tak'n chill. C'mon."

Her erstwhile hostess turned and stomped away, not to the shed, as Jenn expected, but toward the boat—

Presently well down from the pier and bucking wildly with each churning wave.

Oh dear.

Patience was a weapon. Patience was a weapon. Jenn Nalynn knew he was here and trapped. She'd tell his uncle and mother and father, but they'd need time to plan. Time to act. Time his patience gave them, so Werfol kept going even though he was most thoroughly bored.

He was midway through the list of spices traded across the Sweet Sea, in order of economic impact to Rhoth, when his patience was rewarded.

The ground shuddered under his feet. There was a sound like ice pellets hitting the big windows at home and a smell like rotten vegetables, but he resisted the temptation to look.

The voice returned. "You wanted to see me, little one?" Sly and confident.

Wait. Wait, Werfol told himself, keeping his eyes closed. He switched to the list of where spices were grown—

A furious, bellowed, "BEHOLD ME!"

Ancestors Smug and Satisfied, he'd won. Werfol opened his eyes, braced for a monster.

Finding himself gazing down into the limpid brown eyes of an ordinary-seeming house toad, with skin matching the sand's color. Which toads could do, of course, along with swallowing pebbles and making eggs—but near this toad, roughly half as big, lay Goosie, looking perfectly normal, as if her seam hadn't been ripped and he'd been stuffed inside.

Trickery. Werfol just knew it. Tricks made him angry, they always had, as lies now did, but he dared not lose his temper, not here.

"Don't you want your toy, little one?" The same voice filled his head. "Give it a cuddle, now. You know you want to. It'll make you happy."

It thought him a child. Which he wasn't, not the way this toad implied, and Werfol went from angry to sick inside, suddenly sure he wasn't the toad's first victim.

His eyes turned molten gold, the eyes of a truthseer, able to *see* through the tricks.

Where his house toad would have chain mail, this false toad was covered in warts and pus. Instead of medals and gems, it sported a collection of absurdly tiny objects, like the miniature carts and lampposts on the model of Vorkoun Werfol had broken in a temper but was almost fixed—but these weren't whole and clever, these were broken and foul. Skulls the size of his littlest fingertip, stuffed toys like Goosie, shattered bits of wood, and horrible wee skins—

This toad was everything wrong and hateful. "What are you?" he demanded, no longer able to conceal his loathing and disgust.

Momma wouldn't have approved, because an interrogator didn't show emotions unless to a purpose but Werfol was, after all, just turned six and vastly upset.

"You think you see me, little truthseer?" The false toad puffed itself, as if proud, sand crusted on its belly. "THINK AGAIN!"

Then began to grow—

Scourge returned. He arched his neck, nostrils flared until the inner red showed, then gave Bannan a sharp look.

The truthseer returned an innocent one. "Find anything?"

"Yes. What is this?" The kruar circled him, head lowering to stare.

"'This'?" Bannan tapped the gleaming white disc that filled an oval disturbingly like a mouth on the floor, the outcome of the house toads' white pebble vomit. "I believe it's a lock. The toad queen won't use this door again."

The look *that* earned him was almost worth what they'd been through. "There are little cousins here?"

"And nyphrit," Bannan pointed out, "to which you abandoned me, bloody beast. I'd have died, you realize. Quite horribly."

A lip curled in distain. "Yet have not. While I found a way out. Or rather a way in." The kruar gave a prideful shake. "Come."

The truthseer kept his grin to himself. The former general admit a tactical error? Not in this lifetime. He got to his feet, his wounded leg stiff but able, he discovered on careful experimentation, to bear some weight. He paused to consider his companion. "A way into where, exactly?"

"The mountain."

"But—" Bannan silenced his objections, however much the thought of going further underground—away from the sunlight and any chance of reaching Lila—filled him with dread. Let alone, Ancestors Destitute and Derelict, what the landslide might have ripped open. He waved his crutch with what he hoped was nonchalance. "Show me."

A mass of dusty kruar flesh appeared in front of his face. "The path I took is too small for you. You must ride."

The vaulted portion of the ruins was here, not to either side. Bannan mounted, not without misgivings. Sure enough, Scourge bounded into motion, leaping up the slope of rubble like a crazed goat.

The truthseer crouched to protect his head as the distance between it, wood, and stone lessened alarmingly. Something brushed his back, snagging on his coat, then tore free as Scourge abruptly turned left.

And stopped.

They stood on a portion of undamaged floor. Ahead, it vanished into the depths, presumably the kruar's original access. If Bannan reached to his right, he'd touch the wide trunk of a ceiling tree, but his attention was for the paneled wall to his left.

A painting still hung from it, askew and covered in dust and cobweb. He didn't need to brush it clean to know it was a landscape, painted by his grandmother, its once-vivid colors showing the first rows of grapevines that would become the mainstay of the Marerrym fortune. The wide frame had lost its golden sheen but not the embossed vines and wide-eyed owls of the Marerrym crest. His mother had loved—

Scourge huffed. "If you're done staring?"

He gave the beast an apologetic pat. "Where's this path?"

The kruar shoved his nose into the wall panel next to the painting. It swung open with the smoothness of well-oiled hinges.

Sliding to his feet, Bannan hobbled forward, taking hold of the wood bordering this door he'd never known. His parents' rooms had been down the hall. "How did we never find it?" he protested.

Searching for hidden passageways in their big old home had been a favorite game of his and Lila's. They'd knocked on every bit of wall, even inside closets. On one memorable occasion, they'd taken pry bars to the wine cellar after Lila'd read a book about buried treasure—the point being, they'd been as thorough as children could be and he found himself oddly offended. "Ancestors Witness, we looked everywhere. Even here."

"And *you* missed it." With an amused snort.

Implying the ever-canny Lila may very well have found the opening and kept it secret for reasons of her own, a likelihood Bannan acknowledged with a shrug. He leaned into the opening, getting a sense of space, unable to see in the gloom.

"Go on." Hot breath in his ear. "It's safe."

Fine for a kruar, able to see in the dark. Bannan drew on his deeper sight, hoping for reassurance.

Ancestors Blighted and Bent.

A corridor with a plank floor and ceiling led straight ahead, a corridor he *saw* because those immured in the stone walls wept a sickly green light of their own. "What are they?"

"A kin of nyphrit. They hunt in the deep places." Somehow, Scourge's voice managed to convey a shrug. "These are harmless."

He'd seen ants caught in amber, legs splayed and bodies contorted. These—though larger and heavier, with ominous protruding jaws—had a similar look, as if they'd tried to struggle free of the stones only to be trapped. The glowing fluid bled from the exposed parts of their bodies, dripping down the walls, forming runnels along the floor, and he swallowed gorge, unwilling to imagine how long they'd been here.

When the truthseer took a step into the corridor, their eyes shot open. Baleful, accusing eyes. *Or was that hunger?*

Shuddering, he fingered the scarf in his pocket and thought of the toad queen.

All at once, Bannan realized the light didn't come from the fluid alone. There were sparks, pale gold and warm, in a line shoulder high along the walls. He edged closer.

"Harmless," a rumbled warning, "unless they grab you."

He gave an absent nod. Where the sparks were, the creatures weren't. Bending to examine one, Bannan sucked in a breath. The spark came from a sunflower crafted of tiny beads, the whole the size of his thumb, fixed to the stone, and he'd seen the like every time his younger self had snuck to the kitchen for a treat. "Ioana wore one of these," he whispered. "Our cook," he added. Back then, the kruar had avoided the house—to the relief of staff—not yet aware of cheese or bacon.

Greatly daring, he touched the flower, delighted by a faint greeting. *Larmensu.* "These are wishings." At a guess, to keep out what tried to get in—perhaps weakened by the dark magic that brought down the house itself.

Had Ioana—back hunched from work and an old injury, her rare smile missing several teeth, and her smell, to be kind, memorable—been responsible for these protections? He could credit the possibility, having respect for age and accomplishment; Lila would know. Any time his sister wasn't where she was supposed to be, he'd check the kitchen and find Lila sitting at the cook's tiny small table, the pair deep in a conversation they'd stop at the sight of him and Lila not explain.

Though the Marerrym side, their mother's, boasted renowned crafters and artists. To Lila had gone their elaborate scale model of Vorkoun, built over generations, a treasure and asset to her and Emon.

The beadwork, however, was evidence of another art altogether. One frowned upon by Rhothans, if not by their neighbors, the Ansnans, and for the first time in years Bannan remembered his parents speaking of old friendships across that border, sundered by the prince, and didn't that open the door to what else those friends had shared?

"There should be more—" There. A small table stood in the midst of the room. It held a box no larger than his paired fists, with the face of a fox burned into the lid. Without hesitation, Bannan went to it and picked it up.

Larmensu! the box greeted, with what felt like triumph.

He tucked it carefully in his coat pocket. A few steps ahead was

another opening, the wooden lintel aglow with sunflowers and centered with a dark-faced fox. Bannan limped alongside the kruar,
keeping clear of the wall, to find the start of a stone staircase. It
curled down and around, leading into a lightless pit, and the truthseer reached out involuntarily, putting his hand on that big shoulder.

A whoof of kruar-rich breath in his face, Scourge bending his
neck to regard him, curious why he delayed. Or waiting for his rider
to regain his courage, which, Bannan thought shakily, wouldn't
happen while he stood here.

Then, for no reason but there should be a lantern to his right, the
truthseer stretched out his hand.

To find one waiting. *Larmensu.*

The work of a moment to open it. A pure silver light spilled forth,
washing the shadows away, for inside the lamp wasn't oil, but mimrol, the liquid that flowed through the Verge. Sold outside it as the
incredibly valuable 'Silver Tears' and Bannan would have dearly
loved to know how his family, who'd never to his knowledge trav-
elled beyond Vorkoun, came to have a magical artifact from far-off
Mellynne.

A question for Lila. Or Emon, who did trade there.

"What do you think?" He held it up to the kruar, who sniffed it,
then gave a dismissive huff.

Heartened, the truthseer aimed the lantern down, finding the edge
of the first step. "There's not much room," he cautioned, then grinned.
"I'd be beholden if you don't knock me over, you great bloody beast."

Of course, if his injured leg gave out, he'd do that for himself.

The sun came out of the cloud, scattering gems across the bay and
drawing shadows from the bridge. The ebbing of the tide ended and
its flood began. Water swirled around the arches as if dancing, then
inexorably switched from heading out to the Sweet Sea to coming
back. With it would come the fishing boats, their nets full and hulls
brightly painted, and Jenn Nalynn might see them later.

Being, at the moment, in the bowels of one herself. Jenn, feeling much like a fish must, had been dropped willy-nilly onto the deck, her hostess jumping lightly after, then hustled below, down a minuscule ladder, as if they mustn't be seen.

Below was a wonder, if a slightly shabby one. The walls were lined with clever cupboards and racks, like those Zehr Emms had built for his family but even more, space being constrained and tighter toward the boat's front. All wood in view showed ancient traces of paint and newer of grease. Every edge was either worn or splintering. Planks that creaked underfoot covered most of the floor, with gaps revealing smelly puddles implying the boat was prone to leak.

But there was a snug little stove on a counter at the very front and—much to Jenn's relief, being chilled to her bones—her hostess had a battered kettle she set to boil.

If, from the look of it, no tea.

Or conversation. It wasn't for her to break the silence. Yes, Aunt Sybb would say introductions had to come before anything else, and certainly she'd questions and very many concerns, but there was a daunting aloofness about the woman who bustled around the narrow room. The boat's cabin, Jenn remembered, determined to use every boatish word she could remember.

Though stories about pirates weren't necessarily the ideal source.

Bags hung from hooks overhead, making it necessary to stoop. A cot pulled down from one wall. The woman pointed Jenn to it then tossed her a coarse blanket, so she sat, wrapping herself in it, to wait.

She used the time to study the other, taking little peeks so as not to be found staring, which would be rude, though after a while Jenn came to believe the other had forgotten she was there.

Her garments were indeed rags, no longer useable scraps like those Jenn and her sister would collect to make a braided rug or use for cleaning. These were looped and layered around her body and limbs, a shawl like a fish net—that might, for all Jenn knew, be one—holding the somewhat colorful mass in place. Her feet were bare and callused.

As were Jenn's, out of her boots. They'd that in common.

The kettle boiled. The woman, hand wrapped in yet another rag, took hold of the handle and poured some of the water into a cracked cup. She added a scoop of powder from a small red tin, glancing over her hunched shoulder at Jenn as if begrudging the use.

"Thank you," Jenn said politely, taking the cup. It wasn't clean but the gesture was kind and warmed her. She sipped, cautious of the heat and whatever the powder might be, then raised her brows, the taste better than she'd expected, bitter and strong yet flavorful, with soothing heat. She looked up with a smile from her heart.

Startling the other woman, who ducked this way and that, rags waving to either side of her head. "Ye be magic, girl," she grumbled.

It wasn't a question, but Jenn answered. "I am a woman, like you." She wiggled her toes in evidence. "I am also turn-born and, yes, a little magic. Where I come from," she clarified, unwilling to test if this part of the edge would answer her and feeling that the more prudent answer.

The woman whistled between her teeth, the sound more annoyed than alarmed. "Well, don' ye be bringing yo'r magic 'ere. Unnerstan? There's those who'll know-n-some who'll tell. They'll bring dawizards on ye, swift as storm."

Jenn blinked, lowering her cup. "What is a 'dawizard'?" If of magic, maybe they could help her save Werfol.

"Trust ye nah find out. Drink yo'r cafel or giv it 'ere."

Or not. She dutifully took another swallow, paused to relish its warmth, then offered the half-full cup.

The woman snatched it with ill grace, stomping over to the ladder. She leaned there, bringing the cup into cover of the rags drifting around her face, and seemed to stare out the small round window.

A porthole, Jenn told herself, proud to know that one.

Then, abandoned, heartsore, and more than a little afraid, she curled herself up in the blanket and lay down on the cot, facing the wall, and it wasn't mysterious dawizards who consumed her thoughts, or even Werfol or Bannan.

But Marrowdell and everyone she'd deserted, having acted without thought of them and sorry.

Though if she hadn't, maybe she'd never have found poor Werfol.

If and maybes, Aunt Sybb would say, never darned a sock. It meant, Jenn was sure, that dithering about what might have happened wasn't as important as fixing what had.

Although, to be fair, there'd been an unusually large number of socks with holes at toe and heel piled up in Jenn's basket, last spring having arrived with special urgency.

Jenn nodded to herself. She'd trust Wisp to look after Marrowdell, though she'd be curious as to how, her dear dragon more interested in teasing than saving people, but he'd do his best and that was that.

A tear slipped out, wetting the flat folded blanket acting as her pillow.

At least Wisp wouldn't have to worry about further consequences. She'd not be making any wishes in Marrowdell anytime soon.

The toad queen had made sure of that.

Having finished expanding—or so Werfol ardently hoped, the false toad having grown to the size of the Westietas' home plus a barn and quite alarmingly bloated—the monster blinked enormous eyes no longer limpid brown but a sickly green centered with black and waited.

For applause, no doubt. A thing Semyn would whisper to him when they were supposed to be paying attention to a speech by someone who thought themselves important but were, as Momma would say, pompous and uninformed.

Well, what she'd really call such a person, to their father, was pocket lint, but her sons weren't to be *that* disrespectful even in their heads.

The false toad wasn't pocket lint but was, Werfol judged, pompous. Hadn't it insisted Jenn Nalynn call it "your majesty"?

As for uninformed, that was his problem. The majesty-monster was probably full of secrets.

And he'd seen it before—

"WELL?"

Goosie had grown, too, now bigger than he was—unless he'd shrunk, but Werfol was confident he'd stayed as he was. He tried not to look at where she lay flopped on the sand next to him, split seam gaping open as if to swallow him up again.

Werfol bowed, his fingers brushing the sand, and said very properly indeed, "Greetings. My name is Werfol Westietas. What's yours?"

"I RULE ALL!"

It had to be a lie—but didn't feel like one. Uncle Bannan had warned him people could believe something untrue so completely, he wouldn't be able to tell. How annoying. Trying not to frown, Werfol said, "That's impressive, but hardly a name. I can't call you that."

"You've called me before without one, little truthseer," words oozing with triumph. "Seen me before. Admit it."

He'd used his gift on the house toad from Marrowdell, only to be surprised by something else. Rising through, something larger and darker, a something *not happy* with a boy looking back—

It—*she*, Werfol corrected himself, had been there every time he'd pushed his gift to look beneath the surface truth, whether at the scree, or at Dutton's ancestors, or at their tutor, Master Setac. He'd seen a mouth and eerie green eyes.

His temper flared. "You've been spying on me!" he accused hotly.

The majesty-monster rocked back and forth, as if too delighted to be still. "You started it!"

He hadn't, not ever! Which sounded like bickering with his brother, not part of a serious conversation with a pompous—scary—majesty-monster.

Werfol swallowed and settled. "If I did, it was unintentional." A good word that. Semyn liked it, if didn't always believe him when he used it. He narrowed his eyes, staring up. "My being—rude, like that—doesn't give you the right to kidnap me—and Uncle Bannan and Jenn Nalynn." Involuntarily he glanced around the empty plain of sand, as if, named, they'd appear. Sagged a little inside when they didn't. "Where are they?" Stuffed inside a filthy toy seemed entirely possible and dreadful, so he wrapped his arms tightly around his middle.

A slow blink, then, "I sent the man with a gift home to gather what I want. I sent the meddlesome turn-born where she'll have no choice but set me free. And you, little truthseer. Wherever shall I send you?" With a disturbing purr.

He'd lost control of the conversation, letting the subject ask him a question and that, Werfol knew, wasn't good at all. He needed a new question, a better one, and quickly.

Oh, Ancestors Blessed, and he had one, didn't he? The majesty-monster had slipped, to say "set free." It meant she was trapped here, too. While the implication of something bigger and more powerful to have done the trapping was unsettling to say the least, here at last was the chink in her armor Momma said you had to find.

And attack.

Werfol spread his arms. "What would *you* do with freedom?" He couldn't sound as grand and dignified as Jenn Nalynn, so he made the words mocking, his tone dripping with scorn. His aggravating Weedly-voice, Semyn called it, and usually punched him, but not if he ran first.

Running wasn't an option. Besides, the monster wanted to tell him. Had to brag. *I rule all.* He understood that need as only a younger sibling could, and waited.

She lowered herself until he stood reflected in the black heart of a bilious green eye, her hot breath like the bottom of a cesspool. "Why do you want to know?" Suspicious. Wary—of him?

She must have been alone here a long time.

Werfol kept his face, as Momma would expect, set to politely attentive with a touch of disinterest. As if he didn't care, not really, but made idle conversation. "If I were free," he said casually, though his heart felt like a drum in his chest, "I'd run straight to our kitchen. Cook will have a special treat for me. Or visit the stables."

Oh, the thought of having the kruar at his side—though Werfol was almost certain from what he'd overheard that Uncle Bannan had had Scourge with him and even that mighty steed hadn't been able to fight the majesty-monster—

"Small ideas." Matching scorn.

"I am small," Werfol pointed out.

It struck her fancy, as he'd hoped. Pulling up and away, the majesty-monster made a sound like a laugh. Or had something stuck in her throat. He couldn't tell.

"What will I do with freedom?" She shook her bulk, set her terrible collection to a terrible dance, and laughed again. "No longer will I be forced to scavenge these scraps of magic to survive. No longer will I have to trap those who hoard it in their flesh and take it from them."

Those with gifts. Like him. Hearing—*feeling*—the raw hunger in her voice, Werfol eased a step back. What had she done to Uncle Bannan? To Jenn?

"The sei forbade me to take more from the Verge, yet permit mimrol to bleed into your realm. Where it is wasted! Lost!"

And the majesty-monster opened her mouth and it was the size of the sky, ready to consume all there was—Werfol cried out in horror.

—instead of being swallowed, he found himself back in the dark, inside Goosie, who was, no doubt, hanging from a wart like her other trophies.

Her voice followed him, full of spite and malice. "When I am free, little one? When I am done? The edge will have no magic left and I will be mighty enough to challenge the sei! I WILL RULE ALL!"

Werfol covered his ears, feeling alone and very small indeed.

The flood receded as if Marrowdell drank it down, pools becoming puddles, puddles dark stains. The animals were first to cross what had been the river's ford, pushing and shoving one another in their urgent drive to return home.

To Wisp's dismay, having envisioned a dignified return.

To keep the mannerless beasts from undoing the good he—and the yling—had accomplished, the dragon flung hay from the nearest barn into the commons field to head them off. A fodder ignored by the sows and their boar, busy rooting in the mud of what had been their pasture.

The villagers followed on foot, except for Cheffy and Alyssa, who clung to the back of Wainn's Old Pony as it trotted, wheezing, behind the cows. The people moved more slowly than Wisp expected, as if leery of the muddy gravel, unless it was a shared reluctance to face what remained of their homes.

They'd a pleasant surprise ahead. A new and peculiar sensation filled Wisp, his smug anticipation fading to a troubling concern. What would they think? He shouldn't care.

Hadn't, before.

Still, from his perch high in the old oak, safely invisible, the dragon watched closely.

The villagers arrived burdened with bags and sacks—Kydd carried Bannan's broom, once used by that worthy on a memorable occasion to shoo off curious young dragons. The truthseer had survived his daring, becoming of interest.

His latest pestilence would not, if it challenged him again. Wisp canted a hopeful eye upwards.

Glad cries drew his attention back down. "Ancestors Lifted and Loved!" "What is this?" "Blessed Ancestors!" People hurried along paths he'd cleared, under a roof of their cleaned belongings the yling had strung, entering their homes only to rush out again, waving their hands and calling out to one another. "Do you see?" "How is it possible?"

"It must have been Jenn!"

True, the girl had stopped the flood, making all else possible—including consequences to be faced by the villagers later—but Wisp couldn't help a heavy sigh. If Jenn Nalynn were here now, as she should be, she'd be happy to see what he'd done and smile her wondrous smile for him.

Unless she knew it had been Wen Treff's notion for, if he was honest, he wouldn't have helped the village otherwise, it not being a dragonish sort of impulse.

Which the girl would understand.

Though really all he'd done was hurry along a tidying these people were perfectly capable of doing for themselves and while he'd found the experience mildly satisfying—

"Where is she?"

The villagers' joy vanished like smoke caught by wind, taking his with it.

What if the girl was in the clutches of the toad queen? The thought speared his heart with ice, stole his breath.

Meanwhile everyone rushed around, checking back inside houses and barns as if Jenn Nalynn played a game of seek and hide with them. Done, they gathered in a solemn circle around the village's still-pristine fountain and Radd put his arm around Peggs, who began, very quietly, to cry.

As if mourning her loss.

Someone else started weeping, and more and—

Wisp gave a vicious snarl, claws digging into the branch, heedless of the great tree's instant attempt to shake him off.

How dare they give up hope of the girl!

The dragon flew down to stand behind Kydd Uhthoff and his kin, judging the three the calmest present, assuredly a better choice than Hettie and her sniffling babies or Cynd, who wailed against Davi's big shoulder, or any of the rest, for that matter, by now there being not a dry eye or even voice among the lot.

He wrapped himself in light, sending breezes to nip their ears. "Jenn Nalynn went after Bannan." Lost with the other, older fool who should have kept him safe, and Wisp utterly lacked the capacity to worry about them as well.

The three men whirled with gratifying alarm to stare at him, an alarm and notice spreading around the circle until the dragon suffered the regard of every villager old enough to focus.

"She will return," he finished with absolute conviction, rejecting any future in which she did not.

The youngest Uhthoff, Wainn, took a step closer. "Jenn should have saved the hives."

Courage or obsession? Before an aggravated Wisp could judge, he felt a beat of air.

He braced for attack but wasn't the target. The youngling, an ill-controlled shimmer of malice, landed in a sprawl and rushed at Wainn—

Wisp was there first, bowling the other over, readying his good claw to rip out interloper's belly while his wounded jaw—

Stopped, there being a hand in his way.

Both dragons froze in a strained, astonished tableaux.

Wainn, kneeling by the youngling, kept his hand between them as if a dragon hadn't tasted his blood and come for more.

Smiled up at Wisp, as if oblivious to his own peril.

Then spoke with a voice holding mountains.

"TEACH IT."

ᴛHIRᴛᴇᴇN

*A*DREADFUL DREAM IS writ in mystery and symbol. The wise heed them. The foolish do not.

Roche Morrill's eighth dreadful dream took him while he slept in the bed he shared with Flam and Disel, in the coach inn a day from Vorkoun, and while it made no sense then, he never forgot it.

> *He stood with his friends on the road where it passed between mountains and shadows were deep. Shadows that suddenly rumbled and roared as the mountains shrugged, a torrent of rock tumbling all around—and he grabbed his friends to pull them to safety but their arms were gone and before he could find them the road cracked open and something terrible grabbed him to pull him down—he sank, sank, sank and couldn't breathe—*

He gasped for air, his face wet, and Flam's bearded face filled his sight. "You're safe, Roche," his friend told him, a flask in hand that explained the wet if nothing else. "We're safe. It was just a dream."

"It was more—but that can't be—" Roche sat up, Disel behind and bracing his shoulders, Flam sitting on the mattress. They'd lit a candle, its small and fitful light barely enough to show the scarred bare wood of walls and floor, the wide straw mattress and lack of blankets or other furnishings. The poorest room, but they'd thought to save their coin—

"I don't understand," he said at last, trembling with exhaustion and afraid to his bones. Ancestors Blessed and Bountiful, that he'd friends who knew to wake him—saving him twice over. "Dreadful dreams come years apart, not hours."

"Your gift grows," Disel guessed.

"Or the hazard does," Flam put in, the pair never doubting him. "The first warned of flood. What was this one about?"

"A landslide." Roche tried to keep his mouth shut, but the truth vomited forth as it always did. "I tried to save you," he admitted miserably. "I couldn't. Your arms were gone."

Flam paled.

Disel turned Roche so she could stare in his face, keeping an arm around his shoulders. "We were in your dream?"

He gave a reluctant nod. "It might have nothing to do with you." In his first dreadful dream, as a child, he'd tried to save his toys as his home collapsed around him. The next day, his family was exiled from Avyo, leaving most of their possessions behind. "Or mean we'll be separated, soon."

"Or we die," she countered, flat and grim.

Roche shuddered. He drew up his knees, wrapping his arms around them. It did nothing to warm his heart. "Something will change. I can't tell what. I never can."

She gave him a hard squeeze then stood, her hand lingering on his shoulder. "Can't say I'll be able to sleep after that—and you won't want to—" a gentle press.

"Let's see if the kitchen's up and stirring," Flam suggested, his hand on Roche's knee. "Stars know, I'm starving."

Their instinct was to touch him, to anchor him here with them. While brave and kind, it wouldn't be enough, Roche knew. Whatever clawed for him through his dreams was too powerful.

Today might be his last with them.

"You're always starving," he observed, that being the truth and better to say. Disel laughed, Flam pretended to be offended, and the mood lightened as the three pulled on boots and raced for the stairs.

Jenn woke to the strange sensation of being gently rocked and, while Bannan on occasion rocked her in his arms, usually while humming in her hair, this was more as if the entire world shifted back and forth, back and forth.

She opened her eyes to find a face hovering close to her own, managing not to squeak in surprise. "I'm on a boat," Jenn heard herself say.

Teeth flashed; almost a smile. "The *Good Igrini.*"

Boats having names. Jenn knew something about this one. Urcet had claimed his mother warned him to be good or the house igrini would take his nose. It wasn't comforting.

Careful not to move, she gave hers. "I'm Jenn Nalynn."

The smile vanished. "For'n'r name." Said like a curse and hardly promising.

Foreigner. True, if not exactly her fault. "And your name?"

"Ye wan' m'name?" This close, the woman's breath smelled of cafel—and fish, though everything in the cabin shared that reek. She came closer. Jenn pressed back into the cot, hands clenching the blanket. "T'do ye magic agin me?"

The words were fearful and angry, delivered with a fair amount of spit. With an effort, Jenn didn't wipe her face. She circled her heart with the fingers of her right hand. "I swear on the Bones of my Blessed Ancestors, I mean you no harm," she said earnestly, being careful not to wish to be believed. "You saved my life. I'd—I'd like to thank you, that's all."

The woman reared back, her rags brushing Jenn's cheeks. Hesitated.

What would Aunt Sybb do? Jenn went on her elbow to offer her hand. "Thank you . . ." She let the word trail suggestively.

"Nonny. S'what t'others call me. Ye use that."

"Thank you, Nonny," Jenn said. It didn't seem a typical Eld name, by Master Dusom's teachings and her sole living example, the scholar Urcet a Hac Sa Od y Dom. On the other hand, he'd gone by Urcet the entire time he'd been in Marrowdell, so perhaps the rest of his name was an Eld sort of honorific.

She dared sit up, steadying herself against the rocking of the boat with her hands. "I need another favor."

"What, now?"

She made a wry face. "Where do I pee?"

The boat, it turned out, had a curtained closet called a head for bodily necessities, containing a seat over a hole. Jenn apologized under her breath to whatever swam beneath, though she supposed if all boats had the same, the fish must be used to the temporary fouling of their waters.

Of course, fish had to pee somewhere. The notion lent a new aspect to swimming she'd consider later.

Done, Jenn ducked back through the curtain to find Nonny at the stove again. "Ye be hunger'd, I expect," the other said, not turning around. "There's no much."

Her stomach chose that moment to growl, loudly. By the little shake of the rags, her hostess heard and was amused. Jenn took it as a good sign. "May I help?"

"Keep out'r m'way." Harshly.

Jenn set herself against the ladder to take up as little space as possible, holding on as the boat bounced.

An instant later, Nonny grumbled, "I donna 'ave guests."

An apology as much as explanation, though Jenn feared she owed one in return, having disrupted the life of such a private person. And used up supplies, by the look of the boat, in scant supply. In Marrowdell, she'd have added what she had.

Urcet had not only been a scholar, he'd been wealthy enough to fund Dema Qimirpik's expedition to observe the Great Turn, supplying

Eld wagons and gear. The expedition hadn't been wise, since the pair had come to attempt magic they shouldn't, but they'd accepted the advice of those who knew better and refrained in the end.

Urcet, Jenn now recalled, feeling more and more hopeful, had worn gold ornaments, including a bead through the side of his very handsome nose. Surely he'd become famous by now, having planned to write a book on his adventures. Famous enough, perhaps, to be known in a fishing village, for the Eld, she reminded herself, rewarded academic endeavor and treated their scholars like heroes.

"I have a—" *friend* wasn't quite right, although Urcet had paid her flattering attention and listened, "—an acquaintance in Eldad."

Without turning, Nonny lifted a spoon and spun it around in the air. "Eldad's full of 'quaintances. Ye know," this pityingly, "we've more people 'ere than all t'other domains then some."

According to Master Dusom and Bannan and anyone in the village she'd spoken to on the subject, Mellynne, the oldest domain, was also the largest and most populated, but it wouldn't be the least courteous to say so, nor productive of good will.

Jenn paused then brightened. "He'd be famous."

Another droll spin of the spoon implied more of those, too.

Quashed, she leaned back against the ladder. "I only thought he might be able to help, if I could find him. His name is Urcet a Hac Sa Od y Dom. He had an interest in—magical things."

Nonny used her spoon to lift the rags from her face, the better to stare at Jenn. "Urcy? Urcy Shade's Ass?" With incredulity, then a laugh. "Donna that beat all."

Seen clearly for the first time, she'd a strong face, with high cheekbones and broad forehead framing a generous mouth, presently quirked to the side in amusement. The right nostril of her wide nose was pierced with a single blue bead, the color of her eyes, and a tight curl of red hair peeked out from her rag headdress.

Three parallel scars scored her black skin from forehead to chin, just missing her eye. They gave her a distinctly piratical look and Jenn, for one, wasn't about to inquire their source, having other concerns. "That wasn't his name," she countered testily.

"Is now." Nonny barked her laugh again and turned back to her stove. "Man's worse off'n me, and that's not say'n much. Tho' I've m'boat. Urcy beds 'neath a tarp, if he's nah sent pack'n. Help you?" Her shoulders shook. "Best joke I e'r heard."

Ancestors Troubled and Tried, if it were true—and the creature sent her here to a purpose—

Jenn's hands clenched on the shell necklace.

Here, where a man who'd sought magic had come after, by the sound of it, falling from what he'd been to something far less worthy, and Jenn would have felt some guilt in that, having sent him from Marrowdell without the proof he'd wanted—though the dema had promised—

But what if Urcet had found magic here? Of the kind to suit the toad queen, the dark and dire and deadly kind, for it existed. She knew it.

Jenn looked longingly at the ladder. She needed to talk to the large little cousin in the water, the one who'd saved her. Surely the waalum was good, as the toad queen wasn't, and possibly had answers—

"Supper," Nonny announced, turning with a bowl in each hand.

The lantern proved inexhaustible. Not so much his leg, and Bannan lurched down step after step, wanting nothing more than to stop but they'd yet to find an end to the stairs. The passage was too low for him to ride. Scourge, crouching, had taken to holding his belt in his jaws, as if anticipating a fall at any moment.

The grip would have been more reassuring if those jaws hadn't been responsible for his injury in the first place.

Ancestors Battered and Bent, the kruar had tried to save him. Too late now to ask for a different approach. Things were as they were. Including this staircase to nowhere at all.

He was, the truthseer suspected, growing a little punchy. No appetite but the thought of water had grown to a torment. Add it to the list, he told himself glibly. His right foot had blisters forming at the toe, soggy boots and socks the bane of feet, and his back seriously protested being bent this long.

When his next step hit the same level as the last, only the kruar's grip saved him from lurching forward on his face. "Found the bottom," Bannan announced, beyond relieved to be done with stairs. "Now what?"

A eloquent nudge from behind.

He lifted the lantern and stepped forward into a tunnel.

The construction differed here. Timbers framed cut stone. The source of the material used in the building above? No, Bannan judged. Unlike those stones, here the rock was laced with veins of black and red. A mine. An old one, the floor level and worn. The tunnel disappeared in either direction: one surely toward Ansnor—the other to Vorkoun and everything he cared about. But which? He turned right.

Scourge snorted. "Other way."

Within steps, they found another opening, choked with rubble. Bannan looked up, considering. One hidden passage—why not more? "This could have led to the kitchen." Defended from inquisitive children by their formidable cook, and might this be why? Ancestors Perplexed and Perturbed. "How much did we miss?"

Another nudge. *Stop dawdling*, that was.

Frowning, the truthseer tarried a moment longer, using his gift to examine the rubble, startled to find streaks of what wasn't silver but mimrol.

Peering up, he spotted trickles and drips of the stuff, none now within easy reach.

Heart's Blood. The flowers in the wall. The lantern. Their magic hadn't come from Mellynne. Their home had been built on a source of the precious stuff—

Claws poked out from a crack in the rock, making him jump back.

"Can we go?" Scourge said testily.

Nodding agreement, Bannan limped on, chewing on questions no one was left to answer. Had the Marerrym, his great-times-great grandparents, built here because of mimrol—drawn by the magic inherent in the edge?

Had the family kept this secret for their own profit or to stop others having it? If mimrol could be mined within Rhoth, what then of Mellynne's hold on magical artifacts?

What mattered now, he decided, was who else knew of this place, starting with the ones who'd destroyed it.

Limping on, Bannan stepped over rusty paired rails set in the tunnel floor. They crossed to vanish within more rubble-sealed exits to either side, giving him one answer. "Ansnan work."

Scourge dipped his head to sniff the metal. "Cows," he sneered.

Which Ansnans used to pull their carts and minecars, yes, but Bannan couldn't help but snort at this. "You can't possibly smell them after this long."

An eye regarded him. A lip curled. "Still stinks," the kruar affirmed.

Chuckling, the truthseer reached out with his crutch—

It kept going, finding no floor at all, and he staggered back. Gripping the precious lantern tightly to keep it safe, Bannan thrust it out to see what lay ahead.

A wide crack, three times the length of Scourge, zigzagged across the tunnel.

It didn't open into the earth—or not only. The lantern's light caught on what wasn't rock, but an immensity of what appeared pale bone, smooth and curved, and Bannan sucked in a breath.

Let it out. "Sei. What's it doing here?" Under his house, yes, but in this place at all?

"Whatever it wants." Scourge appeared no more eager than Bannan to approach the crack. A snarl of contempt. "The fools who brought your home down with magic risked more than they knew."

Cold slithered down the truthseer's spine. Risk it was. He'd seen no trace of the mad sei in Channen but in Marrowdell? It didn't show itself just as the Bone Hills and Spine, but in terrifying marks left on the landscape, like those of giant claws, scarring the surrounding ridges. Those same claws had brought down the once-great Ansnan refuge, and if it had been roused here?

At the least, Vorkoun would have fallen into the Lilem and

drowned. Keeping his voice calm with an effort, Bannan asked, "How do we pass it?" Ancestors Timid and Terrified, there was no way in this life or any other he'd lower himself into the crack and limp over a piece of what was essentially a god.

"We jump," Scourge informed him with reprehensible glee, considering the paucity of room to land on the far end of the crack. "Climb up."

Muttering, "Bloody beast," under his breath, Bannan did as he was told.

Backing a few steps—an unusual caution for a creature able to leap a hedge from a standing start—the kruar surged forward and leapt into space—

A splendid effort that almost succeeded.

Scourge's back feet scrambled for purchase. Bannan hung on, unable to stop the—"BLOODY BEAST!" he shouted as chunks of rock rained on the sei.

Once on solid ground, the pair froze. Waiting.

A heartbeat. Two.

Feeling Scourge inhale, Bannan started to breathe.

To stop as the world gave a delicate, ominous flutter, like a moth stretching its wings.

Werfol never thought he'd miss being hungry and thirsty. Or having to go to the bathroom, although that was just as well, though he missed being tired and falling asleep. Whatever magic the majesty-monster used on him erased the needs of his body while leaving his mind woefully free to run in circles, so it did.

What was she? Old, he decided, and rotten, not at all like a dried apple that got sweeter with time, a favorite of the pony in Marrowdell—

His limited world shook. *Strained.*

At once Werfol tried with all his might not to think, in case the name he'd thought and feelings he'd felt because of thinking it was the cause of whatever was happening.

And because however horrible it was to be here, the possibility of the majesty-monster reading his thoughts was worse.

The shaking and straining stopped.

Of course not thinking was impossible, since you had to think about thinking to not think which was thinking—Werfol smacked his forehead in disgust.

He had to know. Did she know his thoughts? Or was the shaking and straining merely from an internal upset, like he suffered after beets and heartily wished on her?

Perfect.

The little truthseer thought about beets.

How beets made his stomach hurt and gave him cramps and sent him running to poop until there was nothing left to poop.

He thought about beets as hard as he could, focused until his teeth clenched and ached, and he even grew queasy as if beets were truly involved, but nothing happened.

He let himself stop, relieved.

Thoughts of home sprang up, unbidden and achingly clear. Thoughts of Semyn's laughter and Dutton, with his enormous sword. Of JoJo climbing into his lap, despite having grown too big for it, and feeding the pigeons. Of sneaking bacon to Spirit and Dauntless—who were getting better at not trying for his fingers, too.

Of Poppa and his workshop.

Of Momma—

He mustn't think of her. Momma had a gift and she might hear and if she did she'd find a way to come after him and the Verge would kill her if the majesty-monster didn't—

Werfol urgently thought of Marrowdell and its people. Of Frann, the first person to die who he'd known—and how confused he'd been about the villagers afterwards, and hurt, not that anyone lied, as Uncle Bannan tried to explain, but grieved in their way.

Ancestors Dear and Departed, Frann had been kind and good to them. He'd think of that.

And of Peggs' wonderful pie. Of playing in snow able to play back.

Maybe such thoughts, being of Marrowdell, were a little magical in themselves, for Werfol found himself feeling calmer, more in control.

And when he thought next of Wisp, the dragon who was real and his friend?

He found himself ready to fight back.

The boat rocked without warning, then settled. When Nonny paid it no heed, Jenn focused on supper, having missed every meal this strange long day. Supper, it turned out, consisted of small brown grains, black beans, and slivers of fish, fried together then served in a bowl. The other woman hunched over hers, eating with noisy relish.

Jenn paused to whisper the Beholding, her fingers curled over her heart. "Hearts of my Ancestors, I am Beholden for the waalum and Nonny, who gave help to a stranger, and for this food—" though the dollop of bright red sauce in the midst looked alarming, "—that will sustain me. I would be Beholden if you would keep watch over— over those I love and miss so much. Especially poor little Werfol—"

Her voice quivered at the end. "—Hearts of my Ancestors, However far we are apart, Keep Us Close." Eyes swimming with tears, she blinked them into her bowl, taking a quick mouthful. The sauce was hot enough keep her eyes watering, but she finished her portion, her stomach grateful.

Stacking their empty bowls and spoons, Nonny poured a scant measure of dark liquid into mismatched cups, pressing one on Jenn. "Donna spill it," she warned. "I've naught more." Without acknowledging Jenn's nod, she swarmed up the ladder in a whirl of rags and out.

Jenn followed eagerly, though careful of her cup and doing her best, after one whiff, not to smell the contents. She stepped over a wooden ledge onto the *Good Igrini*'s deck, a fresh little breeze tossing her hair in greeting.

The world had changed while she'd been below, something she should have expected given the presence of tides, but hadn't. Seven

boats, hulls and cabins painted the same bright colors as the buildings, were now tied up by the village, people swarming over them
and along the dock, heaving crates full of fish to one another with
cheery shouts, everyone in a hurry.

The largest boat had two tall masts instead of the usual one, but
its sails were hidden—furled—like the rest.

And water, smooth as glass, filled the bay. It covered the green
slime on the shoreline rocks and stroked the top rung of the ladder
she'd climbed. White birds floated peacefully on it, as did the boats,
including this one, her deck now level with the pier.

Ancestors Timely and Tossed, if only she'd arrived at this moment instead of earlier. It would have been much easier to climb out.
Safer, too.

As if in answer, something rose in midst of the water, wide and
dark and glistening. It paused, then slowly sank again, and whatever
it was, was much much larger than a waalum or this boat, making
this moment no safer at all.

"What was that?" Jenn whispered.

"Basker, come wi't'tide." Nonny perched comfortably on the rim
of her boat—the gunnel, Jenn's pirate reading informed her. She
raised her cup in salute. "Good luck, see'n one."

Disturbed water etched out a circle larger than the boat, sliding
from lips covered in small white lumps and seaweed, an enormous
mouth like an empty pit filling with frantic tiny creatures and water
as it rose. Full, it closed and sank.

The cup aimed at Jenn. "Sit ye down," a snap.

She'd climbed Marrowdell's old oak, a tree that wouldn't have let
her fall. Such courtesy Jenn didn't think applied to a vessel bouncing
excitedly with her steps, but Nonny waited and Nonny, she suspected,
found her nervousness highly entertaining.

Suggesting, Jenn decided, boats moved without throwing those
aboard over, and those who lived on them grew accustomed to it, as
she must.

As calmly as possible, she walked to the side of the boat, took a
resolute look over into the dark water—though it seemed improbable

the waalum would stay near with a basker feeding—then turned and sat as if at home.

It left her facing the mighty bridge, behind Nonny, and gave her a question—as most things here did, but this struck her as important. "Why is the bridge so high?" The arches were easily twice the height necessary to clear the rise of land bordering the bay, including the trees, a waste of stone and labor.

Unless there was a reason.

The mass of rags that was Nonny's head turned to the bridge, then back again. A shrug. "Dawizards said it ha' be th'way. They fear t'magics." She shook with laughter that didn't sound amused. "Joke's on'm who do. Magics donna care 'bout us without."

A feeling, Jenn knew, shared by most of Marrowdell's little cousins—and its resident dragon.

There might be other similarities here. "The edge—the part where magic is—has boundaries," she dared say, careful not to add they defined her existence as well. Much as she disliked secrets, this one, she knew, Bannan would advise her to keep.

"Aie." The cup, contents as yet untasted, swung up to circle the bay. "Top o't'arms. See where t'trees get measley?" Without waiting an answer, the cup lowered and thrust past Jenn, aimed at the fishing village and beyond. "Beyond t'bend in t'road. Shadesport wallows in magic—e'n if folks like t'be blind t'it."

Jenn nodded her understanding. "Where I come from, most people go through their days without noticing anything strange." Especially Aunt Sybb, who found house toads disturbing and continued to harbor a deep suspicion the man Wyll, back to Wisp, had been one. "Though sometimes," she added, "they can't help but see it."

Such as the day dragons plucked them from rooftops to whisk them through the sky—an event some, namely Lorra Treff, might try to explain away in a month or so as a tornado, perhaps.

Invoking a storm felt, to Jenn, less a comfort than what might have eaten them helping instead; she supposed their dear livestock, having a more pragmatic outlook, might now fear dragons more.

Probably for the best.

"Nah 'ere." Nonny settled back, her cup in her lap between both hands. "Nah yet," she qualified wistfully, as if a crisis of magic might improve her neighbors.

Jenn sincerely hoped none happened before she left—leaving only the magic she was determined to do. She gazed at the bridge, then through its arches at the waters beyond. "And what of that way, toward the Sweet Sea?"

"Momma's Basket, ye mean?"

Her map listed the Eld name for the sea as 'Syrpic Ans,' translated in neat script below to 'The Mother's Elbow.' If that were wrong, a discomfiting notion, what else might be?

Nothing, Jenn decided. The baroness had commissioned a most excellent map. This was, as Aunt Sybb would surely say, a local peculiarity, no less valid, of course, so Jenn quickly said, "My mistake. That's what I meant."

"Ye have t'ask t'waalum. If there be any left 'sides t'one saved ye." Nonny's voice turned grim. "Dawizards put a bounty on t'hides. Mor' than a fisher gets in a good year."

Ancestors Perilous and Perverse! "They mustn't!"

And she almost wished it. Came close enough her heart pounded with the effort to pull back from that brink, for there was no way to know how the Bay of Shades would answer but certainly a wave to wipe the boats and fishers from the shore was a horrible possibility—

Peeing on fish, Jenn thought frantically as the water did indeed seem to grow choppy and agitated. Slime on ladders and—

"Nah argument fr'me," Nonny commented, unaware of her peril.

~Elder sister! Stop!~

The waalum. At its plea, she took a breath, then another—having apparently stopped breathing altogether in her distress, which Nonny might notice if it continued and she really mustn't forget what made her flesh—

"I'm very glad," Jenn said, "that no hunter saw the kind waalum who risked itself, coming to close to shore to save me."

Nonny squinted at her. "I n'deaf."

She'd spoken loudly for those ears under the now-calm water, trusting the waalum would hear and exercise greater caution in future—disappointed when the little cousin failed to respond.

Jenn nodded an apology to her companion and softened her voice. "Who lives in the other village?" she asked, after a more peaceful topic. "The one at the bottom of the bay?"

A gnarled knuckle rapped the gunnel. "Donna ye speak o'them, hear!" An admonishment sharp—or was it fearful? "Not t'any."

Well, that hadn't worked. Refusing to be dissuaded, Jenn leaned forward, eyes fixed on Nonny. "Why?"

"Hush." Nonny raised her cup. "It'd be magic's time."

The turn. It was coming; Jenn felt it inside. A tide, like the water's, to change the landscape as the light of this world faded, letting that of the Verge shine through. A brief moment, flowing ahead of night, revealing all in its path.

Unless hidden from view.

In Marrowdell, the sun set behind the Bone Hills, the turn slipping ahead of night's shadow, racing down the valley from her meadow to the village. Here, the turn would start behind the fishing village and come toward them across the bay, ending—somewhere else.

Unless she rushed back down to hide in the cabin, it would find and expose her other self.

Jenn raised her cup, touching it to Nonny's. "About that."

There being no further sign the world was ending, Bannan had lain flat on Scourge's back and signaled the kruar to advance, too worn to dismount. He grew, if not comfortable, then comforted, and had almost fallen asleep when his companion stopped.

"There's a door."

Bannan slipped off, raising the lantern to see for himself.

A door there was, heavy and reinforced with iron, with a ring to pull and lock beneath. Leaning on the frame, he took out the box he'd taken from the table.

Larmensu.

Opened it.

A large key lay on its bed of velvet, the silver bow shaped in the Larmensu crest, the shaft thick and black, the collar and wards—its teeth—silver. The latter were rounded like flower petals, and he didn't need to look beyond the surface to know what appeared silver was, in some part or all, mimrol.

Beautiful work, this key, left untouched in the room above, a room hidden from everyone but known—surely known to his parents. Why?

More to the point, "This was their escape route. Why didn't they use it?"

"No warning."

The kruar's preference, a sudden devastating ambush. Bannan gave a grim nod. "Or they wouldn't leave the others—" It didn't matter, now. He put the key in the lock, felt the bow warm in his hand in welcome.

Larmensu.

Turned it.

The door pulled open with silent ease and light filled the space. Scourge pushed through first and past him, intending to spring any traps.

Bannan hurried behind, in case he did.

Instead, he found a room lit by more magical lanterns, these ornate sconces on the walls. He closed the one he carried and, thinking of nyphrit and things stuck in walls—not to forget the sleeping sei—went to close and lock the door.

Before he could, it shut of its own accord, the lock giving an audible click. Bannan and Scourge exchanged looks, the kruar flattening his ears in his version of a shrug. *Don't loose the key,* that meant.

They were in what his soldier's mind recognized as a resupply room. No, he realized with numb shock, a cache, implying—"My family were smugglers."

Cases of wine filled one wall. Narrow shelves on the opposite were stocked with row upon row of little wooden boxes. He chose one at random to open. It held a vial of black powder and three twists of hair, a bone and neatly handwritten note, and didn't, he noticed wryly, whisper his name.

"These are wishings. Spells. What are they doing here?"

Being illegal, by the laws of prince and land—

He read the note. It referred to curing bunions, one of the more common and lucrative scams in Vorkoun's underbridge market. The truthseer snorted. "Fake. They're all fakes."

Why peddle falsehood when they'd mimrol? Because such fakes had value in Ansnor—let alone those in Rhoth who'd pay anything for what purported to be magic.

Marerrym wine and casks of Ansnan ale. Baskets of cleaned bones—presumably none from an ancestor—destined for the potion market. Behind Scourge was a rack of swords and other gear. Whether taken in trade or for sale, these he understood.

Glaring at the boxes, Bannan ran a hand through his hair. Ancestors Vile and Villainous. The Verge was the source of mimrol, meaning that wouldn't be what the toad queen wanted. What if something *here* was, a real spell of the darkest kind? "We need to check them. Every one." He raised an eyebrow at his companion. "Can you smell anything dangerous about them?"

A tail flipped. Scourge remained in the corner he'd been searching. "What I smell is food and drink."

Tucking two of the spell boxes in his pocket, Bannan pulled a dusty bottle from its case, then joined the kruar, who'd taken a substantial bite from of a wheel of hard cheese, rind and all. A stack of ale casks stood nearby, looking new despite the years. Setting the bottle aside, the truthseer brought down the topmost only to grimace at the date. "I'd best stick to the wine."

A lip curled. "That's not wine."

"Wha—" Bannan snatched up the bottle. Rubbing at the dust didn't help, for the glass was tinted green. The label held the Marerrym crest with an etching of a fox below. He passed his thumb over it and almost dropped the bottle.

Larmensu.

Heart's Blood. If he had dropped it, that would have answered

the question if it contained wine or mimrol, but to what consequence?

Bannan returned it, carefully, to its case. Looked at the rest.
There had to be over fifty bottles, and, if all contained mimrol, represented a fortune.

And why his family was dead. Had he doubts before, they were
gone now. "The murderers failed to find this."

"No key." Mystery solved, at least to his satisfaction, Scourge
chomped another huge bite of cheese, bits flying. "Eat."

The cheese didn't appeal, or maybe it was how his companion ate
it; a drink did, greatly. His last had been some of the Marrowdell's
river.

"Ale it is." Tapping the cask, Bannan filled the metal taster cup
he found nearby. Gingerly he brought the liquid to his lips, ready to
spit it out if foul.

After a tiny swallow, he quickly took a deeper one. "It didn't
spoil," he marveled.

"Magic," the kruar offered slyly.

Not a comfort. Refilling the cup, the truthseer sat on a barrel to
rest his throbbing leg and think. A second locked door suggested an
exit—or more stairs or tunnels—heading, according to his companion, west to Vorkoun, but at some point, they'd go beyond the edge.

This might be their last chance to converse about more than rabbits. Bannan took a breath—

"You worry about the wrong things," Scourge interrupted. His
big head lowered, a lip curled in distain.

Bannan raised an eyebrow. "You're not worried about forgetting
who you are—again?"

"You will remember for me." Smug, that. "You will take us back to
Marrowdell. Once there, you will instruct the turn-born to destroy the
toad queen. There should be," a pregnant pause, "bacon. To celebrate."

As plans went, it had simplistic charm and glaring flaws. "You're
assuming Jenn can destroy the queen and—" Bannan paused mean-
ingfully, "—the house toads agree to it." A certainty, that his beloved
would never act against the will of their small friends.

"They lock the queen from the edge."

"Protecting us from her isn't the same as acting against her." Best not bring up the Rhothan prince who'd sent Marrowdell's inhabitants into exile in the first place and remained comfortably in power. "You're right. Assuming we get out of here, we could take the Northward Road home." The words filled him with painful longing. Hadn't he done it twice in the past year? Jenn Nalynn would be waiting—

"Then we go!"

"I said *could*. Not should."

An unhappy, "Why not?"

Bannan brought out his mother's scarf, holding it in a light fist. "Ancestors Witness, this belonged to Gyllen Marerrym Larmensu. We have to believe the toad queen in this much, that some dark magic brought down our house."

"She wants more," Scourge rumbled, a menacing growl under the words. "Your presence here is a provocation to the enemies of your family. She wants them to strike again. At you."

Or for him to find and use such spells to take revenge. He'd no doubt the nasty creature believed him capable.

Was he? He'd the rage for it, still. Before Jenn Nalynn, he'd a sick violence burning inside him—and there was his answer, Bannan realized with an inward shudder of relief. So long as his heart rested in her sure hands, bathed in goodness and love, he'd a compass to follow. "We won't let that happen," he said firmly, to himself as much as to Scourge.

"Agreed."

"Bringing us to the sticking point. If we return to Marrowdell without doing what she wants, the toad queen will know. She's made one door—what says she can't make another to pull us through again? Or do worse? The villagers suffer already. We can't bring more danger down on them." Bannan drained his cup. "What we need, old friend, are answers—the means to foil her plans for good. Without—" he added dryly, able to read that gleam in the kruar's eye, "—involving our dear turn-born in the struggle."

Scourge took another bite of cheese and stood chewing it, dribbling crumbs and grumbling deep in his chest.

As close to agreement as he'd get, Bannan decided, and pointed to the rock above. "What we know? Someone used magic to bring a mountain down on our house. The question Lila could never answer was why anyone would want to harm our family. Now we know. The Larmensus were smugglers, moving illicit goods, including mimrol, to and from Ansnor." Ancestors Blighted and Bold, didn't that explain a great deal about his sister's peculiar skills?

Had Lila known?

A question to ask later. He sat back, giving the kruar a brooding look. The beast had permitted his uncle to ride him briefly, preferring his father, then—"Did you know?"

An ear flick. A shift of a hip.

Doubt. Understandable. Scourge's memories of events outside the edge were dim, fragmented, and focused on blood. Battles. Code words. Places they'd been surprised and had to fight their way out. Pursuits.

Bannan tried another tack. "Have you been here before?" He tapped the stone floor with his good foot.

"No." Nostrils flared, showing red inside. "I served those who went to war, not those with cows."

A warhorse without peer, Lila'd called Scourge. As well as a stupid lump of rancid meat when he wouldn't let her climb on his back. The kruar had definite and unshakable taste in riders. "Was my uncle a truthseer, like my father?"

"No. I found him in the midst of battle." Coyly, "I chose the winner as my rider."

Still, magical gifts ran in his family, from truthseeing to truedreaming and, for all he knew, others.

Because of the edge or did they simply belong in it? "My father saw you for what you were." And had far too little time to share his knowledge with his son.

Scourge shifted again. "I remember our hunts." A sudden disquieting purr. "Good hunts."

Implying they'd hunted men, the kruar's favorite quarry, and what did that say about Maggin Larmensu, a quiet man who'd preferred the peace of his country household to Vorkoun. That much, his truthseer son fully understood.

Hunting men, he didn't. "Who did you hunt?"

"I didn't ask." Scourge's ears went back, then up again. "Thieves. Poachers. People," darkly, "who liked cows." Finished with a wicked smack of his lips.

"Idiot beast," Bannan complained mildly. "You're less than no help. We need a name. Anything. You went through the ruins."

"The nyphrit left nothing."

His fingers clenched around his mother's scarf, all he had, his mind racing. "The mimrol it is, then. We'll follow its trail to those responsible. I'll wager it leads straight to the underbelly of Vorkoun and its market."

"A trail old and cold."

Bannan tucked away the scarf. "Cows."

Earned him a huff, that did, but also a flare of those nostrils.

He brought out the key and grinned. "Of course, for all we know, the other side of that door is blocked and we're trapped here anyway."

"There's cheese," Scourge reminded him, but there was fire in his eyes at the thought of a hunt. Or something else, for the kruar lifted his head. "The turn comes."

Jenn. His lips shaped her name; his heart held it. Sunset was about her and her magic, his privilege to witness, the myriad ways they found to keep her secret. Most involved a sweet retreat to their bed.

Where was Jenn this turn? Somewhere of her choosing, he had to believe. Somewhere safe.

Bannan looked around the room. An unlikely place for magic to be revealed—

—yet here, too, it was.

The door through which they'd entered sprouted eyes, round as if surprised to see him there, disappearing almost at once into the wood.

A cluster of loose stones on the floor became a group of tiny hunched figures, busy at some work. Noticing the truthseer's attention, they gathered their tools and, muttering darkly, scampered hastily out of view before he could apologize.

One paused between Scourge's feet, brandishing a gleaming sword. The kruar bent his neck to examine it with one red-rimmed eye, even as his dark hide became scarred plates and mane the broken ends of blades. "Don't," he advised grimly, and the overbold little warrior ran off after the rest, giving out a high-pitched squeak.

The turn passed.

They were alone again.

Ancestors Witness, he'd have to avoid kicking any loose stones while in the edge.

TEACH IT?

He'd thought the bizarre punishments of the sei behind him, that he'd earned, if not respect, then their indifference. Having been proved so blatantly wrong, all Wisp wanted was to rip the youngling into small bloody *UNTEACHABLE* bits and be done.

The beardless youngling, well aware its danger, cowered submissively, though one eye stayed open and was that a gleam of defiance?

Wisp let his jaws gape, licks of dragonsfire boiling inside.

"Stay back, everyone!"

He snapped his jaws shut and swallowed the flame, reminded by the hoarse shout they weren't alone. Worse, the girl had expectations of his behavior near her kin and, much to his dismay, Wisp knew those would include not eating the heart of another dragon.

Or searing it, then eating it.

Or—suffice to say, he sat back on his good haunch to regard the instrument of his downfall, defeated.

Wainn Uhthoff smiled happily back, seemingly unaware a moment before he'd used his bare hand to stop two dragons and his voice to change their lives. "You have pretty eyes," he said, as if intent on destroying whatever pride Wisp might have left.

Master Dusom, showing remarkable sense, took hold of his son's arm and gave a gentle tug. "Let's go check on our home."

"It's because of you, Wisp, we have homes. Thank you. Thank you from the bottom of my heart."

He tilted his head to regard Peggs Uhthoff, who stood closer than most, if not too close, while keeping a wisely leery eye on the youngling. "The small ones hung the laundry," he admitted.

Her mouth, so like the girl's, formed a little "o," but she continued valiantly. "Please thank them for us and—would you ask if we could have it come down now? It appears quite dry and we've only the one ladder."

The youngling made a little noise like a hiccup, communicating with small ones or even little cousins a strangeness unimagined by other dragons. Wisp flung his head around to glare at it with both eyes.

Paused to consider, other dragons being, after all, ignorant fools, then lifted his head. ~YOU will thank the yling and pass along this request.~

The youngling gaped at him in horror.

~NOW!~ Wisp roared, sending a wind to tumble the youngling over and over until it came to rest against a hedge. Rather than collect itself, it climbed the hedge then bounded into the air, bellowing for the yling to show themselves.

Remembering Peggs, who would assuredly convey every detail to her sister on her return, the dragon turned to her. She stood with a fist to her lips, eyes twinkling. With great dignity, Wisp sent a warm little breeze to her ear.

"My first lesson concerns manners."

Then he wrapped himself again in light and vanished to watch the youngling talk to its first yling.

After finding one, the small ones having fled the instant a wild dragon appeared and in no sense willing to answer its pathetic bellowing.

This might not be the utter disaster he'd thought. Not that Wisp cared any better for the youngling—a thorough nuisance and burden. Still.

What could he teach it next?

The turn came . . . not that it would help the youngling.

Small ones knew well how to hide.

FOURTEEN

*T*HE TURN CAME.

It snuck as night's leading edge around the boats and build-ings of Shadesport—unnoticed by those gone inside the shacks by each house to deal with the day's harvest—and pricked unexpected flashes from shadows and cracks.

Jenn couldn't tell what made them. Perhaps eyes.

Nor could she, from the gunnel of Nonny's boat, make out what slithered so quickly to hide between the tumbled rocks of the shore-line as the turn slipped past them, though that might be, she thought, just as well.

As the light of this world faded, the light of the Verge reached the bay, or rather, shone up through it to reveal treasure below.

Mimrol.

The magic that flowed as rivers and filled lakes in the Verge did the same here, in the depths beneath the dark water, its silver like some fantastic etching come to life. In Channen, the stuff had fallen as rain, greedily snapped up by the turtle-like nyim—what wasn't collected by those who knew its value.

Suggesting she did, Nonny stood, calmly handed Jenn her cup, then shrugged off her rags. Beneath she wore nothing but a woven belt lined with compartments.

With one smooth motion, she stepped up on the gunnel and dove.

Splash! The boat rocked but Jenn hardly noticed, breathlessly intent on the slender dark form as Nonny cleaved the water and swam straight down. Within a heartbeat, she'd lost sight of her.

Within the next, the turn arrived. Jenn saw herself reflected in the water, a glass woman filled with pearl, glowing so fiercely bright and strange even she flinched.

The turn passed. Flesh again, she leaned over the side, searching anxiously for Nonny. Ancestors Daring and Drowned, how long could anyone stay underwater? Jenn put her leg over the side, preparing to jump.

"'M'ere."

Jenn twisted around to see Nonny step from the ladder at the back of the boat, which of course she would do, knowing it was there, but it didn't stop her from surging to her feet. "Are you all right? I was—worried."

"Tol'ye baskers were luck." Water dripped from long twists of red hair and beaded skin like night, Nonny in no hurry to dress. Ignoring Jenn, she dug into the compartments on her belt, humming tunelessly as she brought out three small flat black bottles and set them on the deck, checking their stoppers were firmly in place. "Best haul in weeks."

Nonny wasn't, Jenn abruptly realized, much older than Peggs. Worn and scarred by a harder life, and were the risks she now took why or because? "If magic is forbidden in Eld," she asked cautiously, "why are you collecting mimrol?"

The Naalish called it Silver Tears; artificers painted their creations with it, adding specific and amazing magic. Bannan's sister—and Frann—possessed amulets able to speak with the voice of a loved one, and hadn't they concluded, she and Bannan and Kydd, that a coating of the tears must have given magic to Crumlin's mirror, allowing the wizard to spy?

Mimrol was scarce indeed outside Mellynne; though listed as an ingredient in many Rhothan wishings, what was sold in markets was fake.

Or so Jenn had thought.

"Canna fish. M'boat's n'seawort'y," the other replied matter-of-factly. "Won't betray m'neighbors." A grim nod to the water—and the persecuted waalum, Jenn guessed. Nonny passed her a bottle. "Be them as pay, no questions. Curs'n Silver, we calls't. For curs'n t'her folk—" in case Jenn missed the point "—w't boils and t'like."

The bottle felt strangely heavy, as if the mimrol inside objected to her hold, or would draw her with it back to the depths. Refusing to let go, Jenn looked up through her hair and asked bluntly, "Did you see me at the turn—magic's time?"

Nonny snatched the bottle back, seeming not to notice its weight. "I be busy. Why?" With sharp new suspicion.

Meaning she'd missed Jenn's transformation. By coincidence or design? Ancestors Perplexed and Puzzled, she'd more questions than ever—

—so must Nonny. Jenn nodded to herself. "You would have seen me become something else. The same shape," she hastened to add, "but no longer flesh."

As she spoke, Nonny picked up her garment. Now she held it up like a shield. "What be ye?" A hoarse whisper.

Heart's Blood. She was in for it now. "Glass," Jenn said, and let herself be turn-born, tapping a finger's tip to her other palm in proof.

Spitting an oath, the other woman threw up her arm to shield her eyes.

Jenn returned to flesh at once. "It's all right. I'm back." She waited for Nonny to lower her arm, pained to see the fear on her face. "I'm sorry, but I didn't think you'd believe me unless I showed you."

"D'ye h'powers—like t'thers?"

Others?

Jenn's heart, the one she most definitely remembered, thudded in her chest. "You've had other turn-born here?" The expectations felt faded and old, as if they hadn't been renewed in generations, but maybe that was normal. Maybe these turn-born saw no need to reinforce them—or had other means—

She focused on what mattered. They'd have a crossing. "Will

they return at the Balance—the equinox?" If they did, she'd know where it was. Knowing, she'd use that weaker spot herself.

Otherwise, she'd have to force herself through—if she even could, not having ever tried, though the Balance should give her the best chance. There'd be, Jenn sighed to herself, unforeseen consequences.

Realization struck like a blow. They weren't unforeseen—not by the toad queen. She wanted out. Ancestors Trapped and Tortured. The Balance. The monster had sent her here, now, to create a brand-new crossing, one the sei hadn't made or controlled. To force her way back to Werfol, because when she did—if she did or could—

It would crack open the toad queen's prison and set her free.

To go where?

Where house toads built, according to the dragon, a throne for their long-lost and despicable queen.

Marrowdell.

To do what? Nothing good. Of that, Jenn was certain.

"T'magic folk?" Nonny, blissfully unaware, merely shook her head, drips flying from the ends of her hair. "T'never leave." A thick-knuckled finger stabbed out over the bay. "T'stay 'ome."

Then angled down.

The key worked, the door opened smooth and quiet—closing to lock itself once he was through, Scourge going first again in what now felt prudence—and the way clear, if yet another tunnel. One that angled up, which Bannan felt promising, but in dire need of maintenance, which was not. Water, not mimrol, trickled down the walls, glistening by the light of his lantern. Fallen stone made walking treacherous.

Unless you had hooves. Regrettably, the roof was too low for Bannan to lie on Scourge's back. The kruar crouched like a cat, moving with effortless menace. Just as well, for things chittered and scrambled out of sight, only to fall in behind them.

The truthseer hobbled along as quickly as possible. This wasn't a place to linger.

Cold drips fingered his neck. Hearts of his Ancestors, he'd be beholden if it was rain seeping through, and not what else it might be.

The Lilem. Still in flood, no doubt, though spring came earlier this far south. If this worn and crumbling tunnel came too close to its banks, they'd know soon.

Ancestors Perilous and Pent. What if it dared go under the river?

Bannan moved faster.

Turn-born, other than her, lived in the Verge and only visited the edge. Moreover, the turn-born who weren't her were terst, who resembled Jenn's sort of person and came from families who farmed the land but, according to her dragon and Mistress Sand, were nothing alike otherwise.

Making the illuminated village in the depths the home of someone new, someone different.

Who had her boots and probably her coat, socks, wool petticoat, and dress, thus likely, Jenn thought wistfully, a poor opinion of her manners already.

The flowing turn had passed the train bridge when she'd been looking for Nonny, the sun set behind the ridge and fishing village; she'd missed what it might have revealed, if anything at all. Stars began to show above a deep blue horizon both distant and—oddly, to her eyes—flat, being the sea.

Jenn lowered her eyes to the bay, its water dark and unforthcoming, and, she admitted to herself, utterly daunting at the moment. She looked to Nonny. "What can you tell me about them?"

Pressing her fist to her mouth, the other woman gave a single harsh shake of her head. Not, Jenn judged, as if she was afraid to answer. She protected a secret, an important one.

Secrets were, Jenn sighed inwardly, often a problem. She lifted the necklace; Nonny flinched.

So. "This belongs to them, doesn't it." It wasn't a question. She let the monster's trophy fall back on her chest. The shells struck her like lumps of ice, bitterly cold and hard. She shivered in revulsion—then for real, the air cooling with night.

Nonny jerked her head at the cabin door. "Ye be sleep'n'ere."

Giving up her bed, that was, the cot narrow for one and no space on the floor.

Before Jenn could refuse, Nonny left her for the shadows by the cabin, the side away from the bay, reappearing with a paddle. She secured it to the gunnel with some rope so it stood, wide end up, fussing a little as if the alignment was significant, not that Jenn could guess a reason.

Satisfied, Nonny sat on the deck by a barrel, curled herself into a ball, and pulled her garment of rags over her head to forestall any argument, questions, or thanks.

She'd kept her bottles of mimrol but left her empty cup by Jenn's. Taking them both, Jenn climbed the ladder into the dark space below, feeling her way forward. The cabin had a door; she didn't try to figure out how to close it. Nonny chose the deck to keep her safe or keep her here. Both might be true, Jenn thought wearily as she put the cups by the little sink, or neither. Her hands trembled with fatigue.

Her heart felt bruised.

Ancestors Blessed—

Stretched out on the hard little cot, she fell asleep before finishing her prayer, the necklace grasped in one hand.

A ghostly white moth settled on a hook above her. After long and curious study, it took a parchment from its tiny satchel and began to write.

Having stayed still and quiet a long time—likely longer than any child in the history of children ever had or would again—when the mended seam gave way on Goosie's side again, tumbling Werfol out on the sand, he was startled speechless.

Which was just as well, because the majesty-monster immediately asked a tricky question. "Why hasn't your mother entered the edge?"

Ancestors Witness, she hadn't been home when the avalanche and majesty-monster took him and probably wasn't home yet and might not, unless she'd truedreamed, know he was lost and come home at all.

Truths to get him sucked back inside the toy.

Werfol got to his feet and brushed off his pants with exaggerated care.

"WELL?"

Best not push too hard. The majesty-monster seemed to have grown since their last conversation—or had he shrunk? Unless it was the smell from her new ornament, a dark flayed hide fresh enough to wiggle with her every move, drips of blood pocking the sand.

Momma had made sure he and Semyn knew how to hunt and skin a deer.

This hadn't been a deer. The majesty-monster had killed and skinned something bigger, something shaped vaguely like a man.

Werfol avoided looking at it. "How should I know?" he replied in his *I'm only a child* voice. "Was she supposed to?"

"She must enter the edge to be found."

Not an answer. Something better. A clue! What the majesty-monster couldn't find, she couldn't grab. Did it mean she couldn't touch anyone outside the edge? Which included most of the people he cared about—

But not all. Not Cheffy or Alyssa or Wainn or—he had to keep it talking. "Why do you want to find her?" A smart monster wouldn't, Werfol knew, Momma being the most dangerous person in the world—not that now was the time to boast.

"Your mother brought her magic into the edge. She used it to save you." A blink drew strings of mucous over the green eyes. "I saw her pretty tears and yours, little one. Tears and tears."

He didn't like knowing the majesty-monster had watched them. He didn't like it at all.

What he liked didn't matter, Werfol told himself sternly. He was the interrogator, after as many secrets as he could while his target remained this—what was Momma's term? Foolishly voluble. That was it. Talking too much.

"Where was that?" the young truthseer asked mildly, as if he wasn't burning to find out. "Wait—I know. On the slope behind my house. You saw us when we gave the scree hammers. I tripped and bumped my knee. That's when—"

"Not there. Not then." Threat, in that narrowing glare, but, as he'd hoped, the majesty-monster had to correct him. "I saw you together in the home of the turn-born and truthseer. Why has your mother not returned to the edge to find you?"

Werfol met the majesty-monster's glare with his most innocent, charming look—the one that made Dutton wince and his father turn him over to his mother without another word. "Marrowdell? She wouldn't go back *there*," as if the creature was being silly. "It's days and days *and days* travel from where we live." He added a dose of fake sympathy. "I guess you can't tell, being stuck here."

"FOOL CHILD!" The shout came with a blast of her foul breath that knocked him back a step. "Every turn closer to the Balance I am less *STUCK* here!" Another step. "When it comes, I SHALL BE FREE!"

He landed on his backside and glowered up at her.

The majesty-monster tucked her stomach over her front feet, settling her bulk.

Smug.

Smug and mean.

"I know what a turn is," he told her. Not that he'd noticed one happening here, or a sunrise or sunset or even the sun. "What is the Balance?"

"Bold little truthseer, full of questions." The hide dangling from the wart near her eye quivered each time the majesty-monster blinked, as if it remembered being alive. "Shall I tell you everything you want to know? Shall I? Be careful. It will make you more afraid, not less."

His heart hammered in his chest already. If only he were as brave as Wisp.

But it was the sort of question people asked without caring about your answer or wanting one, the sort that roused Werfol's temper and always had. So he rose to his feet, glad to be mad. "Tell me!"

"At the Balance, the light of the Verge and edge match. The boundary between thins and thins until—at the turn—" She made a popping sound. "—it is thinnest of all. It is then, little one, the turn-born will come for you."

Werfol choked on joy, his eyes welling up. Jenn would come. Was coming and soon! It was the very best news—until he remembered the source and his joy turned to dread.

The majesty-monster chuckled, a horrid wet sound. "That's right. It won't be a rescue. You've no hope of that. To get here," a lazy toe tapped the sand and shook the ground, "from where she is, the turn-born must rip open my prison and I assure you, little one, I will be ready to take advantage. There are a couple of matters I will attend to at once. Some—final snacks." With a horrible gaping grin.

"Then, after I consume you both, I will cross into Marrowdell. Your world will end, but that's fine.

"MINE WILL BEGIN."

With a sob, Werfol dove for Goosie and squirmed his way inside. Having no where else to hide.

Bannan staggered and caught himself. Again. Walking like a drunk, he was, between the leg and exhaustion, but he wasn't about to stop. Not here. Not now. Not until he found the way out. He tried to swallow, coughed instead, the ale in the smuggler's roost a distant memory and the inside of his mouth gone dry despite the damp. He'd be licking the walls soon.

"Maybe," he croaked, "you should scout ahead. See how much further."

The presence at his back didn't answer.

Heart's Blood. When had Scourge last spoken?

Stopping, he turned and held up the lantern. Eerie flat reflections marked Scourge's eyes. A burst of hot, kruar-scented breath ruffled the hair on his forehead, the beast coming to a halt close enough to touch, and Bannan tucked his crutch under his arm to reach out, finding the warm velvet patch under the jaw, the flat of a cheek. "You there?" he whispered.

When a low rumble was the only answer, Bannan knew himself alone.

In that instant he felt crushed by the endless dark—of the tunnel, of the mystery, of being lost and far from home and love—

"I'll remember for you, old beast. I promise. I—" His courage failed him and he leaned forward in despair to rest his forehead against that massive neck.

Scourge brought his head around, lipping at Bannan's ear, the coarse whiskers of his chin tickling. The truthseer twitched, then couldn't help but laugh. A ragged laugh, sending disturbing echoes before and behind, so he stopped at once, but it healed something inside. "Ancestors Witness, I'm not alone," he murmured, slapping a big shoulder gratefully. "On the bright side, I'll get the last word—"

A hoof stomped, then the not-horse shoved him forward. *Get going*, that was.

—or not.

Bannan limped on, discarding plan after plan. He'd no allies. Showing his face in Vorkoun would be a risk. Captain Ash had enemies. If any recognized him or suspected—

He should have left when he had the chance. Listened to Tir and taken contract as a private guard—better yet, a mercenary. Whatever work took him as far from here as possible, a chance to start again—

His neck *burned*.

Uncertain why, Bannan stopped.

Then, as if pulled across a great void, he remembered a name. *Jenn Nalynn.*

And everything came back. Marrowdell and magic. Wen and the dragon. The toad queen and the spell that murdered his family—

Bannan clapped his hand over the letters inscribed in his skin by the sei's moth, feeling their heat subside, grateful beyond words for them—for without?

Having left the edge, he'd have forgotten what mattered most.

The not-horse—the *kruar*—lipped his hair. The truthseer let out a shaky sigh. "Heart's Blood, that was close."

They'd left the edge. No need to fear an ambush by nyphrit of any ilk. Or dragons, Bannan thought, who weren't safe to be around without Wisp to take charge. "Rats and rocks," he announced with forced cheer. "Might be a bear," for his mute but listening companion.

Rewarded by a throaty purr.

Wait. Was that a light?

Closing the lantern, Bannan quickly pressed against the tunnel wall to present less of a target. A dark mass slipped by him without so much as a click of hoof to stone, Scourge gone ahead to scout.

His wounded leg developed a tremor, and Bannan fought to remain still. Ancestors Impatient and Pent. How long did the bloody beast need?

As long as it took. He'd joked, but an abandoned tunnel offered an excellent refuge to bears and the like, including men who wanted to hide.

Without warning, Scourge was back, huffing and tossing his head. *Hurry up,* that was—

Bannan came off the wall, leaning on his crutch. Sniffed. No stench of fresh blood or worse, but he did smell something—something very familiar indeed. Stale beer and smoked fish, with the tang of wet, rotting wood.

Vorkoun.

Wisp had, in the end, to address the matter himself. The youngling had tried—desperately and entertainingly—to find an yling willing to listen. It even stuck its nose into a toad's burrow, filling its nostrils with dirt. Alas, with night coming, the villagers could wait no longer for dry clothes and bedding, putting the onus of good manners on its elder.

Not a promising start.

Nor did he know what to do about it—or next.

Lacking inspiration, Wisp ordered the youngling to sit by him on the Ropps' barn to observe from safety, that being how younglings learned in the Verge and their original home. It let the dragon keep an eye on the village—and his unwelcome companion—while resting himself.

To his dismay, the youngling seemed unable to rest or sit still, quivering with pent excitement despite its hunt having failed abysmally. Before the lamps were lit in every home, it burst out, ~I need a name, Great Lord of Dragons.~

Wisp, able to list many things this youngling needed, starting with his fangs deep in its hide, was taken aback. ~Why?~

~You have a name.~ Quickly, perhaps aware he'd no patience for it, ~For the convenience of the meat.~

The father had named him on their first encounter, the sei having sent the dragon to the meadow to await the shape of his next penance. It arrived as a crying Jenn Nalynn, mere days old and smelly. The father had knelt in the grass to cry himself, in heavy hopeless sobs, never knowing he was watched.

The dragon, misliking the sound, had sent a little breeze to investigate the wrapping around the babe, and tickle a flushed cheek, and dry her tears. She'd calmed and closed her eyes, falling fast asleep; her father had calmed and taken a shaken breath. He'd whispered, "A wisp to save us. Ancestors Dear and Departed. Thank you."

Wisp he'd been since.

He casually pressed the youngling's snout to the roof with a clawed rear foot. ~Names are *earned*.~

An eye rolled at him. ~How do I earn one?~

This youngling was incorrigible, bereft of the least sense of self-preservation; he'd do dragonkind a favor if he killed it now. Wisp, happy at the thought, opened his jaws.

A moth arrived, perching on a mossy shingle, out of reach but too close.

He closed his jaws, glowering at the reminder of the sei's *interest* in this particular, deficient, youngling.

It misread his inaction as encouragement. ~Will you teach me, great lord? How to earn my name?~

After a bloodless dig of his claws to show displeasure, Wisp removed his foot. ~Learn this. Do not refer to the people of Marrowdell as 'meat.' They are not prey. They are—~ Beloved of the girl and essential to her happiness, thus preserving the edge and Verge.

The truth might not be the most effective approach, Wisp decided, since she wasn't, at this moment, here, nor would he deign to explain her importance to such as this—

Nor, to be honest, did he dare turn his thoughts to where she might be, if not here, other than much too far away and woefully beyond reach.

~The people are mine,~ he snapped. ~That is all you need to know.~

Encouraged, the youngling lifted its head. Not fully, implying it could learn. ~And are the small ones and little cousins yours as well, great lord?~

Much as it pained him, truthfulness in this was required or the other denizens of Marrowdell would rightly take offense. ~They are their own. And not prey. As you know.~

The youngling flinched. ~The little cousins are kin, Great Lord of Dragons. The small ones are not prey, except—~ slyly, ~—nyphrit.~

~Except those.~

~And our blood enemy, kruar.~

About to agree, Wisp paused, sensing a trap. The youngling wasn't wrong about kruar, who hunted dragons in the Verge, but wasn't right, either. ~Do you know what a truce is, youngling?~

Its eyes went owl-wide, pupils narrowed to alarmed slits.

~I didn't think so. Pay attention, for I'll say this but once.~ Being distasteful to admit at all. ~Dragons do not attack any kruar who serve the turn-born and they do not attack us. That is a truce.~

The youngling looked horrified. ~Ever?~

Wisp let himself grin. ~When kruar leave the service of the turn-born, the truce ends.~

~And the old general?~

Impudence! ~HE IS MINE!~ Wisp roared with force enough to crack stone in the Ropps' chimney, then smacked the youngling with his tail, knocking him from the roof and into the muck of the riverbed.

Lesson over.

Neither saw the moth flutter away.

FIFTEEN

MARROWDELL WAS WHOLE again, Bannan and Scourge home, Wen found, and everyone happy. The river sparkled, clean again and well behaved, and Werfol was home with his family, as he'd always been. Life was as it should be.

Jenn kept her eyes closed, clinging to the dream—and good feelings—as long as possible. But a pot clanked and lid popped and she'd no right or reason to linger in Nonny's bed, having taken it.

And nothing was as it should be or where. Not even close. She opened her eyes with a tiny sigh. "Good morning."

"G'day." Nonny didn't look at her, busy at her little stove. She tipped her rag-covered head at the end of the cot.

Sitting up, Jenn found a pile of similar rags waiting for her. Curious, she pulled the nearest close.

The rest followed, for they weren't, she discovered, rags at all. Or had been, but now were part of something else. Tight tidy stitches bound ends together, leaving others to float free. The netting overtop was more careful work, if less finely done. Jenn gave the mass of fabric a shake to reveal a well-crafted garment, the likes of which she'd never imagined, let alone seen. Ancestors Baffled and Befuddled. She snuck a look at Nonny, already dressed, finding no clue how it was worn. "How do I put it on?"

"Take a dip first. Ye stink, Jenn Nalynn." As this came with a grin and a wink over Nonny's shoulder, Jenn couldn't take offense.

And, sniffing cautiously, agreed. Her underdress and simples, though dry, smelled of seawater and what lived in it. Her hair was little better. Gathering her new clothes under an arm, Jenn went to the ladder.

"'Ere." Nonny chuckled and kicked her heel against a bucket full of water on the floor. "'Less'n ye wanna join t'ide go'n out."

"I'd prefer not," Jenn replied hastily. Come to think of it, the boat moved differently, its rocking more abrupt and vertical. She took up the bucket, finding a sponge floating in the water. A block of yellow soap with an embedded rope was looped over a hook on the side, a useful invention she'd try, next time she and Peggs made soap. Thinking of her sister added a husky note to her, "Thank you."

"Use t'head."

Safer and sensible, as she needed to visit it anyway, though Jenn winced inwardly at the idea of pouring soapy water down the hole. The boat kicked again and Jenn grabbed hold. "How many tides are there a day?"

Without looking around, Nonny held up two fingers.

Ancestors Blessed. If she hadn't been exiled here by a monster, she'd think it a fascinating place. Or perilous.

They were, Jenn reminded herself, often the same.

When she went to push aside the curtain, Nonny spoke, and she stopped again to listen. "High tide's w'matters. S'when boats kin clear t'shoals left unner yon cursed bridge." A dry spit. "Quarter-day f'r t'flow t'go 'tween high'n'low. Stay outta t'water when t'currents are strong," she continued rapid and sharp, abandoning her former reticence.

Because this, Jenn realized with a lump in her throat, was a topic of life or death importance.

"'Round now high be dawn'n'sunset," Nonny continued, "low be noon'n'midnight, near 'nuff. S'when t'waalum come t'shore if t'be no moon. Like t'night."

Heart's Blood. The hunters would be out. "Isn't that dangerous for them?"

"'Tis needful." A spoon waved in dismissal, Nonny's briefing done.

Much as she'd have liked to ask more about the waalum and tides, and so many other things, whatever Nonny stirred on the stove smelled wonderfully appetizing. Jenn suddenly realized what she wanted most was breakfast.

A good wash first. In the head, Jenn found a wooden peg high on a wall and hung her new clothes from it, leaving her soiled ones in a corner. To her delight, the water in the bucket was warm; Nonny must have added hot from the kettle.

More unlooked-for kindness.

Ancestors Blissed and Bountiful, sponging herself clean made her hiss with pleasure, even standing over a hole full of ocean in a closet-sized room so cramped she bumped her elbows and a knee. A closet, moreover, prone to unpredictable movement, so more suds splashed in the boat than out.

But the soap had a pleasant spicy scent that clung to her skin and hair after rinsing. When done, Jenn rubbed it over her dirty dress and simples, leaving those to soak in what remained in the bucket.

Bracing herself, Jenn eyed the mass of rags and net on the peg. How hard could it be?

As she went to lift it off, the boat rocked again. Her head hit the wood of the ceiling with a thud and she gave a small cry.

"What was that?"

Jenn froze. It was a man's voice.

She *knew* that voice.

"A love tap from a basker. Get aboard. I'll not conduct business on the dock." Nonny's voice was and wasn't familiar, having shed her thick dialect.

The male voice again, anxious. "I didn't know they'd come this close."

The tide was going out. Nonny'd told her baskers entered the bay with the high tide—making what she told the man a lie. To keep her presence secret?

Clutching her garment, Jenn eased her head past the curtain. While Aunt Sybb cautioned, often, against listening to the conversation of others, saying you never heard good of yourself and rarely better of others, that was more to discourage her nieces from using the hole in the loft floor to listen in on their elders. Who, to be honest, hadn't said much of interest until recently and now knew better than talk beneath their bedroom.

This conversation was more than interesting—it was vital she hear it, for the new voice belonged to Urcet a Hac Sa Od y Dom, the one person in Eldad who'd known her in Marrowdell.

Someone Jenn planned to ask for help, all of which she'd told Nonny.

Why hide her from him?

Jenn listened, hoping for an answer.

Being inside Goosie, he couldn't see the horrible majesty-monster. Not seeing restored some of Werfol's courage.

If not all of it.

Or most, he thought with regret. Learning her scheme hadn't helped. There was nothing he could do about it and very little, in his estimation, anyone could.

Except Jenn Nalynn. Especially if she had Wisp's help and Uncle Bannan's and Scourge's—and while he was at it, Tir and Dutton and . . . he stopped, feeling more alone than ever.

Still, Momma always said to list one's assets before committing to a plan in order to have a sufficiency. Then she'd whispered how a little something extra tucked away was a good idea, in particular an asset no one else knew about—

Werfol held his next breath. Let it out slowly, carefully. Examined the thought, which was more a memory he'd tried to forget but hadn't, of course, that being the way of memories, especially scary ones.

He'd written a story this past winter. About a prince named William and his brother and their adventures—mostly William's because he was older and braver—and a dragon.

A dragon for William, this being a story and not real, however much Werfol had missed Wisp and Marrowdell, and desperately wanted a dragon of his own.

But stories, he'd learned to his dismay and utter peril, could be dangerous. Especially if you were a truedreamer and, as Momma explained, too young to control that gift.

Most especially, if something *real* answered.

The something had looked like a huge and powerful green dragon, a dragon that tried its best to lure him into the Verge and almost took Momma, being dangerous.

Yet had listened to him, in the end. He remembered that.

Werfol wrapped his arms around his knees, holding them tight to his chest.

Having wanted him for itself, surely the green dragon would object to the majesty-monster keeping him. Unless it forgot him.

That wouldn't happen. Dragons had longer and better memories and clung to their notions past when a boy might forget. He was certain.

Plus, Werfol thought suddenly, he was already *in* the Verge, where the green dragon had tried so hard to coax him, which put them closer together.

Unless it didn't.

A tenuous basis for alliance, Momma would say, but she'd approve. He just knew it.

But how? He didn't sleep, so couldn't truedream; a consequence suspiciously convenient for the majesty-monster.

Unless he could.

He'd try his best. It was that, or wait for the Balance and hope he and Jenn weren't gobbled up.

The young truedreamer put his head down on his knees and

thought only of the dragon he'd written, building it scale by scale in his mind, believing in it.

Whispering without making a sound, over and over.

"I'm here. Come and get me."

Vorkoun.

His nose hadn't lied. They'd passed under the once-fortified eastern wall into the city. Bannan leaned his elbows on a beam to survey their surroundings. The beam was more intact than the rest of the jumble of what had been a wooden exterior wall—presumably with a locked door his key would have opened—now effectively bars.

Scourge thrust his nose out a gap above the truthseer's head, giving a cautiously quiet huff.

The alleyway outside appeared abandoned, the few crates and barrels lining its walls broken or overturned, the gaps between filled with debris. A maze to keep out the curious?

More likely years of neglect. Walls rose to either side, gaps between their stones full of weeds, the lowermost rows discolored by repeated floods. Fog hung low, stinking of fish and fumes. It lightened where lamps shone from windows above but concealed what lay beyond the alley.

Trusting Scourge to keep watch, Bannan turned and eased himself down. Considered the now-filthy bandaging on his shin and decided to leave it be. He'd no stomach for disturbing the wound. Come daylight, they'd find a way through and head into the city, or rather—since he'd a good notion where they were—out into the slums below the high bridge.

Then, find those who'd help without asking questions—

Bannan yawned, his jaw cracking. Knew himself done. He slumped, dropping his head on his knees. A moment's rest. His hand sought the moth's inscription on his neck.

Hoping to dream of sky-blue eyes and the smile that filled his heart.

Jenn's hope of fruitful eavesdropping—boats having no eaves, there was likely a nautical term for it, but she couldn't recall—came to an end when the pot boiled over.

Throwing her new clothes across her shoulders, she rushed to save their breakfast, going on tiptoe down the center bit of floor to not rock the boat. Not seeing potholders, a needful convenience she'd be happy to make for Nonny at a less complicated time, Jenn hooked the big wooden spoon under the handle and lifted it off the circle of flame beneath.

"Noemi, I hope you appreciate the risk I take, trafficking in silver."

The device used lamp oil, or something like, and Bannan had told her of the tiny stoves soldiers used, when they'd the fuel for them, which had been most intriguing—

But Ancestors Witness, how was she to turn it off? The pot of, yes, porridge was thoroughly cooked and about to burn—

"All I ask is a fair price, Urcy. For two bottles this time."

As the voices continued above, Jenn looked desperately for a place to put the pot. Spotting the metal hook above the stove, she eased the handle over it, her rag garment choosing that moment to fall to the floor. She caught it before it landed in bilgewater, dropping the spoon.

Ancestors Confounded and Frantic. Jenn kept still.

They hadn't heard.

"Two!" Greed then disappointment. "I can't afford both."

Was that why Nonny, who'd filled three bottles at the turn, offered him but two today? Or did she keep one for herself?

Jenn put the kettle over the flame, after checking it was full of water, so as not to waste the heat. A cup of cafel would be welcome, the part of her not listening decided.

"There's a way you can."

A suspicious, "How?"

"I take what you've brought in partial payment for both bottles. For the rest? Here's my list. I want everything on it by nightfall."

Jenn blinked. A list? Of what?

"This—you can't be serious." Urcet sounded distressed. "I'd be cheating you, Noemi. Let me come back with proper coin."

"It's the deal I'm offering." A thump on the deck as if Nonny stamped her foot. "Here are the bottles. You want them or not?"

"You know I do." Silence. Jenn imagined the exchange, Urcet tucking his prizes in a pocket—if he had a pocket. In Marrowdell, he'd worn tight pants and an ornate jacket, looking most handsome—"I'll be back with your list—as much as I can get of it—after magic's time."

He mustn't leave! Jenn started for the ladder, covering as much of herself as possible, but modesty wasn't as important as catching Urcet—

"Get here soon, Urcy, and watch it with me. I promise it'll be worth your while."

The words stopped her cold. Jenn sank down on the cot, wrapping herself in her rags, wet hair sliding over a shoulder, and frowned.

What was Nonny up to?

Morning. Or what passed for it. The fog hadn't so much lifted as thinned, letting through a dim wavering light, refusing to reveal the sun's direction. Sounds echoed, pots and pans, voices. The city woke with him, though Heart's Blood, he hadn't truly slept.

A purr. Scourge, a cloth bag hanging from his teeth. Bannan squinted at it. The stains weren't reassuring, though he didn't wonder how the kruar obtained it, sneaking and theft among the beast's favorite pastimes. He took the thing and opened it, half expecting dead rats.

Meat pies. Three of them. Fresh-baked and plump, so hot the juices scalded his tongue on his first ravenous bite, and the truthseer stifled a moan of delight.

He held one up. Scourge backed away, licking gore from his lips with that forked tongue; rats on the menu, after all.

No need to share, then. There was for something else. Setting the second pie on his knee, Bannan touched fingers and thumbs together, holding them to circle his heart.

"Hearts of my Ancestors, I am Beholden for this feast, for it probably saved my life. I'm Beholden for this idiot beast and his care." Scourge rumbled in satisfaction. "Above all," Bannan's voice thickened, "I'm grateful for Marrowdell's magic, for it gave me back my true love. However far we are apart, Keep Us Close."

After which, he ate the rest of the pies more slowly, savoring every bit, then shook the bag over his hand, not to waste a crumb.

Replete, Bannan thought about standing, then changed his mind to focus on a less daunting goal—moving his good foot and leg.

The effort brought a wave of agony. "'Flesh wound,'" he muttered darkly. "Bloody beast."

Scourge stomped a great hoof near his foot. *Get up*, that was, callous and pragmatic. A tenet of kruar life, that to stay down was to die.

Might be the case if he didn't get care for his leg and soon.

The truthseer gritted his teeth. Taking hold of the nearest fallen beam, he pulled himself to his good knee, sweat beading his forehead as he tried, nauseous with pain. Heart's Blood, he'd not lose his precious meal.

It came close.

Cramped from the damp and chill, from a night spent on the ground. Moving, Bannan promised himself, would help. He rose.

Ancestors Tortured and Tormented! A whimper escaped his lips as he got to both feet. Wasn't a scream. Had to count.

His makeshift cane was on the tunnel floor, bending to retrieve it impossible and pointless, his hands blistered and sore from its use. Time to crawl or ride.

Assuming he got out. Clinging to the nearest chunk of wood, Bannan searched for a man-sized gap in the chaos. Scourge passing through didn't prove there was one. Tir swore the not-horse could pass through a keyhole.

The beams were huge and old—if not neyet—and the planks between thick and free of helpful rot. Seeing him test each piece, Scourge leaned a massive shoulder against the pile, growling when it didn't budge.

"We'll find a way out," Bannan told him. They hadn't come this far only to be trapped and die. "Jenn's waiting for us in Marrowdell."

Larmensu . . .

"Shh!"

His companion stopped growling.

The truthseer looked deeper, as if wood might lie and ruin hold the truth.

A glimmer from his left. He shifted closer, lost sight of it, paused to catch his breath, then looked harder.

Larmensu . . .

There. Bannan eased down on his good knee. A fractured bit of door panel, complete with now-rusted crest and keyhole. Useless.

He slammed his hand against the wood. "Heart's Blood—!"

Larmensu . . .

"This what you want?" He brought out the key, half crazed with pain and disappointment. Without hope, he shoved it in the lock and gave it a turn.

Nothing happened.

What did he expect? Bannan dropped his head to his arm, the arm with the hand clenched on the key, the key in a lock to a door that no longer existed, and knew himself close to giving up. "I need help," he whispered.

LARMENSU!!!!

Scourge startled.

Bannan's bones shook and he cried out.

It wasn't a sound, but was. Wasn't a bell, but pealed a summons from the tunnel to fill the alleyway, bouncing from stone and cobble—

No one heard or took note, though a sluggish horse shied and birds flew from their roosts—

It climbed a stairwell and shuddered lamplight, slipped under a door and poured into a room—

To wake the one who waited.

Nonny closed the cabin door, sliding a bar across before climbing down the ladder to face Jenn.

Who held out a cup. "Cafel?"

They stood without moving for a long moment. Jenn, for her part, determined to pretend nothing had happened until Nonny told her what had.

While Nonny, by the strain on her face, was determined not to laugh at Jenn's best efforts to cover herself in the rags and netting. Then did, a deep belly-filling laugh that brought tears to her eyes and made her grab for a shelf, and Jenn's lips twitched, it being that contagious a sound.

Sobering, she pushed the cup forward. "It's the last from your tin."

Nonny wiped her eyes, taking a breath like a hiccup. "Waves'n'fishes.'Aven't a chortle like t'at in ages." She took the cup, nodding in thanks. Before she drank, she produced a small cloth bag and held it up, giving it a little shake to make the contents clink together. "Nah worry 'bout t'cafel or 'ther stock. Kin git whatevers now."

Jenn gave her a steady look. "I heard you talk with Urcet, Noemi."

An eyebrow rose. "And you're wondering why I spoke to you like a Shadesport fisher?"

People had their reasons, Aunt Sybb would say, and others no right to pry. Something she'd said to deflect a question about Riss Nahamm choosing to stay with her deaf and oft cranky great uncle when there was room with her nephews, Devins and Roche, their mother having moved in with Anten and his family.

Riss' reasons, Jenn much later learned, had to do with her love of her great uncle, and of peace and quiet—most of all, with proximity to Sennic Horst, whom she'd loved then in secret.

Who was she to question Nonny's? "That's your business, not mine." Turning, she picked up the two filled bowls. "Breakfast is ready. Where would you like to have it?"

The eyebrow plunged, meeting the other in a scowl. "And now you, who arrived talking like you'd been born here, speak to me in flawless Banat, the language of the deep south? How is that, Jenn Nalynn?"

She'd no idea. She'd spoken Rhothan, that being the only way she knew to speak, and sounded the same to herself.

Jenn shrugged. "A small magic," she temporized, though it hadn't been, according to Mistress Sand, and what seemed a convenience might get her in trouble if Nonny couldn't accept it. "It lets people hear me speak as they do." She grabbed hold of her rags, seemingly determined to slide away and leave her naked, and added plaintively, "I don't do it on purpose."

Nonny, watching this, tried to keep her scowl but couldn't. Her lips twitched, then she laughed. "You're an interesting guest, Jenn. We'd best straighten you out or neither of us will be able to eat." A small smile invited her to share the joke.

Jenn wasn't sure she'd an appetite, not without knowing. "Why did you tell Urcet to come here at the turn?"

A sharp tug and Nonny had the bundle of clothing Jenn had tried to drape over herself. "Arms here," she ordered, instead of answering, holding up the garment to reveal a pair of slits.

"To see me?" Jenn persisted as she slid her arms through. "To see me as turn-born?" He hadn't, in Marrowdell. She wasn't at all sure she wanted him to, here.

"Hold still." There were additional slits, these for longer strips of rag that Nonny tied to keep everything where it belonged.

Once properly fitted, it was light and airy, yet warm, and no longer threatened to trip Jenn's feet or catch on the cabin's many hazards.

And Nonny still hadn't answered her questions.

Giving up, for now and to be polite, Jenn nodded, indicating the garment. "Thank you. Did you make this?" she asked, once seated with her bowl on her lap. "Is it—what fishers wear here?"

"It's called a harmoot." Nonny, an elbow on the ladder, gave a humorless chuckle. "My clan's weaving." She sipped from her cup, looking at Jenn over its rim, then went on, "You won't find another Eld in a harmoot north of the Tac Ys—the singing desert—nor any who speak Banat. Other than Urcy, the show-off. Like him, I was drawn from my place to the Bay of Shades—by its magic." A chuckle. "In his case, an affliction brought on by reading too many books."

Jenn doubted that was possible, books always in short supply and precious, but didn't comment. She took a spoonful of what wasn't exactly porridge, but more of the grain from supper with a sweeter sauce, before asking, "And in yours?"

Nonny's gaze grew unfocused, her voice softer. "I dreamed this place, long before I found it." She raised her cup in the direction of the village. "Most of the others were born here. The *Starscaper*—the schooner—came in with the tide years before I came and never left. She's from Mondir. That's a city in Ansnor."

Jenn replied to the unspoken question. "I know of it. Its proper— its Rhothan name is Vorkoun. It was divided as part of the truce this past fall by Prince Ordo of Rhoth—so your people could build a train there."

It was the other's turn to look surprised. "Why?"

She didn't, Jenn guessed, mean the treaty. "To reach Ansnor's mines."

"We've plenty." Nonny gestured up and behind, toward the bridge. "How do you think we built all this?"

"I—" She hadn't thought of it. "It's what the prince claims."

"Your prince should be careful." Nonny's forehead creased, tightening its scars. "We've a saying here. *Nothing binds tighter than rail.* It wasn't an army, Jenn, that conquered the southlands and brought us under the governance of Eldad's Inner Circle.

"It was a train."

"Sir."

Wasn't Tir, who persisted in his 'sir' nonsense despite leaving the soldierly life long and far behind. Tir was with the Lady Mahavar on the Northward Road and Bannan felt himself very clever to remember that through the wool filling his head.

Larmensu.

The faint mutter in his head wasn't, Bannan concluded, Tir either. And didn't come from Scourge—who'd been able, in the edge, to form words with little breezes—even though the bloody beast was here, not there. Close enough to send his hot, smelly breath into Bannan's face and was that drool? He grimaced. Tried to raise a too-heavy hand to fend off such unwelcome attention.

"Sir! Laddie, please wake. Your warhorse won't let us at the door."

Laddie? Ancestors Blessed—he knew that voice, if not this frail version of it. "Tagey?"

"Ancestors Blessed. Yes, Laddie. It's me with some help."

The now blurred with the past, Bannan struggling to separate the memory of those same words and their deepfelt emotion from when the Marerryms' senior groundskeeper had found him and Lila, much younger and lost, in the woods. "Lila—" he heard himself plead, missing his sister's arms warm around him, how they'd kept him safe through the long night—

"We'll get a message to the baroness, Laddie. First to get you out. Your horse?"

Lila was a baroness?

Of course she was, for this was now, with Scourge, Ancestors Witness, overly protective as always. Bannan flailed an arm. "Back off, idiot beast. They're here to help."

A rumble of protest, but the step taken.

"Thank you, Laddie. Be sure you've unlocked the door."

Door? He was dreaming this, Bannan decided. Nodded regardless.

"Good. It'll take but a minute, then."

The truth, however improbable given the daunting task of prying loose the mass of timbers. Bannan squinted to see past the man, making out the figures of three more old men with, yes, hooks in their hands, and a wagon beyond them in the alley harnessed to an equally ancient ox who lowed in complaint at the scent of kruar.

The men placed their hooks around certain of the timbers, pulling together with what seemed no force at all.

The entire mass swung soundlessly open, Bannan barely managing not to fall out with it.

Gentle hands took hold of him. "There," an anxious voice. "There. Did you bring a load with you? We've the cart, in case."

He shook his head, sorry as the world began to spin. "Just us."

Safe in the arms of an old friend—a smuggler, no doubt, like his parents, but he was unable at the moment to care—Bannan lost consciousness.

Bannan's house toad stood before the door of the building it guarded, puffed itself to its full extent and glowered. ~You may enter, elder brother, and be most welcome. You matter to Marrowdell.~ With approval. ~*That* may not.~ With a frosty glare at the shimmer marking the youngling at Wisp's shoulder.

Whose silence might be prudence but, more likely, shock at being commanded by a little cousin.

Wisp felt a stir of annoyance at it himself, having planned to be indoors during the night's chill damp and finish healing his bones by Bannan's deliciously warm stove. Still, the toad's courage deserved respect, an example important to set. ~While I rest, little cousin, this youngling requires—~ he dearly wanted to say *killing* but changed the word in time to a neutral, ~—supervision. It is not to cross back to the Verge.~

Where it might spread word of his intolerable yet unavoidable new penance to others of its kind. Anything, Wisp decided, but that.

The house toad exuded an unusual air of menace for something balanced on an inflated stomach, baring its teeth. ~It is not to attack the wise one again.~

Yet would, if given the chance. Thwarted of its chosen prey, the youngling couldn't help but thirst for Wainn Uhthoff's blood. A dragon's tenacity with a fool's brain. Leaving it to its own devices in Marrowdell was unthinkable.

He needed, Wisp thought wearily and with disgust, help.

The dragon bent to regard the little cousin, who deflated slightly. The youngling tensed, perhaps hoping he'd attack. ~Have you a suggestion, wise little cousin?~

The youngling gasped.

Wisp ignored it, intent on the unblinking toad.

The little ones knew more of Marrowdell and its magic than any youngling—more than he did, much as it galled him to admit it. And, while he'd neither forgotten nor forgiven how they'd stopped his following the girl, the dragon was forced to concede the toads might have had very good reason to spend their precious hoard of white pebbles not for a throne, but to bar their queen from Marrowdell.

What *that* implied about the little cousins who lived here—

A second house toad leapt from cover to join the first. The girl's. Disturbingly ambitious but utterly devoted.

Or so he'd thought, but this toad had proved itself capable of plots and secrets, having made off with a wizard and swallowed a moth.

A snarl bubbled in his chest, Wisp oblivious to the painful grate of partly healed bone. ~You abandoned Jenn Nalynn!~ He reared up. ~Left her with your foul queen! What does *she* want with the girl?~

Both blinked at him, calm and unmoved.

Her house toad spoke then, with the greatest care. ~Jenn Nalynn left me behind, elder brother, as she did you. I swear on my honor we do not know why our queen summoned our elder sister, and the truthseer and general, to her. We do, however, know something that might be of interest to you.~ It paused, head canted hopefully.

Impudent creature.

When the youngling twitched, Wisp smacked it with his tail, patience worth learning.

Summoning his own, he lowered his head, closed his jaws, and made his tone civil. Closer to civil, at least. ~Worthy and esteemed little cousin, I ask you tell me.~

It gave a little shudder as if overwhelmingly relieved to be asked and quite possibly was, house toads adhering to a bewildering set of rules and strictures beyond the ken or care of dragons. ~The sei forbade our queen from exerting her power within the edge, elder brother. To open her door, she used the force of the flood.~

There'd surely been floods before this one, that being the nature of water and seasons. If she could bend such events to her will, the queen's meddling would have been discovered before now.

Unless this was her first attempt.

A shiver not born of the damp fingered every part of Wisp's spine, leaving dread behind.

This spring's flood was different, being the first with a turn-born in Marrowdell. But how did that matter to the queen?

Wisp felt the youngling stir, as if equally unsettled. Or bored. It was very young and foolish.

And tired.

~Thank you for this information, little cousin. I don't know if it will be of use, but I appreciate your candor.~ Betrayed its queen? A title, Wisp began to fear, with no connection to its use in the girl's storybooks, just as what the toads told him they planned to build wasn't in any sense a throne.

Vexing, to discover the little cousins had hidden depths. If he weren't hurt and exhausted, he'd push for more.

Emboldened by his hesitation, the girl's house toad spoke. ~I have a suggestion, elder brother. For the safe storage of *that*.~ Both toads aimed a glare at the youngling.

Wisp was almost afraid to ask, then thought of the stove's warmth, so close, and how heartily sick he was of tending the youngling. ~What is it?~

~Elder brother, the chests in the barn are impenetrable. If you enclose *that* with them, we would stand guard this night for you. We matter to Marrowdell.~

~You do,~ Wisp agreed, thinking over its proposal. Using the turn-borns' belongings to imprison the youngling had a certain appeal—but did it come with consequence? Would they know, when next they crossed? Be amused?

Or otherwise.

They'd not cross until the kaliia was ripe for harvest. He'd face the outcome then, with Jenn Nalynn to dispute any disagreeable behavior.

Immensely cheered, Wisp took hold of the protesting youngling's neck to drag it to the barn, house toads hopping along behind.

To avoid the temptation of dragonflesh within his jaws, he thought instead about biscuits.

Knowing the places some might be hidden.

SIXTEEN

Dear Bannan. Dearest Heart. I pray to my Ancestors Marrowdell survives the flood and you've found your way back, with Scourge, from wherever the toad queen sent you. As I pray this will reach you. I'd wish it with all my heart and magic, but I sense no other turn-born here, nor have there been for a very long time. Without knowing why, I fear to trouble this part of the edge, though I may have to.

For I've dire news. The toad queen stole Werfol as well, and holds him captive inside his own toy. I heard his cries for help. He knows I did and I must hope that gives him courage. I will save him, Bannan. I swear it. Though I face a difficulty. The toad queen has sent me across the breadth of the world and, though safe within the edge, I've yet to find a crossing to leave it.

Where am I? In the cabin of a fishing boat that doesn't fish, writing on the back of a label from a cafel tin. I'm not alone, Dear Heart. The boat and tin belong to a kind woman who calls herself Nonny.

Nonny's boat is in the Bay of Shades, on the northern shore of Eldad and the southern of the Sweet Sea, too small to see on the map your sister gave me. The water is warm and salt and has tides, which are a marvel. The other people here don't like magic or magical beings, which is not good and I keep away. I've encountered the waalum, who are like little cousins but bigger, and one saved me from drowning. There are people here who hunt and kill them. If I could, I'd stop the practice.

It isn't all grim. If you were here, I know you'd see so much more with your gift, for there are wonders I'm sure I miss. There's a village with lights in the depths of the water. Mimrol flows through the bay at the turn and tide, what Nonny calls 'magic's time.' She dives with great skill to collect it in bottles she sells to someone you'll remember: Urcet, who came to Marrowdell with the dema, now lives here.

I rely on Urcet and Nonny to help me find a crossing. Once I have, I intend to free Werfol and bring him home to you and Marrowdell.

If I can't find one, I'll make my own at the Balance. I must save Werfol. I know Wisp—and you—would tell me that's what the toad queen in the Verge wants above all. For me to make a mistake and set it free to—

Ancestors Pressed and Perplexed, she'd written as small as possible and still run out of room.

Dismayed, Jenn turned over the cafel label, but printing and dark colors—likely cafel stains—filled the other side. Well, she'd said what mattered most. Without a word, she returned Nonny's writing stick, then, carefully, folded the paper into the smallest possible square before tucking it—

She stared down helplessly, her harmoot lacking pockets or handy bodice, feeling tears well up.

"You're done?"

"I couldn't fit it all in," Jenn confessed, gripping the little square in both hands. She'd meant to finish with a message of love and hope, for Bannan would be in need of both. To add "Keep Us Close" as she did with every prayer, and she really truly should have added a message for poor Wisp—she sighed. "It's not the best letter."

"Letters." Nonny's tone offered sympathy for the effort, if distain for the result. "What you need is some fresh air."

Jenn held up the square and firmed her chin. "I need to send it."

"We'll just borrow a seaworthy boat, then, and sail to Plentiful Bay, then give your letter to the stationmaster for the next train through. Don't worry. Every train will have a mailcar. From there—"

"Nonny," Jenn interrupted what was fascinating but, for her, impossible. She gazed into the other woman's dark eyes, pleading in hers. "Please. There must be a way. Bannan—he has to know."

"Why? What's so urgent?"

"A little boy, his nephew, is in great danger. I have to tell him."

Nonny's head wove from side to side, like Wainn's old pony when trying to evade his halter.

"Please?"

Instead of answering, the other went to a cupboard, rummaged a moment, then produced an empty bottle the size of Jenn's thumb. "Put it in here," she ordered mysteriously.

Jenn managed to stuff her precious letter into the bottle, though it took more folding and bent the ends.

Nonny took the bottle from her and rammed a cork in the top, further crushing the scrap of paper. "Now," she declared, "we go outside."

So it was Jenn Nalynn found herself once again climbing a ladder, this time to leave the *Good Igrini*'s deck for her ramshackle dock. The harmoot proved easier to move in than a dress, except the hood Nonny insisted she keep up to hide her hair and face drooped into her eyes, limiting her view to her hand and the rung she gripped with it.

The fresh air did feel good, if still foreign with its sea tang and pine.

Nonny had the bottle with her letter, offering no explanation. Ancestors Witness, she'd gambled more on less, and Jenn decided to hope.

A hope lost when she climbed on the dock to find Nonny about to throw the bottle into the bay.

"Stop!" Jenn grabbed her arm with both hands and held on, though Nonny didn't struggle. "What are you doing?"

"You want to send your letter or not?"

She did, but this? Letters had, according to stories, a long history of being sealed in bottles dropped in the sea, to be carried away by currents and found in unexpected far-off places.

Ancestors Tried and Troubled, there might be years between the dropping and finding, if found at all, and the equinox nigh.

Jenn sensed it closing in on her, its distant song clearer, sweeter; the scent of rose stronger or was it summerberry pie? It summoned thoughts of Marrowdell and family. Of Bannan and Scourge, wherever they were. Of how Mistress Sand and the others would cross back to the Verge, bearing the gifts she'd requested, expecting her to meet them and be glad—

She mustn't, mustn't, mustn't unleash the toad queen on them all, yet tomorrow's turn, by her very nature, she'd have to cross—

"Well?"

"Surely there's a better way," Jenn protested, numb inside, meaning more than the letter in a bottle.

"Might be." With her free arm, the Eld pointed into the bay.

Letting go, Jenn looked.

A dark face bobbed up and down in the water. Two, no, three, with gaping mouths, pointy teeth, and huge eyes fixed on her.

Waalum.

She felt the bottle pressed into her hand. "You do it," Nonny ordered.

Heart's Blood. "I need your help!" Jenn shouted, then tossed the bottle, aiming between the waalum she could see so as not to hit any. As it arched through the air, glinting in the sunlight, she circled her heart with her fingers and thumbs to whisper an urgent prayer. "Hearts of my Ancestors, I'd be Beholden if someone reads my letter who can help, though I'd prefer it be Bannan. However far we are apart—"

A waalum, demonstrating more power than she'd expected, leapt half out of the water to snap the bottle from the air. All three sank below the surface and were gone without a word.

"—Keep Us Close," Jenn finished.

Prayers and invocations to the Ancestors, Aunt Sybb would say, were expressions of hope and faith that needed no answer to do a body good, meaning you weren't to be disappointed and complain if nothing happened, which was usually the case.

But if ever an answer would help, Jenn thought, it was now.

Coming back to himself, the ease of a proper bed under him, Bannan kept still, eyes closed, listening for clues. Caution came second nature; wherever he was, he'd no memory of getting here.

That faint unceasing roar—he was somewhere close to the Lilem, the river racing through Vorkoun to deliver Ansnor's mountains' snowmelt to Avyo, there to join the wide sleepy Mila from Mellynne with her barges, and the small but swift Kotor draining the north. The three would braid themselves into Thornloe's vast inland bay, sweeping silt and debris from their domains into the Sweet Sea, spring's gift to its fish and fishers.

First, though, the Lilem would drink from the Ynot, then all the nameless little rivers tumbling from valleys along the Northward Road. Including Marrowdell's, quite possibly carrying the hives of such concern to Wainn, and Bannan's breath caught, to think of the distance between where he wanted to be and was.

"Laddie?"

Caught himself, but reassured by that familiar voice, he opened his eyes.

The room was sparse but neatly kept, with a wardrobe next to the single door, the narrow bed he inhabited, and a deep-set slit window with a bench beneath. Nam Tagey sat there, a blanket across his shoulders for the air was chill. He'd been a big man and strong. Age had shrunk his frame and withered his hands, but hadn't dimmed the warm smile or bright eyes Bannan remembered so well.

Throughout his and Lila's childhoods, Tagey had been both teacher and friend, ever willing to let them tag along into the fields and woodlands above the vineyards. They'd lost touch with him and the few surviving staff once taken to live with their mother's great uncle in Vorkoun, Lila heir to what remained of the Marerrym wealth and having prospects—much to her chagrin—Bannan with her, unwilling to be parted.

He'd never forgotten who'd taught him to make a smokeless fire and follow tracks, to trim grape vines and sharpen a knife—a wealth of small, vital skills part of who and what he was today. Those memories—and overdue gratitude—added a husk to Bannan's, "Ancestors Blessed, it's good to see you again."

"And a surprise to see you, Laddie. A very good one indeed. How do you feel?"

Like he'd been tumbled down the river himself, there not a part that didn't complain when he sat up, but the truthseer grinned. "I'll live, thanks to you."

By the window's style, they must be in one of the towers abandoned by the rich as floods came earlier and stayed longer, eventually consuming the lowermost floors. The destitute lived here, along with those who preyed on them, and Bannan felt a pang of guilt.

It hadn't been his family alone who'd lost everything.

"And Werfol?" Tagey asked urgently, leaning forward. "Do you bring news?"

Bannan froze. "What's happened?"

"Then you've not heard—I'd hoped—" The older man slumped back, a hand waving restlessly in the air. "Day before last, he was caught in an avalanche behind their home—"

Heart's Blood—"He's dead?" The words choked him, thinking of that small, lifeless body, crushed under snow and debris. "Lila—"

"Your sister says Werfol's alive." Quick and firm. "That he's been taken."

Relief, of a sort. Lila's gift was to truedream. Before falling asleep, she'd taste a thread or scrap of paper touched by a person, to find them and look out their eyes.

Which made writing his sister a letter tacit permission to do just that, though she'd sworn not to peek through his without advance warning. Unless perturbed. Or angry at him.

He and Jenn blew out their candle more often than not.

She'd 'dream of Werfol, find him no matter the risk to herself.

He couldn't stay here.

Bannan went to throw off the blanket and stand, subsiding when Tagey shook his head.

"I wouldn't try standing yet, Laddie. I'll tell you what I know." Tagey got to his feet with an old man's care and cane, making his slow way to the wardrobe. "There's nothing hot, but I've food and drink if you're ready for it."

The truthseer forced himself to ease back against the wall and take stock. Clean cloth wrapped his leg from ankle to knee. The rest of him was clean as well, dressed in a coarse nightshirt sure to belong to his host. A thong of leather held the key around his neck. He laid his hand over it. Heard the soft uncanny *Larmensu* and looked a question at his companion.

Wrinkles softened alongside wise pale eyes. "That belonged to your parents, Ancestors Dear and Departed. I thought you'd want it close."

"I do." Bannan closed his fingers around the key. "You hear it, don't you."

"Aie." A nod. "It's more than a key, Laddie. It's a wishing to call for aid when a Larmensu is in need. We'd hoped—" He faltered.

"That it came from Werfol."

The other nodded, eyes overbright. Gnarled fingers reached into a pocket and pulled out a coin. Tossed it to him.

Bannan caught what wasn't a coin, but a disc inscribed with the fox and sunflower. It warmed in his hand. *Larmensu*. When he looked beyond its worn and tarnished seeming, it glittered with the silver of magic.

Mimrol.

Treasure, unspent. Say rather a vow fulfilled, for he hadn't missed Tagey's "we." Stunned, the truthseer looked up. "Who else has one? Mistress Adrianna?"

Their mother's own nurse, become Lila's, then his, Adrianna Mosan had been so valued by the Marerryms, their father had joked her continued employment had been stipulated in the marriage agreement. After the tragedy, before Marrowdell, only three had known

Bannan inherited his father's gift: their nurse, Lila, and Tir. Mistress Adrianna had urged him to keep his gift secret, Lila showed him how, and Tir—Tir had been Bannan's shieldarm through their time in the marches, and kept him, more than once, from descending into the same darkness his deeper sight found everywhere.

As chance would have it, Adrianna had taken a rare trip to Vorkoun to assist a grandniece about to give birth, escaping the collapse of the Marerrym home. Afterwards, she became part of her nephew's household, seeming melancholy but content—certainly glad to see him, when he'd visit.

Not as often, Bannan thought guiltily, on assuming the role of Captain Ash. He should write—

"Dri?" Tagey shrugged. "Not as I was ever told, but I wouldn't expect to be, Laddie. She's blood, you know, from your mother's side. A cousin's cousin, or the like."

Bannan blinked. "I didn't."

Another shrug dismissed the vagaries of family, especially wealthy ones. "Dri could have lorded it over the rest of us but never did, Ancestors Dutiful and Devoted. No, your father, our good lord, gave charms to me and my sister, Ioana, and to Jarratt and Ignace."

The former his mother's maid and assistant, the latter his father's aide. They'd have been on the second floor—

Tagey took back his charm, tucking it away then giving its pocket an absent little pat. "Ioana will have heard you call. She's taken over as head cook for your sister's household."

Making the previous cook likely among those who'd betrayed the Westietas. The baron, as promised, had cleaned house, but this choice?

Was Lila's. His sister would remember Ioana's kitchen as a haven. Want the same for her boys. Boy. *Werfol* . . . Bannan shook himself. "Jarratt? Ignace?" But he knew, didn't he? The nyphrit left nothing.

Grief filled Tagey's face. He turned to face the wardrobe. "Ancestors Dear and Departed." A pause. "Me and my sister—we were the only ones outside, Laddie, when it—when the mountain fell. We tried to dig—found your parents—but there was nothing more. I'm sorry."

The truthseer rose to his feet, heedless of his leg's stinging protest, and went to Tagey. He rested his hand on a stooped shoulder. "Don't be, my friend. You did what mattered. Lila and I—" He'd had nightmares for years of piling out of the carriage to find their home a pile of rubble, Tagey there, covered in dust and tears, taking care, taking hold. "—we'd have been lost without you."

Turning back to him, the old man wiped his eyes. "As I recall it, your sister took charge of us all."

He kept his hand on Tagey's shoulder. Pressed gently. "You said Ioana will have heard." Ancestors Blessed, what a marvel that was—and potential pain he'd not want to cause. "We must get word to Lila it's me, not her son."

A nod, then a practical, "I sent one of her birds straight off with the news. A rider follows."

Bannan nodded, relieved.

A keen look. "We're yours to command."

The truth—and a reminder the former groundskeeper had been—was still—something else. Someone more.

The two boxes of wishings, the key's box, and the magic lantern sat atop his folded clothes, a statement of their own, Bannan judged. Tagey hadn't lied to him in the past. Admittedly, his younger self hadn't known what to ask.

Now he did. "You work for Lila, don't you? You and your fellow—smugglers."

A second keen look, then Tagey smiled. "We serve the Larmensu. Whatever's asked of us, Laddie, no questions. It shall be our duty and joy, Ancestors Blessed, till we're bones and dust."

Neatly putting the onus for any crimes he and the others were asked to commit, or overlook, squarely on Lila's shoulders. Where they belonged. They'd have a talk, he and his devious sister. A long one.

An avalanche, he thought suddenly, so close to Marrowdell's flood.

Coincidence, surely. Spring was the season for disasters.

Unless they were opportunities. Heart's Blood, when they'd been taken, hadn't Scourge heard a faint cry for help—high-pitched, Rhothan—

An avalanche—Bannan took a sharp breath—to disguise magic, used to take a child—Ancestors Dire and Despondent, let him be wrong.

"Did Lila say who took the boy? Where?" Ancestors Blessed, let the list to start with Glammis Lurgan—with someone of this world and reachable—

Not the toad queen—not the Verge—

But Tagey was already shaking his gray head. "All I can tell you, Laddie, is the instant your sister got home she put a stop to those digging in the snow and called off any search. She's looking for Werfol in her own way, if you get my meaning."

—and there flew any possibility of it. "I do," the truthseer said, hearing his voice as if from a distance.

His sister was indeed truedreaming to find her son, an effort she'd make as long and often as her body allowed—no, she'd ignore any limits, he thought with savage despair, knowing Lila, understanding her. Worse, if the toad queen had Werfol in the Verge, Lila put herself in the gravest danger, madness the least of it—

Heart's Blood, he couldn't lose her, too. Bannan found himself leaning heavily on Tagey's shoulder. Tried to straighten.

"None of that, poor Laddie. Let's get you off that leg before you undo all my stitching." An arm around his waist, deftly using his cane, Tagey steered Bannan back to bed.

Seated, Bannan drew up his knee, finding the leg sore and throbbing but without that sickening pain. His fear—there being no ease for that, he tucked it deep inside. Let it give him strength.

"I was told," he complained lightly, for Tagey looked concerned, "it was a flesh wound."

Opening the wardrobe, the former groundskeeper snorted in disagreement. "Looks like you were mauled by a bear. But it should heal fine now." He pulled down a shelf. There was a promising clatter of cups and plates. "With rest."

"I can't—"

"Your family needs you capable of standing on your feet. And shaved."

Reluctantly settling back, Bannan felt the stubble on his jaw and grimaced. "Good point."

A too-wise look. "Aie, Laddie. This part of the city, there's still some around who might pick you out."

Captain Ash had a beard and conducted his interrogations from the shadows, but it had been, the truthseer admitted to himself, hardly a disguise. His gift, that dreadful use of it, had done more to hide who he was, even from himself.

No one from his past better get in his way, Bannan thought grimly, his face hardening.

He'd help. And Lila—more likely Emon, if she 'dreamed—would know he'd get to them as quickly as he could.

On that thought, he looked up.

"Where's Scourge?"

She'd sent her urgent letter—or lost it forever—to Bannan—unless to some perplexed stranger gleaning from a distant beach, and Jenn Nalynn gazed forlornly at the inscrutable water. What was she to do now?

The Balance would take place at tomorrow's turn. Its approach fluttered across her skin, gave little pulls and tugs to what filled her, tempted and promised. Sang of roses and Jenn now understood why Mistress Sand and the others, despite her pleading, refused to tarry in Marrowdell beyond the fall equinox. How could they, when this moment demanded they move with it, cross in it?

That she cross. Ancestors Blessed, she hadn't expected her turn-born nature to have instincts of its own, like a bird heading home.

Home—longing for Marrowdell, for Bannan, filled Jenn. Along with worry and fear—*Werfol*—

"Well? Are you just going to stand there? What of the child?"

She blinked, startled to find Nonny's nose a finger's breadth from hers, face twisted in a fierce scowl, and being startled, spoke without thinking. "It's up to me to save him. I need a crossing."

Or her dragon, who knew ever-so-much more than she did about the matter.

As well, Jenn sighed inwardly, wish for one of Peggs' pies and all that came with it, from cozy dry kitchens to ripe summerberries and everyone safe including Aunt Sybb.

She focused on Nonny, who hadn't budged and whose breath smelled of the minty leaves they'd chewed after breakfast. "A crossing—" Catching sight of the train bridge, Jenn seized on an explanation. "A crossing is like a bridge, only between worlds. That's how I got here."

Best not, she decided, mention the part where she'd passed through a giant evil toad on the way.

The other pulled back, her frown turned thoughtful. "You want a magic bridge. That's why you asked about—" She angled her head at the water.

At those beneath.

"Yes. Werfol—Bannan's nephew—is being held in the Verge— that's the other world from this—by—" and, Heart's Blood, now she had to say it regardless, so Jenn grimly kept going, though Nonny already looked stunned, "—an evil monster who wants to get out and mustn't," she finished, certain of that.

After a moment's contemplation, or so Jenn interpreted the way Nonny's eyebrows kept rising and falling with each pursing of her lips, the other said, "Let's go for a walk, Jenn Nalynn."

And took her arm firmly, so she would.

The jumble of rocks forming the shoreline of the Bay of Shades were possibly climbable in bare feet—if she avoided the wet slimy ones closest to the water and took her time. To Jenn's relief, Nonny led her to a narrow but well-trodden and quite walkable path between the shore and start of the cliff. They took it away from the boat toward the bridge, Nonny promising a fine view into the open water beyond the bay once they got there.

Though that wasn't the reason for the walk, nor the destination.

Thinking of boats and the bay, Jenn grew puzzled why there was a path to walk. "I thought everyone traveled by boat."

Nonny, who walked faster than anyone in Jenn's experience, including Bannan, paused to look back, her face shadowed by rags. "Not the waalum hunters."

The path no longer pleased her. The sun dimmed and Jenn, shivering in a sudden chill in the previously warm breeze, thought hurriedly of buckets and soap and most particularly of the smelly puddles Nonny called bilge that sloshed beneath the cabin's floor boards and meant the boat leaked.

The sun came out and a bird sang as if surprised by dawn.

Heart's Blood. Here she'd thought she was being careful. Jenn paid fervent attention to her feet, setting one after the other, until sure Nonny hadn't noticed the momentary strangeness—or chose to ignore it.

A moment later, she burst out, "Someone else must use the path as well."

"Of course. We all do," as if she'd said something silly.

Jenn felt her cheeks warm.

Nonny gave her a quick look and let out a breath, continuing in a more serious voice. "We must. A body can't live on fish alone, and there's precious little land for gardening and less soil. We find what we need here." She stopped at a jumble of slimy rock like the rest they'd passed and crouched. "We eat the seaweeds with red leaves. And those with green. The brown," pointing to an array of slick flattened leaves, though some were more like long grass and others like moss. "There's meat here, too." Her quick fingers snatched up a tiny yellow crab Jenn hadn't even seen to show her, then put it back. "Low tide's when we glean from the sea."

Making the bay and those who lived here like Marrowdell after all. Jenn resolved then and there to remember as many details as she could, to tell Bannan and Peggs once home.

Which proved easier since Nonny, having spotted these tasty things to show her, couldn't bear to leave them. Producing a small hooked knife, she quickly clipped bunches from this weed and that. "Fool I am," she muttered, "to forget my basket." Undeterred, she tied each little clump of seaweed to one of the rags floating from her harmoot until she looked a bit like a slime-coated rock herself.

None of it looked or smelled the least appetizing.

Neither, Jenn thought practically, did a freshly dug turnip, and yet the tuber was delicious once cooked and mashed, especially with a dollop of butter. She resolved to be hopeful about Nonny's finds, sure to be lunch and supper.

As were the white birds, who appeared like magic, flying over their heads and making their racket. They were properly called seagulls, Jenn had learned upon asking, and were daring thieves. Their beady eyes fixed on Nonny's drapery of seaweed.

Nonny waved away one that swooped too close. "You're for my pot next!" she shouted.

The seagull laughed, safe in the air. Still, the flock lifted up and away as if they'd understood the threat, and Jenn gave Nonny a surprised look.

"They're nesting now and cautious," the other confided in a whisper, as if the birds hadn't left. "Best eggs you've ever tasted."

Jenn, loyal to Marrowdell's house toads, doubted that. She did, however, find herself feeling slightly sorry for the birds.

"Aha!" With a glad cry Nonny jumped agilely between rocks. She used her knife to pry a closed ragged shell from a rock and showed Jenn. "Oyster!" Shoving the knife tip between the shells, she gave a twist and one came free, leaving her with a single shell like a spoon. She cut under the mass inside, then slurped it up.

Jenn, watching this from the path, felt her stomach lurch. Ancestors Noxious and Nauseous, she was not doing that—

—but was, for Nonny repeated her actions, climbing back up to Jenn with an open shell in her hand and a wide smile on her face. "A treat for you!"

Pie was a treat. Summerberries, honey, and syrup were treats, even curds of cheese. The lump of brown and white goo glistening on the shell like an orphaned tongue was, most assuredly, not.

But Nonny kept smiling and holding out the shell, and even demonstrating the proper tilt to aim the goo into the mouth.

With a silent apology to her Ancestors—and stomach—Jenn took the shell and tipped its contents into her mouth.

It tasted like the brine they used to store butter. Saltier, if that were possible. She dutifully chewed what felt like underdone turnip, conscious of Nonny's anxious attention.

Having succeeded in swallowing, Jenn managed a smile. "Thank you."

"It's only right you have a taste. We rarely eat them ourselves. Those inland pay a fortune for oysters, the fresher the better." Her smile widened. "There's more if you like."

Aunt Sybb believed in tactful courtesy. That said, the Lady Mahavar also strongly emphasized the importance of honesty, saying if a compliment wasn't sincere, it was worse than no compliment at all.

On the other hand, a lack of compliment led one into the muddy waters of misunderstanding and potential insult—surely to be avoided at all costs, especially to someone trying her best to be kind, like Nonny, and help despite magic and mystery.

So Jenn Nalynn thought frantically, desperate to find a response that would avoid her ever having to look at another oyster, while respecting her companion's ways—

"Barnacle bellies. Your face!" With a wicked chuckle, Nonny took the empty shell from Jenn, tossing it into the water to join the others. "If I'd any doubt you weren't from Eld, despite your fine accent, that does it. Jenn Nalynn, my word as your host I won't make you eat more raw oysters." She tipped her head, very much like a seagull in her predatory look. "Fried, maybe?"

"I think not, thank you," Jenn said, finding it much easier to be honest with someone willing to laugh at her. Like Peggs would, or Bannan.

And easier to ask what she'd wondered since leaving the dock. "Why have you brought me here?"

"To get you away from your worries," Nonny observed keenly,

then did a little dance, her bare feet stirring dust on the path. "And to talk where they—" that telling nod at the water "—won't hear."

A needle goes in and out,
pulls a thread,
wraps around,
nipped by teeth.
In and out. Pull and wrap.
Nip! InoutpullwrapNIP!

Werfol roused, slumped against Goosie's soft side, his hand clenched around a thread the size of rope. He bit his thumb, quick and hard, before he squeaked or made any sound. He'd done it!

Ancestors Blessed and Bountiful. Every Ancestor Ever, he decided, that being quicker than reciting their names, though he and Semyn could, if asked, genealogy being significant. Not here.

Granted, a truedream of Gallie Emms sewing—at least, that's what he thought he'd seen her doing and hoped it had been—wasn't much and he was ever-so-slightly disheartened.

An unhelpful attitude, Momma would call it, so the little truthseer drew himself up, determined to be proud. He'd accomplished something important. Really, his glimpse of Gallie was what their Poppa would call a proof of concept, though his usually involved blowing up part of his workshop, and wouldn't some of his black powders be handy now?

And a flint. He'd need both. Use both. Werfol indulged in a wonderfully gory and gratifying vision of the majesty-monster exploding all over her stupid sand.

Of course, to do that, he'd better get out first. With any other prisoners. And be sure Jenn and Bannan didn't *need* the majesty-monster's magic to escape where they'd been sent—

The little truthseer shook his head, determined to stick to his plan. He'd truedreamed Gallie Emms in Marrowdell. Yes, he'd meant to 'dream the green dragon, but holding the thread-rope must have messed things up.

Werfol thought for a long long time.

Then he remembered exactly what Momma had said about true-dreaming on purpose. Well, first that he wasn't ever to do it alone, but this was an emergency and she'd understand. He hoped.

No, what he'd forgotten was more important. He needed some-thing touched by the person—or thing—he wanted to 'dream.

For the dragon, he'd used the pages of his story but he didn't have anything like that. The only object in his pockets was a hand-kerchief embroidered with the Westietas' crest he'd used to wipe his nose several times already and some grain for JoJo. Helpful if he wanted to 'dream through the eyes of the Liar Twins who did laun-dry or his bird, which he didn't.

Alone, in the dark within Goosie, Werfol drew up his knees, resting his chin on top. And sighed. And sighed. Sighs that might have been sobs if he wasn't feeling stubborn and determined, but he was so they weren't.

Something caught his attention. Something white and fluttery but very small, so he didn't flinch as it fluttered closer and closer, though he did hold very still indeed.

A white moth, smaller than the tip of his little finger, wings glowing like faint candles, landed on his nose. Werfol didn't blink and hardly breathed, for Momma had told him and Semyn about the magical moths of Jenn Nalynn, sent to find those lost and bring them together, and it had sounded like a story.

But what if it was real?

He looked at the moth with his gift, as hard and deeply as he could, rewarded by tiny, if mysterious, details.

Four of its thin legs wore golden boots. A fifth leg pulled a wee curl of paper or parchment from a satchel hanging from its body, holding it while the moth aimed the tip of its remaining leg like a pen.

Waiting. That much was clear.

Suddenly he doubted this moth came from Jenn at all. It appeared to be a scribe, perhaps sent to record his fate—which didn't, Werfol admitted truthfully, appear destined to be at all good.

Or was it a messenger? If it was, he feared the majesty-monster would overhear whatever he said out loud and that wasn't good either.

~Elder brother, do you have a question?~

A fussy little voice—safely inside his head, though Werfol was at a loss how to reply in the same way. It had his name wrong, for he wasn't an elder brother but a younger one. Unless the name meant something else again.

A wing twitched as if to hurry him up.

Ancestors Tried and Troubled.

It would take his question somewhere. He had to believe that. Out loud it had to be, then. A question to bring him help, while fooling the majesty-monster.

Fighting back a sneeze, for the moth's wings tickled, Werfol thought hard and fast. In a careful whisper, he said, "Is the green dragon truly my friend?"

He watched, cross-eyed, as the moth dutifully wrote, then rolled up the parchment and tucked it in the satchel. Before it left, he whispered, "Thank you."

It fluttered in front of Werfol's face, dipped to his cheek to taste the tear he hadn't noticed, then was gone.

Leaving him in the dark.

But, Werfol thought hopefully, no longer as alone.

Bare toes in a stream . . . tip of a nose smudged with flour . . . dazzling light and sweet, warm laughter . . . golden hair spread on a pillow . . . that smile . . . his heart fills with joy and he falls into the purpled depths of astonishing eyes . . . Jenn Nalynn . . .

Bannan lingered before waking, unwilling to leave the dream and lose her.

Then all at once he saw Jenn standing with Werfol, holding his hand! They were alone on a vast plain of sand—

NO! He shouted a desperate warning—tried to shout—she glanced over her shoulder at him—the toad queen erupted from the sand, festooned with horrific new trophies! Heads, faces set in a rictus of suffering. Lila and Semyn. Peggs and Wainn. More and more—

Her dreadful mouth opened, getting larger and larger, and Jenn wasn't looking but Werfol was and he screamed—Bannan tried to run to them, feet slipping in sand—

With one gulp, the monster consumed the boy and his love, extinguishing her light—strands of her golden hair draped over its hard jagged lips—

"JENN!"

Bannan found himself awake and sitting up, bathed in cold sweat. His heart hammered until he felt sick. He put his feet on the cold floor.

Elbows on his knees, he dropped his face into his still-shaking hands.

Jenn, he told himself—making it firm and sure because it had to be—was in Marrowdell, keeping everyone safe, as Marrowdell kept her safe. Wisp would. The toads with their secrets and Wen Treff with hers—he'd not underestimate her—would.

As for Werfol—Bannan's breath caught. Ancestors Blessed, he prayed, let the boy be in the hands of ordinary evil.

And what did that say? He shuddered. Heart's Blood, who wouldn't have nightmares after encountering the toad queen.

Scourge.

At the thought of his brave companion—lurking, according to Tagey, in the alleyways a level down, helping himself to rats and foolish strays—Bannan took a deeper, calming breath. He raised his head. Patches on the curtains let through pinpricks of light.

Time to go.

"The fishers in Shadesport named them sirenspites," Nonny told Jenn. She sat, a bare foot propped on a rock, outwardly at ease. An ease betrayed by how her fingers fussed with a strand of drying green seaweed, the way Peggs would chew on her hair, drawing it between her teeth—if Aunt Sybb weren't in residence, and sometimes even then.

As she would with her sister, Jenn nodded encouragement. "What do you know of them?"

"Not much," was the discouraging answer. "'Spites listen to us. They hear what's said through boat hulls or on docks—understand enough we move away to talk about them. Not," with emphasis, "that you'll find others in the bay willing to."

"Why?"

Noticing her busy fingers, Nonny dropped the seaweed. A second later, she began absently to twirl the end of a rag from her harmoot. "If something's said or done that makes them unhappy, they sing. I haven't heard it myself, but I'm told it's a terrifying, ominous melody, able to penetrate a hull and sink into bone until any who hear it go mad and throw themselves into the bay to make it stop."

Jenn raised an eyebrow. "A story. One I believe I've read."

The other woman gave an emphatic nod. "Stories come from truth. Most in the village believe it's how the 'spites curse their victims. What's certain? Those who've heard them drowned soon after."

She shivered. Ancestors Dire and Dreadful, these 'spites seemed more likely to be the toad queen's allies than hers. "Then they're evil," Jenn concluded with shrinking hope.

"Depends on your point of view." Nonny tipped her head. The sunlight reflected from the bay, adding a fierce glint to her eyes. "Those who've killed a waalum know to stay on land afterwards."

Justice, then. Of a kind her dragon would approve and made Jenn uneasy. Rather than speak more of it, she pulled out the necklace. In the daylight, the shells had a waxy sheen but didn't smell of the sea. "You recognized this. Does it belong to a sirenspite?"

"I don't know. I saw it around the neck of the last dawizard to come sniffing for magic, the day she went missing. Soon after, a full cohort of them descended on us like wasps on a sweet bun. They searched every boat—even dredged the bay near shore—but found no sign of her. Bloody nuisances the lot, breaking most of what they touched—and pay for damages?" Nonny dismissed the possibility with a spit. She paused, giving Jenn an inscrutable look.

"There's something else," Jenn prompted.

"If there's anything people here agree on, it's that nothing good ever comes of giving dawizards information they don't already have. These left without learning of the necklace—or that their missing dawizard got it from Urcy who stole it from its maker, a hunter named Symyd. Mark that name, Jenn," grim and low. "A foul one, Symyd, with a nose for magical things. He's no friend of mine or yours."

She'd heed the warning, though it seemed unlikely in Nonny's company she'd meet this Symyd or indeed any from Shadesport. "Is Urcet? A friend?" She'd believed so in Marrowdell. Wanted to, very much, here, but—she touched the necklace. His having done the same wasn't good hearing, let alone that he'd stolen it. "This was sent with me to cause harm."

Had already done so, if she was right about the fate of the dawizard who'd worn it before her.

Jenn shook her head. "The Urcet I knew pursued his goals without regard for others."

Nonny snorted. "True, he's a useless Shade's Ass with pretensions of glory, and don't you tell him I said otherwise." Her lips tightened, the corners aimed down, as she studied Jenn's face. She blew out air, coming to a decision.

"Whatever Urcy was," Nonny went on, "he isn't now. The dawizards were waiting when he returned from the north, waiting to denounce his work and ruin his life. When Urcy found peace here, they followed like the pestilence they are, certain they could make him expose the magic of this place." A satisfied grunt. "Not our Urcy. He strings them along, gives them crap like Symyd's, spins his wild tales. A friend to—" She stopped midsentence, raising a hand for silence.

Just as well, Jenn thought, busy trying to reconcile Nonny's version of Urcet with her own, filled with remorse. He'd left Marrowdell charged with hope and ambition, having found the magic he'd sought. Ancestors Cruel and Capricious, how unfair he'd faced such trouble at home because of it.

Because of her.

She realized Nonny was listening and did the same. There! A distant whistle. Three long bursts, a short one, then a final long. Before she could ask, the source came into view.

A train.

Thoughts of Urcet, dawizards, and magic vanished as Jenn jumped to her feet, shading her eyes with her hand to watch the magnificent machine go over the bridge. The locomotive was bright red and gold, with black scrollwork, noisily chugging out a massive plume of white smoke—steam—as it went. The plume curled down and over the sequence of other parts it pulled—like carriages, Jenn decided, because they'd windows, most curtained.

Some were not, and, seeing faces, she raised her hand to wave, to have Nonny pull her arm sharply down. "They don't want us," she hissed. "We don't want them."

Sighing to herself, Jenn had to be content with memorizing every amazing detail. People had made this in order to travel easily from place to place, to carry mail and goods and themselves. Engineers as well as artists, for even from this distance she could make out ornate designs, and the power of it, to move so much so fast.

The train was altogether wonderful and she found herself full of questions—

—until Nonny let out a low cry of distress and scrambled down the slippery rocks to the water.

Where a corpse bumped ever so gently with every incoming wave. A corpse lacking its skin.

He hadn't meant to sleep. Hadn't thought he could, for that matter, and Bannan—though he made no accusation as he stood to be fitted from the bundle of used clothing arrived when he'd been so conveniently oblivious—eyed the empty cup on the tray. Tagey, capable of dosing a man irrational with exhaustion and worry with more than sweet, dark tea?

He should be glad Tir'd never thought of it.

"Most will serve," Tagey approved. "I wasn't sure, Laddie."

Bannan nodded absently. He couldn't argue with the benefits: due to the rest, his leg bore his weight with less complaint and his mind felt clearer than it had since he'd left Marrowdell. Now, inside? He quivered with impatience.

Pre-battle nerves. Riding to the Westietas' estate took him closer to conflict, not, he believed, with anything a sword could harm—

A coat was tossed on the bed. "The larger it is. Your shoulders have grown."

"Farming." The truthseer half grinned at Tagey's look of surprise. "It's true. I've a farm." Complete with dragon and toad. "And I've my very own love, my Dearest Heart, to share it with me. Her name is Jenn Nalynn." She'd keep Marrowdell safe. Be kept safe by Marrowdell—the words didn't dispel the images from his nightmare.

"A farm." With the same disbelief Tir had used, the fate not remotely envisioned by those who'd known his younger self.

It helped Bannan shake off the nightmare. "And my home," he insisted. "Once Werfol's found and safely in his,"—and Lila safe "—I'll be heading back as fast as I can."

"Good. That's good, Laddie." As if his words had lifted a weight from the other's shoulders. "I'd feared—pay no mind. An old man's folly," Tagey dismissed.

A lie—his first. The truthseer knew not to let it go. "Feared what, old friend?" he asked gently, then showed his mother's scarf. "That I'd stay and rush out in search of those behind this?" He folded the scarf with care, tucking the square into the pocket closest his heart. A gift, he decided, for Jenn Nalynn.

After he showed it to Lila.

Bannan firmed his tone. "Trust we'll come for them—when the time is right." *When there wasn't a monster waiting in ambush in the Verge.* "Those who murdered our families and friends won't escape justice much longer," he vowed, his fingers over his heart. "I swear it on the Bones of our Ancestors."

"I've never doubted it, Laddie. Our Dear Heart. Not once." The truth shone in Tagey's face.

If not that—"What worries you, then?"

The former groundskeeper flushed, then pointed to the lantern and spell boxes, still on the bench. "You and me, we know there's more of that under the ground. Far more. Enough to tempt anyone, but it's locked away safe. Only the key around your neck—in Larmensu hands—can open the door again."

The man, his family and friends, were poor. So many were—"Is that what you're asking?" Bannan asked quietly, careful not to show any emotion. Unsure himself what he'd do if the answer was yes.

"Me? No!" Utter and convincing shock. "Up to me, Laddie, I'd bury it and be done. Ancestors Blessed, let the secret of what's down there die with us. If it's ever found, the peace will shatter. Vorkoun—our city will die in flames." Tears filled Tagey's eyes. His outstretched hand trembled with emotion. "Keep your key. Keep it to call for our aid, and we will answer with our last breath. But I beg you, Laddie, don't think to go back there."

Bannan's fingers reached for the key, brushed the cloth covering it.

Larmensu.

Magic waited beneath the ruins. Mimrol, the gift of the Verge, and he'd be lying to himself if the extraordinary wealth it promised didn't stir his blood.

That the sei showed itself? Warning enough to still any such urge.

Yet the toad queen had sent him there. To what end? To find the mimrol? To give into greed and bring it above ground?

He'd come to believe she relished disaster—how much greater than flood or avalanche would be a war? For that would be the outcome, should Rhoth reveal a source of the silver tears outside of Mellynne, should Ansnor want a share, should, Heart's Blood, the Eld—who so loudly eschewed magic—prove interested after all—

An anxious, "Laddie?"

He'd spent too long in his thoughts. Bannan put his hands on the other's shoulders. "Ancestors Beloved and Blessed, we both know that's not my decision to make, old friend, but Lila's." Who'd tell Emon, the incorruptible pair of them dedicated to the good of Vorkoun's people above all else. "If she asks me," he said solemnly, "I'll say the secret should die with us."

Hoping it could.

Above all, hoping Lila would be awake and aware when he arrived.

Tagey stood back, watching Bannan load his pockets, for he'd refused to keep any magic but the charm he'd carried these long years. He ran a knowing eye over an outfit suited to someone who lived beneath the bridge, poor but well patched and clean. "You'll do," he pronounced.

Bannan took his hands. "Thank you. Hearts of my Ancestors, Keep Us Close."

"Keep Us Close," Tagey echoed warmly. "Give m'love to my sister." The truthseer nodded.

But as he went to close the door behind him, he heard Tagey call out, "Good luck with the crowds."

Bannan stuck his head back in the room. "What crowds?"

Knock, knock. "I know you're in there!"

The deep voice belonged to the smith who, despite his assertion, had no way to tell where a dragon was or wasn't.

Therefore Wisp—having, in the interest of proper healing and with pleasant thoughts of the youngling freezing in the barn, piled every pillow, blanket, and quilt in the building on top of the mattress, and spent the night contentedly curled within that nest—ignored the interruption.

BANG! The door flew off its hinges, skittering across the floor, followed by the largest man in Marrowdell. He stomped around the main floor, knocking furniture aside with the huge iron hammer he carried, eyes searching every corner.

Unable, of course, to see what didn't choose to be seen. Including Bannan's house toad, who, sheltering beneath the stove, now ventured a hopeful, ~Elder brother, is this a new guest?~

Hopefully not. ~We'll see,~ Wisp temporized.

Without warning, the man dropped the hammer and collapsed on the side of Wisp's nest, sitting so close the disgruntled dragon had to shift to make room.

As if that weren't annoying enough, the smith covered his face with his hands and began to sob, loudly, sputtering out words. "I've—lost—her. Lost—her!"

The *her* not, Wisp realized at once, referring to Jenn Nalynn who was lost, but his sister, Wen, who wasn't, having left of her own accord.

To avoid such scenes, the dragon dourly suspected.

Against his better judgement, Wisp sent his little breezes to right the toppled chairs and table, then fan the banked fire in the stove and nudge the still-full kettle into position. To finish, he set the damaged door against the wall, unable to repair the hinges.

~He is a guest!~ the toad concluded with regrettable glee.

A guest who kept wailing and weeping wasn't much of one, in Wisp's estimation, but the girl, being kind-hearted, would insist on compassion.

Though his had limits. When the kettle boiled, though he waited expectantly, the man didn't stir to make himself tea.

So the dragon heaved him off the mattress with his tail.

The smith tumbled on the floor, rolling over to glower at the stack of pillows. "I *KNEW* you were here. Where's my Wen?"

~I'M HERE, LORD!~ With that battle cry, the youngling flew through the door opening, cracking the frame.

Wisp blocked him with a breeze, only to have the girl's house toad leap after in futile pursuit, shouting, ~COME BACK HERE!~

And Bannan's house toad, again with unwise bravado, jump to the attack, bellowing, ~YOU ARE *NOT* A GUEST!~

"WHERE'S WEN?" the smith added his voice, not that he'd have heard the roar, shout, or bellow from the rest.

Wisp sent a breeze to sweep up the highly exercised toads, holding them in midair, a stouter one to pin the enraged youngling against the broken door, then wrapped light around himself, silencing the smith.

"There is," he said, in a testy little wind directed at the man's surely ample ears, "no need to shout."

At the sight of him, the smith had risen to his knees and grabbed his hammer. Common sense prevailing, he set it down, his face working. "Help me, dragon. I must find her."

"Wen will be found when she wants to be."

With comical unison, every head—of dragons, toads, and man—turned to stare at the doorway.

Where Wainn Uhthoff stood, he the one who'd spoken, with his brother Kydd at his side, a hand on his shoulder.

Bannan's house toad, spinning slowly in the air, legs akimbo, caroled out a delighted, ~Guests, elder brother!~

Wisp, giving in to his fate, lowered the toads and sent a breeze to lift the boiling kettle suggestively.

"Tea!" Wainn said, smiling. He held up a basket. "Peggs sent biscuits. It's to thank you, Wisp."

The still-pinned youngling asked, with dawning and understandable horror, ~Is this another lesson, Great Lord of Dragons?~

~Of course.~

If hardly intended, Wisp admitted to himself as Kydd helped the big smith stand, then sit at the table. Nor was he sure for whom.

He settled back on the pillows, disappearing from sight. Two large, warm, and well-buttered biscuits floated from the basket to disappear as well, and Wainn laughed.

~Do I get one?~ the youngling dared ask.

~Biscuits are mine. As are pies and whatever else the villagers make.~ There. More worthwhile lessons.

"Dragon."

Wisp gazed warily at Kydd Uhthoff. Unlike the pitiful smith, he wasn't a man to take lightly. "I'm listening," he sent, just to Kydd's ears.

"This is addressed to you." The beekeeper reached into the basket and produced a piece of notepaper, holding it up between two fingers.

A letter.

At best such missives were perplexing—at worst, full of peril. Wisp wasn't about to touch this one.

Kydd fanned the air suggestively with it.

~Great Lord of Dragons, what is this? Should I take it for you?~

Requiring he release it, demonstrating a pleasing deviousness in the youngling. ~No.~

Besides, thanks to years in the girl's meadow, poring over the books on her lap, Wisp was, regrettably, the only dragon able to read. He sent a breeze to snatch the paper from Kydd's fingers and brought it to the pillow nearest an eye.

Dear Wisp,

There are no words to express the depth of our gratitude for your aid. Without you and your kin, we'd have drowned. Without you, we would have returned to ruined homes. Most importantly, without you, we'd mourn Jenn instead of awaiting her return with all our hearts.

Our river's disappearance was her doing, I'm sure. It doesn't seem very sensible thus I fear she was forced to act in haste. As I fear Jenn's continued absence means she and Bannan cannot return on their own.

Wisp, please give us no further thought. You've set us on our feet and we can manage henceforth on our own. Instead, I implore you to seek Jenn wherever she is. Help her and Bannan find their way back to us. Please.

I urge you be careful of yourself as well. To you I'm but Jenn's sister, the one who bakes, and I hope you enjoy the biscuits, though made in haste and not my best.

But to me, Dearest Wisp, you're family. My brother of another shape. I shall keep you close to my heart forever and vow to teach our child to do the same. However far we are apart,

Keep Us Close,
Peggs Nalynn Uhthoff, of Marrowdell

PS Please save Scourge while you're at it, though he appears well able to care for himself, at least where bacon is involved, and brave. What Jenn's told me of the Verge is as terrifying as well as wondrous.

At the mention of biscuits, Wisp sent a breeze to steal a third, to check its quality. It seemed suitably delicious.

At the mention of family, hearts, and forever, he felt very strange and might have clawed the pillows and bedding to shreds, disliking the feeling, but for Peggs' urging to do what he wanted most of all to do.

Find Jenn Nalynn.

Agreeable.

Wisp had a breeze fold the now-precious piece of paper into a tiny square, then sent it to land on the house toad's snout. ~Keep this safe for me, little cousin.~

The toad's eyes crossed, trying to see what *this* might be. Its mouth opened slightly.

~No. I'll want it back,~ Wisp commanded, before the silly thing swallowed it, and before he dared examine too closely why he chose to keep a piece of paper with words on it.

Other than the need to have the girl read it and explain to him.

Seeing the letter disposed of, Kydd looked at Wisp—or where the pillows were dented—taking a slow sip of tea before asking mildly, "Will there be a response?"

~What is happening, Lord?~ the youngling whispered, well adrift in this play of manners. ~What 'response'? Do we attack?~

Wisp stretched, testing sinew and bone, muscle and skin. Found himself intact—as intact as he'd ever be again—and well rested. Relished a welcome surge of anticipation.

~Elder brother, would you like assistance to write your reply?~

~That will not be necessary.~ The dragon glowered at the too-helpful little cousin, who'd conspired with yling to sew words stolen from Bannan's book—also stolen and torn apart—into letters for the girl, and, while there were books in great number in this house, he'd no desire to attempt a letter of his own ever again.

The things propagated without warning. There'd be no end to them.

"Tell the girl's sister—Peggs," he corrected, judging it more appropriate in response to a letter addressing him by name, "that her biscuits are sufficient. Tell her I will—" On a whim, Wisp paused to assess the youngling.

Powerful, if foolish. Close to full growth, if less than likely to attain it. A formidable ally, if it learned to listen.

Bait, he decided cheerfully, if it didn't. "—tell Peggs *we* will do as she asks," Wisp concluded.

"I'll convey your response," replied Kydd, his face turning an odd color. Perhaps he wondered what his wife, a Nalynn, had asked a dragon to do.

~*We*?~ the youngling echoed uncertainly.

~Time for your next lesson.~

With that, Wisp dropped the breeze pinning the other dragon to the door. He lunged and took a solid grip on its neck before the youngling did more than flinch in reflex at Wainn, then hauled it outside.

To find the girl's house toad already there, in the way.

SEVENTEEN

*I*F, BEFORE LEAVING Loudit, Roche and his friends had given the slightest consideration to *when* they'd arrive in Vorkoun, they might have realized the city—and its university—would be shut down for the celebrations around the spring equinox.

Including their rooms. A terse note on the gate stated students should come back in three days, after observing the festivities with due care and common sense.

Though they'd few coins to spare—and knew nothing of cities—adventure beckoned. The three dashed away in search of the nearest street party, following the sounds of wonderful music.

Music emanating from one of Vorkoun's upper levels, the realm of the rich, where people gazed down at the streets from balconies and patios, admiring lavish parades of horses and tall horned oxen pulling decorated carriages full of musicians—

Frowning at those who didn't belong. A series of bored guards chivvied the three students along, the last saying, with a friendly wink and grin, that the best partying happened under the nearest bridge, and pointed the way.

She was right. Roche, Flam, and Disel joined the celebrating throngs, welcomed and made at ease and given, to their vast delight, great mugs of ale. So welcomed did they find themselves that Disel, on meeting a cheery pair of Rhothan smiths—large and healthy ones—promptly abandoned Roche and Flam, promising to be back on the morn.

Or the day after. Surely by the start of classes, and they weren't—with a stern look—to come looking.

That had been—yesterday? Wonder was they hadn't been fleeced yet, Roche thought blearily, though the new day had, Ancestors Witness, barely started. The hour didn't slow Flam, who raised his mug to keep time, more or less, with the latest offering from the ever-present mass of celebrants, then began to sing at the top of his lungs. Well, but loudly.

Wincing, Roche slipped away, in search of relative quiet. He was drawn to the wide, low stone wall that ran alongside the road under the bridge, by the famed Lilem River. He found himself too exhausted to care how huge it was or how powerful. Stains and dried bits of fish gave the stones a rank smell. Droppings from birds nesting under the bridge added risk.

If the combination kept the crowd at bay, so much the better.

Roche's ninth dreadful dream took him where he lay snoring on top of the stone wall, and he never forgot it.

> *Roche stood on a wall, by a river wider and greater than any he'd imagined, surrounded by laughing strangers who sang songs he didn't understand. Strangers who were innocent and didn't deserve what was coming, for the river rose before him, coming over the wall, sweeping out his feet and theirs. He shouted for help—everyone did—he couldn't hear words over their screams and his as bodies disappeared into the water, then something grabbed his legs and pulled him down faster and harder, and he couldn't breathe, he couldn't breathe, he couldn't—*

Roche woke, gasping, to find his face wet with beer and revelers standing nearby, staring down at him. When he blinked, a young woman tossed a handful of flowers at him but they rolled off into the river—

None of it mattered. His heart protested each and every beat. His

limbs trembled violently. The effort to breathe made his head spin
and the fight to stay conscious took all he had. His third dreadful
dream in the space of two days and he told himself the truth. The
next might be his last.

Worse? Something terrible was coming. Here. Very soon. To
harm these people. He struggled to stay awake, to warn them away—

*—he couldn't hear words over their screams and his as bodies
disappeared into the water, then something grabbed his legs and
pulled him down faster and harder, and he couldn't breathe, he
couldn't breathe, he couldn't—*

The sad, bloated mass looked disturbingly like a woman as it floated
and bumped the rocks, but had been, Nonny assured her, a waalum.

"This happened last night," she concluded, rising from her crouch
by the body. She used a stick to push it further out. Waves brought it
back, as if they weren't to dismiss it so lightly.

Jenn certainly couldn't. "The hunters did this?" She looked back
at the fishing village, as if guilt stained its prettily painted walls.

"They wouldn't waste the meat."

Gorge rose in her throat. Waalum weren't like cows or pigs. One
had spoken to her—saved her—

Ancestors Horrible and Hateful. Jenn fumbled for Nonny's shoulder, desperate for her attention, seeking support. "Heart's Blood. I
know who did this, Nonny. The toad queen—the monster from the
Verge that exiled me here." And had Werfol—

Who lived. She had to believe it.

"Why?"

Because it was evil—

Labels, according to Aunt Sybb, belonged on pickle jars, not
people.

So Jenn said what was harder. "I fear this was the waalum who
brought me to you."

Nonny turned, seizing her elbows in a hard grip. "How did your monster know?"

The air grew damp and chill. The sun dimmed. Silver fish who'd begun to approach the corpse disappeared with a flash and, this once, Jenn didn't immediately counter the edge's response to her feelings.

"She's watching."

Centuries of building overtop flood-ravaged lower levels—with a lack of forethought for the movement of people and goods bordering on criminal—made Vorkoun what she was today: a maze of under-bridge slums and soaring overbridge accessways, of secluded gardens and unavoidable cesspools, the whole a seething busy mass best viewed from the top floors of her many and intricate towers, or from a bridge over the Lilem River.

Add the typical heat of late spring, a river full of spawning fish and their spent corpses, and it was easy to see why most of Vorkoun's wealthy fled to estates in the mountains, while the rest of her popu-lation endured.

Except during festivals. Then the entire city turned out on her cobbled streets to celebrate. Like now, hence Tagey's wish for luck with the crowds. Luck?

They'd need wings, Bannan thought with disgust, to get through these.

Scourge gained a grand total of three forward paces before being stopped again by a line of dancing dogs in costume. The truthseer dug in a toe before his mount could do more than snap at the last. The dog cowered and sped on, one of the few animals in sight. This was a gathering of people.

All happy. Most drunk.

He mustered his patience. Tomorrow's equinox might be a time, according to Jenn, full of meaning and purpose for turn-born, but here?

It marked the beginning of spring. Rhothans and Ansnans alike filled the streets and bridges, crowding balconies and patios until three paces in a row was, Bannan judged, blinding speed.

The Rhothans wore spring flowers and grape vines, and some only that, to celebrate the Green and Growing Day, the time of new blessings, when livestock gave birth and salmon ran the river and buds promised fruits and flowers. Considered the luckiest of birthdays, little wonder pregnant women queued outside the local ossuaries, to obtain the special attention of their Ancestors and possibly hurry things up a bit.

Ansnans, for their part, believed an equinox to be a solemn meeting, when the Celestials—the stars of the night sky who watched and judged the worth of souls—glanced away from the world to plead with the sun for more time observing those beneath. An argument the Celestials won every autumn, marked by a solemn day of fasting and heartfelt promises to be better.

An argument lost each spring, inspiring liberated Ansnans to bolt outdoors, wear bright colors, and dance barefoot in the streets while the sun shone. Preferably while drinking and coupling like mad rabbits, which, though hardly sanctioned by the Celestials, had the predictable result of a host of new arrivals by the winter solstice.

Scourge slipped his bulk between two overloaded carts only to be thwarted by singing children pushing barrows of flowers. He growled helplessly, ducking his great head. Bannan rubbed his neck in empathy. Ancestors Stupefied and Stunned, there couldn't be a slower path to the nearest bridge.

It'd be fastest above, where the roads were wider and straighter—and less prone to dead end in a wall. But higher levels meant horses—and other livestock—sure to react poorly to the proximity of what wasn't a horse at all. Let alone those experts who valued well-bred horseflesh and be shocked by Scourge's odd, if heroic proportions. His balls alone—

Attention they couldn't afford, Bannan nodded to himself. Meaning this step-by-step progress through the oblivious and loud.

And the unexpected. Everywhere he looked, Rhothans mingled

with Ansnans, dancing and singing, their songs different but their joy patently the same. How was it possible?

His city had been cut in two by the treaty, half given back to Ansnor, those Rhothans displaced and homeless. Angry. Lost.

Ancestors Blind and Blissed, had no one told these people?

Oh, but hadn't Lila told *him*? Bannan thought suddenly. Sharply, when he'd turned his face like a petulant child and scowled. She'd said peace would be good for their city. Insisted nothing else could heal the wounds of war. Words he'd been too bitter to hear.

An Ansnan and Rhothan came down the stairs, arm in arm, singing badly at the top of their lungs. They waved at him.

The truthseer let out a long shaky breath as he raised his hand in answer, feeling a knot deep inside loosen. His lips twitched. Lila, right as usual. Seeing Vorkoun—and Mondir—come together in celebration? Ancestors Witness, three days wouldn't heal all the hurts, but it was a promising start—

Scourge abruptly shied, snapping Bannan out of his reverie. The idiot beast refused to step on so much as a flower petal.

Odd. He didn't see any bouquets in their path, only a steaming pile of dung, probably deposited by cart horses delivering ale last night. Into which the kruar deliberately planted a great hoof.

Bannan covered his nose with his sleeve, shaking his head in disgust.

Their surroundings grew more and more familiar. They were almost to where this road slipped to run beside the river and under the first bridge. He and Tir and Lila had spent a memorable night drinking on its floodwall—well, more than one.

Once past, a tight turn and a curling ramp would get them on the overpass, the quickest route from the city—

The kruar plunged again, front feet landing in a dung pile slick enough to cause him to slip. Recovering, he gave a happy little trot, clumps of manure flying up.

"Bloody Beast!" Bannan shouted, flicking a stinking clump from his pants. "What are you doing?"

"Blending."

At the droll little breeze in his ear—at the overwhelming and impossible relief of it—the truthseer froze, legs clenched around that massive body. Leaning forward, he mouthed, "Scourge?" The larger question loomed like the bridge and the wide dark river flowing beside them. "Heart's Blood, we're back in the edge."

Within Vorkoun. On the same neglected, so usefully out-of-the-way street he and Lila had always sought for their nefarious adventures. Pretend duels with third-hand swords—bags of candy stolen for practice, with double the coin left behind—that stranger's head in a sack Lila'd never explained—

Ancestors Witness. They hadn't found this place by chance or cleverness. They'd been drawn here—by their gifts, magic calling to magic.

As memories tumbled through his thoughts, the truthseer looked beyond the scattered partiers and cobblestones, the familiar shabby inns with dust-streaked windows and crude patios lining the road opposite the river. The Dragon's Nose pub—

Things scampered up the walls and out of sight too quickly to make out. Above, hanging under the bridge, were slings of silk—ylingwork, though he was disappointed not to spot one of the shy beings. A lump under a patio bench blinked wise limpid eyes at him. Before Bannan could call out, the house toad slipped out of sight.

He kept looking. The long, low floodwall on which they'd fought with knives and drunk too much ale wasn't only stone. It held trapped little faces that scowled, being noticed—

Scourge sprang forward as if nipped by an invisible dragon. Which weren't in his city, Bannan told himself, hanging on—

—unless they were—

On hearing they might be watched, Nonny pulled her rag hood over her head and gestured furiously for Jenn to do the same, hers having slipped down while examining seaweeds and shells. "There's but one safe place," the Eld whispered hoarsely, after looking over both shoulders and glaring out at the bay. Seizing Jenn's wrist, she towed her along the path to the bridge.

A destination that seemed reasonable until it dawned on Jenn they were rushing toward what was also the boundary of the edge.

Ancestors Frazzled and Fraught.

She grew more and more concerned. Finally she dug in her heels and refused to take another step, even when Nonny took her wrist in both hands and pulled.

"The edge," Jenn whispered urgently. She waved her free hand wildly at the bridge, the bridge over which the marvelous train had passed moments ago, and under which fishing boats would return at day's end, the tide having swapped directions, knowing now was no time for secrets. "If I leave it, I'll cease to exist!"

Dark eyes squinted, as if trying to assess her sincerity—or sanity—but Nonny merely said, "We're not going that far."

"How can you be sure?" Jenn fought to keep her voice quiet and calm, but she'd her life—and Werfol's—to protect. What would Bannan say? "The waalum. Do they pass under the bridge?"

Not that she knew if leaving the edge for the less magical world of people mattered as much to little cousins, for they didn't disappear, though kruar forgot themselves and Wisp hadn't cared for it. A brave yling had accompanied Bannan beyond in Channen but returned looking most bedraggled, so there was that.

"I don't know," Nonny admitted at last. She opened her hands, releasing Jenn's wrist. "Hunters stick to this side of the bridge. I'd thought it was because of the cliffs beyond." The flash of a humorless smile. "Not to mention the longer you pull the carcass through the water, the more come to feast on it."

Like the silver fish who'd tried to feast on her, Jenn thought with an inner shudder, and waited for the poor waalum's corpse.

"I can't prove it's safe for you," Nonny said, her tone matter-of-fact. "Not unless we come and watch during the turn—but that's when Urcy expects us at the *'Grini.*" A pause. "Or we try your necklace."

Which wasn't hers, but stolen by the toad queen from a vanished dawizard, a woman more likely than not a skin or skull hung from a wart. A fate Jenn would wish on no one. Queasily, she touched the shells. "Try it how?"

"If it's sirenspite magic, maybe it will disappear or change beyond the edge. Let me take it—"

Jenn instantly stepped back, wincing as her heel found a stone, but determined in this. "The toad queen put it around my neck, Nonny. I won't risk your life with it."

A nod. "Then it's up to you." The Eld pointed to the nearest foot of the bridge. "My secret place is there."

They were near enough Jenn expected to see imperfections in the stonework, but there were none. It rose and widened into arches to either side, an awe-inspiring monolith whose sole purpose was to keep trains and those they carried safely above the contamination of magic—

Though the edge must extend to the sky, for Wisp and other dragons flew there, Jenn realized, and maybe even the stars—a question to save for Mistress Sand, to be sure, but it made the grand efforts of the Eld builders seem overwrought and foolish, if all they accomplished was a lie, and she felt sad.

"You can't see it," Nonny continued, lowering her arm. "I found it, my first night here." Her voice took on a reverent tone. "It was as if it called my name. I touched the stone and it let me pass into a room full of blue light. And locked trunks," she added, as if reluctant to mention anything so prosaic.

The turn-born! "Ancestors Blessed!" Jenn spun on her toes, snatched up the startled Nonny in a tight hug, then resumed walking as quickly as she could toward the promised sanctuary where, she was sure, they'd be hidden from the toad queen's baleful eyes—

—and, even better?

She'd find her crossing.

Scourge plunged to halt before a small crowd of people staring at a section of the floodwall. Or rather, Bannan saw over their heads, at a man writhing in agony atop it and likely to fall any moment either into the river or onto the road. Heart's Blood, why was no one helping?

The truthseer drove in his heels, sending Scourge forward. The kruar shoved the nearest onlookers out of their way with his mighty head, his growl dispersing the rest.

Bannan slid from his mount.

The man's face rolled toward him. Bloody foam erupted between clenched teeth, and his eyes weren't just shut, they were squeezed tight in a rictus of pain—or was it horror—

A face he knew, however distorted. "Roche! Hold on!" he shouted as he ran to him.

Suddenly Roche gasped as if drowning, back arched as if there were no air—

"I have you!" Bannan wrapped his arms around the stricken man.

Who, though unconscious, fought to free himself—but before being a farmer, the truthseer had been a soldier. Bannan held firm until Roche went limp, then gentled his grip at once, cradling the younger man through more of those deep and surely hurtful gasps, a wary eye on the dark water lapping against the floodwall near his boot. "Easy. Easy."

A breeze nipped his ear. "What's wrong with him?"

"I don't know." Whatever it was, it wasn't drink or sleep.

Another gasp and Roche's eyelids shot open. Revealing what weren't his eyes, brilliant green and clear, but dull black pits. The truthseer flinched, but held on, looking beneath.

To his gift, the black parted like wind-driven cloud, revealing the eyes he remembered beneath. "Come back, Roche," he urged, greatly relieved.

A blink. An exhale surrendered the final tension from the form he held, and Roche stared up at him, conscious again.

And instantly alarmed. His hands plucked frantically at Bannan's arms. "Run! Everyone has to run! It's com—" Roche froze mid-plea, his eyes wide with dread, and his mouth worked, forming words without sound. "It's here." He shouted a name. "EDIS!"

The wall beneath them *GROANED.*

People screamed.

"EDIS!"

An Ansnan name, one Bannan didn't know, though he heard the passion in the cry, and if the young man had found someone here to care about this much, he truly hoped she was safer than they were—

With a second sickening *GROAN,* the stone wall began to crumble beneath them. They could barely scramble to stay on it, let alone get off.

"EDIS!!"

The crumbling stopped. The world seemed to hold its breath—other than Scourge's grunts of effort as he tried to reach them—and time itself to pause.

Beneath their feet, Bannan saw how the small inset stones, the ones with frowning faces, had produced hands to grip the larger rocks around them—while through the wider gaps flowed, or swam, or oozed—what might have been a snake.

Save it had a face, a woman's face, stern and crowned in a helmet of stone, and wherever her strange body passed, a glow of blue remained and the rocks settled.

"Edis," Roche breathed, leaning on him. "You came."

The creature *smiled.*

Not a lady met dancing on the street. Nothing so benign. This was a being of magic and peril, and Bannan resolved to have a talk with Roche, after this. A long and serious one. Given they survived—

BANG! A shockwave hit, taking the wall and most of the road with it. The mighty Lilem rushed onto the street it had been denied all these years, sweeping away flower petals and lives and little stones with faces.

Edis vanished.

Desperately Bannan kept hold of Roche as they were sucked down into the depths together, knowing this wasn't death but might be worse.

The toad queen had them.

She'd come. She'd come.

Edis had promised to answer him the next time he stepped into the edge, where he must have stumbled unknowingly, and, while he'd believed her, he'd called more in despair than hope.

And because Jenn Nalynn had wished him to be truthful, and he was, even to himself, now Roche Morrill told himself he'd called his friend to her death, for nothing could have survived that.

He hadn't. Unless this was another dreadful dream, for the riverside street and partiers, the bridges and horses and cows, the entire city of Vorkoun had been replaced by a flat featureless plain of sand, and he stood here alone.

Then he looked up at the impossible sky and cowered, covering his eyes. "The Verge," he said, or wanted to say, but the words dribbled from his nostrils and bounded away like rabbits, for the Verge was her place, her true home, and deadly to him. "Edis—help—"

"Roche, take my hand." Words slapped his skin and cut his ears. Crying out, he tried to flee but had no legs—

"EDIS!" he shouted then, with his heart and soul and need, her name falling from his lips or did it soar—

But how could she find him when he'd lost himself—and—there'd been someone else, someone holding him—

Ancestors Destitute and Despairing—

He'd lost Bannan, too!

Green dragon. Werfol concentrated, mouthing the words, his mind's eye seeing it perfectly, from snout to—

Goosie split open, dumping him on the sand. For a glorious second he thought he'd been answered and saved, but no.

Not yet, anyway. Werfol picked himself up, annoyed at the interruption, and brushed sand from his pants. The majesty-monster squatted like an enormous heap of rot, eyes gleaming as she watched. She looked unpleasantly cheerful.

And maybe it was the moth, or maybe thoughts of the dragon, but the little truthseer couldn't resist giving the shortened bow Momma called cheeky and wouldn't permit around company. "Good morning. How are you today?"

The majesty-monster's wide lips moved sideways as if trying to decide whether or not to spit. They made a nasty crunching sound. "I have a present for you."

The truth. Werfol, who'd recently had a birthday and gifts, couldn't help perking up at this, however much he distrusted the source. "What is it?"

She gave a shimmy and shake, burrowing herself in the sand. Sand that rose and flowed under his feet, knocking him down. Werfol fought to keep from being dragged down with her, using his arms as if swimming, and if this was her present he might die from it.

The ground stopped moving. Werfol, spitting sand, found himself alone on the plain under its wildly colored sky. At least the hateful majesty-monster was gone—

A lie. She was somewhere beneath him, the sneak. Hiding. Why? "EDIS!"

Leaping to his feet, Werfol looked around frantically. Nothing. Nothing. There! Two figures stood on the plain, facing away from him. One dropped to his knees, the other touching his shoulder.

Her present?

A mean trick. He knew better than move or call out. If he did, the majesty-monster would send them away. Or they weren't really there and she waited to laugh at him when he found out. Or—

She'd no patience. A wave of sand swept him forward, and he tumbled helplessly until landing at the startled strangers' feet.

"Werfol!"

More than anything, ever, Werfol wanted to throw himself into his Uncle Bannan's open arms. Instead, he stayed out of reach, fingers flying in the signs for *danger* and *enemy*. Pointed down, then held a finger over his lips.

Saw instant comprehension fill those apple butter eyes, with their gleam of gold so like his own. *Well done*, his uncle signed, the motions crisp and sure, filling Werfol with a flood of relieved joy.

But they weren't safe yet, in any sense. He signed *under surveillance*.

With a nod, Uncle Bannan reached down to the dark-haired man at his feet—the one who'd shouted the strange name, Werfol realized. Now he sat, rocking himself in a tight ball of misery, like Werfol had when he was scared.

Worried, he signed, *hurt*, with the question sign.

His uncle gave a meaningful shrug. Said, low and calm, "Roche, take my hand."

The man named Roche flinched as if the words were weapons and wriggled away. He put his hands flat on the sand and, before either of his companions could stop him, raised his head and shouted again. "EDIS!!"

A scream, more than shout, echoing like thunder across the plain. Werfol bolted for his uncle, who knelt to hold him tight and press his lips to his hair, and the feeling of being safe and saved was better than anything—

—even if temporary. The stupid man's scream had to rouse the majesty-monster—

Nothing happened. After a long moment of nothing happening, Werfol raised his head. His uncle looked as puzzled as he felt. Well, if the majesty-monster hadn't cared about a huge noisy scream, he'd dare to talk. In a whisper. And it had to be important talk, not *I love you* or *take me home*, because he just knew they didn't have much time. A proper briefing, like he'd give Momma.

And had imagined doing, Werfol thought wryly, over and over in the dark inside Goosie, meaning he knew exactly what to tell his uncle now.

"She wants the magic from the edge, including from anyone with gifts, like us." Werfol glanced at Roche, back in his ball, and decided there was no need to mention empty skulls and flayed skin. "She plans to grow strong enough to challenge the sei, whatever they are, and rule the Verge, but first she has to get out of here. She sent you, Uncle, to bring her something and didn't say what." Unless it was a who and here already, a grim possibility he saw in his uncle's quick look at Roche. "She sent Jenn away—"

His uncle started violently, his grip shifting to Werfol's shoulders, eyes searching his face. "Jenn? She—she was here?"

Werfol nodded. "Right after you, the first time. Uncle, Jenn heard me. I was inside Goosie—" he added, understanding his uncle's now-horrified expression, "—so you couldn't. It's all right."

Though Uncle Bannan saw that was the truth, Werfol found himself pressed against his uncle's chest again anyway, only this time it was his uncle who shook uncontrollably and needed comfort.

Feeling oddly older, Werfol patted him gently, then pushed away. "Jenn promised to come back for me, but that's what the majesty-monster wants. For Jenn to come at the Balance and free her—what day is it?" he asked urgently. "When's the equinox?"

Uncle Bannan stood, keeping a gentle grip on Werfol's shoulder as if afraid to let him go, his face pale. "Tomorrow. Do you know where Jenn is now?"

"FAR FAR AWAY!" roared the majesty-monster, surging up from the sand.

Only to stop with her mouth sealed and her feet and body trapped as the sand around her turned to stone.

As her eyes bulged in helpless fury, a woman with a body like a pale white snake emerged from the still-soft sand, rising tall and straight. "You may not have him," she told the majesty-monster, her voice like the strike of a hammer to rock. She tucked Roche under one arm and began to sink.

"Edis, wait!" Uncle Bannan called out. He took hold of Werfol. "Take the child with you."

She hesitated, looking at Werfol, who looked back. Her head was like a statue of ancient Ansnan warrior he'd seen in a museum, with a helmet of stone instead of hair, and dots like pearls lined the outside of her arms and he couldn't tell if she'd legs, beneath the sand.

Her expression was stern and resolute, her eyes large and purple, a bit like Wisp's but not, eyes edged in lines like those from squinting too much at the sun—or from laughter, lines like Dutton's, his guard and friend.

Suddenly he wasn't afraid. "And my uncle," he urged quickly. "Please. We all need saving. The edge behind my home. Take us there." Home, to his Momma and Poppa and Semyn and Dutton and JoJo—Werfol trembled, wanting that so much it hurt, and felt his uncle's hands tighten.

"I cannot contest the toad queen much longer," Edis answered, growing paler even as she said the words. She held out her free arm. "And take only what I can carry. Choose, child."

And it was the truth and terrible and was the stone already starting to crack? Biting his lip, Werfol squirmed deftly from his uncle's grip and backed away. "My uncle."

"No!" Uncle Bannan started after him, eyes wild.

More stone cracked. *GROANED!*

"I'll be safe." He hoped. "You won't." Werfol looked past him at Edis. "Take him."

She snatched Uncle Bannan mid-stride, though he cursed and fought. Dived headfirst into the sand with a man under each arm, leaving sparkles in the air.

And Werfol to his monster.

The forbidding stonework soared up and up until Jenn's neck ached trying to see to the top. "How do we get in?"

Tossing back her hood, Nonny pressed her right hand to a stone outwardly the same as any other. "It's Nonny." She glanced at Jenn and smiled. "I've brought a friend. We seek safety."

A thin black line outlined a section the size and shape of a door. The stones within it faded away and Nonny boldly stepped through an opening that hadn't existed a moment before, pulling Jenn with her.

Into darkness, laced with the still-firm expectations of the turn-born. *Stay strong. Stay hidden. Be a refuge.* And, *light.*

Suddenly it wasn't dark but softly lit, the ceiling giving forth a lovely blue glow to illuminate a simple room. It was this light Jenn imagined whenever needing comfort; the same filled Wisp's sanctuary in the Verge and was the doing of the sei, not turn-born.

She hadn't thought they worked together.

Alas, if there'd been a crossing, there was none now. To be sure, she walked around the entire room, fourteen steps to a side, ending in the middle where Nonny stood watching beside the stacked trunks, five in number. "You were right," Jenn told her. "This is a safe place." Safe from the toad queen—from any harm—and, despite her disappointment, her tension and fear faded. "But I don't sense any crossing."

"What about in here?" Nonny toed a trunk.

Ancestors Blessed. Jenn supposed it was possible. After all, she and Bannan, with two kruar, had entered a raindrop to cross into Channen—and hadn't she and Nonny just walked through a stone wall?

Three trunks on the bottom, two on top. She ran her finger over the nearest, a trunk that might have sat in Bannan's barn every winter. "These belong to my friends." Five, not seven. Her finger left a mark in the thick dust coating the top, and she felt a flicker of doubt. "Or those who came before."

"They're locked," Nonny warned, giving a little shrug when Jenn looked askance at her, a bit of drying seaweed coming loose. She stooped to pick it up, popping it in her mouth. "Don't worry," while chewing gustily. "I know better than touch them."

They had what looked like massive closed locks, but appearances could deceive, Jenn thought, trying a lid.

Instead of the sharp ~*OURS!*~ that denied her attempt in the barn, this came open easily. They looked inside, standing shoulder to shoulder.

Nonny gave a disappointed huff. "Empty." She raised an eyebrow.

"And no crossing," Jenn admitted.

She opened the next on the top row to no better success, then, with Nonny's help, eased those to the floor to try the rest, the pair having agreed to check them all.

The second-to-last trunk rewarded their effort. "My clothes!" Clean, dry, and neatly folded, and Jenn couldn't have been more shocked if she'd found a waalum inside. "How did they get here?" She bent and brought them out, holding them tight as if they might disappear.

Nonny picked up what had been under them. "Yours, too, I take it?" She held out Jenn's boots.

"Yes, but—I took all of this off while swimming in the bay. Let them sink."

"They didn't stay—" The Eld tilted her head, a finger up for silence.

Listening, Jenn heard it, too. A faint, irregular whoosh.

It was Nonny who recognized it. "The tide!" She shoved at the final trunk.

Rather than slide across the floor, it tipped on its end, proving to be hinged to the stone. Under it was a hole in the floor. A neat, square opening leading straight down, and, at the depth Jenn surmised would match the water outside, passing under the bridge, there was water here as well, churning and whooshing. If it sank with low tide, it must rise almost to the floor at high.

By the light from the room, for there was none below, she made out rungs cut into the stone on the wall of the shaft. A ladder, in other words, one disappearing into water. "Someone came up this way—with my clothes."

She and Nonny stared at one another, both reluctant to say it. Finally Jenn did. "The sirenspites." She leaned over the opening, trying to see more than black, angry-seeming water. "The turn-born didn't come for the bay. They came for what's under it." She felt their expectations holding the stone firm. Had they been here when the bridge was built?

Had they influenced its builders to ensure the train passed beyond the edge, far from their concerns? She hadn't thought they'd care. Then again, Eldad was a dangerous place for those with magic, having waalum hunters and dawizards and who knew what else.

She summoned her courage. "I have to go down there. It has to be where the crossing is—"

"Oh, no, you're not. Not," Nonny temporized, seeing Jenn's face, "without a strong rope and me at this end of it." She tipped the trunk over, closing the hole, and gestured to the various gleanings tied to her harmoot. "Besides, it's time for lunch. We'll make a plan."

The 'we' warming her heart, Jenn smiled. "No oysters."

Nonny smiled back. "No oysters."

Between one step across the wooden porch and his next, Wisp felt the girl's presence within him, the reassuring glow faint but still real and vital—

Felt it *stretch*.

He paused, youngling in his jaws. What was this?

Stretch and stretch until all at once, his sense of her SNAPPED!

Jenn Nalynn was gone.

The sei's doing. His first thought and one that saved the youngling's neck.

The sei imposed his connection to the girl, and he'd grown foolishly complacent, hadn't he? Believing they'd forget their own meddling, as they often seemed to do, and leave it in him, so he'd have the comfort of her presence even apart. So she know he'd hear her call and come to her, always.

He searched for a prying moth, finding none, but no matter. The sei spied when least wanted. This unconscionable, unwanted severing— was it because of where he planned to go in search of her?

HOW DARE THEY—

~Elder brother. Take me with you.~ The girl's house toad squatted beside a bulging bag with a strap, and Wisp's furious attention jumped to it.

~WHAT?~

~Where?~ the youngling added querulously. ~What's happening?~

Wisp gave it a silencing shake, his greater concern the determined look of a toad who knew perfectly well a dragon hadn't the power of a turn-born, to cross with anything but themselves. ~Impossible, little cousin.~

~I may have a way, elder brother.~ A foot pushed at the bag, the contents of which had hard edges, disturbingly like a box.

Not just any box. The one, Wisp feared, made by this same toad from a traitor's blood and hero's tunic, from iron that had dared bind Jenn Nalynn, and silver threads cast by yling.

—and from who knew what else the little cousin might have consumed when unwatched. A dragon daren't think about it.

All to create a prison for Crumlin Tralee, a wicked man and evil wizard, letting the girl keep her reckless promise to return him to Marrowdell while keeping him from causing more harm.

When neither dragon proved willing to ask, the girl's house toad gave its bag another nudge. Out rolled a white pebble, hastily tucked back inside. ~We entice the queen to take us, elder brother.~

On hearing this, the youngling began to struggle wildly—and understandably—to escape Wisp's hold.

Wisp gave it a harder, quelling shake, his eyes never leaving the toad's. ~How does that bring me to Jenn Nalynn?~ he demanded, a snarl under it. The house toad best not answer in riddles or he'd break a peace between their kind that extended to the beginning of time. ~Explain yourself!~

~We have watched. The queen values certain prey above all others, elder brother. That which possesses magic from the edge. Even more, that has a connection here, to Marrowdell, such as this box and its contents. Once she's made aware, she will take it. She will not expect us to come as well.~ A meaningful glare at the youngling. ~*That* need not risk itself.~

~I fully agree, Great Lord of—~

Wisp's jaws tightened in warning. The youngling stopped. ~My student goes where I go. The sei order it.~ Not that he'd any idea if they did or would care regardless, but it satisfied the toad.

Who rose to its full, if small, height. ~Then we are agreed, elder brother? To leave at once?~

Impatience, when house toads tended to cautious thought and hesitancy. Why? A dragonish urge to battle? Concern for the girl?

Or had it other reasons?

The girl's absence a wound in his heart, Wisp spat out the young-ling's neck, keeping a clawed foot on a wing. Lowered his head until the house toad was all he saw and said, very carefully, ~I go to find Jenn Nalynn, little cousin, and see her safely home. I have no inter-est in your queen.~

And no intention of confronting such power.

The youngling nodded quickly, a deplorable gesture it must have picked up from the villagers.

The toad didn't flinch, though they were nostril to snout. ~What if our elder sister is her captive?~

Wisp reared back, flames boiling from his jaws, wings mantled behind him. The youngling cowered.

The house toad stayed as it was and where, as if prepared to wait till the end of the world.

Then—a *whisper*—then warmth!

The girl's glow was back, no brighter, no closer, but real and vital and his again. As if she'd stepped through a door and back—

Sei mystery. Her magic. He cared not, the relief so great, a lesser dragon would have trembled.

Wisp stretched a wing.

~We will set her free, no matter the cost.~ He paused to consider the toad and its offer. Shuddered inwardly. Openly encourage the queen to take them prisoner as well?

He'd far rather use his old enemy's tactic: sneak up from behind and pounce—not that he'd ever tell Scourge.

~We will scout ahead,~ Wisp concluded. ~Keep your bait ready, little cousin. We may need it yet.~

The youngling gave an unseemly whimper, stealing the last word.

EIGHTEEN

*B*Y THE TIME they left Nonny's room, the turn-borns' sanctuary, though Jenn had started to think of it as an entrance and exit for something else entirely, the tide had, indeed, reached its lowest ebb. Seaweed-coated rocks glistened in the sunlight, and seagulls ignored their passing, busy hunting the myriad little creatures left dry and exposed. Shrinking pools trapped fish and brightly colored pincushions—urchins, Nonny told her—and she stopped hurrying long enough to point out a small octopus, which hid itself as if noticing their attention.

A bird caught a silver fish and flew up and away, its companions quick to pursue, calling noisily.

Ancestors Benevolent and Blessed, there was no sign of the dead waalum. She'd been afraid they'd see it stranded and covered in birds.

Following Nonny, whose feet fairly flew down the path, Jenn carried her precious clothes under an arm, her boots in her free hand, and thought about the beings who lived under the sparkling wild water who must have rescued her clothing and tucked it in a trunk. It was the drying and neat folds that perplexed her most. How had they known? If she'd found something of theirs on the shore, Jenn couldn't imagine noticing, let alone knowing how to return or care for it.

It implied, she decided, an awareness of those who lived on land as well as a grace of manners akin to Aunt Sybb's, making the sirenspites—or whatever they called themselves—someone she earnestly wanted to meet and soon.

And feeling that way, the path became shorter, or their steps covered more of it, for in far less time than it had taken to reach the bridge, they were stepping on Nonny's dock.

Nonny let out a low whistle and, lifting a corner of her hood, peered suspiciously at Jenn. "What did you do?"

Nothing deliberate, which wasn't, Jenn realized, a comforting answer. Nor was suggesting the path, and by extension the world, might have shortened itself to accommodate her. "When I'm in a hurry, sometimes I get where I want to be a little faster than expected."

"Is that all?" The Eld made a show of patting herself through her rags, as if to check all her parts had arrived "a little faster" with them, and Jenn chuckled.

She stopped when a glance from the dock showed the boat far below, straining against its ropes with every wave. Heart's Blood. How had she got down there yesterday?

Meanwhile, Nonny scampered down the ladder with enviable nimbleness, then balanced on the pitching deck to raise her hands. "Toss them."

Her boots. The rest. Of course she should, and Jenn did, then resolutely turned to go down the ladder herself, gripping the wood as tightly as possible. Her foot felt for the next rung. Missed. Tried again.

"Arrive a little faster, Jenn," Nonny called up, cheerfully mocking.

Smiling made her braver. Jenn still took her time and, when she was close enough, Nonny grabbed her waist and swung her on board.

In their absence, three filled sacks had been left next to the cabin door—Urcet's payment for the mimrol, Jenn guessed. She helped Nonny carry them—stow them, she was told—inside the boat.

To her surprise, after a quick look at their contents, Nonny put two aside and handed the third to Jenn. Without her hood, it was easy to see her wide grin. "These are for you."

"What is it?"

"I sent Urcy shopping," the Eld reminded her.

Sitting on the cot, Jenn opened her sack and pulled out its contents. First was a brown woven belt. Then a white underdress so sheer Jenn dropped it to her lap at once, her face hot. "I can't wear this," she protested. Unless at home, where Bannan would surely—she hauled her thoughts from that unhelpful direction—"There's nothing to it."

Nonny, who'd sat across from her, pointed to her recovered clothing. "That's proof, if I needed more, of where you're from, Jenn. Fine for the cold, I'm sure, but you'd regret wearing any of it here. Trust me." Her grin. "Keep looking."

Next from the sack was a brown dress, not at all sheer but soft and light. The fabric felt like Aunt Sybb's scarf, a treasure of painted silk, and the faint scent of it was like her aunt's, too. Jenn's eyes prickled and she choked down a sob. Blinking rapidly, she held up the dress.

The fabric had appeared plain—most was a simple, but rich brown—but the work was not. The hem featured a band of the most delicate embroidery she'd ever seen, also in brown. Each sleeve had a clever strap and button to shorten it—a feature Jenn resolved to remember for her own dresses, once home. The number of times she'd wet her sleeves—

"Oh." Holding the dress by the shoulders, Jenn finally saw the collar. It was gold, with green leaves—that looked like the tastier of the seaweeds, so Jenn quite approved—sewn on it. "It's beautiful," she murmured, then looked up at Nonny. "And expensive. I can't—"

"You will. It's a disguise," Nonny replied firmly. "Looking like another me won't pass. There are none. This, though? It's what every woman in Shadesport wears to do their work. Easy to wear and simple to clean." A fond smile, as if at a memory. "We love our colors, in Eld." She took the dress, stroking the collar. "Dawizards, mind, wear no color but white, like the belly of a shark. Normal folk? We can't resist adding some even to what's ordinary, and when there's a celebration?" Her eyes lit. "Our dresses put flowers to shame."

Oh, how she'd love to see such a dress—and buy one for Peggs. Kydd would paint her portrait in it, then those with clever, careful fingers, like Riss and Cynd, would pluck apart the threads and use them to brighten shirts and coats—Marrowdell would shine!

"They sound wonderful," Jenn said, which was true. "But I must leave by tomorrow's turn." Thinking of the Balance, she heard its song, more insistent now and almost clear, and reached into the sack to quiet it.

Finding a green and gold hair ribbon, matching the collar.

And a wicked curved knife, like Nonny's, but with a bone handle. Jenn looked a question.

Taking the knife, Nonny gave it a twist through the air. "We all carry such. To open oysters," a grin, then abruptly serious, "or spill an enemy's guts."

Jenn shook her head. "I don't like oysters," she pointed out, deliberately ignoring the part about enemies and their insides, the knife much too small to harm the toad queen.

"Dawizards. Waalum hunters. People who get in your way. People who mean you harm. Strangers!" Reciting her appalling list, Nonny grew more and more exasperated. "I can't always protect you!"

Careful to avoid the now wildly waving knife, Jenn stretched her hand across the small cabin to touch Nonny's knee. "And you mustn't try, Dear Heart," she warned quietly. "What I am is not flesh and blood alone. What I can do, if not careful, is far worse than stabbing someone. Which I won't," she finished.

Nonny's eyes narrowed. "More than 'a little faster'?"

Thinking of what she'd done to Marrowdell's river, Jenn could only nod. "Don't fear me. Please. I would never hurt anyone."

With a grunt that might have been disbelief or an understandably wary agreement, Nonny dropped the knife in the sack and took the ribbon. "Let's tidy that mop."

"WERFOL!" Bannan stumbled to his feet, standing on round little rocks instead of sand, under a normal cloud-whipped sky, and looked around frantically for the child. "WERFOL!"

"He chose," the Ansnan creature told him.

"YOU DID!" Enraged, he lunged at her—it.

Roche got in the way. Bannan raised his fist, ready to strike, desperate to pound something.

Lowered it, his heart cracking with grief, to whisper, "How could we leave him there?"

"He chose."

The truthseer dragged his eyes to where Edis stood, or coiled, or whatever her body did to hold her upright. "Heart's Blood, he's a child."

"Who knew what he was doing," Roche blurted out. "The creature would have killed us both and hung our skins on her—on her—" He gagged and fell silent.

He told the truth, horrible as it was to hear, because Jenn Nalynn had wished it upon him. As Werfol had, or believed, and Bannan forced himself to think past his despair. "Edis, can you go back for him?"

Large purple eyes regarded him. She gave a single nod. "We leave no one behind."

As a soldier said and a soldier did—

"You go—you'll die!" Roche objected. "You've lost too much, Edis. You must go to the pool. Seek the olm and heal yourself."

For the first time, Bannan noticed how her body had become wizened and dull, as if it had dried out—or the magic sucked from it—and how she trembled with effort. Still, she shook her head at Roche. "I must—"

"No. Care for yourself," Bannan heard himself say, the hardest words imaginable, the right words. "Werfol said he'd be safe. That means we have time."

She flowed to stand in front of him, her hands hovering beside his face. This close, he saw her as a person, and questions boiled up he pushed ruthlessly aside. "I ask your name," she said.

From a being of magic, not a simple or innocent request, and Bannan hesitated.

Roche couldn't. "It's Bannan Larmensu, Edis. He's a truthseer and soldier who came to Marrowdell after the treaty and loves Jenn Nalynn. He was good to me when I didn't deserve it."

"Stars Witness, what we deserve finds us." Her body swayed. "I'll return when Roche calls me, truthseer, but I ask you keep my friend out of the Verge in future. His dreams are burden enough."

His dreams?

Before Bannan could ask, her eyes gained a faraway look. "You have another name, truthseer. Captain Ash. We met once." A predatory smile. "To my cost."

He remembered nothing of her, nothing *like* her, but there'd been so very many Ansnan soldiers, Ancestors Dark and Despairing—

"Larmensu," Bannan said, insisting on it. "Werfol is my sister's son." He pulled out the scarf with the Larmensu crest. Thrust it in her face. "This is who I am. Who we are."

She snatched it from his hand before he guessed her intention, rearing back, her face convulsing. "How got you this? How!"

"It's my mother's, lost with her when she died. The toad queen gave it to me before sending me into the ruins of our home."

Roche went to her, looked up. "Edis, what's wrong?"

She stared down at the scarf. "I was there," barely a whisper. "I saw it happen. What they did. They used this—" Her eyes flashed up to Bannan, an accusation in their depths. "Now our enemy can."

The scarf fell from her hands; Roche caught it as she sank through the rocks and vanished. Wordlessly, he returned it to Bannan.

The two stood staring at one another for a long moment, as if suspended in the aftermath of a spell, or the way soldiers stood when the battle paused but wasn't close to over. The latter, Bannan decided grimly, tucking away his mother's scarf. Changed by a whisper into something other than a memento, something possibly—probably— dangerous.

He'd not leave it lying here.

"Don't summon Edis until the last minute, when we're ready," he told Roche. "We'll give her all the time we can."

Roche nodded. Though haggard and worn, his green eyes bloodshot, he appeared remarkably composed for someone who'd survived the Verge, as if accustomed to stomach-turning strangeness. "Do you know where we are?"

The truthseer glanced up the rock-strewn slope, startled, then overjoyed to recognize landmarks. "That's the Westietas' ossuary," he said, pointing, then turned to the forest below them. "The way to the house." And Lila—

Roche's weary face filled with wonder. "Ancestors Blessed. Werfol asked Edis to take us home. To his home. How did she know where it was?"

The truthseer let himself see beyond. Several of the round white rocks looked back at him—with much happier faces than the ones in the floodwall. A couple waved toy hammers.

His heart pounded. "This is in the edge." Which wasn't an answer— unless it was. Wisp and Scourge were able to find crossings; he'd never thought to ask how. Never guessed there'd be one near his family.

For all he knew, the toad queen, who must have taken Werfol from here, left a trail—

—into the edge. Where it touched Westietas land; where the Marerrym had built their home and the Larmensu come; where he and Lila went to drink in Vorkoun—and Roche Morrill; and, Ancestors Wary and Wise, it couldn't be coincidence.

Lila hadn't told him the edge lay within the estate grounds. Did she know?

Heart's Blood, she would now, if she truedreamed her son and touched the Verge.

"It doesn't matter how we got here, only that we are." He put his hand on Roche's shoulder, feeling the tremors the other tried to conceal. The man was done. "We have to get to the house, and quickly. Come."

An arm supporting Roche, the rocks uneven and inclined to roll underfoot, Bannan headed for the path leading to the Westietas' estate and Lila, distracting himself from his fear for her by trying to come up with a way to tell his sister he'd left her youngest behind.

He supposed it was cowardly to hope she'd be unarmed when he did.

Having just been braver than ever before—even counting the time they'd been attacked on the Northward Road before he'd known there was magic but known there were lies—Werfol Westietas' courage deserted him the instant Edis disappeared into the sand with Uncle Bannan and Roche. Tears running down his cheeks, he stood before the majesty-monster as she lurched free of the sand-turned-stone, giving a miserable, terrified sniff loud enough to echo over the plain.

If she'd threatened or puffed up or roared at him, he would have collapsed into a useless puddle.

Fortunately, she laughed.

A mocking, wheezing, stinky laugh, and, as anyone who knew Werfol would know, it stiffened his little spine and made him angry. He wiped his face with his sleeve, his eyes glowing molten gold, and shouted, "I saved them!"

Which it wasn't true, Edis had, but he'd made the choice for her so he had as well. And Werfol used the tone that warned Semyn he spoiled for a fight—and their parents to expect very poor behavior—and it made him feel gloriously brave so he said it again. "I SAVED THEM!"

The majesty-monster settled on the rubble, rocking to aim a huge green eye at him. Her latest acquisition, the animal hide, twitched as if somehow still in agony, and this close, Werfol saw there were three new hooks, empty and waiting, so he'd been right. Uncle Bannan hadn't been safe this time. None of them had.

Wait her out. It was almost as if Momma whispered in his ear. Werfol spread his feet and put his hands behind his back, the perfection of his parade rest owing much to Dutton's example. He waited. And waited, the majesty-monster apparently having the same tactic in mind, but whenever his courage threatened to fail him, he'd glance at the hooks and his anger grew.

An eyelid twitched.

Ancestors Tested and Triumphant! Werfol schooled his features and waited.

Finally, a frustrated bellow. "I'll have them yet, little one. Including your mother and the turn-born and all who think to help you! At the Balance all gifts will feed ME!" Her dreadful mouth gaped in anticipation, letting out its stink, and Werfol trembled on the inside.

But not on the outside. Refusing to cough or cover his mouth, Werfol looked into the abyss of her greed and, deliberately, smiled his mother's smile.

The one that turned the guards, even Dutton, a little green and made bad people run—or confess with all haste if they couldn't, even then unsure it would be enough to save them.

"That isn't what will happen," he said, still smiling.

Her mouth crashed shut, her trophies jiggling. "OH NO?"

What had Jenn said? "No. Tomorrow you'll get your comeuppance. And the very next day," the young truthseer added, aiming the words like a spear, "we'll forget you." Not that he ever could—but he knew her sort of monster rather well and that had to sting.

A huge clawed foot, bigger than a carriage, rose in threat, and Werfol had barely time to regret having gone what Momma would call "a little too far" before it came at him as if to wipe him from the world.

He couldn't outrun it. He didn't try. Without him, the majesty-monster had nothing to lure Jenn Nalynn back and would be stuck here forever. She was either bluffing and he was safe—

Or he'd be dead, saving those he loved—

The foot stopped before it hit, its arrested motion sending a blast of air that made Werfol stagger, but he didn't fall.

"Clever, clever little one," she said, her tone now cloying and too friendly. "You know your worth—or think you do. Aim to distract me—but don't, not at all. To get to you, the turn-born must break open my prison. She will release me and I will start to feast. Starting with Marrowdell." The majesty-monster gave a bizarre wink. "Then your home. Then every home and place of thieves who've dared to steal what is rightfully mine—and now I think I will keep you with me, little one." Her foot moved like lightning, sweeping up Werfol in a cage of her claws. She brought him to an eye. "I will keep you and let you watch. You won't forget me. I promise."

Hands gripping her claws for support, Werfol glared at her and shouted, "Comeuppance!"

He found himself in the dark, inside Goosie, again.

Trying not to cry.

Jenn stared down at her knees—her fully exposed knees—and tried not to imagine what Aunt Sybb would say.

While that gracious lady might accept and applaud the diversity of dress worn in varied locations—being fond, for example, of the handweaving done by the hillfolk of northwestern Rhoth, and having a wonderful summer shirtwaist of their work—she would absolutely not condone a hem that revealed knees.

And calves, Jenn thought, bending to confirm those were in plain sight as well, though her aunt had almost given up on her ankles. As for her feet? Those were, in her aunt's words, a lost cause—other than requesting they be clean and in shoes at their shared meals.

Her arms, also mostly bare, revealed her scratches healing nicely, the stinging salve the Eld had applied to the worst of them having done its work.

Nonny, smothered from head to ankle by her harmoot—a garment Aunt Sybb would find far more suitable even if of rags—busied herself putting away supplies from the other sacks, oblivious to her guest's crisis of modesty.

Or entertained and trying not to laugh.

The boat rocked and Jenn swayed with it.

Her extremely short dress, and sheer underdress—the two were worn together, according to Nonny, which was a relief—moved as well, sliding soft and cool over her skin. It was, Jenn admitted to herself, the most comfortable clothing she'd worn in her life, mostly because it was like wearing nothing at all.

If she wore it to Marrowdell—under her cloak, of course, and with her boots—the look in Bannan's eyes would be worth it. And what would doubtless follow, both of them apart too long. Contemplating their passionate reunion, her heart lurched—

As did the boat, making her companion curse and grab for a hold.

Jenn thought quickly of oysters. The water calmed again and she relaxed.

"And what was that about?" Nonny inquired, her head turned so far around she resembled a gull more than usual.

Nothing Jenn wanted to share. "I've never worn anything this short," she said instead, tugging at her new dress as if that might lengthen it to Aunt Sybb's satisfaction.

With a derisive snort, Nonny spun around and hitched her harmoot up over her knees, tying rags to hold it there with the ease of long practice. "You can't follow the tide out and dig for clams in anything longer."

A practical, sensible reason for a style Jenn shouldn't find embarrassing at all. And wouldn't, she told herself, twirling in the small space to prove it.

"That's it. The length's even better for dancing," Nonny added cheekily, lifting her knees and kicking out her feet in demonstration, rocking the boat until it danced as well.

Jenn laughed. "You're right. And it's very comfortable." She swallowed the logical question of why didn't Nonny wear the same, not wanting to pry.

The other woman guessed, plucking at her rags and giving Jenn one of her keen looks. "I dress to remember where I came from. And," this with a mischievous grin, "to keep the very helpful, very fine, very curious people of Shadesport off my boat and out of my business." Her grin faded. "Being thought a harmless hermit—slightly

crazed at that, I'm told—I'm of no interest to the dawizards. I plan,
Jenn Nalynn, to keep it that way."

Meaning she wasn't to do anything to attract attention to Nonny
or her boat, and Jenn nodded, quite sure that was to her advantage
as well. "And Urcet? Are the dawizards interested in him?"

Nonny went back to putting away supplies but without her earlier care, shoving cans and little bags on shelves roughly, a hunched
shoulder her sole reply.

Making the question of Urcet and dawizards important, Jenn
thought worriedly.

Important indeed.

Within the embrace of mountains, the forest surrounding the Westietas' summer estate resembled those in Avyo and southern Rhoth,
in spring filled with light and bursting with ferns and flowers, before
leaves opened fully to create a soft dappled shade. Birdsong came
from every direction, not that Bannan had time or inclination to
notice, for at their second step on the path into the forest, he and
Roche were accosted by a pair of well-armed guards.

Ancestors Blessed and Benevolent. Relief weakening his joints,
Bannan went to introduce himself—

"We left Werfol with the monster!" The words shot from Roche's
mouth like vomit.

—to be as poorly received. "Take us to the young master now!"
the younger guard ordered furiously, a grip on her pistol as she drew
her short sword. "Or pay with your lives!"

Ancestors Witness, he should have tucked Roche in the hut
they'd passed. Preferably gagged.

Done now. Bannan raised his free hand in surrender, the other
keeping Roche on his feet. "Let me explain. I'm—"

"No talking!" The older guard drew his weapon with a menacing
rasp. "You too, Sillan," without looking at his partner. "Mum's the

word. Anyone we find goes straight to the baron. Our lord will sort this out."

The truth. But it made no sense. Emon left the questioning of intruders to his exceptionally capable wife, and Lila was here—Tagey'd been sure of it. Bannan tensed. "Why not to the baroness?"

They exchanged fleeting, troubled looks, justifying his fear. His sister was truedreaming. Had she been trapped already by her gift—or, Heart's Blood, caught by the toad queen?

"I'm Lila's brother, Bannan Larmensu," he said urgently. "Tell me what's wrong!"

"Doesn't matter who you are, orders are orders." The senior guard gestured with his blade. "The baron'll tell you what he wants you to know, good sir," he added with gruff courtesy. "You'd best make ready to do the same. Go on."

"I know my way," Bannan muttered and, ignoring the guards, started down the lovely winding path at the best rate Roche could manage.

Catching up, the younger guard took Roche's other arm, sharing what was quickly becoming dead weight. The older paced behind Bannan, sword no doubt aimed at his neck, and he couldn't fault the attitude, given how they must look. Roche, straight from an Ansnan village by the cut of his clothes, the worse for wear and smelling of cheap beer.

As for Bannan? He'd make no better first impression, dressed by Tagey like a dock worker and a poorly paid one at that. Let alone they'd been dunked in the Lilem then dragged to the Verge and back.

Leaving Werfol—

When they reached where the path forked, the rightmost leading to the house, the guard behind him ordered, "To the left, good sir."

Emon's workshop. Sure of his goal, unable to hurry to it, Bannan's every step felt like moving through mud. If ever he could have used Jenn's ability to shorten the road, he thought desperately, it was now, through this awful stretch of beautiful spring forest, leaves budding out, shrubs in flower and how dare birds sing—

A snort. A huff. The ominous plant of a hoof.

Two horses, a chestnut with a short black mane and a bay with black points, abruptly blocked their way. While the size of a normal horse, these proved they were something else again as lips curled from fangs and eyes glowed red.

Kruar. That the mighty beasts announced themselves instead of attacking from ambush was a courtesy they accorded very few and never a trespasser. Seeing that realization cross the face of the guard helping him with Roche, Bannan dared give her the man's full weight.

He limped to the prancing, snarling creatures, hands wide in welcome. Most likely the guards expected him to be savaged.

Not by these. Nostrils flared, taking his scent, and the pair settled. "Spirit," he greeted the bay huskily. "Dauntless." The chestnut. He'd named the kruar after they'd almost killed themselves to bring him and Lila to Werfol in Marrowdell in time to save the boy's life. Watched them leave with his sister and her sons, trusting their loyalty to the young truthseer to keep them safe outside the edge, and he couldn't be happier to see them now. "Take me to Emon."

The mare, Dauntless, his mount on that incredible ride, knelt to let him climb on her back. She wouldn't remember him. Couldn't speak, outside the edge.

But obey him? Spin to leap down the path with all the haste he could ask?

That she'd do.

Wisp led the way, flying over the drying fields of the efflet and abandoned farm, swooping low over the old trees, the neyet, home to yling who danced in excitement—being prone to such displays—and watched by nyphrit who gnashed their teeth in panic then bolted into hiding places.

Being wise to the nature of dragons.

The youngling kept pace, silent and sorely puzzled.

There was no explaining, Wisp knew, or he'd get the same reaction as from nyphrit and have to root the terrified youngling from some hole or cave.

He'd something of the feeling himself, but used it to goad himself onward, not away. An advantage of surviving this long—or why he had.

He landed in the upper meadow, its ground crusted with old snow and new ice. Was pleased to find stubborn thistle stalks erupting here and there, the bones of last summer refusing to be forgotten, their heads topped with the fluffy remnants of last year's seeds, and he'd have paused to blow them into the air, but there wasn't time.

The youngling hovered, though it took work, as if landing might commit it. As if it had the illusion of choice. ~Come down,~ Wisp ordered, cracking the new ice with each halting step. ~NOW.~

The other dragon dropped to the ground only to slide along the ice. It recovered with a wild flail of wings.

A new lesson.

~Who is that, lord?~

And now distraction. Annoyed, Wisp turned his head to see a woman sitting on a brown cloak. Her back was to them, for she looked out over Marrowdell.

~Wait here.~ Much as he wanted to, Wen Treff wasn't to be ignored. Wisp changed direction, his intact legs dragging his useless ones, and sent a chill breeze to snap against her ear. "Why are you here and not in the village?"

She didn't look around. ~I might say the same, dragon lord.~ She spoke like a little cousin, or fellow dragon, but unlike her earlier and truly painful efforts of before, this sending was smooth.

And ominously powerful. Free of the youngling's uneasy attention, Wisp would have bid her good day and gone about his business, unwilling to trouble hers.

But he wasn't alone, and the girl, the dragon sighed to himself, had asked him to find her strange friend, who didn't want to be found, but was.

He moved between Wen and her view, wrapping himself in light. He couldn't escape the uncomfortable feeling she saw him regardless.

Wen sat cross-legged, hands under the bulge of her unborn, a house toad on one shoulder. The little cousin, being wise, peered from the cover of her wild hair and offered a rather faint, ~Greetings, elder brother. This past moon I laid—~ It desisted at the lift of his jaw.

Not the Wen of before, Wisp realized. Her eyes had become like flecks of old snow, her hair shifted its color, and she wore clothing like a villager—

—but at times a perilous light.

Little wonder she'd left her family behind—they were safer for it. Wary, the dragon settled himself on his haunches despite his impatience. ~We return to the Verge.~

~By this crossing?~ Her lips curved. ~Bold dragon lord.~

It wasn't approval. The youngling whimpered.

This was the girl's crossing, entering the Verge closest to his goal. Wisp snarled, deep in his chest. ~You won't stop me.~ Even if he suddenly feared she could.

~Brave dragon lord.~ The curve deepened, almost a smile. ~I would not tamper with the freedom of any being, having waited so long for my own.~ In a flash, her face turned grim. ~But have you thought of Jenn, should you fall? Of this?~ Her long white hand left her bulge to stroke the air, encompassing the valley and more.

He'd thought of little else, which she didn't need to know. ~My place is at the girl's side, not here.~ *Not waiting and useless,* he left unsaid.

She seemed to hear nonetheless, for her expression grew less stern. ~I've never doubted you.~

He bore her long, searching gaze, refusing to twitch a muscle. The youngling, amazingly, remained still. The world turned under them, or so it felt, before Wen gave a nod, copied by her ridiculous house toad.

Wisp eyed the little cousin, and it eased back into her hair.

~I don't know what you will face, dragon lord, only that the power opposing us continues to feed and grow. It seeks to swallow all there is and will do so at the Balance. Unless thwarted. Unless challenged. Unless the brave and bold and good-hearted face this threat together. Are you willing?~

They weren't words, they were the heartbeats of Marrowdell itself, driving the blood through his body, magic through his bones, lifting his wings. Roaring in glorious fury, Wisp found himself on his feet, dimly aware the youngling stood as well, that it roared with him, the pair cracking stone. Dragonkind called to battle—

Yet what looked out at him through Wen's eyes, what rested tender hands on her unborn, wasn't fierce or angry, but dispassionate and calm. She unleashed dragons, yes, but demanded more than their heedless rage, however potent.

It wouldn't be enough.

Hard as it was, Wisp drew himself from that brink, embracing the coolness of reason, remembering the war he'd won with cleverness, not claw. Gave the still-aroused youngling a smack with his tail, to calm it, and bowed his head, ever so slightly, to Wen Treff, as he might to an equal.

Not, Wisp reminded himself, that he'd any. ~We will not fail.~

She inclined her head to him and vanished.

As people and little cousins couldn't, while dragons could. Shaken, Wisp resolved then and there to have nothing more to do whatever strangeness Wen Treff was becoming if he could possibly help it.

~Follow me.~

The girl's crossing was between these two eruptions of the Bone Hills, part of what the villagers called the Spine and Wisp knew as the body of the trapped mad sei. A creature soothed and healed to obliviousness, or so he hoped.

They were almost to the spot when a moth landed in front of him, forcing him to drive in his claws and stop.

~Where are you going, elder brother?~ Said in its fussy little voice, but something else listened.

He felt it as weight.

Wisp absorbed the blow as the youngling slid haplessly into him, the lesson of ice apparently yet to be learned, preoccupied with a second disturbing conversation. At least this one he'd half expected.

~We go to the Verge. Jenn Nalynn permits me to use her crossing.~ As the girl herself claimed the terst turn-born would approve of her opening their trunks, but, as neither were here to disagree, Wisp stood firm. ~Let us pass.~

Foolishly curious, the youngling stretched his neck alongside Wisp to sniff at the moth.

Which took two dainty steps back, slipping a little, then spoke as a mountain.

~GO WHERE I SEND YOU!~

The upper meadow and Spine faded, replaced by the warm brilliant sky of the Verge as they crossed. As the youngling spun in mid-air, jaws agape with relief and joy, Wisp opened his wings to glide in a slow easy circle, eyes checking for threat.

Interfering sei. It was worse than Wen and her toad.

Where had it sent them? Some unfamiliar place, not where the girl's crossing had opened before. As well, he thought grimly, expect help from a snowflake.

His sense of her remained weak and distant, ending his hope he'd regain it in the Verge, afraid what it meant. He'd seen her precious map. Knew, from the turn-born, that the edge writhed through far more than Marrowdell, and Jenn could be anywhere if—

The youngling came close, breath heaving like a bellows. ~We can't be here! We must leave! We must go!~

Peeved, Wisp slanted his next downward spiral to see what so alarmed the youngling, gratified by what he found. The mad sei had been of use after all—and what that implied about the danger they faced? Wen's words came back to him. A power feeding, growing, preparing to strike.

That a sei might fear it as well was in no sense a comfort.

White towers cut the sky, their base lodged in a dry empty cup of wasteland, sending shadows in every direction. A dark, fell place where no one came and nothing lived. For long, anyway.

The palace of the toad queen.

~Come, youngling,~ Wisp told it cheerfully, feeling dark and fell himself. ~Let's see if the hag is home.~

And ask her about Jenn Nalynn.

Suiting action to words, and, in truth, action preferable to thinking about what they were about to do, what no dragon ever had and survived to boast of it, Wisp snapped his wings shut and dove for the towers' heart.

NINETEEN

JENN HELPED NONNY prepare their supper, one of Urcet's sacks supplying two of the silver fish with nasty teeth, bundles of fragrant fresh-cut herbs, and four long twisted tubers her companion called potatoes but which weren't at all like those of Marrowdell.

Making a special meal was. Jenn thought wistfully of Peggs and her kitchen, regretting, now that she couldn't be there and might never be again, the number of times she'd showed up late only to find her share kept warm on the oven, her sister doing extra especially for her.

She'd been, Jenn realized, careless of irreplaceable moments, caring overmuch for what weren't. Listening for frogs, collecting thistle seeds, and dancing with Wisp could be done at any time; she'd missed too many lovingly prepared suppers by thinking only of herself and, while she didn't wish, Jenn firmly planned to do better.

Nonny gutted the long fish, saving their insides for bait—without clarifying what might consider the stinky mess appetizing. Fortunately the little bucket she used had a tight lid, and, when she stuffed the hollow fish with crushed handfuls of herbs, the smell in the cabin improved at once.

After looping white thread around the fish until they looked intact again, if sad, she chose a wide-mouthed jar from her shelf. The jar proved to hold a creamy substance that looked like butter but smelled interestingly pungent. "Garlic," Nonny explained when Jenn asked. "About the only thing we can grow." Using her fingers, she took out a good-sized blob and proceeded to rub it over the outsides of the fish.

A mystery, how they were to cook fish the length of Jenn's fore-arm, Nonny having winked and refused to say. There wasn't room on the burner for a frying pan of sufficient size, not that she'd seen one, nor was there an oven in sight.

Meanwhile, finding the biggest pot, Jenn peeled the Eldad pota-toes, charmed to discover they were bright orange inside instead of white.

Definitely not like those of home, where they'd plant the next crop soon, using seed potatoes saved from last year's harvest and carefully stored in baskets covered with sand to keep out the light and damp.

Before the flood, had anyone thought—or time—to move the baskets to safety?

Jenn had a sudden vision of baskets of potatoes on beds and tucked into loft corners. Of their contents sprouting and potatoes growing down through soggy ceilings—which might be convenient for har-vesting, except no one could live there and then what would they do?

"Jenn!" Nonny seized her hand, taking the knife and wrapping a rag around the cut in her left palm. "Pay attention."

"I was—I wasn't," Jenn admitted, the cut throbbing now that she paid attention. Ancestors Dreaming and Distracted. Bright red drops spotted the potatoes she'd peeled, though not her new clothes, giving them a measled look. "I'll clean them." She reached for the pot.

Nonny pushed away her hand. "I'll do it." She poured water from the kettle over the potatoes, shaking them clean. She glanced at Jenn. "What was it this time?"

Jenn sat on the bench, the cot being tucked out of the way. "It wasn't me—or magic. I was thinking about my family. When I left—" She couldn't say *taken*, having willingly followed Bannan and Scourge, even if she had been taken as a result. "—there was a flood. I'm wor-ried." About everyone and everything. "Because it's spring, you see."

Though a person from a land seemingly always summer wouldn't, so she went on miserably to explain. "When we have to plant the gardens and everyone must help, but Bannan's gone and so am I. And—" She had an urge to hiccup and stopped. "—and they won't have water, other than the well, because I took away Marrowdell's river."

The pot froze in midair. Nonny stared at her. "You what?"

Heart's Blood. That had been her and magic, hadn't it? Jenn gave a helpless little shrug. "It was in my way—" which, once said, didn't sound good in any sense, so she kept going. "The water's not gone, I swear by my Ancestors. I dammed it up, that's all." By collapsing a small mountain and Jenn knew better than mention *that*, a similar ridge ringing the bay. "I'll fix it when I'm home again. I hope to fix it," she added, to be honest, for she'd no idea how.

Nonny's eyebrows danced and her nose wiggled. Finally, words escaped her pursed lips like steam from a kettle. "You 'HOPE'?!"

"I haven't done anything like that before," Jenn admitted. "I've only been a turn-born since my birthday, last fall." Though at times it felt like forever, at others she found herself astonished. "What matters," she stated, quite firmly, "is to save Werfol. After that—I'll see about the river."

"You should do that, yes," Nonny agreed rather numbly. She turned and put the pot on the burner, faced away from Jenn as if collecting herself.

"Bannan!" With that glad cry, a man brushed aside those with him, rounding a workbench covered in maps to rush to where Bannan stood in the doorway. Even dressed in rough outdoor clothes, like the rest, the Baron Emon Westietas was instantly recognizable, with curly reddish-brown hair, gentle brown eyes, and a round, still-boyish face that tended to fool those as yet unaware of his brilliant intellect and knowledge—let alone a boundless curiosity that put their boys', according to Lila, to shame.

As Emon neared, Bannan saw eyes framed in lines of worry and smudged by lack of sleep, a face pinched with anguish. The two met in a tight embrace, then the baron seized Bannan's shoulders and thrust him back to give him a searching look. "We heard the impossible. You, in Vorkoun and coming here. Have you news?"

Ancestors Dire and Despairing. "Werfol's alive," the truthseer responded quickly—and quietly, not being alone, but Emon had to know this before all else. "I know where he is, but it's—" at the sudden desperate hope blazing in the other's face, "—nowhere easy to reach."

"But alive." Emon breathed the words. Releasing Bannan's shoulders, he ran his hands down the other's upper arms, gripping once to be sure he was real. "Ancestors Beloved and Blessed, I should have guessed you'd be the one to ease my heart, brother."

I, not *we. My* not *ours.* Bannan's blood froze in his veins. "Lila—?"

"Sleeps—" Before Emon could say more, they were interrupted. A guard stepped to his lord's side, face grizzled and familiar, for this was the Westietas' seniormost guard, the formidable Dutton Omemee, who, before Bannan's eyes, had saved his lord's life in Channen.

The truthseer nodded a curt greeting, returned by a flicker of expression. Dutton spoke, his voice deeper than Scourge's rumbling growl. "I suggest you take the good sir to the kitchen, m'lord. He's been hard-used and injured. Sendrick can adjourn the meeting on your behalf."

"'Injured'?" The baron took hold of Bannan again. Moved him this way and that, seeking the injury. Finding it. "You're bleeding!"

The truthseer glanced down, unsurprised to find his left pant leg soaked with blood. About to say it was nothing but split stitches, he caught Dutton's hand signal. *Get to a secure place.*

Bannan leaned on Emon, saying in his best strained-but-brave voice, "Mauled by a bear," he said for the benefit of others. "My companion needs care, too. He comes behind with your forest watchers." To Dutton, low and firm, "Don't let him talk to anyone else."

Lila relied on her brother do as she would. Let Roche walk into this room of strangers to spew the incredible truth?

She'd take his head first.

Nonny's boat, it turned out, had a metal box hanging from the stern, kept filled with driftwood and tinder and covered against the dew. She'd slipped out earlier to open it and start a fire while Jenn tucked her Marrowdell clothing and boots into a sack, setting that near the coil of rope ready to take to the sanctuary in the bridge.

Not so ready herself as it happened, climbing the ladder into the black water a thought to send shivers down her spine despite the day's heat, unless it was when they planned to try it. At tonight's low tide, when the water would recede, and there'd be no watchers.

Midnight.

They spent the rest of the day doing chores, Nonny following Peggs' rule of busy being best, and the ' *Igrini* receiving more care than Jenn had expected, given its state. She dutifully scrubbed the deck from aft to bow with a brush and buckets of water drawn from the bay, while Nonny hung over the side and applied warmed tar to the boat's seams, dropping to stand in the shallows before the tide turned to reach as low as she could. She used a hammer and chisel to pry off barnacles above the water line and muttered darkly about the cost of something called dry dock to get at the rest, and Jenn wasn't, she was informed bluntly, to ask about fancy paint. Whitewash was good enough for her.

Water flooded back into the bay, bringing home the boats out fishing for the day. They had white sails and hulls of gold and green, matching her collar, with dots of red and scrollwork of black on other woodwork, which didn't.

Ancestors Frugal and Care-Filled, anyone from Marrowdell, Jenn included, understood making do with what you had and not fussing about what you didn't. Still, after catching Nonny's longing look at the bright, colorful boats, she wished she could give her all the paint she needed.

Then changed her mind, Nonny having bought her new clothes

and food—and the unwanted, but well-intentioned knife—and if she really wanted paint for her boat, Jenn realized, she'd get it herself.

No, Jenn thought, feeling the truth of it, the *Good Igrini* looked exactly as Nonny wanted, shabby on the outside while functional within: a disguise as effective as her harmoot.

Sails flapping, then snapping taut, one of the fishing boats veered, coming daringly close. There were three people on her deck, two men without shirts and a woman wearing a dress just like Jenn's, her hair in a similar braid. Seeing her, they smiled and waved vigorously. Jenn waved back, it being polite, and smiled.

Nonny hissed and tried to pull her behind the cabin, out of sight, but it was too late to hide and the effort, Jenn firmly believed, would make those watching suspicious. So she resisted, staying where she was to give a final, carefully casual wave, before turning to pick up her bucket.

"Spying," Nonny grumbled, unhappy, if not with her. "That Symyd. Always spying."

Jenn looked at her. "Will harm come of it?"

Their eyes met, something grim in the Eld's. "Only if a dawizard's in the village."

Once the fire became hot embers, they placed the herb-stuffed fish, rubbed with garlic butter and wrapped in layers of damp salty seaweed, on top. Nonny shut the box lid with a satisfied chuckle. "Wait till Urcy smells that cooking."

"Do you eat together often?" Jenn asked, taking her spot on the gunnel. In the distance, she heard the villagers, hails as boats arrived and were tied off, cheerful chants beginning as the day's catch was unloaded. Strange, how quickly she found the routine of the place, though it wasn't, she thought, so different from Marrowdell, where outdoor chores were best done before the sun set.

And the turn came.

Pouring for them both, Nonny handed her a cup of the same drink they'd shared last night, then leaned an elbow on the roof of the cabin, gleaming with fresh polish. She'd tied back her harmoot while working, leaving off the hood once the boats were safely out of sight. Twists of her red hair bobbed with the motions of the boat, and Jenn waited patiently, for Nonny, she'd learned, was thoughtful and never rushed her answers.

Sure enough, a few moments later, Nonny aimed her cup at the building on the shore, more shed than shelter. "He's asked." A shake of her head. "I've no interest."

Because being a private and solitary person wasn't the same as being lonely, a revelation Jenn wouldn't have had before meeting Nonny, who seemed quite happy as she was.

The water was settling, sunset's high tide almost complete; the boat rose slowly but surely to meet the dock, a timely welcome for their guest. Tall billowing clouds lined the horizon showing beyond the bridge, but the air was still, scented with sea and pine, and wonderfully warm.

"You love it here," Jenn said, taking a cautious sip, this time ready for the burn down her throat.

Nonny looked surprised, then pensive. She took a drink. Another. "It's my right place," she replied at last. "I wouldn't be myself anywhere else."

"I'm glad for you." Ancestors Rare and Remarkable. It was, Jenn decided, an answer worthy of Aunt Sybb, and most inspiring. Marrowdell was, in this sense, right for her, she'd no doubt. Didn't she long to be home with all her heart? Most especially with Bannan, with his warm smile and glorious apple butter eyes—

And yet—"I don't think I've found all of myself yet." Which made her sound as if she were in scattered pieces and she wasn't, of course, having lately understood she was a flesh woman, a turnborn, and part sei, all at once and whole. "I can't explain it."

A lift of the cup. "A place includes purpose, Jenn Nalynn. My guess is yours lies ahead of you." Nonny didn't smile and her voice grew solemn. "Take my advice and don't rush to find it. You won't leave it again."

She fell silent, staring out at the bay.

Jenn didn't speak either, for the words made her feel peculiar, as if the deck tilted under her, or she wore shoes, which did tend to shift her perspective. It might, she thought, be the turn coming, for it was, or her sense of the Balance closing in, for it did.

Unless it something else again.

A warning.

Kitchens were a home's heart, be it in the farm he shared with Jenn Nalynn, or in the Westietas' old and famed summer estate, and Bannan closed his eyes for a fleeting moment as its warmth and aromas wrapped around him.

Then arms did, unexpectedly. "Laddie!"

"Ioana," he greeted, bending his head over Tagey's sister, their former cook and bearer of the other charm, to kiss her on the cheek.

She blushed and fussed at this, as he'd hoped. Grew serious at once, as she should, and took his arm, ignoring her baron and lord, steering the truthseer to the small table in a corner, with a chair facing the doors to the outside and dining hall. "Sit you down. I've cheese buns."

Ioana leaned close, then, smelling of soap, cinnamon, and sweat, and whispered, "Now you're here, Dear Heart, the poor lass will come out of her 'dreaming. She wouldn't stop for me, and that's not for lack of trying, I swear by my Ancestors' Bones."

Those conversations in the kitchen, hushed when he'd arrived. Their cook had known about Lila's gift all along—perhaps even helped her with it—and she mustn't have hope of him, none of them should. Bannan put his arm around Ioana's stout waist, his head against her arm. "I don't know how."

"It's not you who needs to," she said mysteriously.

The truth. For no reason, Bannan took heart. Rising, Ioana pinched his cheek between thumb and forefinger. "Glad we are to see you, Laddie. Ever so glad."

"Uncle!"

He found his arms full again, this time with Werfol's older brother, Semyn. Who collected himself quickly and stood, inclining his head politely to his father, then to their other guest, arriving on Dutton's sturdy arm. "Greetings and welcome. I'm Semyn Westietas."

Roche's hand shot up to his mouth, his face strained as he tried not to respond.

Taking pity on him, Bannan rose, supporting himself on the table—his cursed leg threatening to collapse—to make a quick introduction. "This is Roche Morrill, late of Marrowdell. Devins' older brother," he added, that a name Semyn well knew.

It seemed, however, he knew more. Emon's heir's eyes widened briefly before he composed his features and swept a deep and respectful bow. "And rightful lord of the Sensian District of Avyo. You honor us with your presence, Baron Morrill."

Roche's hand dropped, face drained of blood, mouth open and not a word coming out.

Feeling much the same, Bannan stared at his slim young nephew, seeing the truth shining in his face.

Jenn had told him Roche and Devins' father had been a baron in the House of Keys before their exile, but never had it crossed the truthseer's mind—or Roche's, by his shock—that Prince Ordo hadn't stripped the title from the family along with the sum of their worldly goods.

Emon stepped forward, assuming control with looks to guard and cook. He pushed Bannan down in his chair with a gentle hand. "Dutton, please escort—" with a hint of hesitation, but no doubt, not of his son's scholarship, "—the baron to the guest suite and see to his needs. Personally."

Stay with him, that meant, and Bannan gave the now-anxious-looking Roche a quick nod of reassurance. "I'll be right up," he promised, heart thudding in his chest as he thought of the cook's cryptic assurance. A being of magic pitied Roche the burden of his dreams—the toad queen who collected magic had taken him—

"Nimly, take up our guest's tray. Careful, mind," Ioana ordered, handing it to the scullery boy who'd sat through all this, eyes carefully averted. He rose willingly to work.

Roche, seeing the filled plate and mug, looked more nauseated than pleased. "Come along, m'lord," Dutton said gently.

Emon nodded to a smaller door, off to the side. "The family stairs, Dutton." An expression of trust—and not to pass their new guest by anyone else in the house.

"Yes, m'lord."

Once the door closed behind Roche, Dutton, and the tray-laden Nimly, Bannan said quickly, "I know Lila's stuck in a 'dream, hunting Werfol. Roche might be able to help." He glanced at the cook.

Who, to his disquiet, shrugged her hunched shoulder and turned to pour tea.

"He doesn't look able to stand. Nor do you." Emon brought two stools to the table, gesturing to his son to sit with them. "We'll go to Lila shortly, I promise. Tell us of Werfol."

Ioana, setting cups in front of them, stopped to look at Bannan. "Our wee laddie?"

But it was Semyn, sitting with un-childlike patience though tense as a bow-string and pale, Bannan addressed. "Your brother's alive. At least—he was when we left him."

"You—what?" Emon half-rose, his face distorted. "How could—"

Semyn touched his father's arm, waiting until he sank back down before leaning forward, blue-green eyes intent on his uncle. "It's all right, Poppa. Uncle Bannan would never leave him of his own accord. Weed sent him away—to us, to get help. It's what Momma taught us." As matter-of-factly as if they discussed the weather or a piece of harness. "Uncle, who has my brother?"

Emon's heir, Lila's son—the legacy showed, Bannan thought, in the boy's restraint, his sharp insight. He answered in kind. "A creature not of this world. Can you remember Marrowdell's magic?"

Emon choked.

Nodding grimly to herself, Ioana shuffled away, her fingers working a knotted string. Like the one, Bannan suddenly remembered, Lila had worn under her sleeve when they were children, and he bit his lip, holding in questions not urgent, not now, but oh, so important, about beaded sunflowers and foxes and what a cook might know of the fall of their house.

"Weed does," Semyn said calmly. "I've promised to believe what he tells me and I do. About dragons and yling and the rest." Then, somber as any adult, he concluded, "But Werfol isn't in Marrowdell."

Would that he was—"No. He's trapped in the Verge."

Semyn and his father shot looks at each other, then turned back to Bannan.

"Then so is Lila," Emon said heavily. "She refused to let us search, certain only her gift could find him. Ancestors Dire and Disastrous, she's—" A ragged breath. "—she's been 'dreaming ever since. Nothing we do will wake her."

"Werfol could." Semyn's chin trembled then firmed. "Werfol will. You'll see, Poppa."

Speechless, his father put an arm around his small shoulders.

The toll of the toad queen's crimes continued to mount. Bannan forced his fingers to hold the cup, his hands to pick it up, his mouth to drink what he couldn't taste. Whatever it took to gain strength enough to climb the stairs to his sister's room and see her for himself.

Stairs. Heart's Blood. "My leg," he grimaced, reluctant to waste the time, knowing he mustn't squander Tagey's healcraft.

"I'll see to it. Not the first time, is it, Laddie?" With a gap-toothed smile, Ioana plopped a broad basket full of bandages and ointments on the table, the three hurriedly moving their cups out of danger. "Off with your—"

THUD!

They all looked up, for the sound came from upstairs—

The scullery boy burst into the kitchen, signing with such frantic speed all Bannan made out was—

Dead.

Roche stood in the entryway to the guest suite, unable to take another step. It wasn't that he hadn't been in a room as rich as this since younger than the boy downstairs, brother to the brave child they'd left behind, and who'd said the strangest thing he'd ever heard.

It wasn't them, either.

It wasn't that his empty stomach cramped and his dry mouth fill with drool at the meal the servant set out on the ornate table under a sunny window, bowing awkwardly to Roche. Nor that his every bone ached with longing at the sight of a bed better than any he'd known—

The servant stopped, staring up at him. Made quick signs with his hands.

"I don't know what ails him, Nimly. M'lord?" Cautious, that question. Wary.

He was, Roche realized, behaving very oddly, and it wasn't even the large and daunting stranger, with his sword and pistol and weapons he couldn't see, or that he'd been sent to keep him here.

His lips moved. Formed the shape of "My—" and the truth he needed so badly to say, that they mustn't let him sleep, that his next dreadful dream would kill him, stuck in his throat as his heart stuttered violently and his lungs refused him breath, and everything from the supper to the bed and window spun as he fell—

Roche told himself the truth, for he must, even now.

This was death.

"—got you, Roche. Dutton, a healer, quick! I've got you."

He rolled his head, unable to focus on Bannan's face, mute though desperate to speak—felt himself slip away—

"No you don't." A shake rattled his teeth. "Stay awake! Stay with me—"

Ancestors Beset and Beleaguered, the effort was too much.

His heart gave out.

The tenth dreadful dream of Roche Morrill took him in the truth-seer's arms on the floor of a baron's guest room, the moment he died.

He stood in the hall outside, looking down at the body that had been his and the friend he'd found again. Turned away for they no longer mattered, hearing a sound like a song or weeping or a battle cry. He moved toward it or floated or fell, went through a door closed and guarded without stopping, to find there a body as empty as his, but pulled by the sound he turned from it too and floated or fell through a bookcase and mirror and walls—And there she was, standing over a little bed, strong arms outstretched as if to gather up a child, face utterly still and calm—

And the sound became louder and a name . . . WERFOL! WERFOL!

So powerful was her voice it had pulled him from his body and brought him here to her and she could be only one person, the boy's mother, but she called in vain and forever, for Werfol wasn't here and couldn't come—Roche moved toward her and she whirled, crouched like a fighter—shouts GET OUT! YOU DON'T BELONG!

But he's died already and left fear behind. He hasn't her power to speak inside a dream, but truth fills him to bursting and somehow he knows. If he touches her, he can share it—Roche holds out his hand, waits an eternity—Feels hers take it—even as the floor turns to sand and she does and he falls and falls . . . and can't breathe . . . can't breathe . . .

She has him. He catches an unexpected and wonderful breath, then a second. Opens his eyes as if they'd been closed. Sees her smile. Hears a word. No, a command—WAKE!

Too late.

"Ancestors Blessed—Lila!"

At Emon's startled, if happy, cry, Bannan looked up through

tears to see his sister—dressed in, of all things, a nightrobe with her sword belted at her hip, her hair loose and wild—push by her husband and son. The twins who served as upstairs staff stood frozen in the background, clutching linens.

Lila dropped to her knees beside him, but he didn't stop cradling the dead man in his arms, this young and good man who'd never see his own mother again.

"Ancestors Bloody and Bent," Bannan whispered hoarsely, crushed by guilt and grief. "This isn't right, Lila. This isn't right."

"Brother," he heard her say, but her hand cupped the dead man's cheek, not his. "Thank you." A whisper making no sense.

Then Lila slapped the dead man's face. "Wake up!"

Sunset came in reds and oranges this night, torching the distant clouds and setting fire to the bay. Baskers slipped under the bridge made by those with hands and feet, of metal and stone, affected by none of it. Jenn Nalynn found the changed light more ominous than magnificent, as if the sky tried to warn those heedless below.

The fish had burnt and turn was nigh and their guest being late for both wasn't rude, from Nonny's pricklish mood and brooding stares inland, but a dire worry.

The turn came, finding quick motions and bright eyes in the fishing village and shore. Mimrol welled up, but, unlike yesterday, Nonny made no move to strip and dive for it. Instead, before the turn reached the *Good Igrini*, she put up her hood and went to the ladder. "Keep hidden," she told Jenn, adding a muttered, "Fool man," under her breath as she climbed the couple of rungs to the dock. Darting into the shadows, a shadow herself, Nonny went to the shack, only to fly out again within a heartbeat, leaving the door ajar, and took the path to Shadesport at a run.

As she watched, Jenn circled her fingers and thumb over her head, supper being the time for a beholding, even if the food was spoilt. "Hearts of my Ancestors, I'm Beholden for the help of my friend Nonny and ask you keep her safe. As I ask the same for Urcet, who might be worse than late. I'd be Beholden if you'd watch Werfol and help him be brave, and to please find a way to let Bannan know where I am and that I'll come home tomorrow." Which she didn't make a prayer, it being up to the toad queen and powers untried and factors surely beyond her Ancestors Dear and Departed. "However far we are apart, Keep Us Close."

The turn arrived as she prayed. Jenn became a light of her own, however briefly, a light caught in the huge eye of a curious basker and surely visible for a distance, explaining Nonny's good and reasonable advice to hide herself.

Too late now. Seeing no boats away from their docks, Jenn relaxed. The turn passed her by.

She took the fish, more charcoal than flesh, from the box. Breaking it in half revealed some of the insides weren't burnt at all, so Jenn scraped those out, saving most for Nonny and Urcet, but tasting some for herself. The seasonings were different than she'd experienced—as was the fish, for that matter, with rich flesh that left a slick feeling in her mouth—but the sum was delicious.

The inedible charred bits she left where Nonny had shown her, in the bucket for bait.

Earlier, she'd drained her potatoes and mashed them with some of Nonny's unusual butter, pleased with the result. Jenn filled a bowl with the orange stuff and added more of her portion of the cooked fish. She took her supper on the deck, sitting on the gunnel to eat, though she paid less and less attention to the food.

Where was Nonny? Why had she run?

Shadesport lit lanterns to hang from posts and at the side of doorways. More of the soft yellow light peered through slits in windows. Curtains, Jenn decided, having not noticed this before and thinking curtains something Rhothans and the Eld had in common—

~Elder sister.~

A waalum. Jenn swung her leg over the gunnel as she'd seen

Nonny do and looked for the little cousin. Spotted it bobbing in water that reflected the village lights, much too close to hunters.

Worse, too close to her. "Go away!" she ordered. "It's dangerous near me!" Grief bowed her head. "The waalum who saved me yesterday died for it. Please, you must stay away."

To her growing dismay, Jenn saw two more of the rare little cousins had joined the first. ~Elder sister, come with us!~

It was like arguing with a house toad. The trio bobbed up and down in synchrony, their huge eyes locked on her, and whatever was she to do with them? It wasn't as if, Ancestors Witness, she could throw rotten apples at them, the way she'd chased away Roche when they'd been children—much to Wainn's pony's delight—nor did such powerful and important creatures seem the sort to enjoy the nastiness in the bait bucket, though they might.

She'd not, Jenn decided, take the chance. "Go!"

~The walker-with-treats is in grave danger, elder sister!~ A deeper tone to this voice. ~We cannot reach them.~

The first voice again, ~You can! Hurry, elder sister!~

Walker-with-treats. Easy to imagine Urcet earning that name by trying to entice the waalum to shore. He'd tried, as had the dema, to catch a house toad—

Jenn got to her feet, leaving the bowl on the gunnel, and leaned over the water. "I won't risk harm to you."

The necklace leaned as well, aiming at the water and, all at once, exerting a force in that direction as if to pull her in! Grabbing it, Jenn jumped back. "Stop that!"

~It is not our doing, elder sister.~ A waalum stroked its big flippers, rising higher in the water. ~Swim with us——~

Wisp was far more reasonable. ~I won't risk it. The toad queen—she'll hurt you.~

~Then you must walk.~ With disapproval, the waalum plainly considering her desire to protect them neither important nor wise.

That didn't, Jenn reminded herself, make her wrong. "And go where?" she asked.

~The far shore.~

She looked up and across the bay. Twilight now, the moon yet to rise, but—there. A lantern. More than one, and moving. They shone like wicked little eyes.

Waalum hunters.

~Make haste, elder sister. Save the walker-with-treats!~

Jenn glanced wildly at the village. Heart's Blood—if Nonny didn't trust them, how could she?

An enormous mouth broke the surface in the distance; it wasn't alone. The boat rocked, a second basker moving beneath.

The boat.

She'd apologize to Nonny later.

"Little cousins, I need your help."

"I can't lie. I tell you I was dead," Roche protested.

"You dreamed it," the beautiful—and scary—woman assured him, tucking a third blanket around him, for he shivered uncontrollably and, despite the fireplace cheerfully burning nearby and heated bricks at his feet, was convinced he'd never feel warm again.

"My heart—" He looked beyond her to where Bannan sat nearby, resting his bandaged leg on a stool. "I felt it fail. I know I did."

The truthseer smiled and raised a glass of amber liquid. "Our good healer calls it seriously strained, but as you're young, you'll recover—given rest."

"Which I order," the woman commanded, her voice low and potent. She opened her hand, showing a small vial. "Roche, this is the potion I use, to sleep and truedream."

Roche flinched. "I mustn't dream again—"

"No. At least, not yet," with an assessing look. The vial disappeared into a pocket of the jerkin she wore over light armor, for the Baroness Lila Larmensu Westietas dressed for war. She held out her hand, and her husband the baron stepped forward with a cup. "This, on the other hand, contains a draught to ensure you won't. It contains a wishing that temporarily smothers a gift. One with which my brother is regrettably familiar."

Bannan made a face. "I promise it works."

Ancestors Blessed. To close his eyes and sleep without fear—"I'll still tell the truth," Roche warned them, eyes riveted on the cup. "That's not my gift, it's Jenn's, to make me better than I was, and it has, I swear. But you can't trust me with secrets. I can't keep them safe." Hearing himself, he found an excuse. "My friends will worry— the school—" He tried to move.

Lila's touch kept him still, but Roche couldn't stop. "I have to leave."

Emon gazed down at him. "What are you studying?"

Lila put the cup in his hand as words fell from his mouth. "Engineering. I want to make things that matter. That last. Like Vorkoun's bridges," Roche finished, face hot and embarrassed to his core.

The baron's face filled with sudden interest. Seeing it, the baroness snorted. "Heart's Blood. Another one."

Confused, Roche lowered the cup. "You don't seem like fools. Surely you see I mustn't stay here."

"Quite the contrary, Roche," Emon countered. "Stay as long as you wish. You've no idea how much I look forward to the company of a fellow tinkerer who is an honest man—and potential colleague, Baron Morrill."

Defeated by kindness, Roche sagged back against the pillows. "Even if somehow I am a baron, I don't know how to be. I wouldn't listen to my mother's stories about Avyo and the courts. They made me angry. Angrier."

"Drink," Lila told him. Her smile developed an edge. "Anger can be power."

"Lila—" Bannan closed his mouth, shaking his head.

"I've heard everything you told us, little brother." Her eyes softened. "Trust I plan no hasty misadventure. Thanks to you, we know to avoid the edge until ready—which you are not. Our resources muster as we speak. I've sent my birds with urgent messages to those in Vorkoun and elsewhere. We will be ready before the hour Werfol said she'll strike."

Taking all this in, Semyn sat quietly at the table by the window, his gaze going from person to person, his face calm and composed. A grave nod acknowledged Roche's attention.

A house toad like any in Marrowdell sat on the boy's lap, its big eyes closed. Roche wanted to ask but was afraid to know. No doubt, if he stayed, he'd hear the story of the toad and more about the Westietas, a ghastly responsibility they appeared willing to dump on his shoulders.

He wanted, with a sudden desperate longing, to learn from this remarkable child, this baron-to-be, who listened to his parents' plan to delay the rescue of his little brother with more self-control and composure than he'd had in his entire life.

If he stayed—

"The cup, Roche," Bannan reminded him.

The drink tasted like the sour medicine their mother would give him and Devins at the first sign of a cough, meaning it tasted of home and love; Roche drank it eagerly and was sorry to be done.

"Nothing from this world will help," he heard himself say then. "You need Jenn Nalynn's magic."

Bannan's eyes shot to his, molten gold; Roche looked away, unable to bear the naked emotion exposed in the truthseer's face, but didn't stop, for he couldn't.

Tried to keep his eyes open, but the lids drifted shut as he spoke. "Without her, there's no hope for any of us."

The pale palace was deserted. The dragons flew through winding corridors, wingtips brushing dust from the walls, unchallenged.

Being a fool, the youngling grew brave, landing to push its head through an open archway. It roared, only to be sorely startled by its own echo and crash into a wall.

Wisp didn't laugh.

He listened, but there was nothing to hear. Sniffed, catching a fleeting hint of dried leather and fresh blood. Used his eyes most of all, unwilling to risk setting foot anywhere here.

If there were traps, let the youngling stumble into them.

The immense towers were hollow inside and connected, as if they'd grown from the centermost with no plan or reason obvious to a dragon. The highest portions featured airy ledges open to the sky, the sort dragons liked for basking, but no dragon would live here.

Down and down they went, around and around they flew, the corridors always the same width, sloped and twisting like intestines. In places, ceilings were hung with slender spikes and hooks. The youngling gave them a worried look and wide berth; Wisp recognized them as how yling supported their cities, but no yling would live here.

Peculiar and puzzling, to find places fit for company, as the girl would say. The dragon began to watch for more, discovering wide rooms floored in dried-up pools that would have held mimrol before the toad queen drank it all for herself, pools a pleasing home for some.

There were rooms sized for terst, empty and bare, and great pots for what grew, filled with dry powdery dust.

The toad queen had robbed this place of life as much as magic, and Wisp found himself consumed with rage as much as grief. He flew faster, determined to find her before she alerted to their trespass, the youngling straining to keep up.

They reached where the towers merged, ending at a rare solidness of the Verge, and could go no further without flying through the earth.

It was an empty, hollow place, lit through cracks foretelling the demise of the arches and ceilings and walls above.

In the center of the open space was a ball, suspended by no obvious means in midair, easily overlooked, for it was the size and shape of a marble the girl had brought to their meadow to show him, a toy made of hard glass and color.

Perhaps mistaking it for an eye, the youngling went to eat it.

~Do not,~ Wisp commanded.

Size and shape meant nothing here.

Avoiding the uncanny ball, filled with sudden unease, Wisp let himself land, lightly, lightly. When his feet touched, the ground gave and the scent of dried leather and fresh blood surged up, as if he'd disturbed a crust keeping it back.

The youngling descended. Wisp snarled a quick denial. ~Stay aloft.~

He eyed the floor. Pressed and pulled with a single claw. Came away with a withered scrap of dragon hide.

He stood on unfathomable carnage.

A drop of fresh-seeming blood clung to the scrap, the healing magic of a dragon the last to fade. A magic stolen!

All at once, a forest of whipping tendrils rose up around him, to harm not heal, aimed for his heart.

Her trap! She'd sprung it, but where was she?

Wisp deflected the tendrils, gave them his crippled foot and leg to toy with, thought furiously.

~How do I help, Great Lord of Dragons?~

~Don't distract me,~ he growled, though he was now, by the unprecedented offer. Any other dragon would seize the advantage and attack him, or flee to save itself.

Teach it, the sei had ordered.

He hadn't taught it this—*unless he had?*

Of course not. The youngling must be, as he'd suspected, deficient in proper instincts. Still, Wisp found himself unwilling to throw away its life. Much as it pained him, he looked up at the youngling and delivered his command. ~Return to Marrowdell. Tell the elder sister what we've found.~

It twisted its neck to bring an eye to bear on him, wings beating. ~What have we found, lord?~

A floor no dragon could fly through, a trap no dragon could escape.

~It doesn't matter. Tell her to send the villagers to the road beyond the edge.~

It might save them from the queen.

It might not, should the mad sei join the battle and tear their worlds asunder.

~I will do it. Then I will come back for you!~ the youngling proclaimed, valiant, if short-sighted.

~Do not.~ Tendrils clutched his shoulders and wings. *PULLED.* Wisp resisted, holding his place, bones cracking. ~You have a greater purpose. Earn yourself a name, youngling. Stay in Marrowdell. Fight with the little cousins and small ones.~ Wisp let fire fill his mouth. ~Die well.~

~YES, GREAT LORD OF DRAGONS! YES!~ With a roar of joy, the youngling whirled in midair and flew up and away. ~A NAME! A NAME!~ Suddenly faltered as if trapped itself.

Wisp threw a blast of wind to send it up and away. Silly creature. Should they survive, he supposed he'd have to name it, unless the girl would, for him.

Now. To the toad queen.

With a roar, he stopped resisting the *PULL* and went with it instead, flying where she wanted him to fall, through the floor of hides and death magic, a force greater than any dragon before him.

Springing a trap of his own.

TWENTY

*T*RAVELING BY BOAT, Jenn discovered, was not only easier than swimming across so much open water but decidedly quicker, the baskers more enthused about the game of "nudge the boat" than she might have expected. To the point where she'd have been alarmed, but the waalum assured her the giants were gentle and merely enjoying themselves, this a form of play they did together in the deep.

Leading Jenn to wonder what other wondrous things took place beneath the surface where people couldn't see, so when they reached the middle of the bay, she hurried to the bow and leaned well over, hoping to glimpse the lights of those living below. She couldn't, of course, from this high above—which was another strange way to think about water—and there was a white froth leading the boat, thanks to the baskers' speed, blocking much of the view. Trails of glowing blue-green spread out, altogether beautiful—

Jenn sank back on her knees, arms crossed on the prow, to watch the far shore approach. A splash caught her attention and she glanced down again.

A big dark body swam powerfully alongside. It leapt clear and dived into the froth. A second took its place. Were the waalum leading the way, despite her warning to keep clear, or was this, too, their form of play?

Her dearest and oldest friend Wisp loathed water with a passion and would grumble at the lovely drops of morning dew; he wouldn't enjoy this. Resting her chin on her arms, the warm night air teasing at Nonny's braidwork, Jenn thought of Bannan, who would. Of how this moment would be absolutely perfect if he were here, with his arms around her—

And, of course, Werfol home where he belonged, and Urcet not in danger—

But hadn't Aunt Sybb said it was more important to dream of good things and hope for better, than to dwell on what wasn't and mightn't be?

Advice, decided Jenn, well suited to the quandaries of being turn-born. Thinking happy thoughts about those she loved, even when apart, gave her the patience to wait. That she would make a wish—that it must be tomorrow at the equinox and any choice fraught with danger—wasn't in question.

She tried not to think of what lay ahead tonight, which was.

The distant shore came closer and closer, until the moonlight slipping past the clouds showed her the shapes of rocks and cliffs and trees. Nothing of Urcet. Those with him had doused their lights or gone into some shelter.

Jenn trusted the waalum to know where to send her. The curved knife Nonny had tried to press on her remained in the cabin. She'd neither skill nor inclination to use it, unlike Bannan's warrior-sister. Lila might, it occurred to her suddenly, appreciate such a gift.

She'd keep it for her.

~Prepare to jump, elder sister. You will have to swim to shore.~

Seeing the waves crashing into the rocks should, Jenn thought wryly, have forewarned her. At least her new clothes would be easier to swim in than her old. The boat slowed, the baskers abandoning it to follow the tide out to the sea, and she wished she knew how to thank them.

She stepped up on the gunnel, arms out for balance. She'd jump, Jenn decided, swallowing hard. Like everyone did, into the trout pond on a hot summer afternoon. Leap as far out as she could, arms around her knees, and hit the water as a ball.

She drew a deep breath.

The sea boiled in every direction! The *Good Igrini* creaked and groaned, as if fighting her fate, and Jenn had no more time to think, only jump.

When she surfaced, the boat was gone. Bits and pieces of Nonny's precious gear swirled in the whirlpool where it had been, and she swam as quickly as she could away, not to be sucked down as well.

How could she have forgotten? The toad queen's obscene trophies hadn't only been stuffed toys, skulls, and hides.

She'd collected boats as well.

"I've a present for you, little one."

It might be someone he truly didn't want to be here, or a nasty surprise. Whatever it was would be to the majesty-monster's advantage, not his, and Werfol stayed in his tight little curl, arms around his knees. "No, thank you. I don't want it."

Goosie's seam split open, dumping him out on the sand, taking his choice away.

It had been worth a try, as Momma would say.

Werfol jumped to his feet, finding himself alone, but that was a lie. The majesty-monster simply played her favorite boring game and hid under the sand.

He looked quickly around. Uncle Bannan and Roche had been at a distance.

This time, her surprise was at his feet.

Werfol picked up the toy boat. It was of wood and shabby, with splintered holes in its hull. Where her claws had grabbed it, he decided, feeling queasy as he brought what wasn't a toy at all but a real fishing boat to his eyes. "Is anyone here?" he whispered, trying to see inside.

Then pulled back hastily. Ancestors Dense and Difficult. A giant eyeball peering in wasn't at all reassuring. He should know. "I'm sorry."

The boat seemed empty and sad. Werfol set it down carefully, arranging the sand to hold it upright.

For naught, as the majesty-monster surged up from her hiding place. Werfol grabbed to save the little boat only to have it slide away. Fought to keep his feet, only to be tossed this way and that as if the sand had become an ocean. Covered his ears as the majesty-monster hissed like the biggest kettle in the world and, through his very natural alarm at all this commotion, felt a leap of hope.

The majesty-monster wasn't happy, wasn't smug. Was—if his eyes didn't deceive him and this wasn't another of her tricks—writhing in pain, falling over on her side with all four tree-sized legs flailing, her trophies flying off and through the air.

Werfol ducked as a skull sailed past him. Lunged to grab Goosie and—there, the boat!

Everything stopped. He waited, panting. Was it Jenn?

Suddenly, the majesty-monster's stomach bulged, swelling like an enormous hideous balloon, *something* struggling under the skin—

She POPPED!

And out flew a dragon, roaring with rage and covered in gore.

It wasn't the green dragon from his story. This was—

"WISP!" Werfol shouted, on his feet and waving the toys, so glad tears poured down his face and he didn't care one bit. "There's your comeuppance, Stupid Monster!" Momma said never taunt a fallen enemy but he couldn't help it. "TAKE THAT!"

And everything would have been perfect, except the gaping hole in her belly began to seal itself and Wisp to tumble from the sky, and he heard her dreadful horrible voice ask in her nasty, coy way.

"Do you want your new present, little one?

"OR SHALL I SKIN AND EAT IT?"

There'd be rest but no sleep this night for any but Roche, who'd succumbed to the gift-numbing draught and snored peaceful as a babe, reported the healer. Who'd stay at his side, implying concern for the young man's heart remained.

He was glad for Roche's sake, but there'd be a conversation, Bannan vowed grimly. He might have guessed Lila would learn the spell Lurgan had used on him in Channen and add it to her arsenal. But the other—the one to enslave a truthseeker's will and gift—Ancestors Beset and Besieged, surely his sister had it destroyed.

A conversation that had to wait.

They'd cleared the oval table, moving it to the middle of the room to continue their work as sunset approached and they lost the light. Answering his heart, Bannan stood and went to the windows to watch the last beams sift through the forest and down the slopes. The light from the Verge didn't reach beyond the edge, behind the house.

If he closed his eyes, he could see it shine inside his love, like the glow of her warm and wonderful heart.

Where was she now, at this moment?

Far, far away.

Of course Jenn had come after him and Scourge—how not? To be trapped even as he'd fussed about the fall of their mother's house and stumbled in the dark.

Far, far away.

Most of the world was. The truthseer didn't dare look at Emon's magnificent globe on its stand in a corner. Hardly dared take breath, lest he believe Jenn truly and forever lost—

A touch on his elbow, the telling fragrance of leather and fresh oil. Bannan roused to put his arm around his sister, the pair gazing into twilight.

"I'd 'dream Werfol," she whispered, her voice terrifyingly calm. "Every time, what I saw through his eyes was either the blinding madness of the Verge or utter darkness. Over and over."

"Remember the stuffed toy Werfol brought from Marrowdell? The—bird?" A charitable description, the thing loved to anonymity. "The toad queen keeps him inside it."

Pulling away, Lila stared at him, her expression fortunately in shadow. "Goosie? But it's—" Her hands cupped a small space.

"House toads can change the size of things. So can their queen." He sighed. "Werfol believes he's safe from harm. I saw the truth in his face. That's still no reason to—Lila—Dear Heart—I—" He hadn't told her he was sorry. There weren't enough words in the world for how much—

"Hush," she chided, refusing to hear them. "I trust our sons. Don't think for an instant we haven't prepared them to be taken hostage. Werfol understands he has value to his captor. Up to a point and certain to expire, yes, but he knows to gather information while he can. Didn't he brief you, brother, with what we have to know to save him?" With pride.

"He's a little boy," Bannan protested.

"He's *my* son."

He conceded her point with a nod, taking heart from it. Glimpsed their reflections in the window, the world dark beyond, comforted by kinship. The same shape to their faces, their mother's heritage. Their father's nose. Lila's eyes, like their mother's, were vivid green; his—when not gold—brown with dark flecks. When not in a tight Ansnan-style battle braid, her hair tumbled in a mist of brown curls. Though delicate in frame, beneath Lila was whipcord and steel. Her head came to his ear.

He'd despaired of being taller until a final growth spurt, when he'd gained breadth and weight as well. Not that either helped when sparring. They'd the same reach, but Lila?

Fought to win, and usually did. Even when he cheated. Especially then.

Emon poured over lists at the table, eating one-handed while murmuring to himself. His crows, Scatterwit and Cheek, slept on their perches, having done their work by day. Lila's birds, bred to fly home even in the dark, continued to travel, conveying messages back and forth. Those already received curled in piles, like shavings. Every so often, Emon would dig one out to check against his lists. They left nothing to chance or guess in this world.

The Verge beyond their reach.

Lila drew her forces to her, a few from here, a couple from there, no single mustering sufficient to call attention or raise alarm, but the sum should be, as she'd put it, *adequate*. To deter the more ambitious among their non-magical enemies, ever ready to take advantage of disruption.

To cover a needful retreat, Lila preparing for that as well.

Semyn had gone to bed, Dutton staying with him to be company on a troubled night, as much as protector.

Emon's gaze shifted their way every few moments. Bannan didn't take it amiss. A long-standing habit, to watch for Lila's signals, even here and now and safe.

Did he not do the same?

"I admit to curiosity, Brother. What have you brought?" Lila nodded to the bundle he'd left on a chair.

What he'd been frankly astonished had stayed in his coat pockets, after the toad queen's second attack and crossing with Edis. On changing into clean clothes from the assortment Lila kept for him here, he'd wrapped the assortment in his old shirt to bring here, oddly loath to carry them in the open or leave them in his room.

"What you need to see." Leaving the window, he collected the bundle and brought it to the table.

Emon rose and Lila came to stand beside him.

The truthseer looked from one to the other. "Roche Morrill mustn't know of these or what I'm about to tell you."

Emon's high forehead creased. "You disagree with my invitation."

"I respect the power of Jenn's wish. So should you. Roche wasn't just angry. He was full of rage. He grew up a compulsive liar and disruptive influence. As far as I know, no one in Marrowdell ever knew he suffered from dreadful premonitions."

And didn't that explain a great deal, a boy growing up afflicted, without help.

Bannan steeled himself and continued, "When Jenn lost her patience with his lies, she did more than make him truthful. Roche is as compelled to tell the truth now as once he was to twist it to suit himself. Much as he would wish otherwise—for under it all I believe he has a good heart—that includes any and every secret he learns."

His sister's lips quirked. Emon smiled as if reassured. "Good," he said. "One day in the House of Keys and he'll hear what none of them want known outside those walls. The baseless slanders. The futile postering. I'll wager if Roche shares the least of it, our fellow barons will realize they have to do honest work or keep quiet so others can."

"Or," Bannan cautioned, "he'll be assassinated."

Lila moved her head slowly from side to side, her green eyes—so like Roche's—glinting. A promise, that was, and the truthseer glimpsed what should prove a very interesting future ahead for the lad from Marrowdell.

Should they survive the toad queen's plot.

Shrugging off a chill, Bannan brought forth the key. Taking it from the thong around his neck, he set it on the table. "Speaking of keys . . ." He paused, looking at his sister. "Touch it."

Her long fingers brushed the key, eyes widening. "It speaks."

Emon tried it and shook his head. "Not to me. What did it say?"

"Our family name. Larmensu." Her eyebrow lifted. "Why? What does it open?"

A topic he chose to evade, for now. "The important thing is the key calls for aid for any Larmensu from those given matching charms. Father gave one to Tagey. And to Ioana."

Emon grimaced. "Ancestors Witness, I owe Cook an apology. When she burst into my meeting claiming a Larmensu needed help, I judged her forgetful with age, that she meant Werfol—or Lila—" His fingers found his wife's hand. "Until, that is, the first pigeon arrived with Tagey's message about you, Bannan."

"Old maybe," Lila commented dryly. "The Ioana I know has a mind sharp as my sword." A lift of a brow acknowledged Bannan's evasion; accepted it, for now. "Who else has a charm, Brother? Mistress Adrianna, surely."

As he'd thought. When he shook his head, did Lila's eyes narrow? The truthseer went on, "Jarratt and Ignace. Our parents' personal staff," for Emon's benefit. "They perished with the house."

"Can a charm be used by someone else?"

Trust Lila to see opportunity.

"I don't know. There's more." Bannan opened the bundle, revealing the lantern, two boxes of wishings, and the key box.

Lila touched each in turn, nodding after each. Done, she picked up the key and aimed it at Bannan. "What's all this?"

"I found them in the ruins of our family home." He nudged the key box with a finger. "This was in a secret passage next to our parents' bedroom."

"Heart's Blood!" Her eyes fairly glowed. "I knew there had to be one! How did you find it?" With gratifying pique.

Bannan didn't quite grin. "Scourge sniffed it out," he admitted. "Look." He opened the lantern.

Emon leaned in to inspect it, his eyes glittering in its light. "I've not seen the like in Channen."

"It wasn't made there," the truthseer confirmed. The baron's eyebrows rose.

"And these?" Lila waved at the boxes.

He opened one, showing the contents: a vial of silver liquid, a wizened black pit, a sliver of bone, the scrap of paper.

"A wishing," Emon identified grimly. "But for what?"

"This one? An ever-faithful wife." Bannan closed the box. "I found racks of them hidden in a storeroom beneath the house. I can't say if any are real,"—other than wine bottles full of mimrol; a revelation for another time—"but it's clear our family was in the token business."

His sister stilled, hardly seeming to breathe, her face expressionless. Reframing a lifetime of memories, at a guess. Hadn't he done it? The conversations overheard, the visitors who came and went.

They'd lived in a house of secrets.

Bannan turned his hand palm up, sweeping it over the display. "The home built by our mother's ancestors—our family home—is as much in the edge between our world and the Verge as Marrowdell. Magic is our rightful heritage." He brought out the toad queen's cursed gift and spread it on the table.

Lila took a tiny quick breath; from anyone else, it'd be a shout.

"And magic," he went on grimly, a finger pinning the scarf their mother had loved and worn often, recognized by a former Ansnan soldier as part of a catastrophic spell, "is what brought our house down."

~Let us help, elder sister.~

The waalum, distressed and anxious, kept pace with her shoreward strokes, risking themselves. "No," Jenn managed to sputter. "Thank—you."

Once again she fought a tidal current determined to sweep her out to sea, but this time Jenn was ready for it. Slowly she moved closer and closer to where waves crashed against black, slimy rocks. Jagged rocks with sharp edges like teeth, quite unlike the rocks on Nonny's side of the bay, making her arrival there and not here a very good thing.

Yet here she was.

A small relief, the necklace no longer pulled her down, implying it was content to be in the water or slept.

Closer in, the current eased, confused perhaps by the rocks. The waves swelled at the same time, letting her see where she was going, then hiding it. Those on land should have the same difficulty seeing her.

~Pick a big wave and ride it in and up, elder sister. Watch. We'll show you.~

Jenn moved her arms and legs to stay in one place, giving up the effort to argue with the creatures. To be honest, their presence was her sole comfort, though she now had to worry about hunters on shore.

Who'd best worry about her, she told herself, grim and resolved.

A waalum broke the surface beside her, waiting, letting wave after wave lift and lower them.

Without warning it drove its tail powerfully in the water, propelling it forward as the next wave, much larger, arrived. Catching the wave's crest, it rode it into shore, and just when Jenn thought for certain the waalum would crash on the rocks, the water deposited the large creature neatly atop one.

Where it proceeded to scrape the rock with its formidable teeth, presumably—though she couldn't see in this light—grazing on seaweed, much like a cow.

A second waalum surfaced. ~Go with me, elder sister.~

She wasn't at all sure she could swim fast enough to catch a wave, but having no choice, Jenn prepared herself.

~Now!~

She threw herself forward, arms moving, legs kicking with all her might. Suddenly, she felt the wave lift her up, thrusting her ahead faster than swimming alone. Exhilarated, she almost forgot about the rocks—

~Change, elder sister!~

—as turn-born, Jenn met the rock. It cracked and gave as she tumbled and bounced, then slid a good distance back again, the rocks slick. The next wave arrived, tossing her further up. Before it could drag her back with it, she changed to flesh and grabbed for the bush overhead.

A bush that, though stunted, must have endured tides and storms for years, requiring deep and strong roots—or so she had to hope, using it to pull herself to solid, dry ground.

Drier, Jenn realized as a wave crashed the rocks, sending spray to drench her. She scrambled higher.

No sign of lights.

~Elder sister?~

The waalum remained nearby, one grazing peacefully, the others showing as watchful eyes, bobbing up and down in the water some distance out.

Not far enough. "Ancestors Blessed, I'm beholden for your help, little cousins, but please, you must go," she urged. "Hide—" Jenn stopped, distracted.

The necklace. It tugged at her neck, harder and stronger than ever, as if determined to return her to the bay. Jenn pulled it off before it could.

The shells stuck out like rigid little fingers, aimed at the waalum on the rock. On impulse, Jenn stepped back on the wet rocks, easing closer to the creature. Who was, this near and out of the water, very much larger and utterly strange.

But a friend. "What is this?" However much she wanted to know, Jenn took care not to wish them to answer. "Please."

The waves seemed to still. Moonlight gilded the bay, glinted in the unblinking regard of the waalum's eyes, and Jenn held her breath, knowing this was important.

~It is what fills you, elder sister,~ with a note of puzzlement.

Without question, Jenn thought wryly, waalum shared the house toads' assumptions of what she knew of their world. "What fills me," she replied cautiously, "are a sei's tears."

~Yes, elder sister.~

Jenn stared down at the shells in her hand. They felt light as air, no longer pulling toward waalum or water, as if content.

Or relieved.

Or neither or both—sei, in her experience, rarely made sense to those who weren't sei, at least not in the moment and not always afterwards.

Ancestors Perplexed and Perturbed.

She was sei, as the waalum declared, as much as flesh and glass. Raising the necklace, Jenn examined a shell. It had two parts, like Nonny's oyster, and what looked like a hinge on one side, like Aunt Sybb's locket.

The locket held a minuscule portrait of her husband, their Uncle Hane. Peggs and Jenn took their aunt's word for its being an excellent likeness, though privately agreed the painting might have been of their father, or even Zehr Emms.

The point being, the necklace's shells might contain *something*. It did seem unlikely a sei—at times mountain-sized—could fit inside, though her moths came and went from the palms of her hands.

Really, she'd no proper sense of a sei's size at all.

The waalum waited. A little crab tiptoed over Jenn's foot. The party from the fishing village—with Urcet their prisoner—would be coming.

While she contemplated a shell.

Jenn's lips twitched.

Nothing for it but open one and see.

Sorry, now, to have left Nonny's clever knife behind, Jenn pried at the shell. To no avail. Nibbling a broken fingernail, she eyed the shell, glistening in the moonlight.

Smashing it with a rock felt disrespectful, if not foolhardy.

With a sigh, Jenn went to put the necklace around her neck, a mystery to take away and solve later.

~Elder sister? If you wish the shell to open, should you not ask it?~

Out of the fanged mouths of—not that waalum, any more than toads or dragons, spoke with their mouths—but Jenn dipped her head in gratitude. "Thank you, most esteemed little—"

A hand seized her, thrust her aside. A greedy whisper, "Symyd be right t'send us'here. T'be waalum! Scads o'm!"

Two others appeared, these aiming spears like giant forks, and as the waalum in front of her lunged for the water, trying to escape—

Jenn Nalynn said, "No."

And made a wish.

Having tried very hard to call a dragon, Werfol told himself to be grateful to receive one, even if not the one he'd planned. Quite possibly, he should be sorry to have done so, since now Wisp was trapped with him and might still, according to the majesty-monster, being meaner than usual, become her supper.

But how could he be sorry, having company and a friend with him at last?

Admittedly, sharing Goosie with a dragon wasn't comfortable, Wisp being mostly sharp and inclined to snarl if crowded. Worse, he wouldn't answer a single question or even play riddles, that being something Werfol had thought dragons might like and having made up several while waiting for his.

Who was here, if rightfully not friendly about it.

The little truthseer sighed and curled into a tighter, smaller ball of woe.

Wisp, he thought, had reason to complain. The dragon suffered, body and pride badly bruised, and had more important concerns than to entertain a sadly bored child. He vowed not to bother him again.

A tear escaped his eye.

A tiny whisper of a breeze stole the little droplet, then found his ear. "Has she harmed you?" With a not-tiny, quite ominous growl.

Werfol cheered at once. "The majesty-monster? No." Unless he counted being kept away from his family and scared, but those weren't, he guessed, what the dragon meant.

"'Majesty-monster'?" with amusement. "Ah, the toads' queen."

"She—Is—Not!" Werfol contradicted, in his outrage forgetting about manners or who might overhear. "The majesty-monster doesn't care for anything or anyone else and thinks she's SO impressive and SO important even though she's not. She's awful. Toads," he finished decisively, "aren't like that."

"Curious, isn't it?"

Which was exactly the right thing to say, because Werfol understood at once that Wisp agreed with him and, moreover, Wisp had questions of his own about the majesty-monster and what she claimed to be. Relieved, he stretched out his hand.

The dragon shifted hastily so what his fingers found was a hide covered in scales as fine as linen, and not claw or fang. It pulsed with deep, steady breaths, alive and safe.

Without hesitation or second thought, Werfol tucked himself against the dragon. "I'm very glad you're here, Wisp," he whispered, closing his eyes. "So very glad."

He felt something hard but sinuous slip around his legs and feet, pulling him close. Felt a breath like the embers from a fire.

"As am I, Dear Heart."

He'd more to tell them, starting with the Ansnan tunnels beneath the house, but reading his face, Lila shook her head. "Not now, Brother." She waved him to put away the objects, though her fingers brushed the key a final time. "We haven't time to be distracted by the past," she dismissed. "Unless you found anything to help us rescue Werfol?"

"What's below the house would but feed the toad queen." Bannan tied the key around his neck and wrapped the boxes in his shirt. About to put away the lantern, he pushed it to Emon instead, who tucked it out of sight with a determined little nod. He'd have its secrets in short order, of that Bannan had no doubt, and be able to match the maker to anything else they might find.

Lila, taking this as permission, reached for the scarf. The truthseer put out a hand to stop her. "This isn't what it seems," he cautioned, eyes turning gold as he stared down at it, confirming what he'd seen earlier. To his deeper sight, vile red threads desecrated the Larmensu crest, distorting its sunflower and blinding the fox. "A spell's been sewn into it. Maybe more than one," he added.

Her fingers curled but didn't withdraw. "It was Momma's," faintly, and oh, the pain in that.

Pain he shared, but pushed aside. "I didn't find this in our home. It was given to me by the toad queen—I'd no idea why and, Ancestors Unwary and Undone, no thought to look past what it was and meant to me, to see what it is. A trap."

Lila's tiny shrug absolved him. She gave him a sharp look, not missing the implication. "What made you look now?"

"I received a warning." Tucking the scarf in a pocket, Bannan sat, followed by the other two, and lowered his voice. Not that they'd eavesdroppers other than Ryll Aronom, Lila's seniormost guard, standing by the closed door, but his news was dire.

"I told you Roche and I were saved from the toad queen—and sent here—at Werfol's order. I didn't say how." The truthseer paused, but there was no saner way to say it. "Roche summoned help, a friend able to cross from the Verge. Her name is Edis and she's a woman. Or rather, she was."

Silence, thick and slightly appalled, filled the room. Even Ryll stiffened.

The truthseer smiled grimly. "Not a Blessed Ancestor or haunt, I swear. Edis was somehow changed into a magical creature, one at home in the Verge. And the earth," he said thoughtfully, that being true as well. "What matters to us here and now is Edis resisted the full might of the toad queen. Briefly."

Lila's eyes narrowed at his qualification.

He'd known she'd catch that. "The toad queen steals magic at every chance. Her intention is to take it all, from everyone she can catch." He moved his finger between Lila and himself. Saw her mentally add Werfol to the list and begin to frown. "We're safe as long as we're beyond the edge."

Unless, Heart's Blood, the monster broke free at tomorrow's turn and changed the rules, a concern neither helpful nor, Bannan reminded himself, theirs alone.

At this table, Werfol was. "When Edis answered Roche and came to his aid, she'd barely time to flee with two of us before the queen drained too much from her. Edis has gone to where she can restore herself. She's promised to go back for Werfol when summoned."

Faces brightened. Letting out an exaggerated sigh, Emon wagged an accusing finger. "You might have started there, brother of my wife."

Lila lost her smile. "An Ansnan name. Who was Edis?"

He'd never been able to keep the truth from her. "A soldier. One who knew me as Captain Ash."

"Yet was willing to help?" Emon showed his doubt.

"The toad queen's her enemy, too." Bannan's lips twitched. "And she listens to Werfol."

The baron's face cleared. "A good sign."

His sister's expression was impossible to read. Bannan kept his similarly bland. Lila might guess he planned to go with Edis tomorrow, to do whatever it took to distract the toad queen and aid the boy's escape. She mustn't suspect he'd no intention of escaping himself.

Wherever she was now, Jenn Nalynn would come at the Balance to save Werfol and vanquish the toad queen. Bannan knew it in his heart. When she did, he'd be there. To tell her the boy was safe. To help however he could.

To be with his love once more, no matter the outcome.

"Speaking of Ansnans," his sister said, lifting a finger to stir the guard from her post. "Ryll, invite Master Setac to dine with us in the small room." She looked at Bannan. "Time, Brother, you met Semyn and Werfol's latest tutor." Her smile was the one to send a shiver down any spine. "A man claiming loyalty to no one domain, who knows our world is not so simple as most believe. He speaks of unseen forces at play, some peaceful, others disruptive, and some as yet undeclared."

Heart's Blood. The truthseer tensed. "A dangerous man, then." In this house, near his nephews—though their father, he noticed abruptly, looked unperturbed.

"I'll let you discover that, dear brother, for us all. For a bonus, I believe cook's prepared your favorite treat: cobbledeedo. We'll enjoy some with our—conversation."

If Lila sought to distract him from the prospect of this stranger with regrettable knowledge, it would take more than a word from the past, albeit a rare happy one. Bannan frowned a warning.

One Lila deliberately ignored.

A lesser dragon would have railed against captivity, thrashing about in powerful, futile protest proving nothing. Harming the child.

Being, as he was, the greatest of dragons, Wisp remained motionless, saving his rage for when it would be of use. He became cramped in short order and would be stiff, minor discomforts—the potential to be a difficulty.

In a day or so.

When they'd best not be here, inside what he'd dourly recognized by smell and taste as the inside of Loee Emms' toy, given to Werfol Westietas because the villagers of Marrowdell couldn't bear the sight of a child in need and shared what they had without stint.

A dragon, stuffed in a fake goose. He'd believed living under the turn-borns' kitchen the low point of his life. Could he make this a lesson for the youngling—?

Werfol took a deeper breath, ragged at the edges. Let it out with what came close to a whimper but wasn't, courageous beyond his size, patient beyond his years.

Like a dragon, in that. Wisp sent a soft breeze to feather the hair on his forehead.

Rewarded by Werfol's protest. "That tickles!" The boy rubbed his face and sat up.

Wisp took the opportunity to stretch, carefully. Like the girl when younger, the boy moved unpredictably and with a worrying lack of foresight.

"I tried again to call the other dragon," Werfol burst out. "The big green one from my truedream. He won't answer."

And like the girl, full of surprises. "Green is not a—" a dragon color, Wisp almost replied, then didn't.

When a sei thought to communicate, did it not present itself thus?

"Green isn't what?" Werfol asked innocently.

"Common."

"I knew my—that dragon was special," with such immense satisfaction the dragon present might have taken offense—

If not shuddering inwardly. "I suggest you refrain from further attempts to summon it. Until free of here," Wisp added quickly, remembering the girl's dislike of orders and her reaction, which as often as not was to creatively disobey. "The toad queen might attack it."

A brooding silence. *Disagreement?*

No, for Werfol came close, felt his way along the dragon's side to his head, then pressed his soft little cheek to the Wisp's broad hard one and breathed two words. "She's listening."

"Let her," replied Wisp. Knowing a truthseer in the Verge would hear, he spoke directly to Werfol, as he would to a little cousin—or the boy's uncle. ~As we speak, I'll tell you what the toad queen mustn't find out in this manner, which she will not overhear. You will respond with what makes no sense to her but will to me. Do you understand? You must be very clever.~

"I am! Layer Talk is Momma's favorite game!" Louder and with dragonish glee. "And mine. You go first."

Aloud, for the toad queen, Wisp said, "Do you agree not to summon the green dragon?"

To the boy, ~What you describe is a seeming of a sei. If you had its attention once, you have it still.~ *Terrifying to think, however true.*

"I don't think it would come anyway. A moth with boots asked me to give it a question. I said, 'Is the green dragon my friend?' but I didn't get an answer." With exaggerated woe, "I don't think it is, not like you."

Clever indeed. A moth, here? Wisp strained to see, but their prison was lightless. "I will always be your friend, Dear Heart," he said absently.

To the boy, ~An excellent question, but know that moths are chancy creatures. There's no telling of whom or what it will ask your question, nor predicting when you'll get an answer.~

Or if you'd survive the answer you received—

A little hand patted him, unaware of such dark thoughts. "I'm glad you found me. How did you know where to look?"

"I hunted the toad queen. With some success," the dragon added proudly.

"It was fun watching her blow up," the bloodthirsty child said. "I want you to do it again."

Oh, so did he. To the boy, ~I came searching for Jenn Nalynn.~

A gasp, quickly smothered.

Claws of ice found Wisp's heart. ~Tell me. Forget the game. I must know.~

"The majesty-monster caught Jenn and sent her far far away, but Jenn heard me. She told the majesty-monster it will get its comeuppance and it wasn't a lie. I saw!" A pause, then Werfol said the rest. "Jenn promised to come back for me but—I don't think she should. It's what the majesty-monster wants."

Why?

Because she'd have everything she needed. An uncontested turn-born, one with the power of the sei and thus able to open a crossing of her own. Easiest at the Balance, when the boundary thinned—

Exactly when she mustn't, for such a crossing would become a tear. Their worlds would flood into one another, magic spilling.

As would blood.

Had the toad queen squatted here, the dragon thought darkly, spying and waiting this moment, since the girl's birth?

~Trust Jenn Nalynn,~ Wisp told the boy.

To know the consequence. To find another way.

For all their sakes and hers.

TWENTY-ONE

"*N*O!"

The echo came higher pitched and from much lower down, startling Jenn Nalynn, whose furious expectation faltered mid-thought.

Not before frost rimed the hunters' eyelashes, hair, and whiskers, ice coating the rock at their feet. The hunters, a woman and two men, dropped their gear and fell to their knees, clutching each other and hiding their faces. "A 'spite!" came a horror-filled whisper. A second, "Come t'kill us!"

She wasn't—but had thought to do them harm, hadn't she? Jenn felt shamed, seeing their fear, and the air warmed at once, frost disappearing like a dream. Stirring, the three looked up, thoroughly cowed.

The woman squinted. "Flesie?"

"'At's me, Lenzi!" crowed the child smiling brightly up at Jenn. She was no bigger than Loee, her puff of black hair just topping Jenn's knees yet, by her voice and features, she might be Werfol's age or older.

Before Jenn could utter a word, Flesie spun to face the hunters, her fingers wrapping confidently around Jenn's thumb, her free hand pointing to each in accusation. "Lenzi, Heathe, n'Marni. Ye knew—all o'ye knew—" this stern "—there'd be a price t'pay f'unting t'waalum."

They scrambled to their feet, protests spilling out. "We need t'feed our kin—" "We'll starve—"

"Find another way," Jenn said, a remnant of frost in her voice.

Robbing them, it seemed, of theirs. Heads bobbed in defeat and fingers touched throats in the salute she remembered from Urcet.

Aunt Sybb said those knowing they'd erred suffered most in the wait for their comeuppance. Which at the time had to do with a much younger Jenn losing their aunt's prized brooch—which she wasn't to play with, especially in the privy—only to endure agonizing days without Aunt Sybb mentioning her missing treasure at all. Until a tearful Jenn had confessed and all had been forgiven.

~Elder sister.~

Jenn turned to see the waalum had resurfaced, riding the swells close to shore.

~There was, in the older times, a bargain.~

"A bargain?" she repeated out loud, glancing at the hunters. "With the waalum?"

"Aie, t'was," gasped the one named Lenzi.

"Th'old tale—" Scorn, from Heathe, the younger of her companions. "N'sense!"

"M'gran swear'd it were true on 'er last breath, she did." Offered by Marni, the third and oldest hunter, his tone wistful. In his eyes— was that a glimmer of hope?

Little fingers squeezed an encouragement. Jenn looked down at the child, thinking of Aunt Sybb, and her lips twitched.

She turned back to the waalum—who were, after all, the aggrieved party in this. "What would you say to those who hunted your kind?" she asked, her tone carefully neutral.

~Say we bear no malice, elder sister,~ in its deep, ageless voice. ~All things hunt in their own way. Though we would,~ this with an unexpected note of amusement, ~prefer to renew our bargain and no longer be their prey, but partners.~

The waalum went on to explain.

"An'at's it? Piney cones?" The hunters looked dumbfounded.

A request reminding her of the turn-borns' delight at Wainn's simple gift; Jenn vowed to pay greater attention to plants in future.

"They must be hard to come by in the sea," she pointed out, the nearest sizeable trees well up the slopes. "In return for a basket of pine cones left on this rock, the waalum promised to leave you a black oyster each new moon at the start of tide's ebb, so long as the bargain stands unbroken." It seemed a poor exchange, given oysters were easy to find while Nonny'd said the hunters earned a year's wage for a waalum hide, but the little cousins sounded confident.

And were right.

"Black oyster?! One a'month?!" The three fell on each other, hugging and slapping backs. When done, they turned to her, faces glistening in the moonlight with joyful tears. Lenzi spoke for them all. "We 'ated t'hunt t'waalum but couldna stop. We're most grateful t'ye." She looked past to the dim shapes of the waalum. "Mor'n grateful."

"Black oysters 'ave pearls inside," Flesie explained to Jenn. "Big'uns." She cupped her hands as if around a good-sized plum. "They live way way way too deep f'us t'get." A wise look. "Not w'out being gobbled first."

The hunters—who were now, Jenn supposed with some bemusement, traders—couldn't stop smiling. Heathe looked poised to start collecting cones this minute, though the moon was high overhead and full.

Flesie made little shooing motions at them. "Time t'get ye 'ome."

"Wi'ye, Flesie." Marni held out his gnarled hand.

Instead of taking it, the child wrapped her fingers around Jenn's thumb once more. "We'll com'by after. Tell Granny Bunac I said so."

To Jenn's surprise, the man gave a calm nod. "Aie." With that, the three picked up their gear and made ready to leave, clearly accepting the notion of leaving the child with a stranger with more ease than she would.

Nor was she certain they should, given who else was coming this way. Before she could protest, the waalum spoke again. ~Warn them, elder sister. The dire-ones must not learn of the bargain.~

Dire-ones? No doubt the waalum referred to the Eld's dawizards, but to expect these people to keep such a secret—

Ancestors Foolish and Fraught, it wasn't up to her. Drawing herself up, Jenn passed along the little cousin's warning. "There are dawizards nearby. They mustn't find out about you and the waalum."

The three grew serious; none showed surprise or dismay. "Shadesport folk know a thing o'two 'bout secrets," Lenzi stated, flat and sure.

"'Specially from t'like o'm." All spat to the side, including Flesie.

Jenn supposed it would have to do. She was more reassured when the three didn't climb back to the path but set off for home along the water's very edge, their callused feet wonderfully sure on the slippery uneven rocks.

Thus avoiding those taking the safer route, the path Jenn must take, with the child, if she was to help Urcet escape the dawizards.

Ancestors Challenged and Conflicted, she'd still no idea how. She stared helplessly up at the black wall of dense shrubbery, broken only where the hunters had pushed through. Bannan would know what to do, though she should be glad he wasn't here to face such danger and knew how he loathed the idea of taking up his sword again, being new to peace and treasuring it—

Jenn found herself quite unable to move.

"We'll bide 'ere awhile," Flesie told her, sitting on the rock.

It seemed most excellent advice.

Namron Setac arrived in the small dining room promptly and fully dressed, implying he'd awaited a summons. Concern for his youngest charge? A reasonable assumption from the shadows beneath his blue eyes and worried creases by his mouth, but, in Bannan's experience, assumptions were dangerous. He'd reserve judgment.

Setac didn't smile when introduced, only gave those seated respectful nods before looking to Lila for cues. The man's clothing added to the puzzle he presented: a mountaineer's coat from Mellynne, with its cape-like collar, over a Rhothan shirt, with boots surely from Ansnor. He'd a red scarf tied in Eldani fashion at his neck. A compact man, neither tall nor short, wide nor narrow. His skin was brown with the sun or by nature, his short black hair shot through with a single streak of white; the truthseer waited with anticipation for those first, telling words.

They came from Lila. "Werfol's been taken to the magic realm by a monster—the toad queen. What can you tell us about her?"

The man groped for the back of the chair in front of him. Steadied. "I don't know that name."

The truth. Bannan nodded when Lila glanced his way.

Setac's eyes widened. "Truthseer." He breathed the word as if relieved, only then moving to sit. He folded his hands on top of the table. "I'll tell you all I can, but first—is Werfol safe?"

"For now," Bannan told him.

The hands trembled and the tutor lowered his head for an instant as if overcome. If an act, Bannan saw no sign of it. Setac looked up again. "Yes, 'for now.' You're aware, then, that tomorrow's sunset, on the equinox, is a time of great peril for our world—all worlds." His lips twisted. "From those of power and those fools seeking it."

Lila gestured. *Tell him.*

Bannan leaned back in his chair, easing his leg. "I'm familiar. I'd the privilege of experiencing the last one in the company of both. You won't surprise this company, Master Setac."

A whisper of a smile played over the tutor's thin lips. "Not even when I tell you the name of what we most fear will rise tomorrow is *Syrpic ac Ukellak*?"

"Mother of All Disaster," Lila translated. She raised a brow at Bannan.

"We've met," he announced baldly.

Setac's mouth opened. Closed.

"We call her the toad queen. A creature of foul magic who profits from calamity here, within the edge. You are aware of the edge, Master Setac? Where parts of our world overlap another?"

The smallest possible nod. The man might have been frozen.

"Floods let her capture me—twice." Bannan didn't elaborate. "An avalanche let her take Werfol, and we're far from the first. The toad queen keeps trophies. The wrack of boats. Bones. Toys." He didn't—couldn't—look at Lila or Emon. "It's my understanding she's constrained to the Verge, the magic realm. At least for now." Seeing Setac's eyes widen, the truthseer held up his hand. "Your turn."

When the tutor hesitated, Lila tapped her slim finger, once, on the table. *No more secrets.*

Swallowing, Setac produced a well-worn leather notebook from his pocket. "This is a tally of people discovered to possess unusual abilities and where they may be found. Not all, of course, and there are always those of whom we lose track—individuals who've chosen to hide or abandon their gifts."

Or discovered the existence of a group dedicated to recording them—Bannan shot a look at Emon, whose calm, almost bored expression spoke volumes.

He'd known. They both had.

There'd be, the truthseer resolved, a long-overdue discussion about sharing critical information before it became life-threatening. With shouting, if need be.

His sister, meanwhile, sat with her chin on the back of her hand, elbow on the table, her attention never leaving the tutor. "Some were taken by those desiring magic."

And oh, the threat in that.

"Our shared goal is to end that loathsome trade." Said with an involuntary glance at Bannan.

She'd told the tutor about Glammis Lurgan.

Of course she'd told him, Bannan raged inwardly. Lila collected allies the way others collected dead bugs, sticking them to her purpose with pins no less substantial for being constructed of her will.

Seeing Setac flinch, the truthseer schooled his face. "The toad queen," he said pleasantly. "Do you have anything relevant to add or not?"

"Yes. Yes, I believe so," the tutor replied hastily. "You mentioned constraints. Those may be failing. Nineteen years ago, the number of inexplicable disappearances began to climb, a trend continuing to this day—"

The love of his life was nineteen.

Bannan shoved the thought aside as if it burned. A coincidence, nothing more. It had to be.

"—loved ones left without bodies or answers." Setac's voice lowered. "One at a time. Here, there. Without this," he raised the notebook, "we wouldn't have detected the pattern. Each loss followed a natural disaster in the area. A forest fire. An earthquake. Floods, of course. While it made the disappearances seem natural—"

"Something was hunting. You came here knowing it hunted my son," Lila accused, cold and hard, "and didn't tell me."

To his credit, or perhaps unaware his danger, Setac met her glare. "You were already on guard."

"So this was our fault?" Emon said in a dreadful voice, and the guard put her hand to her sword.

"None of that matters," Bannan interrupted. "The toad queen hunts magic of any kind, anywhere she can reach. None of us— *none*—" he emphasized "—could have stopped her taking Werfol once he stepped into the edge."

Like a hound on a scent, Lila refused to be distracted. "Why nineteen years?"

Bannan tried not to hold his breath.

The tutor closed his notebook, steepling his fingers over it. "We have only conjecture. It concerns a rare recurring phenomenon. An eclipse of the sun, in conjunction with the autumnal equinox."

"The Ancestors Golden Day," Lila offered, and oh the restraint, that she didn't so much as glance at Bannan. "Good for weddings."

"Such an eclipse occurred seventy-one years ago, to the north.

During it, an Ansnan refuge was destroyed by an earthquake. We've records from survivors," said earnestly, as if Setac thought he'd need to convince them. "At the same instant, the very same—" A pause to be sure they listened; Bannan thought even the walls paid attention. "—other earthquakes occurred in every domain. Small, yes, but intense local tremors, all confined to what you call the edge and we refer to as the *semnem fal*, those places where magic is remembered. We've uncovered no satisfactory explanation."

In other words, Bannan judged, those survivors hadn't confessed how Ansnan priests in Marrowdell used magic to try and breach the Verge, wounding the sei, who, according to Wisp, *flinched*.

A flinch affecting the edge, the Verge, and the worlds they linked. Thinking of the sei—or portion of it—quiescent under his former home, Bannan wondered why there was no family history of a quake there.

Unless it had been kept secret like so much else.

"History," Lila dismissed with a snort. "Make your point."

"The next such celestial combination occurred nineteen years ago, at the start of the rise in disappearances."

"Positing causality between the sky and doings on earth?" Emon raised his eyebrows. "Sounds more Ansnan liturgy than science."

"I heartily agree, Baron Westietas, but such is the lamentable state of our understanding of—mysterious—occurrences." Setac started to put away his notebook.

Emon held out his hand.

"It's in code—"

A finger beckoned. The tutor relinquished his appallingly dangerous list, and Bannan had no doubt at all Lila's husband would break the code and put those named under the protection of his house.

"In fact," Setac continued, clearly flustered, "I've pointed out to my colleagues there was a similar conjunction this past year and nothing changed."

Heart's Blood. *Everything had*, Bannan thought with despair.

What Setac so blithely listed were Great Turns, special moments—as the sei promised, or threatened—when anything was possible.

A Great Turn nineteen years ago had seen the birth of Jenn Nalynn.

The latest, her change from flesh to magical turn-born, able to move between the edge and the Verge—able to bring others with her.

Ancestors Bloody and Bowed, Jenn *was* the explanation, her birth sparking the toad queen's plot, the years of her life marked by the list in Emon's hands, of the gifted gone missing. Consumed by a monster.

Jenn Nalynn, good-hearted and kind beyond measure. To think of her finding out—

This Setac and those behind him? The truthseer slid a look to his sister, catching her eye. Moved a finger.

They must never learn the truth.

Jenn sat with the miniature child on the waalum's rock. Quiet shrouded them. Moonlight bathed them. The waalum floated at ease on waves oddly slower and calmer than before, and she felt herself come adrift, out of step with time.

She really should be alarmed, but wasn't at all. It seemed important to count the drips from her braid as they soaked her back. To breathe in rhythm with Flesie. To let the world wait.

Not that it could. Jenn spoke at last, nodding at the bay. "I'm not a sirenspite." It seemed important to get that out of the way. "I'm a person. My name is Jenn Nalynn."

"'At's a nice name," the child decided. "Flesie's all o'mine, 'cause o'being an orphan. Everyone in Shadesport cares f'me—till I get old n'pick more names 'f m'own."

The words curled around Jenn's heart. "You've a fine village."

Moonlight picked out bright eyes and a cheery smile, hinting at the hues of Flesie's dress. "We look aft'ours." Matter-of-factly. "Mean'n ye shouldna jump inna bay. Nah by night. Nah alone. It be fearsome danger."

Jenn found herself protesting, "I didn't mean to—" She caught herself before blaming the toad queen, who likely was unknown to the child and more *fearsome* than a splash in the water. "My boat was sinking—"

"Be Nonny's boat," Flesie corrected, her smile wiped away. "Nonny knew better n'take out t'*Igrini*. She weren't seaworthy. Now she's at t'bottom 'f t'sea n'Nonny's lost h'ome."

"I'm sorry. I'll do my best to replace her boat," Jenn promised, not that she'd any notion how. Those in Marrowdell had had little to spare before the flood.

The smile flashed again. "Good, aie." Feet no longer than Jenn's thumb drummed the rock.

"YOU DON'T BELONG HERE, JENN NALYNN."

Spoken in a voice deep and vast as the ocean, impossible from a child's mouth.

Jenn tensed. "What did you say?"

"Tis good," the words high-pitched and soft, normal as the words before hadn't been, and she knew someone like this, who spoke at unexpected times as the edge itself.

Wainn Uhthoff.

Heart's Blood. Had she found an ally? Or one found her?

Jenn leaned forward eagerly. "I want to leave—to go home— more than anything. I can't until I rescue my friend Werfol from the Verge. Can you help me?"

Little feet drummed, making no sound; the water of the bay shook and danced in matching rhythm, tossing the waalum.

"TURN-BORN ARE SELFISH. TURN-BORN ARE HEEDLESS. TURN-BORN AREN'T WELCOME. IS THAT WHAT YOU ARE, JENN NALYNN?"

"I'm turn-born, yes," Jenn admitted, "but I mean no harm to anyone. I swear it by the Bones of my Ancestors."

Suddenly she felt watched by more than the child, the subject of a directionless, intense *scrutiny*, and kept very still indeed.

It became harder and harder to breathe. Though sorely tempted, Jenn remained flesh and blood, like Flesie, at a loss how else to prove her good manners and intentions, if saving the waalum and sparing the hunters hadn't been enough.

Come to think of it, her wish at them might well have attracted the attention of whomever—whatever—a consequence, she thought wryly, she might have guessed.

She'd one thing left to try.

Jenn brought out the necklace of shells, their golden hue muted by moonlight.

To her dismay, Flesie curled into a ball as if to hide from her, feet under her dress, arms tight around her knees. "Wrong thing!" cried the child, shaking her head vigorously, condemnation in her high-pitched voice. "Wrong!"

The shells imprisoned something they shouldn't, that much she believed. Two-sided, this *gift* of the toad queen's. Intended to cause trouble here, but might it offer an opportunity to prove herself? "I hope to fix that," Jenn said gently.

"'Ow?" With an adult's dark suspicion.

The waalum had told her to ask. Ancestors Trusting and Truthful, could it be that simple? Placing the necklace on the rock between her and Flesie, Jenn said, feeling ever-so-foolish, "Open, please."

Nothing happened. Ancestors Flummoxed and Fooled, of course nothing happened.

The child's finger grazed the back of her hand.

The too-vast voice said, "ASK."

And Jenn finally understood. Not as flesh. Nor turn-born.

She held out her free hand and a single moth, tiny and white, bubbled from her palm to flutter into the moonlight, making Flesie giggle.

Jenn envisioned blue, her blue, her sanctuary and power. Held the color close as she whispered, "Please help me free them."

And the Bay of Shades answered.

Pale little crabs swarmed up the rock, over their toes and legs. A few climbed her dress only to drop off again, for their goal was the necklace and they were determined.

Some severed the knots holding the shells, then crab after crab took hold, dragging the shells, twice their size, into the water. Jenn knelt beside Flesie, the pair of them leaning out to see.

Crabs held on, drifting down, their claws busy cracking free bits of shell.

All at once, the halves fell open. The crabs let go, floating away.

From each gaping shell emerged a butterfly, a different sort than Jenn was used to in Marrowdell. Instead of bodies, these had shells of their own, dangling like little pearls, but were the same in having paired, beautiful wings. Wings that undulated slowly rather than beat, sending the sea butterflies flying through the water, away from them and deeper, until the last disappeared from sight.

Flesie clapped her hands.

Jenn sat back, shaking her head in wonder. A solitary crab dragged off the final remnant of the foul necklace, as if collecting a trophy of its own. The oppressive sense of being watched was gone. Had she done enough?

A tiny hand slipped into hers, as if in answer, then Flesie announced cheerfully, "He's 'ere a'last!"

Who—? As Jenn thought the word, an anguished cry startled her. "NONNY!"

A man crashed through the brush, skidding heedlessly down the slope toward them. He might have wound up with the waalum if Jenn hadn't grabbed his arm to stop him.

To be grabbed in turn by Urcet a Hac Sa Od y Dom, that being who the man was, and Jenn found herself speechless, having come to save him.

"You're not—" He shot a wild look at the water. "Where's Noemi?"

"Safe on shore," she answered at once, grasping what he feared. "She went to the village to look for you."

"Jenn—" He froze, incredulous, hands still tight on her upper arms. "How is this possible—I don't—"

"Let'r go, Urcy!" When he remained stunned and unmoving, Flesie tugged his shirt. "Jenn's Nonny's friend." Another tug. "'N t'waalums." Giving up on the shirt, the child kicked the poor man in the ankle. "'N she's mine, so let'r go!"

His hands loosened at last. Slipped down to collect Jenn's fingers in his, as if afraid she'd vanish, and, even by moonlight, Urcet remained the most handsome man she'd ever seen or imagined.

With a self-conscious cough, Jenn gently freed herself. "The waalum brought me here. They said you were in danger from the dawizards."

"I led them here, away from Noemi." A harried look over his shoulder. "They're right behind me. I ran ahead when I saw—her boat go down—someone jump." He took a tellingly sharp breath. "I thought the worst."

Flesie kicked him again, lightly. "Ye thought dumb, Urcy. Ye know Nonny swims better than t'fishes. Drown? She'll smack ye silly f'fuss'n," with satisfaction.

Urcet pressed a hand to his heart. "I'll take any punishment, so long as we get Jenn away before the dawizards arrive. They mustn't find you," this to her, low and frighteningly earnest.

Jenn looked to the water. The tide was going out, exposing more rocks and the slippery weeds coating them. "I don't—"

"Dawizards nah matter." Her thumb was claimed in a firm grip. "Granny Bunac's 'pectin us f'supper f'sure."

He regarded the child gravely. "You've a most excellent champion—" Urcet paused, his head tilted.

Listening, she thought, for sounds of someone approaching. "What happened to you?" Jenn asked urgently. "You were so—"

"Arrogant?" he supplied in a light tone she didn't believe for an instant. "Overconfident?"

"Happy." She went on, "You were to write a book. Share your adventures."

"The dawizards got to me first. After confiscating my notes, they stripped me of funds and reputation. I've been banned from speaking in any way about the north."

"Ye went nor'?" Flesie asked, peering up at him in amazement.

"As far as the road would take me," he told the child. "That's where I discovered magic has a beating heart and warm smile."

Flesie nodded. "Ye met Jenn."

"Indeed I did." Urcet reached for Jenn's free hand, searching her face in the moonlight. "I shouldn't be surprised by anything you can do, Dear Heart. But why come here and put yourself in such danger?"

Sticks cracked. Gravel shifted under booted feet. They'd run out of time. Jenn whispered, quick and low, "Ask Nonny."

She dropped Urcet's hand, stepping away from him as newcomers came through what was now a wide gap in the brush. No need of the waalum's cry of ~Beware. The dire-ones!~ She knew who'd come.

Two were from Shadesport, dressed like the hunters in loose-fitting pants and shirtless, chests covered in tattoos. The larger man had skin pale as hers, a surprise until Jenn remembered the crew of the Ansnan schooner that had found the bay and never left. The pair supported a pole on their shoulders, the sort Davy and Anten might use to carry a slaughtered calf or deer, only from this hung a long black box with holes in the sides. It was heavy, for they set it down on the rock with relief.

Heavy and secured with chains and locks. They'd come prepared to catch something, Jenn realized, dry-mouthed. What tale had Urcet spun to lure them here?

After glancing around, the pale man crouched before Flesie, a hand tenderly cupping her puff of hair. "'Eard ye be wander'n alone ag'n, li'l one," he said, so quietly Jenn almost couldn't make out the words, a grim note to his voice. "Ye shouldna. Nah ever. Ye know why 'at's so."

Flesie stood on her toes to kiss his cheek. "But I'm nah alone, Nis. Jenn came. Nonny's friend."

Nis twisted his head to stare up at Jenn, scowling. "Sink'n Nonny's boat's nah much a friend," he grumbled, but his scowl faded as his hand brushed Flesie's shoulder. "Ye being 'ere with Flesie, tho. 'At be a good thing 'n we thank ye."

Jenn gave a nod, suddenly realizing her mistake. When the waalum insisted she protect the walker-with-treats, she'd wrongly assumed they meant Urcet. Who didn't need her help, being well able to take care of himself.

The person she had to protect was Flesie.

Nis jerked to his feet, hurrying back to the box and his partner. The reason came through the opening, two figures with lantern-topped metal poles they used to steady themselves down the small slope.

~The dire-ones, elder sister! Beware!~

And it wasn't fussing, as little cousins were admittedly prone to do, but a sincere warning Jenn vowed to take to heart.

Despite the warmth of the night, the dawizards were swathed in white cloaks from head to polished boots. Deep hoods hid their faces, and they were taller than any Eld Jenn had met. Thin black chains looped over their shoulders, secured at their waists; each link possessed a sharp little hook, which didn't appear the least sensible and probably, Jenn judged, snared their fine clothes more often than not.

Better to think of that, than what the hooks held.

Ovals of tanned hide, the edges neat and trim, hung from most. Heart's Blood, if each represented a different murdered waalum, the carnage—and their pride in it—made her sick. Between the hides, little sacks were hooked by their ties, bulging with what might be pebbles but might be bones. Then and there, Jenn decided the dawizards were too like the toad queen. There'd be no trusting anything they said.

From the chain on the closest hung a small bottle twin to those Nonny had sold Urcet, filled with mimrol, and the dawizard's gloved finger stroked the air over it possessively. They ignored Flesie entirely, reminding Jenn of Wainn's Old Pony, who'd pretend not to see the apple in your hand until close enough to snatch it.

Feeling cold in the pit of her stomach, she kept hold of Flesie's small hand. Ancestors Untimely and Unwanted, she'd made a terrible mistake not jumping back into the bay and taking the child with her.

The bottle-dawizard dipped his lantern pole in front of her. "Stupid woman," he said. By the light, Jenn glimpsed a thin mouth and short gray beard ending in a black bead. "The water's treacherous. Why were you out on that boat?" His tone was indifferent; his words, their intonation, were nothing like Nonny's or Urcet's.

She guessed he spoke Crucib, what Master Dusom said was the Eld's special tongue of knowledge, a dawizard hardly concerned if a Shadesport resident understood him or not.

She mustn't say a word, Jenn realized with growing alarm. If she did, they'd hear her as using the same and rightly be suspicious.

She didn't have to feign a shiver, being damp and afraid. Hunching her shoulders, she reeled slightly, like someone about to faint, hoping they'd take the hint and let her go. Hoping, not wishing, not anywhere close to such as these.

"A novice's mistake," Urcet dismissed. "She's survived it. Let's keep moving—any delay could cost our prize."

The hood of the second dawizard aimed at Jenn, then lifted as the wearer regarded the bay. She had to trust the waalum had submerged. "It would be unwise to lie to us."

"I brought you proof," Urcet snapped back, undaunted. He pointed to the bottle and the dawizard cupped a protective hand over it. "The living source comes ashore just up the coast. By the full moon—which we're wasting, standing here."

He was most convincing, Jenn decided, proud of Urcet, but the dawizards remained as they were, their unnerving attention on her.

Why? She shouldn't look out of place here, thanks to the clothes and Ansnans. Unless they possessed some sense of magic—could they tell what she was?

Ancestors Furious and Feisty, if they thought to take her away for study, Jenn told herself firmly, she was *not* going in their box. Not that she'd fit inside it, for that matter—

A tremendous thump and splash from the bay drew everyone around in time to see a second basker surge from the black water. The immense creature seemed to hang suspended in air before toppling over to land with an incredible whoosh of displaced water.

Flesie laughed.

"'At's t'best o'luck," announced Nis.

And most excellent timing, Jenn thought, wishing she knew how to thank the creatures, while slightly aghast something *that* big had pushed the boat along in play.

Urcet shoved by her, climbing past the dawizards. "Let's use it then."

The bottle-dawizard stepped toward Flesie. Jenn eased in front, feeling a squeeze on her thumb.

"We'll be go'n t'Granny Bunac," Flesie said loudly. "We're 'pected."

"Not so fast." The dawizard swung his lantern close. Jenn squinted, unable to see beyond its light. His voice had an edge. "I don't know you."

"This be Nonny's friend, Jenn," said the irrepressible child. "She dunna come t'village cause'n ye be there a'times. Nonny nah like ye," she added pertly. "'Caus'n ye pry n'make a big mess."

The villagers snorted, composing their faces when the other dawizard turned to the sound.

Flesie leaned comfortably against Jenn's leg. "Jenn's m'friend. An' needs her supper. An' dry clothes."

What a dear, thoughtful child. Jenn smiled down at her, a smile from her heart, seeing the little face fill with delight.

She raised her eyes to catch a strange look on Urcet's. It changed to resolve. "We leave now, your graces, or fail."

Urcet played a perilous game, trying to control where the dawizards went. He'd given them Nonny's bottle so they'd come away from the village. Jenn was certain he'd stolen the necklace to use as similar bait for that other dawizard, the woman missing and doubtless killed by the toad queen—

Who'd tossed it at Jenn. A thing touched by too many hands with misery involved. Jenn was gladder than ever she'd freed the sea butterflies, with the help of several crabs.

White hoods aimed at each other, as if the dawizards conversed in silence. Then aimed at her. "We'll have questions for you, woman," one said ominously, "on our return."

Questions she wouldn't be able to answer, nor should, not when asked by those who hunted magic.

Pretending to be overwhelmed, which wasn't hard at all, Jenn bent to hug Flesie and nodded.

Wishing she dared thank Urcet, who'd proved a true friend after all.

Goosie shook more often, annoying Wisp and worrying Werfol. The dragon did his best not to bump into him, but sometimes couldn't help it, and there'd be, the boy could tell, bruises.

Unless bruising was like eating and drinking and sleeping and going to the bathroom and everything else suspended here, which made the young truthseer wonder what would happen when he wasn't.

Another, larger shake that sent him flying, only to be caught by a wing. Twitching while waiting wasn't something Momma approved, but was often impossible to stop, as Werfol knew full well. "She's getting impatient," he whispered. "Is that good or bad?"

Once more he felt rather than heard Wisp's reply, like a tickle inside. Which would have been fun and remarkable and something to brag about to Semyn, except for what the dragon had to say.

~The toad queen believes nothing can stop her.~

"You can, though. And Jenn. And—" Remembering who listened, Werfol changed what he would say before sharing his new and very interesting thought. "—everyone who doesn't like the majesty-monster. That's everyone, everywhere, isn't it?"

A soft breeze found his ear. "It should be. Some," pensively, "care nothing for others."

Then he didn't care about them, Werfol decided.

~What has occurred to you, young truthseer?~

He chose his words with extra care, taking his time. "I miss Semyn. He's really good at strategy. Because he reads so much about old battles," which was true and Werfol thought in future he shouldn't complain of being neglected and maybe read more himself. "He told me about one where defeated soldiers hid in a safe place for a long, long time to build up their strength and prepare. When they counterattacked, it was a big surprise and they won."

In case Wisp missed his meaning, Werfol's fingers found his snout and pretended to hop like a toad along it.

~The little cousins were trapped in Marrowdell.~ Said with doubt, not outright dismissal, as if he'd posed the dragon a worthy puzzle.

Werfol almost glowed, but didn't lose his caution. "I wish we had an army like that." He made himself sigh and sound forlorn. "But if we did, we wouldn't know, would we?"

~We will know everything come the turn of this day, Dear Heart.~ Grim and dark.

Even so, the words made Werfol braver, to know the dragon took him seriously and treated him like a battle comrade.

But he would have liked to be sure about the toads.

Every step of the path, Jenn expected a shout to stop or a rough hand on her shoulder. She put her trust in Flesie and refused to look back. Harder, when they reached the gravel roadway leading to—and away from—Shadesport.

All the dawizards would have to do was try to take her with them, on this very road, and she'd cease to exist before the crest of the hill.

Jenn didn't realize she'd halted, transfixed by the ominous gloom of the tree-cloaked road, until Flesie tugged impatiently. "We be most o'way there, Jenn. Com'ye."

Ancestors Wool-Headed and Wandering. With an inner shake, Jenn looked down at the child. "Lead on."

It turned out she could have found Shadesport by following her nose. The potency of the smell took Jenn by the throat as the road rounded the tip of the bay to end at the dock itself. The reason hung from racks behind and beside every building, hung out like laundry to dry.

More fish than she'd ever imagined.

Most were oompah, headless and gutted, yes, but the shape and size matched what Jenn had seen in the barrel. Had Marrowdell's, which was to say Lila's, come from here?

Apparently not. Flesie, clearly glad to be home, skipped and chatted nonstop, and informed Jenn these were to just to feed the village. Only in the big runs, later in the season, would there be so many they'd salt the extra to trade in the nearest inland town.

And maybe this season—this proclaimed with eyes wide as an owl's—they'd catch enough that they'd be rich and Granny Bunac would take her for a train ride!

The coast of the Sweet Sea lined with fishing villages, according to the dots on her map and Master Dusom, Jenn found it hard to imagine there were sufficient oompah for them. As for being rich, the fish might be expensive delicacies served at Midwinter Beholdings across Rhoth, but it was unlikely much wealth trickled down to the fishers. Enough to fill oil lamps and flour sacks seemed likely the realistic answer.

But a train ride? Jenn sighed wistfully. Ancestors Blessed, what a grand adventure it'd be, to ride with Flesie, maybe the one crossing the bridge high above the bay—and how impossible, since it would surely pass beyond the edge at once.

"'Ere we be!" announced her charming guide.

Shadesport's dock was a wooden road perched on pilons and stone, supporting the buildings of the village while providing mooring for the boats bobbing gently alongside. Metal rings and hanging chimes made a soft melody; overlapping circles of lamplight from the houses made it easy to step around purposeful coils of rope and piled gear. Jenn remained leery of the drop to the restless dark water and kept herself between it and Flesie.

Who probably thought her overcautious and a little silly, having lived here all her life, but, as Aunt Sybb would say, better a precaution taken than a problem result—which had to do with Jenn's reluctance to use a thimble and a pricked finger, but suited this and many other moments.

And with Aunt Sybb so very far away at this one, it helped to think of her voice and wisdom.

Most of the houses had open shacks attached to one side, where, Flesie explained, everyone old enough helped chop off heads and tails and pull out guts, the offal to be bait for the long-lines. Which was how, she said with some pride, they caught the fish in the first place.

Shadesport's houses were small, simple structures, each painted with vivid colors and no two the same, making the village resemble a collection of pretty boxes. When they reached the third, done in blue, Flesie stopped skipping to drag Jenn along faster, as if hungry for supper.

Unless it was to hurry her by this particular house.

Jenn glanced at it, feeling the hair rise on her neck. Its lamps weren't lit, which seemed inhospitable. To be fair, the occupant might be the frugal sort, there being abundant lamplight from the rest of the village.

There wasn't the typical shed; what she could make out in the deep shadow beside the house appeared to be a mass of broken barrels and poorly stacked crates. Maybe the occupant did repairs—

Something stirred the window curtains.

Something malicious, like a nyphrit, but not, and Jenn decided then and there to pick up Flesie and run—

Before she could, the door flung open and a figure stepped from the dark to thrust a hooked pole in their way.

And a figure with huge eyes like glowing red embers ordered, "Nah so fast!"

Roche Morrill's eleventh dreadful dream was less dreadful and more dream, perhaps because of the potion given him by the Baroness Westietas, or perhaps because he isn't alone. He would never forget it.

The sky is a maze of wild nameless color, the ground flat and endless. He stands with Lila and she raises her sword, aims the tip at the distant horizon, and waits. She's ready. He waits with her but is not. He feels the floor beneath his bare feet about to shift into sand, into falling stone, into water, into a mouth to suck them down and swallow them whole, but he doesn't cry out in warning. These are shades of dreadful dreams past and harmless. What she seeks—what they seek—is now and perilous.

And has her son.

They turn and turn around, seeing only the maddening sky, the pointless ground. Around and around, until suddenly, they go down. Down. DOWN!

"That's enough."

Roche blinked, opening his eyes to meet a steady gaze from those as green but uptilted and full of purpose. "Did it work?"

His heart felt as if he'd run up a mountain. Though he made no sound, Lila put her hand on his chest and frowned. "At some cost, it seems."

"So it did. The cost doesn't matter. I'm expendable."

A tiny smile denied the last. "Sustainability does matter, my brave friend. Yes. We truedreamed together while awake. But what we saw—that wasn't through Werfol's eyes."

"It was through hers," he guessed, feeling sick.

Lila's smile grew wicked. "I certainly hope so."

"Symyd, ye stinky crab!" Flesie squirmed so fiercely in Jenn's arms she had to put her down. The irate child stepped in front of her, fists on her hips like a miniature Peggs. "Git!"

The pole lowered. It wasn't, Jenn noted, her mouth dry, withdrawn from their path. "Settle, Flesie. Heathe said ye 'ad a new friend. I wanna meet'r. 'at's all." Sweet, the voice, over-friendly.

False as the toad queen's.

Symyd clawed the strange pair of red-lensed wire spectacles

from his face, to dangle from a cord around his neck, and Jenn recognized him from the boat that had come too close to the '*Igrini*. Spying, Nonny'd accused. This man was foul and not a friend—to be avoided.

A warning impossible to heed now, Jenn thought with some frustration. She stood behind Flesie, determined to keep her temper. It wouldn't do to antagonize a villager—especially the one who'd made the shell necklace, with its imprisoned sea butterflies.

Otherwise, she'd have judged the rude young man to be rather ordinary, slender, compared to the waalum hunters, with close-cut black hair. A red bead was embedded outside his left nostril and pale tattoos crisscrossed his bare arms. Small tools filled slots on a belt slung across his chest and he wore a leather apron that hung past the knees of his pants. Deep lines furrowed his forehead and the corners of his mouth, as if nothing gave him joy or ease.

Flesie pushed at the pole, her hands too small to take hold of it. "Git!"

"I nah think so," Symyd said slowly, tucking the pole against his side as he put himself in their path. His gaze never left Jenn, moving over her from head to toe in an examination like Devins with a new calf, but with none of the latter's kindness.

What had he seen through those red lenses to draw him out?

She'd no desire to know. Taking Flesie's hand, Jenn went to move around him, but Symyd was faster, crowding them back until they were closer than she liked to the edge of the dock and her heart was racing. Then she thought of Roche, who'd relished any sign of fear, and stiffened, raising her chin. "You will let us pass. Now."

"Or what?" He tapped her shoulder with the blunt end of the pole. "Glass cracks."

She froze. "What did you say?"

His eyes gleamed, lips twisting unpleasantly as if he'd forgotten how to form a smile. "I know what ye be. T'spites know too. They tol' somma us, t'smart ones, how t'deal w' y'kind, girl, long ago. So ye'd best play nice or—" He went to tap her again.

Jenn grabbed the pole and tossed it in the bay. "I don't know what you're talking about. Get out of our way."

Heart's Blood, but she did, didn't she? Expectations worn thin with time. Five trunks in the sanctuary, dusty and unused. A voice accusing turn-born of being selfish and heedless—they could be, it was true—and saying they weren't welcome.

What had happened here?

An arm slipped around Symyd's neck and Nonny's scowling face appeared over his shoulder. "Ye deaf, Symyd?" she asked in a low tone that made Jenn shiver. "M'friends said t'git."

"I—" He jerked and closed his mouth, giving a terse nod.

"Better," Nonny approved, pushing Symyd aside. He staggered, collected himself, then went back to his house, pausing to give them a baleful look from the entry before closing the door. "Thought I warned you to keep clear of him, Jenn Nalynn."

Jenn glimpsed a familiar knife before it disappeared inside the harmoot. "I—"

"Di'ye see, Nonny?" Flesie interrupted, bouncing with excitement. "T'baskers tak'n t'*Igrini* 'cross t'bay! Sommat pull'n 'er down so Jenn had t'jump n'waalum helped 'er! 'N then t'dawizards—" She stopped to gulp a breath.

Jenn seized the chance to speak. "I'm sorry about your boat." And all of Nonny's belongings—really, a proper apology would take hours.

Time she didn't have. No sign of lanterns on the road yet, but surely Urcet's ruse would fail soon and the dawizards insist on returning to the village. She had to leave here. Get to the room in the bridge, take the ladder down—

To go where enemies of those turn-born might be.

Ancestors Witness, there were, Jenn thought wearily, no easy choices left.

Nonny shrugged back her hood, revealing an impassive face. "Supper first," she said, as if that were what mattered most.

Because it was what Peggs would say, Jenn could only nod.

Flesie led them to a house that was bright yellow on the outside, with red trim and chimes to catch the breeze. "'Ere we be. Granny Bunac's t'best cook n'Shadesport. Ye nah wannat t'eat elsewhere, less'n it be Nonny's."

That worthy chuckled.

Keeping hold of Jenn's thumb, Flesie pushed open the door. "Granny Bunac! I bring'd ye my friend Jenn n'Nonny want'n supper!"

The door revealed a large single room, filled with tables and benches, hammocks slung to the side, for though some here took their well-earned ease, others were busy about their work. The woman Jenn took to be Granny Bunac stood hunched over an enormous pot, stirring slowly. She looked up, blinked, and gave a nod.

Flesie rushed ahead to received a bowl sized just right for her. She went off to sit with other children, starting to talk at once.

Possibly telling a story of crabs, a necklace, and butterflies swimming in the deep.

At a push from Nonny, Jenn stepped up to face the most wrinkled and bent person she'd ever met, and quite possibly the oldest, though the fishers' life doubtless wore on a body, making it harder to tell. Wearing a vivid yellow and red dress, with bracelets jingling on withered arms, Granny gave Jenn a toothless grin and keen look before filling a bowl for her. "Sit ye dun," she ordered, aiming her spoon at a row of barrels before using it to fill a bowl for Nonny.

It felt very much like home. As well as themselves and Granny, there were three other adults present, possibly a father and mother and aunt, though it was hard to tell, for there were children of a variety of ages coming and going without warning until Jenn quite lost track. Everyone gave her shy smiles and sidelong curious looks but didn't offer speak to her, as if a guest of Flesie should receive particular treatment.

A few stared at Nonny, smothered in her harmoot, as if more

startled by her presence than a stranger's. With her boat gone, Jenn supposed she'd have to move into the village.

Jenn made herself smile back and keep eating despite an appetite vanquished by the sounds of spoons and dishes, calls and laughs. With each mouthful she thought of Peggs. Of Hettie and the tiny twins. Of her father and the rest of Marrowdell. Ancestors Blessed, she'd be beholden if all sat to supper together, right at this moment, to plenty. But what if they still struggled? What of Wen and her baby-to-come?

Let alone Marrowdell's suffering livestock. She had to believe she'd left the valley better for them as well, letting them cross the river and go home, but had anything been left unspoiled for them to eat?

Aunt Sybb was fond of saying the best way to ease a worry was to appreciate what was in front of you, usually before she hugged Jenn and Peggs ever-so-tight and bade them sweet dreams. They hadn't known, then, how great the challenge she faced to reach them each year and how much worry filled her winter until she did.

As always, Jenn thought, hers was good advice and helpful. She paid closer attention to the supper in her nicely turned clay bowl, a meal more like breakfast, being the grains and sauce Nonny'd prepared for that meal, but with the addition of thick chunks of spiced seafood she tried with caution only to relish. A hearty meal for, from the conversation around her, these people had worked very hard all day and would again tomorrow, those going out before dawn in their boats to catch the high tide beyond the bridge, into the Momma's Basket.

Today's catch was deemed better than most. For that reason, a bottle of the dark liquor Nonny had served her made the rounds, Jenn declining with thanks, Nonny taking her share. An older child played pipes, if quietly, and a man sang, the key strange to her ears, almost sorrowful, but others smiled and nodded.

There was, she was learning, a great deal more to fishing in the sea than tossing a grub on a hook into the trout pond. Fine black nets hung from the rafters, where in Marrowdell there'd be drying spices or sacks. There were stacks of some kind of trap without doors. Immense lengths of thin strong rope with hooks braided into it were coiled into barrels, after inspection, and Jenn thought these must be Flesie's "long-lines" to be baited and let out once the boats reached the fishing grounds. The younger women and two boys sat at a table mending tears in a net using large flat needles and black thread. There was a clever trick to it and she'd have liked to watch and perhaps help—

But the Balance grew nigh. It made her light, almost dizzy, as if she'd been spun madly in circles. As happened often, dancing with Bannan, though he'd catch her before she could stumble and earn a quick kiss.

Jenn swallowed another spoonful and choked back a tear.

The song only she could hear floated around her head, louder at times than the soft murmur of voices.

Nonny believed the villagers avoided magic. It might be they simply absorbed it into their lives, as did those of Marrowdell, meaning it could be everywhere. To take her mind off her worries, Jenn began surreptitiously to watch for house toads or their ilk, checking under the benches—

"Time to go," Nonny said abruptly, leaping to her feet and heading for the door.

Relieved, Jenn hastened to follow, pausing to give the bowl to Granny and offer her thanks. On the way she looked for Flesie, to say a proper farewell, spotting the familiar puff of hair in the midst of the curl of rapt children at singer's feet.

She wouldn't disturb them.

Still, as Jenn stepped through the door, an impulse made her look back.

Sure enough, Flesie had stood to watch her leave. Jenn blew a kiss and the dear child giggled, pretending to catch it.

Nonny—unusually patient through this—led Jenn quickly along the dock, their way lit by escaping lamplight, beside boats moving restlessly with the tide, past colorful little homes, and around racks of drying fish. Jenn tried to memorize what she could, suddenly certain she wouldn't pass this way again.

Unless caught by dawizards. The thought gave her feet wings. She caught up to Nonny. "The dawizards saw me," she whispered. "Urcet led them away, but they'll be back soon, looking for me. And the man, Symyd? He knows what I am, Nonny." She hadn't done well at all, Jenn scolded herself, from the instant she'd decided to use the boat to ignoring Nonny's excellent advice about avoiding the village.

"Symyd has a reputation. Trust me, without proof, the dawizards won't credit a word he says." A gleam of teeth. "As for our Urcy—I was following the lot of them till I saw my poor boat in the middle of the bay." They reached the end of the lamplight and a hand shot out to take Jenn's wrist, holding her in place. "Why, Jenn Nalynn?"

"The waalum told me Urcet was in danger. That I had to go and help at once."

"By name?" This so incredulous Jenn felt her cheeks grow hot.

"Not exactly. They said the 'walker with treats.'" She hesitated, then went on in a rush, "Now I think the waalum meant Flesie, not Urcet."

"Of course they did." With an exasperated huff Jenn didn't think was aimed at her, Nonny dropped her wrist and started walking again, so she followed.

After a moment, Nonny spoke. "Flesie's forever wandering off for reasons of her own, coming home when she's ready. She'd have been fine this time if Urcy hadn't led the dawizards straight to you both."

And if she hadn't lingered with the child until they came. "I wouldn't have let them take Flesie," Jenn said, feeling a strange heat. A wind whipped spray up to the dock. The wood beneath them creaked. Calming herself, she made herself ask, "Will she be safe?"

A grim chuckle. "No one here will let any harm come to our Flesie."

Nor would the Bay of Shades. Not, Jenn decided, a comforting thought to share.

Leaving speech and explanations for later, if they'd a later, she jogged after Nonny, jumping down with her from the dock to the narrow shoreline path, glad of the other's speed, for she found herself unwilling to shorten the way.

There were those watching.

This child was far more interesting than most of his kind, Wisp decided. Certainly clever and brave, but also wise—that rarer and essential. He would stay with him.

He'd surreptitiously tested a bit of the Goosie-bag, easily ripping a hole with a claw. They'd make their escape at his timing, not the toad queen's.

Werfol's suggestion regarding the little cousins, however, bore pondering. Far from a dragon to admit being fooled, but he'd never asked—why would he?—questions that now seemed significant. Such as "why are you in Marrowdell?" and "why revere a monster as your queen?" and, oh yes, "what are you going to do with all those white pebbles?" it having become obvious house toads could do quite a bit that was unexpected and unforeseen.

The dragon sighed inwardly. Life had been simpler, once.

The idea of an enemy mustering its force in hiding sounded more kruar than dragon, not that kruar ever cooperated on a kill.

Luckily for dragons.

There was a concept he'd like not spread about.

Still. If Marrowdell's house toads sought to depose their queen, they'd need a way to reach her in the Verge.

Wisp felt a chill run down his spine.

Unless they planned for her to come to them.

No. It would make Marrowdell their battlefield. Whatever else he might think of the little cousins, they were honorable to a fault and careful of the homes they guarded. He refused to believe they would put those at risk.

Unless—the prize was worth it. *What did he really know of the little cousins?*

The boy made an unhappy little sound, not quite asleep, not quite awake. He faded, Wisp feared, the toad queen unable to resist sips of his magic, his life. Thus far, not enough to do him lasting harm, but her restraint wouldn't last.

~Elder brother.~

Wisp opened his eyes to find a moth perched on his left nostril, wings fluttering. ~Be of use or be gone,~ he snarled at it, out of patience.

The moth turned green and grew, expanding to fill the space and more. Curled protectively over the little truthseer, crushed under the belly of the sei-dragon, Wisp dared show a fang. ~You heard me! Help or be gone!~

~You cannot stay here.~ The bone-wrenching timbre of the voice was dreadfully familiar.

~I won't desert him.~

~You must go to her.~

Jenn Nalynn!

Wisp curled tighter. If the sei sought to divide his loyalties, it underestimated him—as it did all those of flesh and courage. ~The girl will save us!~ he boasted.

~Not without your aid.~ The terrible weight bearing down on him vanished.

Leaving that on his heart—

But the sei wasn't done. ~You will know your moment. Do not fail us, dragon lord.~

~Moment for what?~ he demanded. ~Fail how?~

Oh, and now the sei left?

Wisp snorted to himself. Jenn would have him stay with the boy. If the sei thought otherwise, it was mistaken—

"I did it, Wisp," exclaimed Werfol, pushing at him. "I 'dreamed the green dragon and it came! It said it was my friend."

And wants me to abandon you. The dragon swallowed the words and a growl.

"As am I, Dear Heart. As am I."

TWENTY-TWO

NONNY'S ROPE—ALONG WITH everything else Nonny owned— had vanished with her boat, except for what went out with the tide. To be, she informed Jenn, gleaned from shores further to the east, that being where currents took lost things beyond the Bay of Shades, and she wished those who found them good use. Words she said to distract her, Jenn knew because, lacking a rope to hold the end of, Nonny hadn't a good reason to come along.

Ancestors Blessed, Jenn was glad she did, for she couldn't imagine making this trip through the dark alone, but she couldn't say so. Once on the path, Nonny insisted on silence, and they went as quickly and quietly as possible. There was no telling how soon the dawizards would give chase.

Neither doubted they would.

Knowing she mustn't wish, Jenn tried her best not to be afraid or sorry or even overly brave and found her best approach was to think of how much she hadn't liked the oyster and how well maintained the path was for something pounded by bare feet over rock and gravel.

Though with the moonlight now behind clouds, they stubbed their toes every so often.

Which was what Jenn assumed happened when Nonny abruptly stopped, but the other pointed wordlessly at the bay.

Waalum swam there, heads up and aimed at them. Dozens—a wonderful unthought abundance and certainly more than she ever would have guessed—pacing them, Jenn realized, more easily than any runner on land. She spared room in her thoughts to be glad they'd be safe. Safer, the water having perils, she was sure, of its own.

Water she was shortly to enter. Oh dear. Jenn caught up to Nonny, on the move again.

They reached the leg of the great bridge, its stone softened by moonlight. As Nonny raised her hand to enter, Jenn stopped her with a touch. "By my Ancestors, I'm truly beholden for all you've done for me, Nonny," she whispered. "You need come no further—"

Eyes glinting, the Eld turned and put her hand on the stone. "We seek safety." The doorway formed, stones faded, and she stepped through, leaving Jenn no choice but follow.

Inside, illuminated by the glow of the room's light, a surprise. The trunks stood side by side on the floor, open.

And full. "Someone else was gleaning," Jenn said, staring around.

There was Nonny's mug and Nonny's kettle. A harmoot in an almost neat pile and a very tidy stack of blankets. More and more until it appeared possible to be everything, Jenn thought in amazement and growing relief, flung into the bay as the toad queen clutched and cracked open the *Good Igrini*, retrieved, dried, and left here.

"Will you look at this," Nonny said, walking around, touching this and that, seeming amazed herself.

Those below must be kind, Jenn decided, or at least thoughtful in their treatment of belongings. Heartened, she went directly to the still-closed trunk that lidded the hole in the floor, tilting it back and out of the way.

The roar of churning water greeted her, not at its final depth, for they'd been forced to come before low tide, but the drop took away her breath. Worse, the ladder's inset rungs were dripping wet and treacherous.

"Jenn."

She looked up, trying not to as appear alarmed as she felt, though Nonny wouldn't mock her for it, it being an alarming prospect indeed to climb down the ladder into the ebbing tide and unknown below. Really, by rights, she should be terrified and show it—

Jenn blinked, finding herself in a knot of showing and not, to find Nonny holding out a bottle. "Look what was waiting."

"But—that looks like—"

"It is," the other confirmed, tossing it to her across the hole.

She caught it, barely. "My letter. No one's read it," Jenn concluded, disappointed. Which was ridiculous. What kind of foolishness had it been, to toss a letter into the sea? Yet—"I'd wished—" she confessed.

"For what?" Nonny's eyebrows wagged at her. "Someone who'd help. Someone who'd care. I'm guessing those below know exactly who that is."

Drawing the bottle close, Jenn stared at her friend. "You think the waalum took my letter to the sirenspites and they brought it here—for me?"

"Along with your old clothes—again." Nonny held up Jenn's wool petticoat and let it fall with distaste. "Well?"

Ancestors Teased and Twisted, it made a sort of sense—as much as anything about being turn-born did—that her wish for help had found her here.

So she could help those she loved. Whoever she was about to meet agreed with her decision to come to them—encouraged her to do so—

She wasn't, Jenn decided, to lose the bottle. It might prove her introduction to those below. She tucked it inside her belt, checking it was secure, and imagined pulling out her letter to surprise Bannan when they were together again, at last and forever.

Jenn stood straighter, eyes shining.

"That's it," Nonny declared, grinning.

"I'll write to you," Jenn said impulsively. "And send you a pot-holder. Two."

The other pretended to scowl. "I've only one pot."

"One for each hand." It was a silly notion but wasn't, and she knew Nonny was pleased.

And then it was time. They stood side by side to stare down the hole, shoulders touching. "A rope, now," Nonny muttered under her breath, that not among their findings and Jenn had to suspect for good reason.

Throwing an arm around the Eld, harmoot and all, Jenn gave her a tight hug. "I'll be all right. What about you? You've nowhere to live. Will you go to the village?"

A snort. "Not me." Nonny tilted her head like one of the big white birds. "Dawizards hate whispers of magical doings spreading about. I do believe they'll want to hush any word of how a fishing boat was sunk by magic right under their noses. Why, I think the very least they'll do is replace that boat, don't you?"

"Be careful," Jenn warned, feeling cold inside. "I don't trust them and you shouldn't."

Nonny's arm went around her waist, strong and tight. "Who taught you that lesson, Jenn Nalynn?"

She pressed her lips to Nonny's forehead. "Be well," Jenn said, and made it a wish. The light of the room pulsed a richer blue than before and the air filled with the scent of roses.

A promise being made.

She laughed and Nonny did, and if those laughs sounded unsteady and closer to sobs, this was farewell and they'd become friends.

"Please explain what you can of matters to Urcet, Dear Heart," Jenn said then, lightly, "and thank him for me. Hearts of my Ancestors, however far we are apart, Keep Us Close. It means I won't forget you," she finished, it being a Rhothan saying and not Eldani, then smiled from her heart.

"Better not." Nonny rapped her on the head with a knuckle, but her eyes glistened. "Now git. I've business of my own waiting."

As did she.

Becoming glass, light, and pearl, Jenn Nalynn stepped into air.

And let herself fall to what waited below.

The front door had opened and closed through the rest of the night, arrivals given quiet commands and a hot meal in the kitchen. The summer estate had been built to entertain goodly crowds, and the hall, with its dance floor and wide windows, quickly became home to what bode to become, to Bannan's amazement, a small and well-equipped army.

Whose role would be to guard the baron and his heir in case enemies thought to take advantage—to see them to safety, if the house fell, and he hadn't the heart to remind his sister that if the toad queen won, there'd be no safety at all.

Lila was aware. She prepared for foes of flesh and blood, none better, and put an appalling trust in her little brother who'd fallen asleep in a chair at some point only to wake, groggy and stiff, shielding his eyes from the first rays of sunlight.

Dropping his hand as realization struck. Heart's Blood. The equinox. It'd be today, whatever happened.

Good, he thought grimly, rubbing his neck as he stood.

The house felt deserted. Brushing off his clothes, Bannan made for the kitchen, changing his mind at the last minute to check first on Roche.

To his relief, the younger man was awake and sitting up in bed, Semyn at the foot, the healer gone.

Replaced by Dutton, still on duty, and Bannan exchanged nods with the guard as he entered and snagged a chair with his foot. "So, Roche, how are you feeling this morning?"

"Like I died and came back to life," the truth, softened by a half smile. "Grateful. Unutterably so."

Semyn, dwarfed by the immense book open on his small lap, looked wan but determined. He hadn't slept, Bannan guessed, despite going to bed. "I've been explaining to Roche why he's now Baron Morrill."

Roche made a face. "It's not what I want." A green-eyed, sober glance at the boy, who gave an encouraging nod. "But is what I am. Semyn's proved it." His lips twitched. "Ancestors Blessed, what I'd give to see Uncle Jupp's face when he hears."

The heir paled. "Had Master Jupp access to current records, he'd have doubtless seen the significance of your third cousin dying without issue—"

"He'll be proud of you," Roche told Semyn, putting a hand on the book. New was the knotted string bracelet around his wrist. A trinket from Ioana or Lila; if it helped, the truthseer was glad.

The confidence—that was new as well, and Bannan wanted to ask—

"And we've been talking about Marrowdell, Uncle," Semyn announced. "The potential for—allies—there. Magic ones."

Lila'd warned him Semyn didn't remember outside the edge; that the boy made himself believe what must seem impossible spoke volumes for his strength of character. Perhaps knowing Roche couldn't lie helped.

As for lies, of omission at least, Bannan hadn't told Roche—or anyone—about the flood. Hadn't wanted to think of what he couldn't help, was the truth, if cowardly, but the pair looked at him with such expectation, he had to say something. "Those of Marrowdell hold you and your brother in all good will, Semyn, but we've no way to communicate with them, not in time."

And no Jenn Nalynn waiting there.

Roche reached under his quilt to produce, of all things, a house toad. "Are we sure we fight alone?"

"You have a house toad," Bannan observed numbly. "Here."

Dutton snorted. "Came home with them, sir, hidden in the luggage." He almost smiled. "Worst-kept secret in the house."

"It hasn't wanted to leave our bedroom or be seen," Semyn said quickly. "I'd promised Weed—but then I thought, maybe the toad could help."

From what Bannan could see, the little cousin, busily tucking itself against a pillow, was more interested in staying close to Roche. For all he knew, it was the Morrills' house toad. Had it come with the boys in search of him?

A question for the dragon.

The matter of house toads, however, had rested uneasily in the back of truthseer's mind since discovering their secret pathways within Marrowdell, a disquiet not helped by meeting their despicable queen. Bannan found himself staring at the toad on the bed, letting himself consider the possibilities.

Was it here to help—or spy?

The toad, meanwhile, stared back, having the advantage of larger, unreadable eyes, then closed them, as if in dismissal, putting a long-toed foot over its snout.

An answer of a sort. "I'll find out." A promise to his nephew— and warning for the toad. "Roche, we move before sunset." Bannan got to his feet.

"I'll be there." When Roche struggled to sit straighter, the toad hopped to sit on his stomach. "Apparently after more rest," he added wryly.

Bannan looked at Dutton, who gave a tiny shrug. The guard wore light mail, his sword and pistol at his hips, and if surprised by an opinionated toad, he'd be the last to show it.

"If it's all right, I'd like to stay here, with Roche," Semyn volunteered. He made a face. "Momma wants me out from underfoot."

Ancestors Witness, his heart hurt just looking at the boy. "We'll get—"

A small hand, palm out, stopped the promise he shouldn't, in conscience, make. "You'll do your best, Uncle Bannan," Semyn stated in his high, oddly adult voice. "Everyone will, for Werfol and our family. I ask no more and thank you."

Dutton straightened, hand to hilt. Roche nodded, eyes bright.

Bannan gave a short bow. "I—"

Which was when doors slammed, men cursed, and the unexpected thunder of hoofbeats careened down the hall—a vase smashing—

"Easy, Dutton," the truthseer said, smiling even as the door burst open.

And a big ugly head of what wasn't a horse pushed through.

Scourge had arrived.

But Jenn Nalynn did forget.

The instant water closed over her head, muting the light above, she didn't care, for above, she knew, was nothing and no one.

She sank, arms outstretched, fingers sending forth beams to catch in eyes, on sides, from scales and fins and teeth, for beneath was plenty and everyone.

Shadowed shapes with huge eyes swam close, scattering the rest, and it was right, she knew, they did so, being in charge.

The shapes guided her deeper, taking her below, and it was good, she knew, they did so, being certain where she was to go.

Not that she remembered where.

Or why.

Once convinced it wasn't an attack, those gathered were more amused than startled, the vase a gift from an aunt Emon did not favor, and Scourge purred with relentless satisfaction as he followed Bannan down the flight of stairs he'd apparently leapt in his hunt for his rider, drooling as he caught scent of the kitchen.

"No, you don't," the truthseer commanded, leaning a shoulder into Scourge's. "I'll take care of it," he promised before the kruar's dismayed huff became all-out revolt. "Semyn, some bacon, please!"

The heir, already burdened with the house toad, nodded and smoothly changed direction, Dutton following.

They'd an urgent use for the kruar, one occurring to Bannan— and by the fire in Semyn's eyes, to the heir as well—the instant the bloody beast shoved his face in the room. They'd needed a messenger—

He'd no idea if Scourge would do it, or could, but they had to try. Using a quick flash of signs, he'd drawn Semyn and Dutton along, the guard giving Roche a hasty excuse involving breakfast that worthy accepted with a bemused look, likely glad enough to get the kruar out of his room.

A clot of new arrivals hurriedly backed out of the doorway to let Bannan and his four-footed companion pass. Outside, he saw Tagey still mounted, with others stepping from horses who rolled eyes at Scourge and might have bolted but for the quick action of grooms.

They'd head to the stables.

He'd another destination in mind.

Semyn and Dutton appeared at the side of the house, prudently going through the kitchen to avoid the congested front hall. The guard carried a sack and Scourge lifted his head, nostrils flared. "I keep my promises, Idiot Beast," Bannan said fondly.

He took the stone pathway to the patio behind the house, those posted taking alert then subsiding at a nod from Dutton—who'd trusted him thus far.

Ancestors Brash and Bold, he'd best deserve it.

The first private spot under the trees, past the wide brick-lined firepit he remembered from more cheerful times, Bannan stopped, taking the sack. Before he could offer it to Scourge, the kruar neatly nipped it from his hand, barely missing fingers, tossing the entire thing down with a joyful snarl.

Answered by two more.

Semyn's eyes widened, but he didn't back up as Dauntless and Spirit materialized from the forest, the pair weaving, heads down, to growl the greeting of their kind to the significantly larger Scourge.

If they thought to get a share of his bacon, they were, Bannan thought with amusement, too late and sadly mistaken.

As for why they'd come—while glad of it, he'd no idea, unless—

He gave Scourge a suspicious look.

In answer, the bloody beast licked his lips with a forked tongue. Had he understood?

No, he smelled battle and drew in resources.

Well done, the truthseer decided, regardless the reason.

"What's this?" Dutton demanded, low and worried, disturbed by the presence of what might seem mounts for the three of them. "We can't leave."

"We're not," Semyn countered at once, his bright gaze flashing to the kruar and back. "They are."

Bannan nodded. "That's my hope. But they can't understand me here."

"Werfol told me. You have to be in the edge."

Dutton's forbidding hand dropped to the heir's shoulder. "You'll not take him there." In a growl worthy of Scourge, who wrinkled a lip in response.

"No need," the truthseer reassured the guard. "Might I borrow your little cousin, Semyn?" He'd questions for a toad and, while he couldn't talk to it except in the Verge, in the edge Scourge could.

If willing. So much depended on the chancy natures of the beasts, and loyalties, but this was a toss of the stones worth taking. "Advise your mother I'm sending word to our more—unusual—allies." He half smiled. "At your suggestion."

The boy's eyes lit up, but his face remained serious. "Be careful, Uncle Bannan. You'll be in danger."

"I won't stay long." Heart's Blood, Semyn wasn't wrong. On the thought, the truthseer pulled the thong with the Larmensu key over his head, careful not to touch it. Brought out the cursed scarf, tying it tightly around the key as Dutton and Semyn watched in silence, then went to give the result to his nephew. About to say, "—for your mother if I've made a mistake and fail—" he changed his mind.

They all might fail.

So Bannan went to a knee before the one who was, in truth, his heir as well, witnessed by the man who'd not desert the boy or be daunted, no matter the size or shape of their enemy. "Semyn *Larmensu* Westietas, I leave these with you in trust until my return. Hearts of our Ancestors, Keep Us Close."

"'Keep Us Close'." Semyn's eyes were as round as the house toad's, his voice shaking, but he freed a hand to take the bound key, and Bannan helped by taking the toad under his arm.

"It said our name, uncle," Semyn gasped. "I heard it."

Bannan glanced at Dutton, then nodded to the boy, meeting those earnest hazel eyes, his flashing gold. "The key is magic and will summon those loyal to Larmensu, should you be in peril. Do not trust the scarf," he added, because that was true as well.

Then he turned and mounted Scourge, sending him toward the edge, the other kruar following like echoes of thunder.

W

Without any warning whatsoever, not that there ever was, Goosie's seam split open, dumping Werfol and Wisp and the tiny boat on the sand.

At a hiss from the dragon, the boy froze in place. This wasn't like the other times the majesty-monster had freed him, not at all.

For one thing, she was right there, looming over them. Not hiding.

For another? The eye he could see was shut tight, the lid stretched thin over the bulge. If the other was closed, she either ignored them or slept.

Ignoring them seemed unlikely, unless to be annoying, which was entirely possible, as far as Werfol was concerned, and had to be more likely than sleeping with them outside and loose.

Especially with a dragon able to blow her up.

Making this another of her tricks. Werfol signed that caution at Wisp, who eyed his flying fingers then said, in his inside tickly voice, ~If you warn we mustn't trust what we see, truthseer, be sure I don't. Has this happened before? Without words, please.~

Werfol gave a minimal shake of his head, wishing he dared move a little more. Or a lot, since they'd landed with him sprawled over the dragon who was—not that he'd ever say so—about as comfortable to lie on as lumpy rocks.

No, rocks would be easier; they didn't have blade-like fangs or a temper. Why had he thought of temper?

Because Wisp's wings were spread in the air to either side, motionless but so tensed they vibrated, like one of Momma's hawks when seriously pissed and ready to take a finger.

Maybe moving might be a bad idea no matter how lumpy and hard Wisp was as a mattress.

~Look at her eyes.~

Wisp's inside voice didn't sound angry. Maybe, the little truthseer thought in some sympathy, the dragon hadn't been comfortable either, while inside Goosie, and was happy now to stretch his wings.

Despite thinking it an odd request, and able to see but one, Werfol did as he was told. There. Her eye moved beneath the lid, the movements restless and abrupt, as if she tracked something elusive—

She was dreaming!

Werfol was off the dragon in a heartbeat, launching himself from Wisp's snout at the majesty-monster's front foot, the nearest part. He threw the boat at her then began kicking a toe wider than his body with all his might, shouting as loudly as he could. "WAKE UP!! WAKE UP!!" His mind white with fear, with thinking over and over: *She mustn't find Momma! She mustn't find Momma!* Because that's what dreams were for, to hunt someone else, and he wouldn't let—

The toe, and attached foot and leg, rose into the sky, shadowing Werfol like doom as the entire mass came hurtling down, intent on squashing him like a bug once and for all.

To be disappointed, for Werfol wasn't there, but snatched up by a dragon and saved. He cheered wildly, sure they'd escape.

Until, hanging from Wisp's gentle grip, he saw the majesty-monster rise and fill the air in front of them. The dragon roared and whirled away, only to have her appear in front again. Again. Again. Powerful wing beats.

Impossible monster.

Who enjoyed this. His friend wore himself out for nothing. "Stop, Wisp," Werfol urged at last, quiet and sure. "This isn't the way out."

Unsurprised that when, the instant the dragon slowed and her fun tormenting them ended, they found themselves in the dark, confined inside his toy.

This time, with nothing to say.

At the bottom of the abyss was a lake of mimrol, like molten silver poured in a mold. Surrounding it, attached to massive smooth white walls, climbed dark featureless buildings. They looked like columns.

Or trees without branches.

They might be, Jenn Nalynn thought, hollow straws, for instead of roofs they'd round openings, and from those streamed bubbles of light, some tiny, some bigger, never a rhythm or pattern to them, random making them lovelier, and sea butterflies flew in and out, their filmy wings catching this color or that, strange colors and wondrous, for the light was of the Verge.

And lit all else.

Straws. She hadn't had a thought in forever and thought of straws. Her lips stretched in a smile.

Lips. She'd lips?

Jenn forgot again, her gaze caught by new arrivals.

She'd been left by the lake, let fall gently and slowly by her guides to lodge rather than sit between two small columns. That blinked at her with hundreds of little black eyes and burped, squatting then growing, so weren't columns, unless these were baby ones.

And the grand ones reaching up and up were not—

Babies. Did she know babies?

Jenn forgot again, a boat, or something like, coming to rest at her feet.

People were on it, several, though they looked nothing like what the word meant in her head. She could see through them, for one thing, except where they had organs; they'd hearts or what beat, but no heads.

For another, they were connected one to the next and to all by sections of their flattened bodies. As a result they moved, as she saw when they left the boat, in sequence, like a ribbon in a breeze. Slowly, each lifting and lowering, the next lifting and lowering, afloat in the water resting atop the mimrol lake.

How extraordinary. She'd love to tell—

Jenn forgot, the connected people forming a ring to enclose her.

The baby columns shot up and spurted away.

The connected people began to vibrate, this one and that, driving waves of pressure against Jenn. It tickled and she wondered if that was their intent.

Until words formed inside her, overlapping and rich, like lyrics sung by multiple voices formed harmonies, adding meanings.

"You belong. You belong. Stay."

"Flesh drowns, you won't. Flesh rots, you won't."

"You belong. You could belong. We'd like you to stay."

"Selfish are turn-born but not Jenn Nalynn. Heedless are turn-born but not Jenn Nalynn."

"You could belong. You should belong. Stay, please."

"Turn-born aren't welcome but Jennnnnnn Nalynnnnnn . . ."

Her name went on for quite a long time, given warm flourish and rich depth and what might have been a triumph of horns, and she felt—she felt—

Jenn forgot the word.

The song stopped. Changed. Became distant and troubled. Came close and more urgent. Reached into her and tugged after her until she let out a cry of protest.

Astonished to watch bubbles drift up past her face. *She'd bubbles inside?*

"Jenn Nalynn. Who belongs and is welcome but must not stay." A deep tone. "We need you to go. All need you to go." Waves of pressure beat against her, louder. Stronger. "GO. GO. GO!"

She huddled and tried to hide.

Grew flustered and angry.

So Jenn wished the people to stop.

Their bodies blew open, becoming strains of pale jelly and pointless parts. Fish with needle-like teeth crowded to the feast. When done, they snapped at each other, then flashed away in pursuit of other connected people, who undulated slowly, so slowly, too slowly for shelter, only to be eaten alive. More and more fish, less and less people—

Consequence.

She hadn't meant this to happen. It shouldn't happen.

So Jenn wished the fish to stop.

A great shape came down, down, down, blocking the bubble lights, dimming the mimrol. It opened its mouth and sucked in all the fish, then all the connected people, then squat little columns with hundreds of eyes, then the other columns crusted on the white wall began to shake and move—

She didn't know what to do. Didn't know how to fix it. Didn't—

A sea butterfly, its twirled shell hanging down, fluttered up past her face. Jenn reached out and it came to rest on her fingertip. The creature was unutterably fragile and precious, the more so for the destruction happening around it, destruction she'd caused.

A voice like a mountain shuddered through her. "REMEMBER WHAT YOU ARE."

Remembering nothing, Jenn looked past the tiny creature, seeing the massive white walls, for the first time noticing how they glistened on their own, how they drew all light. How curious—

A pull at her waist. A host of sea butterflies appeared, dragging with them a bottle. They rose with it, letting it fall in front of Jenn, and her hand found it.

Knew to open it.

To pull out what was inside.

A label with inked words. Words dissolving in the water and she let another cry for she mustn't lose them. Water rushed into her open mouth, for she'd a mouth. It brought ink and the ink made words on her tongue, for she'd one of those again.

Words to fill her heart. *Dearest Heart. Bannan. Marrowdell. Wisp.*

Words to restore her courage. *Nonny, tin, kind. Waalum, little cousins.*

Words to give her purpose. *Werfol. Captive.*

Words to give her direction. *Crossing. Balance.*

Last of all, words to return everything Jenn Nalynn forgot.

The toad queen.

With the name came a flood, not of water, but of faces: Peggs and Kydd, their father, Aunt Sybb, Tir and Werfol's family, Old Jupp and Riss and Uncle Horst, Treffs and Ropps, Cheffy and Alyssa. The Emms. Hettie with her babes. Master Dusom and Wainn.

Wen, turning to look back at her, the Verge in her eyes and a smile on her lips.

And when Jenn Nalynn opened her eyes, for they'd been closed and she'd been gone, she found herself surrounded by connected people and bubbles of light, embraced by the love in their music.

Nothing destroyed, nothing changed.

All as it was.

Except her.

"I'm ready," she said, and was.

A sea butterfly stroked by, wings catching the color shining from within her. White walls rippled with blue.

"YOU WILL HAVE A GUIDE," came the promise.

Being sei and hers.

If Bannan thought to make a cautious, knowing step from this world to the edge—Lila showing him the map and there being, had he noticed the first time, chiseled stones set as a discrete boundary— he'd reckoned without the nature of kruar.

Who'd raced, not run, from the back of the house, Spirit and Dauntless tantalizing glimpses of sleek hide between the trees, Scourge owning the path, until they flew past the forester's hut and careful stones, over the slope of talus that were the scree, and almost out the other side into another forest before the bloody things came to a halt.

Scourge curved his mighty neck and pranced in place. *Smug, that was.*

Dangerous, and Bannan didn't move for a long moment.

"She's not interested in us," a warm breeze assured him.

Smug and overconfident.

With him, again, and the best help of all. Bannan gave that neck a brisk rub before throwing his leg over and jumping down. "Welcome back, Idiot Beast. I've a job for you."

"And us, truthseer?"

Necks not as boastfully curved, but when he looked beyond their seeming as horses, he saw how they rattled the blades kruar wore as manes, and their armor caught the light. They'd a right to their pride and names.

Scourge stamped a hoof.

Spirit and Dauntless rolled their eyes but settled, their posture submissive.

An opportunity he'd not thought to have—if they were willing.

The house toad under his arm stretched a leg, reminding him who else was present. Bannan set it down where, to his deeper sight, the rocks didn't have faces.

A wind sighed down the mountain, chilled by the snow lingering above. Storm clouds brewed far to the west, coming from Avyo, from Channen and points further, a spring storm, with its promise of drenching rain and hail, thunder and lightning.

Heart's Blood, the worst would arrive late afternoon, as if nature intended to be involved.

No matter. Bannan looked to his waiting companions. "Today's turn, the Balance, will see battle. I need your speed and courage to take word to our allies."

Dauntless tossed her head. "What are allies?"

Scourge snapped his jaws and she subsided. To Bannan, crisp and cold. "You want the dragon."

He nodded. "And to warn Marrowdell about the toad queen."

A wail, high and tremulous. The young kruar shied back, eyes wide with fear and ready to bolt; Bannan couldn't fault them.

Scourge reared, holding at full extent against a backdrop of cloud like a statue of ancient glory, and they stopped and stared.

Calmed and stepped close again, nostrils flaring and lined with red.

They took courage, these brave youngsters, the truthseer thought, and lacked only a cause. "We will not let her keep Werfol."

Oh, and now breezes like fetid hot winds struck his ears. Cries of "Ours!" "Save our truthseer!"

Scourge dropped his front feet to the ground, rattling stones. "Do your part to save him! Go to Marrowdell. Tell the dragon to warn the people then come to join our fight." A sly, "If he doesn't roast you first."

"Wisp won't. He knows them," Bannan said hastily, though it was true the dragon didn't care for surprises. But desperate for news? That he'd be. "Tell him the toad queen sent Jenn Nalynn far away. To Eld," a guess, but fair enough. "Most of all, let him know she'll be with us at the turn."

A chance, a hope—but one he'd risk the world against.

Scourge went to Dauntless, nipping her shoulder. Turned and pretended to kick at Spirit. Heads raised, the two ran for the distant trees.

Vanishing before they reached them.

Bannan tried to mark the crossing, Lila surely wanting to know, but the rocks were all the same.

"I stay with you," Scourge predicted, eyes bright.

That wasn't the plan. First, the truthseer crouched to meet the house toad's patient gaze. "We need to talk," he told it. "Scourge, listen to the little cousin for me."

A big black nose reached past his shoulder, blew hot breath at the toad, as if to dismiss it. The toad blinked but didn't budge.

"There's no one here but us," the truthseer said, hiding his impatience. Ancestors Prideful and Prejudiced, cows he understood—but what was it about kruar and house toads? "Bloody beast, this is crucial."

The nose withdrew. "Be warned. Little cousins are at best confusing." A plaintive pause. "I'll do what I can."

The truthseer nodded gravely and addressed the toad. "The time for secrets is over. We've traveled your passages in Marrowdell. We've met—" the word *your* stuck in his throat, "—the toad queen and know her vile intentions, to break free and consume all magic. To destroy. What we don't know are yours. Are you with us?"

To his deeper sight, this house toad appeared like any of Marrowdell, its skin chain mail, its warts gems worn like medals, for this was a fighter and defender.

As if hearing his thought, it bared rows of fine, pointed teeth.

Scourge gave an offended huff.

"What did it say?"

A growl. "The little cousin dares claim 'all are where they should be.'" A furious hoof slammed near the toad, who flattened but didn't budge. "WERFOL IS NOT! WE ARE NOT! THE TURN-BORN IS NOT! YOU ARE A WASTE OF BREATH!"

Bannan winced, lifting a quelling hand. The house toad puffed back to normal size and a little more. Resolute, he thought. And was that *confidence*? "And at the Balance?" he asked carefully.

A toe stretched toward him, pulled back.

"Scourge?"

This time, the breeze in his ear held a note of uncertainty. "It says 'all will go where they must.' What is it talking about?" Darkly. "Perhaps this little cousin has been damaged by its time beyond the edge."

The house toad aimed its limpid gaze briefly at the kruar, blinked, then resumed staring at the truthseer. Scourge growled, not sharing whatever passed between them.

Bannan rocked back on his heels, regarding the toad. "I see nothing wrong with this inestimable little cousin," he concluded, bowing his head to it. Nothing wrong or ill about any house toad, other than an obsession—likely necessary—with secrecy.

Had they escaped the toad queen to await this day and time?

Had they planned for it, all the years of Jenn's life?

Ancestors Blessed and Beloved—the potential shook him to the core.

He refused doubt. Refused hope, for neither helped him now, settling on a profound gratitude he'd found Marrowdell and its denizens—or they'd found him.

"A last question before I send the bloody beast where he needs to be." Bannan ignored the hoof striking a sharp objection into the rock beside him. "Shall I take you back to Roche or will you wait—" for what, he refused to predict "—here?"

The answer, an armful of clammy toad, needed no translation.

The boy, like the youngling, was foolishly, recklessly brave to attack the toad queen. While Wisp knew he should point this out, he declined, full of pride. What a remarkable dragon this boy would make!

Not, Wisp decided, feeling the boy shaking, that he'd suggest it to the girl. ~You feared she dreamed your mother.~

He felt a nod. Heard a sob-filled whisper, "Momma's not going to stop trying to 'dream me, to find where I am. It's not safe, Wisp. It's not safe."

A deplorable gift, the dragon concluded, blissfully free of dreams. Though he'd waking nightmares, being confined here and helpless while matters came to a head newly chief among them.

The sei wanted him to leave. Would, he feared, insist on it. There might be no warning—

~Soon, no one will be safe, Dear Heart. You will need all your courage.~ He tried to think how best to soften the blow.

Forgetting the quick mind with him.

"Because you're going away." A pause, then a somber, "It's all right, Wisp. I understand why you have to leave me behind."

As everyone had, from the girl to his uncle and even the wretched old kruar. The dragon coiled protectively around the boy, feeling soft arms attempt to wrap around his neck, growing more and more enraged. Who were the sei, to force *HIM* to such betrayal? ~I won't do it,~ he vowed. ~The sei can eat their own tails.~

A swallowed hiccup, then a bold, "The green dragon has a really long one."

In company with the boy, Wisp let himself relish the image of stuffing the entirety of it down that insulting throat—

All at once, Werfol said, his voice a little too calm, "The moth doesn't have a tail."

Wisp stiffened, opening an eye.

The moth perched on Werfol's shoulder lifted a thin leg in greeting, its wings exuding a soft blue-tinged light. Light that reflected into eyes of molten gold, the little truthseer willing himself to see the truth.

Never flinching from it. A lesson there, worthy of a dragon.

Who'd learned others from a great-hearted girl.

~I won't leave him.~

~This is your moment,~ the moth said in the sei's voice. ~You must.~

All at once, Wisp heard another voice, other words, those of the strange woman, Wen Treff, sitting on a frozen meadow, atop the Spine . . .

. . . It seeks to swallow all there is and will do so at the Balance. Unless thwarted. Unless challenged. Unless the brave and bold and good-hearted face this threat together . . .

"Go, Wisp."

Werfol was the brave. The good-hearted, Jenn Nalynn.

Leaving him to be bold. Still, Wisp hesitated. ~Promise to stay with him.~

The leg brought an antenna down before a fathomless black eye. Considering. It was more than he'd thought to achieve.

Even a dragon might hold his breath, asking favors of a god.

The leg folded. Every leg did, the moth settling on Werfol's shoulder like a dragon on a ledge.

Wisp sent a breeze to ruffle the little truthseer's hair, tenderly brush his cheek, then find his ear.

Then, the dragon told Werfol Westietas exactly what he'd need to hear, roaring.

"NOW WE END HER!"

His claws shredded the cloth holding him in—his wings opened even as he passed through—and when the toad queen roared in outrage—

Wisp flew into her gaping mouth.

ᏖᏇᎬᏁᏖᎩ-ᏖᎻᎡᎬᎬ

ON THE DAY of Balance comes a moment exquisite and fraught, a moment when those born at the turn feel drawn through the thinning curtain between Verge and edge. To cross. A moment between the lift of a foot and the set of it down, between a remembered breath and forgotten one, between magic given—

—and magic found.

So it was, in that moment, Jenn Nalynn answered the same call, seeking to cross from the edge held in the Bay of Shades, into the Verge.

Long ago, the sei had sealed this undersea crossing against turn-born, those here once betrayed and demanding that protection.

Now, waalum towed Jenn over the mimrol lake and through columns emitting bubbles of light, to face a wall of white stone.

The toad queen had been wrong about this as with so much else. Jenn need not force a new crossing against the will of the sei, need break nor harm a thing.

She need only be herself.

Pressing her hands gently against the wall, Jenn Nalynn said, "Please take me where I must be."

And took her step—

He'd sent Scourge into the Verge, to the enclave of Mistress Sand and the other terst turn-born, a mission that had the great beast flatten his ears but make no other protest.

Knew a last resort, did he?

Bannan shook off the tinge of ill feeling. Nerves were normal—healthy. Jenn had told him the turn-born would cross at today's turn, expecting her to meet them and see the gifts they'd obtained.

An expectation to become curiosity and even alarm, meeting Scourge instead with his warning. To the good, the truthseer told himself, to have such powerful beings aware and ready.

Unless the ever-cynical dragon was right and those turn-born, while they must know of the toad queen, would consider her thefts from the edge beneath notice. Had they not abandoned the little cousins?

Or had they?

Heart's Blood, he couldn't rely on anything he'd been told—

"Little brother, if you keep slowing down we'll miss the turn."

Bannan looked up with a start to find Lila gazing down at him from her halted mount, a leg crossed over the saddle. Emon rode to the other side. He didn't speak. Hadn't, since they'd bid a quiet farewell to Semyn, his face set and grim.

Emon's would be the harder task, to turn back and leave them before the last of the forest, to assemble those gathered into a defense of the house, perhaps of this part of their world—they'd no way to know, Lila had warned.

Roche sat behind Lila, clinging to the saddle ties as if in absolute terror of touching her. The house toad had, to Bannan's surprise, elected to stay with the heir.

Perhaps knowing something of last resorts itself.

"We won't," the truthseer declared. The rain had started before they left, become the drenching waterfall he'd feared; thunder rolled through the mountains, half deafening them. Without help from the sky, they'd set off based on Emon's clocks and calculations.

He'd no need for them. He'd feel this turn in his bones. Refusing to doubt, Bannan lengthened his stride.

When the forest ended, Emon sent his horse close to his wife's. In the gloom, they searched one another's faces. Of a sudden, Lila reached and Emon did—

—to stop short, clasping hand to wrist in a soldier's farewell. Each gave the other a single nod, then their hands parted.

The baron turned his horse, disappearing behind gray sheets of rain.

It was up to Bannan to touch Lila's leg and whisper, "Time to go."

Goosie stitched itself up again after Wisp left and before Werfol could follow.

Not that he was supposed to, but he couldn't not try.

Alone. *Again.*

"Aren't you glad, little one?" came the majesty-monster's horrid voice. He covered his ears but couldn't keep it out. "You should thank me for getting rid of the dragon. They aren't good company at all."

Wisp was the best company. The very best.

Werfol swallowed the words. Battles hung on threads, Semyn had told him. Let your enemy make the mistake, Momma said. Know how things work, Poppa taught.

His heart pounded. *'NOW WE END HER!'*

Her comeuppance was coming. On the wings of a dragon. By the hands of his uncle and mother and more. Through the magic of Jenn Nalynn, who wouldn't, couldn't fail him.

The little truthseer sat nice and still—glad of the light from the moth who hadn't left though didn't seem much use otherwise—and thought very carefully before he said, "Would you tell me again how you'll rule everything, your majesty? Wisp didn't believe it but you're so—" he needed a word, the right word, now, "—*malevolent.*"

Werfol covered his mouth, but it was too late.

"I am, aren't I?" She preened, it was in her voice, like JoJo after a sand bath, and he should have known she'd take it as a compliment. "My first act will be—"

He didn't bother to listen.

Let her talk. Wisp had told him all he needed to hear.

'NOW WE END HER!'

Roche Morrill stood, pale but steady, at the limit of the edge. "I'm as ready as I can be."

Lila nodded, holding the scarf up in the rain. Lightning flashed.

Bannan, as far from ready as ever in his life, thought of Jenn Nalynn. Of her purpled eyes and golden hair and most of all of her smile. Answered the desperate longing of his heart and put a hand to Roche's shoulder and one to Lila's.

Now.

They stepped together into the edge.

"Edis," Roche called at once, his voice cracking. He coughed to clear it. Shouted at the storm, "EDIS!"

And was answered. But not by his friend—

As the ground shook beneath them, Bannan thrust Roche back, out of danger. Lila drew her sword, teeth bared. "Come and get us, you soulless bitch! FOR LARMENSU!"

"FOR LARMENSU!" Bannan shouted with her.

A mouth gaped before them, terrible, fetid, and moist.

Even as it swallowed them whole—

Even as he lost sight of Lila and despaired—

Was that a glimpse of white?

Goosie bounced and Goosie shook and Werfol's teeth met in his bottom lip. Something was happening. Something, he hoped with all his might, bad for the majesty-monster.

The seam split and out he dropped, landing on his feet. He wiped blood from his chin with the back of his sleeve, as he'd seen Momma do in practice, and smiled her smile. It was time. He knew it. So did the moth, who wrote something down before leaving him.

"I've new treats for you, little one," the majesty-monster prattled and cooed, not the least noticing.

Which was, Werfol knew, foolish of her but typical. "Show me," he dared, bracing himself for anything.

Except the sight of his mother, writhing on the sand.

"Momma!" He ran to her, dropping to his knees. Her eyes were squeezed shut and she moaned. One hand clenched a scarf, but the other flailed out, reaching for him.

He seized it.

"Now, Edis!"

Werfol looked up to see Uncle Bannan, and beside him rose the magical being who'd taken him to safety before with Roche—

Who could only take two—

And it wasn't fair, but nothing was—

Werfol squeezed his eyes shut, pulling his hand from his mother's. "Leave me."

"Not this time," he heard Uncle Bannan say.

And as the majesty-monster roared, loud enough to break the world, Werfol found himself held tight—

—felt himself pulled through the earth—

—and deposited, ever so gently, on a pile of stones.

Wherever the toad queen had thought to send him, if not to eat him on the spot, the dragon neither knew nor cared, for the sei had, at last, been of use.

Wisp found himself in her empty, lifeless palace, flying through a corridor. With a roar and tilt of his wings, he sent himself down and down, flying faster and faster, around and around.

The turn was almost here and he knew where the sei aimed him.

Back to her trap, where tendrils sucked away magic and life, where so many dragons had perished.

To where a marble hung in midair.

TWENTY-FOUR

*J*ENN NALYNN'S BARE foot finished its step, landing on what looked like a floor, but gave underneath. She wrinkled her nose at the stench. Then, so delighted was she to have a nose again, she reached up her finger to touch the tip, going cross-eyed to watch, and almost laughed.

But this wasn't a place for laughter. Lowering her hand, she turned around slowly. The floor rolled away from her, uneven and brown, like old cracking leather. Met walls ready to crumble that rose and rose. Her gaze followed them up and up until she saw where the walls reached a ceiling more like a honeycomb than other ceilings of her experience, possessed of openings as well as solid parts, and it might have been magnificent and certainly impressive—

If not so sad. She stood in a place that had forgotten what it was supposed to be, become something dreadful and foul. If there really were ghosts, like in Roche's favorite stories, she supposed they'd be here if anywhere.

A ghost—*something*—glinted high above.

Before she could find out what, Jenn was grabbed from below. She glanced down to find black tendrils winding around her feet and legs. "No, thank you," she told them, ready to wish.

But they withdrew with a snap, letting her look up again.

The glint came closer, closer still, until she saw what it was and the whole of her heart cried out, "Wisp!"

As her dragon roared with joy.

They came together in a rush and confusion, Jenn quickly turn-born and glass, for her dragon lost all restraint and grabbed her in his claws, sweeping her into the air. Which was lovely and wonderful but—"I've come for Werfol!"

Her dragon kept flying upward with strong, steady beats, lowering his head so she saw herself reflected in a wild violet eye, and Jenn grew still and ready, remembering what the sea butterfly promised. She'd have a guide.

Who better than the one who'd guided her from the start?

Wisp slowed, then hovered. ~There she is, Dearest Heart. And Werfol.~

At first, she saw nothing.

Squinted at a speck. A speck sending back her own light, and with a glad cry, Jenn stretched out her hand and plucked the pale blue marble from the air.

Time seemed to stop. Shadowed by the toad queen, breathing her foul stench, Bannan waited.

Then, in a terrible cold voice, the monster spoke. "The turn of the Balance has passed."

Relief drained the blood from his head and shoulders, threatened to stagger him; somehow he held firm.

Ancestors Witness, it wasn't the ending he'd hoped by far, preferring any version with Jenn Nalynn in his arms, the toad queen belly up and croaking her last.

But if the monster was here, Jenn hadn't broken open her prison.

Everyone—everyone but him—was safe.

Bannan grinned. Ancestors Bloody and Blessed, he'd take it. He'd more than take it. "We've won!"

"The game's far from over, truthseer," the toad queen told him, lips cracking open. She did an obscene little dance, shaking her trophies. "The turn-born will make her mistake."

Then the monster laughed.

She was here! She was his! The void inside him where Jenn Nalynn belonged was full once more and Wisp, were he honest, wanted nothing more than to never have it empty again.

And to be anywhere but here.

But here they were. He hovered, unwilling to risk landing. The floor writhed and swarmed with tendrils, drawn by the girl's magic as well as his, and leaving seemed a very good idea, except for one vexing problem.

"I don't know what to do with it." Jenn looped an arm around his leg, helping support her weight as she studied the marble. "You're quite sure she and Werfol are inside?"

~Yes.~ Well, he couldn't be *sure*, but the sei sent him here and the marble was inexplicable—making it, the dragon told himself, something sei.

"It's growing."

That couldn't be good. ~We take it away,~ Wisp decided—before it became too much for him or her to hold. He began to fly.

Only to have another dragon veer into him, almost knocking the girl from his grasp!

~HOW DARE YOU!~ he roared.

The youngling swooped down, curled, and used the momentum to soar again, a pretty maneuver that would, Wisp judged grimly, bring its fool throat to his waiting jaws—

~I've a message! I've a message!~

He closed his jaws as the youngling skimmed by, head whipping around to follow. ~Hold still,~ he ordered peevishly. ~What are you talking about?~

The youngling came to hover in front of them, its attention torn between Wisp and the famous turn-born he held. ~The elder sister said to give these words to Jenn Nalynn.~

"That's me," the girl said quickly, her voice filling with hope. "Do you mean Wen?"

The youngling, addressed directly by a turn-born for the first time in its life, lowered in the air to regard her with dumbstruck awe.

~Speak up!~ Wisp ordered testily.

~Yes, Great Lord of Dragons. The elder sister's words for Jenn Nalynn were: 'What do you do with a house toad's gift?'~

Gibberish, the dragon thought, despairing.

But the girl made a happy sound, as if understanding immediately. Before Wisp knew what she intended, she smacked the marble against one of his claws.

Cracking it open.

Out exploded the toad queen, expanding as she fell.

And someone else.

TWENTY-FIVE

*H*OUSE TOADS LAID eggs. Eggs you cracked open and she'd been so sure she understood Wen's message Jenn hadn't hesitated.

Now this. Heart's Blood, she hadn't even made a wish and there were consequences—

Thoughts to which she gave no attention, of course, being much too busy holding on to a leg as Wisp and the other dragon dove after the person who fell—dodging the ever-growing bulk of the toad queen, and her waving feet—though Jenn couldn't yet tell if it was a little boy and Werfol—

Until recognizing it was a grown man and—

"Bannan!!" And it wasn't a wish, but the dragons were suddenly *there*, where they had to be, and the strange one had her love in its claws—hastily adjusting that grip as Wisp roared, and all at once they were rising again, heading for the nearest hole in the vast ceiling.

"Not so fast," said the toad queen, and the holes snapped shut.

Wisp caught hold of a crack in the wall. The other dragon did the same, as close as it could, having an easier time with four good legs even with two wrapped around—

"Werfol," Jenn whispered, aching with conflicted joy.

"Safe. With his mother and safe," her dearest love said, his eyes glowing gold, the news music to her heart. His lips curved up as if there was nothing but happiness in the world, and for this instant, it was true, she thought. "Been here long?"

"I let the toad queen out," Jenn confessed, because he should know. "Wen told me how."

Astonishingly, his smile grew. "Did she now? That's good."

~I see nothing good, truthseer,~ snapped her dragon.

"Werfol's free and we're together." Jenn reached out to pat Wisp, feeling him strain, but he'd die before letting her go, so she wasn't afraid. "Who is your friend?"

The other dragon twisted its neck to look at her, being remarkably flexible; did that make it younger than Wisp or merely intact? ~I am as yet nameless, elder sister.~

Younger, she decided, on hearing its voice, and a great deal so. Bannan, able to hear in the Verge, gave it a wondering look—aware, as she was, how dragons, to be blunt, ate their offspring when given any chance, making this—

~It is not a *friend*,~ Wisp corrected testily. ~It is my student. A pettiness of the sei.~

Who were, Jenn knew, many things, but never petty. With Werfol safe, she'd ever so many questions—

A tremendous SCRATCH!

She looked down, appalled to see the toad queen had grown large enough to reach the walls on either side, driving in her claw-tipped toes to hang above the floor.

And continued to grow. At this rate, her bulk would squeeze them to death against the ceiling—

"I SHALL FILL ALL WORLDS!"

Or do worse.

ℳ

When Werfol rolled over, his face filled with rain so he had to spit and sputter to find his voice, and rain meant something wonderful, but also something terrible, and where was everyone and where was he—

"I've got you, Dearest Heart."

—in Momma's arms!

"Uncle—!" he protested at once, while squeezing as close to her as he possibly could, closer than any child ever had, noticing his Momma felt more like a dragon than he'd realized, and that was just fine with him.

"Bannan's gone to help Jenn Nalynn."

"You must both leave the edge, daughter of Larmensu," said another voice. *Edis'* voice. "This isn't over."

Momma didn't let go, standing with Werfol in her arms. Through the rain, by flashes of lightning, he barely made out the snake-like figure rising from the ground. "No, it isn't, Edis Donovar," he heard his mother say, in the tone meaning more than now and this.

Did the figure bow?

"Then I look forward to our next meeting," Edis said, surprising him and it seemed Momma—which never happened, so he must be wrong. "Should we survive this one."

Momma dipped her head. "We are forever beholden for your help."

With that, she turned and half-ran through the rain, surefooted as a goat on the stones despite carrying him, a desperate flight with who knew what might be coming. The only thing Werfol could think of to help was to use his true sight to know when they'd passed the edge, though it took most of his strength. "We're safe here!" he gasped when they were.

She ran a few more steps beyond, being Momma and prudent, before planting a wet kiss on his forehead and setting him on his feet. "Can you walk?"

But men and horses were already bursting from the trees, sending up spray and glad shouts, and when Werfol's father dropped to the ground and swept him up, Werfol heard Momma scold him quite fiercely. "Ancestors Foiled and Flummoxed, Emon! What good's a bloody plan if you won't follow the least—"

Which is when his father kissed her soundly and Dutton took hold to hug him, feeling rather dragonish, too, and even Roche turned up. And all Werfol needed was Semyn—and somewhere dry—for this moment to be the best of his life.

Suddenly the ground shook, knocking everyone flat, and *SOME-THING* began to form, like a black dangerous storm cloud boiling up from the earth—

The majesty-monster!

He hung from a strange dragon's claws—several of which plunged into his flesh—hovering over a terrible and growing monster determined to rule everything—and Bannan Larmensu was deliriously, thoroughly happy.

Jenn Nalynn. She was here. She lived and was here. His brave nephew was—he had to believe—where he belonged. While he was here, where he did—

The love of his life flashed him a smile and look that said while she felt the same they both best pay attention to the situation.

The truthseer nodded and looked around. The wall nearest him was riven by dark and deepening cracks, including the one to which his dragon clung. It crumbled alarmingly as the toad queen dug into the stone below—

Something looked back at him from inside.

Quickly, he checked other cracks, found paired eyes in every one, and if they were about to be attacked by nyphrit as well as the toad queen he'd—

A foot worked at the crumbling edge, making it worse—

No, as if what was inside wished to come out. And it wasn't the foot of a nyphrit, being gray with tidy, clawed toes—His dragon lost that grip and heaved up to seize another, and more eyes looked back.

"Jenn, look!" he shouted, the words lost in the cacophony of shattering stone. "Toads!"

Care about us! Jenn wished at the toad queen, but nothing happened. *Turn into stone!* she wished next, which might have changed them all to rock had she considered.

But nothing happened, except for a heart-stopping chuckle from the monster that she somehow heard over the deafening racket. Jenn looked despairingly at Bannan, who seemed to be searching the walls.

~You must stop trying, Dearest Heart,~ the words wistful as a sigh, sorrowful as a sob. ~She feeds on our magic.~

Was that why her fervent desperate wish wasn't working? Was she *feeding* the toad queen?

Oysters! Jenn thought at once. *Dirty diapers!*

Bannan turned to her. His mouth worked but she couldn't hear the words. He pointed at the wall.

"I can't hear you!" Jenn shouted.

But it was the other dragon who answered. ~He's found little cousins. They're digging out from the wall.~ With a note of distinct offense. ~Make them stop, mighty turn-born. It makes it hard to hold on——~

~FOOL YOUNGLING!~ Wisp roared.

Bannan was right! Eyes peered from every opening, catching her light—eyes that seemed hopeful and determined—and if ever she trusted in the goodness of house toads, it had to be now.

"Help them!" Jenn ordered, kicking her feet at the nearest crack. "Hurry!"

Wisp obeyed at once, pulling away from the wall, using his free foot and fangs to break away chunks of rock, sending breezes to erode away more. The youngling didn't move until Bannan bared his teeth and began swinging his legs to kick at the wall, doing better with his boots than Jenn with her bare feet.

House toads started to pop free. They leapt into the air, bodies puffed like balloons, drifting down toward their queen. More and more, for each opening they helped make brought forth not one toad but dozens. Popping free. Leaping out. Drifting down.

Faint, at first, Jenn heard them. ~Get her!~ ~Me first!~ ~We need more!~

The youngling, finally catching on, launched from the wall and, holding Bannan with its rear feet, clawed at the wall, flinching as house toads came free and bounced off it.

They bounced from Wisp, careened into Jenn and Bannan, like puffs of snow with intent eyes and bared teeth.

Making as much impression on the monster below, who looked up and laughed. "Silly little things," the toad queen said dismissively. "So that's where you've been hiding. You're too late."

Another bumped, gently, into Jenn's nose. ~If you please, we need the rest of us, elder sister.~

Reminding her again how she'd once promised a Marrowdell house toad to find its kind in the Verge, and how she'd thought she had, finding the toad queen, but that hadn't been what the little cousin wanted from her at all.

Letting go of Wisp, Jenn Nalynn fell.

As she fell, she held out her open hands and made her wish.

Moths bubbled forth, more and more and more. They went to the walls and ceiling, so many they papered it in white, scratching with their tiny feet. Toads emerged, more and more and more. So many toads, the dragons could no longer beat their wings and had to perch and the young one dropped Bannan.

Other moths caught him, as they caught her, keeping them aloft as the flurry of house toads around them became a blizzard. Being done, Jenn held out her arms and the moths brought her and Bannan together.

They spun ever-so-slowly in midair, where once had been a marble cage, and it was just like dancing. She smiled and he did—

While below, the toad queen, coated and covered and crushed in house toads, hissed and spit and shouted. "STOP THIS!"

Bannan looked down, so Jenn did.

A single house toad was an armful. Thousands were an army.

One of the toad queen's clawed feet lost its hold on the wall, sliding down, ripping a gash in the stone. House toads poured out, adding to those on top of her. They were silent now.

Certain.

Another foot slipped, freeing more.

The toad queen opened her terrible mouth, trying to swallow them, but the house toads were ready and simply moved to her head and her sides. She kicked at them with a foot, but that only hastened the inevitable.

Suddenly, the toad queen plummeted to the floor.

The house toads jumped off as she fell, disappearing into the walls.

The moths flew back into Jenn Nalynn and, just before there were none to hold them—which was a worry—dragons swooped down to catch them both, hovering with great beats of their wings.

All as black tendrils erupted from below, wrapping the struggling toad queen, sinking into her flesh. "NO!!!!!" she shrieked.

~YES!!!~ roared Wisp, who seemed to know what was happening.

But not even her dragon, Jenn discovered in the next instant, could have guessed what would—

Ancestors Tormented and Tortured, thus far his reunion with Jenn consisted of being grabbed by a careless young dragon, dropped, a too-brief moment together surrounded by moths, only to be grabbed again—

Not that Bannan had a complaint. Anything was better than the floor and what grew from it. He might have mustered some sympathy for the suffering toad queen if not for suspecting she'd been pushed into her own trap—

And if not for Werfol.

Jenn Nalynn, being kinder-hearted, looked away; the truthseer made himself watch, seeing the monster writhe and shrink, seeing her trophies become black tendrils themselves, plunging like knives—

"Bannan!"

He looked up, relieved to have reason, then stared.

Jenn was smiling.

Beyond Jenn?

Was transformation.

More tendrils, these of gold and green and orange—of every color and, this being the Verge, more without names—were growing up the walls.

Where they touched, healing spread like wildfire.

Stone became living crystal, glittering blue. Bubbles rose and popped, leaving tidy cubbies, each quickly filled with its house toad, toes curled under, eyes content and watchful. Different from those of Marrowdell or Vorkoun, lacking armor or medals.

Brave as any.

Plants sprouted, the Verge sort, with feathers instead of leaves, and there were myriad little waterfalls—of mimrol—sending dances of silver spray.

While above—Bannan craned his neck, trying to see past his now excitedly flapping dragon—

When the tendrils reached the ceiling, they tore it away, expanding and growing up and through, letting in light.

Letting out dragons.

Centuries of magic stolen by the toad queen and hoarded inside her released in a flood, and Wisp was just as glad to be away before any of it found him and, he shuddered, sought to remake him. He glanced back every so often. Mimrol flowed and spilled from the now-living palace behind them, rekindling the land around it. An appalling toll in one sense, for how could she possibly have wanted more?

She'd been stopped and that was that. Satisfied, Wisp eyed the youngling flying beside him, tempted to praise it. Decided it was time for another lesson instead. ~Spill one more drop of the truth-seer's blood—~ there being spots on the man's shirt, ~—and the turn-born will turn you into an efflet.~

The youngling eased its grip.

Not that the girl would. Wisp felt her joy warming him, warming the Verge. He'd have cautioned her about excess, the terst turn-born home again and aware, but this wasn't an expectation.

Unlike a new crossing inside the palace.

He'd felt it. Known better than draw attention to it, but what it meant? Settled like a sharp new stone in his gut. Only sei could create a crossing. Only sei close them.

Doing so for reasons utterly different from any that might occur to Jenn Nalynn, with her joy and warmth. That they'd allowed her this once, to end a threat, made a dragonish sense. That she'd do it again?

A thing to fear. There'd be repercussions—

"Wisp," Jenn called up, her voice caught by the wind of their passing. "Do you know the crossing to take us to Werfol? To Bannan's family? I want to go there first, very much."

The youngling angled closer, volunteering, ~The kruar came from there, elder sister. They know the quickest way across the Verge.~

"Spirit and Dauntless!" The truthseer shouted to be heard as well. "I sent them to find Marrowdell's dragon!"

~THAT'S ME!~

There was but one dragon of Marrowdell, a dragon presently restraining himself from ripping out the heart of a presumptuous youngling with supreme effort, a dragon succeeding only because if he did Bannan would fall and Jenn be unhappy.

~I saved everyone!~ the youngling crowed, having completely failed to read the threat to its life in striking distance.

Wisp felt himself about snap. *Maybe the truthseer would bounce—*

"We all did, including my brave Wisp," Jenn shouted brightly, to forestall outright violence. "To Marrowdell, then Werfol. Home," she added with longing.

Needing no more encouragement, the dragons began their descent.

TWENTY-SIX

*T*HE INSTANT HER feet touched ground in the unintended pretty and utterly normal meadow created by her very first wish in the Verge, Jenn ran for Bannan.

Who'd landed upright only to be knocked on his behind by a wing as his dragon pulled up late, flailing to rise in haste.

Probably afraid of her meadow, Jenn thought pragmatically. It was a little shocking in the Verge, even to her.

The truthseer sat, legs out, amongst clover. He plucked a flower and held it up. Already in motion, she landed in his lap, quite possibly squashing it, and would have been sorry—

—but the lips she'd dreamed of found hers and the arms she'd missed more than anything held her tight, and nothing could be better—

Except that Bannan squirmed uncomfortably and eased her off his lap. "Ack," he said apologetically, or something like it, his face going pale. He waved at himself in explanation.

Blood oozed from small punctures in his shirt. Having seen the like before, Jenn glared up at the one responsible. "You hurt him! You hurt Wainn, too!"

Wisp, looking unusually pleased, knocked the younger dragon from the sky, sending it crashing down on the meadow. It curled into itself, head pressed flat to clover, and gave her a decidedly humbled look. ~I'm still learning, elder sister.~

Her dragon landed, blood still up by the cant of his head and the fire licking the fringes of his closed jaw, eager to pounce.

Ancestors Fussy and Frustrated. Holding Bannan tenderly, Jenn gave both dragons her best scathing look. "I expect you to cooperate. We're almost home. Bannan needs care." And she needed clothes, her Shadesport dress—which didn't cover much at all by her love's new and distracting attention to her knees—hardly suited to a Marrowdell spring. "You!" This to the younger one. "Apologize and promise not to hurt another person."

She could wish it and the turn-born wouldn't stop her. Hadn't she done it to poor Wisp, after wishing him a man, because others feared his magic?

She'd rather not, Jenn thought with sudden weariness, be responsible for another's behavior. Heart's Blood, she hadn't needed the sei's harsh lesson: the collected people, the escalating carnage a wish meant to help, to tame, could cause—she'd never wanted to rule others.

Unlike the toad queen, whose fate she'd like to know—after getting Bannan to care. "Please," she added, meaning it.

The younger dragon, clover stuck to a fang, aimed an uncertain eye at Wisp. ~I don't understand, Great Lord of Dragons.~

~You say the words 'I'm sorry'.~ Wisp said cheerfully. ~Be suitably humble and use the air. Gently!~

"I'M SORRY!"

At the blast, Bannan covered his ears and Jenn winced. Maybe Wisp shouldn't encourage it.

The youngling's head rose slightly. ~And the rest, lord? 'Promise'?~

~If you hurt a person Jenn Nalynn cares about again,~ replied Wisp, being a little too helpful, ~I'll eat your heart. That,~ he finished succinctly, ~is a 'promise.'~

To Jenn's surprise, the youngster's head rose as far as it could, its entire demeanor one of vast relief. ~I understand, lord! Thank you!~

Jenn felt Bannan fight to repress a laugh, sure to hurt. She wasn't, however, quite done.

"And you," she told her dragon, sternly, careful not to smile at her first and best friend, who'd been so brave and found her. "Have your student practice carrying what isn't a person before carrying anyone else. Maybe a—" Melons wouldn't be available for months and it mustn't use piglets—

"A toad?" Bannan suggested.

~Must I?~ the young dragon asked, eyes wide with horror.

That did it—they broke into whooping wild giggles, hardly able to breathe before setting off again, draining the tension and fear of days and nights past.

Leaving poor Wisp to explain to his student.

Eyes closed, Jenn knew where she was. Marrowdell. Not so chill a night as when they'd left—to the good, her far from dressed for it and Bannan wounded—with spring anointing the air. The scent of spring-berries. They bloomed first of the year and most welcome. Dense thickets of the hardy shrubs lined the ridges around the valley. By day, in flower, they made it seem the snow hadn't quite left.

Springberry and, yes, the tang of healthy rot as last year's leaves came out of the snow, looking like lacework. What disappeared fed the soil and other plants, Master Dusom taught and farmers knew.

"The flood's over," Bannan exclaimed softly.

"About that—" Jenn began, opening her eyes, and stopped.

The moon did them a service, full in a cloudless sky, shining down brightly enough to pick out colors here and there.

Limning every stark detail of what had been a lovely river and wide fields. She stared out over a home she couldn't recognize, one hand fumbling for Bannan's, the other at her throat. "Heart's Blood—what have I done?"

A breeze found her ear, Wisp no longer visible—nor, more disquieting, was the other dragon, and she hoped not to stumble into it. "You took the water away before anyone died, Dear Heart. I did the rest." With pride.

The rest—Jenn dragged her eyes to the village, sagging against Bannan as she saw the buildings were standing. Her stomach chose that moment to remind her of Peggs' pie, starting her feet in motion.

Beside her, Bannan limped heavily and muttered in pain; she stopped at once, not pleased, not pleased at all, to think this more of the young dragon's mistakes. "What's wrong with your leg?"

His teeth flashed. "Merely a flesh wound, Dearest Heart, incurred when Scourge tried to save me from the whirlpool."

"Ancestors Blessed, I should wrap you in bandages from head to toe, Bannan Larmensu," she said archly, hiding her concern.

He kissed her cheek. "I'm agreeable—if you stay in this dress." A whisper, but with such heat Jenn felt a delicious flush run down her arms and grew quite, quite sure she would.

The breeze flipped her bangs. "I've sent the youngling to fetch aid. Unless you'd rather fly across the valley, truthseer."

"In no way, friend dragon," Bannan said promptly. "Grateful as I am for the help earlier," he added courteously. "Does your—student—have a name?"

Silence, then a pained, "I suppose it's earned one. Dearest Heart?"

Name it? She hardly knew it and doubted she'd be able to pick it out should it be amongst other dragons the same size.

Except for being overeager and regrettably clumsy for something large and dangerous—"Let me think on it," she evaded.

"Nothing grand," Wisp qualified. "The youngling is stupid and lacks instincts. It may—" pensively, "—not survive the week."

For all his talk, Jenn knew her dragon was proud of his, and would want a good name, one thoughtful and appropriate. "I'll do my best," she promised, and would.

Bannan lifted his head. "They're coming. That was quick," as if something was wrong in such excellent news.

She turned, hearing hoofbeats, and felt her own doubt. No matter how eager those of Marrowdell would be to reach them, horses had to be disturbed from their sleep first, and saddled. Come to that, none but Perrkin were particularly fast or agreeable to being called out at night, so what was running up the Spine?

Jenn had time to exchange a questioning look with Bannan before two kruar raced into the meadow, followed by a now-visible earnest young dragon.

And no one else.

They'd been about to die.

Sure of it, Roche had rushed to stand between the family and their son and whatever surged upward, flinging himself into the edge without hesitation. Water streamed down his face and from his fingers. Slammed into his mouth as he shouted, "GO AWAY!" and he expected at any second to be swallowed by a monster.

Only to be shocked to his core when the ominous swelling darkness shrank away to nothing.

He was left standing, unable to move, not daring to believe.

"Roche. She's gone. I promise."

He turned his head. Edis stood with him, smiling, skin glowing through the rain. By lightning flash, she seemed more snake-like olm than ever below the neck and strange.

But more the woman he knew and his special dear friend above, and before he thought or if he even did, Roche leaned over to kiss her lips.

They tasted of rain, at first, and were cold. Parted slightly, a little gasp of her breath filling his mouth, then her hands seized the back of his head to pull him closer and he took hold of whatever she was to do the same, for there mustn't be space between them, he couldn't bear it, even as he felt himself growing dizzy and the world to spin.

Staggered, his arms empty.

Smiled in the rain, his heart full, as glad cries rang out from those behind him.

Marrowdell had emptied on the word of a dragon, and Bannan knew he should be proud of their care and caution—

And would, but for the anguish in Jenn's face. The villagers had gone beyond the edge, where she couldn't. Everyone had left, even the livestock.

The kruar, they learned, had helped with that. "The animals didn't like to be near us," Spirit explained, breath hot, showing a fang.

"We weren't going to eat them," Dauntless added, as if a point of honor.

"But when will they be back?" Jenn pleaded.

The long faces of the kruar lowered. The youngling, who allowed them to see it, shifted uneasily. Jenn's attention flashed to it. "You told them to stay away until it was safe," she said with disbelief. "How did you expect them to know?" she demanded of the three. "Most of them forget magic, beyond the edge." Her wild-eyed gaze found Bannan, locked on him. A whisper, near panic. "The flood— I sent it down the road—"

Bannan took her in his arms. "I'll go at once. Find them."

She shook her head, raising her tear-streaked face to his, and composed herself with an effort. "That isn't the least bit sensible, Dearest Heart," his love disagreed, the tone her sister's. "If they're fine now, they'll be fine tomorrow, while you can barely stand. If they aren't—" She swallowed, then went on bravely, "—if they aren't fine, Ancestors Blessed, tomorrow will be soon enough to know." Jenn put her hands on his chest. "Let's go home."

They rode the kruar down the path to the Tinker's Road, grateful to be mounted for the road hadn't fared well, dried so quickly after the flood, and would need grading as well as ditchwork near his farm.

And because nyphrit hunted. Though, catching Jenn's hard look after a particularly loud snarl in the dark, Bannan judged they'd be wise to stay away.

Two house toads waited, on either side of their door, creatures appearing unfamiliar by moonlight and in the aftermath of so much, though when the truthseer looked at them with his deeper sight, their chain mail and gauds seemed unchanged.

Maybe it was his perspective. He understood why Jenn went first to greet them and dipped in a curtsy. "Thank you," she told them.

The truthseer bowed as well.

They went inside, too weary to care their home was as when they'd last seen it, disheveled and bare. Bannan limped to find a lantern and light it, Jenn to fill the stove and start warming water for tea. Homely tasks made almost unbearable by worry of how those they loved fared this night, without stout buildings.

There were bears, beyond Marrowdell. Bandits. Let alone the flood.

They'd Sennic Horst and Davi. The rest were all capable, all experienced. He forced his concerns aside, seeing Jenn step out the door.

Giving her time, he made tea, then went outside after her, gathering the quilt from the mattress as he went.

She sat on the porch step, her bare toes on the dried mud of the farmyard, arms wrapped around herself and face to the sky. Her outstretched hand rested on a bare knee, a moth perched on the palm.

After setting the cups on the porch, and arranging the quilt over her shoulders, Bannan eased himself down at her side, it now habit to silently curse Scourge for his sore leg, though he'd dearly love to see the ugly beast. And to know if he'd reached the turn-born and what they'd had to say.

The house toads roamed the farmyard, hunting any foolish nyphrit.

Counting on Edis, refusing to admit the least doubt she'd saved Lila and Werfol, the truthseer had sent Spirit and Dauntless back to them with orders to remain in the edge behind the Westietas' estate until someone came to hear what they had to say.

That the toad queen was vanquished. That he and Jenn were home again and fine.

Nothing of Marrowdell.

Not yet.

Stars gazed down, those bright enough to elude the moon, and he shivered inwardly.

The valley felt lifeless.

Jenn Nalynn sensed Bannan arrive, the warmth of the blanket over her shoulders, the scent of tea, but paid little attention, being busy with a wish.

A little wish, to be delivered by this single moth. Yes, she might have drawn on her mother's magic and willed those lost to be found and here, but knowing they'd fled in fear, it wasn't right to draw them back, regardless their situation—though she guessed it uncomfortable at best and perilous at worst.

They must be ready and willing to return.

Jenn considered the moth, considering people. She must send it to someone who'd remember her and believe, but most couldn't, beyond the edge. According to Bannan, she could be sure of only two: Kydd, who'd been disbelieved about magic once before, and Tadd, whose parents would argue and overrule him, meaning well.

Ancestors Beloved and Blessed.

There was, indeed, one more. Someone all would follow.

Making her wish, Jenn tossed the moth into the night air.

While it was the best possible news Roche had shared, that the toad queen was gone, and while Werfol would very very much like to have been home and in bed, they hadn't budged from the forest's end. Momma had ordered up tents and provisions as if mounting a siege of the edge, and nothing would dissuade her, though no one really tried.

Her brother remained missing.

Semyn sat on a camp cot with Werfol, both holding cups of hot chocolate they weren't about to taste, Semyn having overheard cook boast she'd "put in a little something to help the lads sleep." As for the cot, they'd stripped it of blankets and pulled it to the front of the tent, hooking the flap open just enough to keep watch.

A lot of people did, Werfol knew, but none with his sight.

"Anything?"

"Not from here. I should be in the edge," he complained, as he had regularly and which wasn't fair to his brother, but he'd no one else to listen. Poppa wasn't pleased to have them this close, but with Momma ordering her guards here, everyone agreed it'd be safer than home.

Besides, Werfol thought, Momma knew he had to be here. She'd need his gift.

If she let him use it.

Stuck in a tent. It was like being stuck inside Goosie—except without the toad queen and thinking he'd die—and while Semyn was staunch comfort, he could really use Wisp—

The house toad pressed against him. Werfol looked down. "What is it?" Not that he spoke toad, but even in the dark, its eyes seemed to be trying to tell him something.

"Weed—look."

He did and shrugged. "Just a horse." They were everywhere around, most with people riding them, but some roaming. Remounts, the word was.

"Is it, though? It's not acting right. You should really look."

Huffing a breath, Werfol stared out of the tent. It was a stupid horse—

Trusting his brother, he squinted and looked deeper, not that he'd see much outside the edge which was why he needed to—

Then what stood in the dark stamped an impatient hoof, pulling lips back from what anyone could tell weren't normal horse teeth, and glared back at him with red-rimmed wicked eyes.

That was no horse!

Overjoyed, Werfol punched Semyn in the shoulder. "You're right! It's Dauntless—or Spirit." He wished he could tell in the dark, but it didn't matter. "You told me Uncle Bannan sent the kruar away with messages. It's back with one for us." Shoving his cup under the cot, Werfol jumped up, grabbing a raincloak. "C'mon."

He might have known his careful brother would hesitate. "We should tell someone."

"It can't talk outside the Verge. You know kruar are impatient. If it leaves we'll never get the message."

"We don't know there is one." But Semyn was moving, getting his cloak and holding up the flap. Of a sudden he reached back, producing their child-sized practice swords, which were useless—

Only these weren't wood, Werfol realized, feeling the weight and balance. He eyed his surprising brother.

Who shrugged. "We'd be using them soon anyway. Dutton said so. You ready?"

Werfol beat him out of the tent.

They kept low, weaving between scattered shrubs, stopping at random as Momma had taught them to listen for pursuit. To Werfol's relief, the kruar hadn't budged.

Semyn pulled him sharply down. Pointed to the ground ahead.

A wire. Momma'd set a trap and, while it probably led to a noise-maker, there was no saying it didn't connect to something deadly.

It being Momma.

Werfol signed to split up. Shaking his head, Semyn mimed going first.

Then the young truthseer had a wonderful, spectacular idea. As his fingers flashed, he caught the glint of his brother's grinning teeth.

Stepping over the wire, eyes peeled for more, Werfol headed straight for the kruar, counting. One. Two. Three. All the way to fifteen and—

CLANK . . . RING!!!

Semyn, having tossed his sword on the wire—a sword they weren't to have, so couldn't be blamed for losing—would be running for their tent, where he'd dive on the cot with pillows and blankets to pretend, to a quick look inside, that his brother slept with him through the racket, drugged by the cook.

Serve them right, Werfol thought, who wasn't happy about that.

He dropped to his stomach, going on elbows and knees. Almost there. Almost.

A hoof slammed next to his head. Nostrils huffing hot breath investigated his face. At last, a breath, warm and welcoming, formed words in his ear. "Little truthseer."

A second. "We bring news."

Ignoring the commotion around the tents—including a very loud yell—Werfol listened, smiling more and more.

News as wonderful as this?

Would make Momma forgive anything.

Well, almost anything.

Jenn cleaned and bandaged Bannan's wounds, leaving a kiss over each. Not that her kisses had healing ability, a fact she'd tried earnestly to point out several times.

Only to have her beloved wrap his arm around her and kiss her back, soundly, in proof that kisses did.

It had, therefore, taken a while to finish his care and been good, she knew, for them both. But after tucking Bannan in their bed, Jenn had gone downstairs, taking the quilt, to sit outside and wait.

An hour later, or maybe two, she discovered she'd company.

Wen Treff sat beside her on the porch, wrapped in a blanket from the barn, another, of finer stuff, rolled up in her arms. She smiled, being noticed at last. "Welcome home, Jenn Nalynn."

It was as if the valley spoke. Feeling that, Jenn straightened. "How have you been?"

"Busy." Wen held out the blanket. "Meet Delfinn."

Awestruck, Jenn took what was, in fact, a baby, swaddled in fabric so soft and fine, she suspected the yling and was glad Wen had had help.

By starlight, Delfinn looked like any baby, those tending, in Jenn's experience, to be of a sameness their first months.

Still—curious, she used a finger to tease open the blanket, hoping to see more, and accidentally touched the baby's forehead.

An echo resonated through her entire body. It wasn't sound, exactly. Wasn't anything she'd felt before but—

Heart's Blood. Jenn's gaze shot up to Wen. "How did this happen?" she demanded.

"You know how, Dear Heart. I gave birth at yesterday's turn." Wen half smiled. "What you want to know is why."

"I know why," Jenn snapped, and the air grew chill around them. "To make your child turn-born and powerful. You've cursed her with my fate." Ice cracked and she saw her breath—

Jenn thought hastily of warmth and soft things, having not intended to—"I'm sorry," she said, to Delfinn and Wen. An apology she should extend to the poor house toads, briefly frozen in the yard.

"You are not cursed, Jenn Nalynn," Wen told her, though it wasn't Wen, but Wen and something more. "You are Marrowdell's steward. Our savior twice over. What you really are is alone."

Thus vulnerable. The reason the toad queen had wanted her. The reason Jenn had to stop her own wishes and so greatly feared one day she'd make a mistake. The sole turn-born outside the Verge, having none to counter her merest, heedless wish.

Now, one day, there would be. Overcome, Jenn gazed down at Delfinn, glimpsing the future. "You'll be nineteen when it happens," she whispered. "I promise to explain." On that thought, she looked at Wen again. "I can't be her mother."

"You didn't have one," Wen pointed out, blunt but kind, her voice hers again. "She'll have a village to raise her—will have a village," she corrected.

Jenn gazed into the chill night. "If they come back."

"They'll be back." Wen stood, taking her daughter. "When they do, I'll come. To introduce Marrowdell's newest member."

Jenn stood with her. "And to say goodbye. I wish—I mean—" She sighed from her heart. "Are you sure you can't stay with us?"

"Yes, Dear Heart."

And light flowed through Wen's hair, cloaked her body, caressed her child, a light not from the moon or this world's sun. "Don't worry, Jenn Nalynn. I'll be going home."

Jenn blinked.

Alone on the porch.

She gave a little shiver. "Wisp?"

~I'm here, Dear Heart.~ A pause. ~I heard. A second turn-born. Mistress Sand will be pleased.~

She hadn't thought of that—of them. While a relief to hear from her dragon, Jenn wasn't sure about sharing the news. "Need they know?"

~I don't see how you could stop them. Turn-born recognize one another, do you not?~

The echo. "I suppose we do," Jenn agreed, feeling quite odd. Her thoughts raced, her heart thudding in her chest. Tiny, unknowing Delfinn would, one day, change her life as she—being, she supposed, something of an aunt—must find the wisdom and patience to guide Delfinn's.

Nonny had said finding a place—her true place—meant she must discover her purpose there. That once she found it, she'd wouldn't be able to leave it again; beset by fear and dread, she'd taken that as a warning.

And been wrong. A smile played across Jenn's lips and sang in her heart. Why, it hadn't been a warning at all, but a hope-filled promise. Didn't Aunt Sybb always say you made your place in the world and were responsible for it?

Which sometimes referred to sloppy bed-making, true, but she'd really meant this, that to feel you belonged somewhere, you needed a way—your own special way—to care for it. Her purpose. Her place.

Marrowdell.

Ancestors Daunted and Delirious. She'd so much to learn first.

Peggs and Hettie counted on her to be a good and joyful influence on their children—and help with diapers—as Aunt Sybb was and had been all her life.

Why, she was about to be busy. Very busy indeed. And her first task, Jenn realized, thinking of her father and Uncle Horst, would be a heavy one, however vital to Delfinn's future.

A turn-born existed only within the edge.

The people of Marrowdell must know to help keep Delfinn safe. On the bright side, the baby wouldn't be crawling down the road anytime soon. She'd time.

"No one is to learn Delfinn's true nature except from me," Jenn said pointedly, looking up at the roof.

Addressing another dragon.

He heard voices, or dreamed them. It wasn't until Jenn Nalynn returned to their bed, her feet cubes of ice, did Bannan come fully awake and aware. "Any sign?" he mumbled, drawing her close.

"I met Wen's baby. Her name is Delfinn and she's turn-born."

No, *now* he was awake. Sitting up, the truthseer lit the lamp by the bed, then returned to look at his love, searching her remarkably calm face for clues. "So—this is good news?" he hazarded.

"I think so. For me. For Marrowdell," that with quick assurance, but the corners of her lips pulled down. "She has no choice in it."

Nor had Jenn, but Bannan, who knew something of unsought gifts and power, and a great deal about his love, fought to keep a straight and somber face. "Delfinn has what matters more, Dearest Heart. You, to show her the joy and wonder of what she'll become."

"And responsibility," she countered, though her lips began to curve up again and the lamplight caught a twinkle in her eye.

"Absolutely," he agreed equably, picking up a lock of her hair and bringing it to his lips. His other hand strayed.

Jenn narrowed her eyes. "And consequences. There are always consequences. She'll need to know—what—Ban—"

He collected the rest of his name with his mouth, urgent and warm.

The rest of the night theirs.

~Do I get one?~

Wisp, curled by the stove, reluctantly cracked open an eye. He suspected he'd be sorry he asked. ~One of what?~

The youngling, curled just inside the door, the furthest into the house the toad would allow, raised its head, looking at the ladder. ~Since there are, or will be, two turn-born, Great Lord of Dragons, and two of us——~

~There is no *us*, youngling. There is you and all other dragons. And there is me.~

~Yes, lord, but I thought——~

Wisp let a snarl vibrate the floor. The youngling, wisely, fell silent. He'd no doubt it kept thinking.

A nuisance, that.

He'd have to come up with more lessons. Or eat it, the dragon thought contentedly. There was always that option.

The truthseer wisely distracted the girl, whose emotions about the new turn-born were unsettled at best. She'd have his help, Wisp vowed. Not with messes—he'd done his share.

Thistles, though.

By fall, the baby would be old enough to giggle. Giggle and, he imagined, wave wee fingers in pursuit of fluffy seeds he'd toss in the air—

Share the new turn-born?

The youngling better think of something else.

TWENTY-SEVEN

*O*VER BREAKFAST, THE house toads providing eggs Jenn had cracked more thoughtfully than usual, she and Bannan shared their adventures. Though his, she decided when done, seemed more like trials filled with danger and death, and said so.

Nodding sadly, he settled his sore leg on a stool and eased his wounded shoulders against the blanket she'd folded as padding for the chair. A brooch winked below the opening of his shirt, his father's brooch, a keepsake hitherto kept in his trunk without mention, though it was a fine piece of copper, the edges smooth with long use. He brushed it with his fingers. "The toad queen did me one kindness."

Jenn chuckled. "She'd be sorry to hear that."

"Nonetheless. I've spent too long thinking of what I lost. It's time I realize how many good memories I have of my parents—my childhood. I wish—"

Jenn tilted her head, guessing what he didn't say. "You wish you'd had time to learn more of them. To have stayed in Vorkoun."

Bannan shook his head, a lock of clean hair tumbling over an eye. They'd taken bucket and sponge to the well at dawn, bathing one another. She'd told him about washing in the head of a boat on waking, then of swimming an ocean.

He'd told her of magical keys and sunflowers. And of Roche Morrill, who'd found himself and, perhaps, his place to belong.

"I belong here, Dearest Heart," the truthseer told her, his apple butter eyes warm. "Never doubt it." He turned over his hand and she laid hers overtop. "That said, I've letters to write."

"I wrote to you," she blurted out, and then, why then had to explain the whole of it, and he laughed at Nonny and the bottle and wondered at the waalum.

While Jenn tucked Bannan's wish beside her heart.

Once rested as much as either could bear, Jenn and Bannan walked to the village. She'd have shortened the distance for the sake of his leg, though it was already improving, but he said they should take their time and see what needed be done.

Marrowdell wounded.

The kaliia fields were in shambles. Patches looked tended, with healthy rows of plants, but most showed dry, cracked soil with no sign of green.

"Wisp says there aren't enough efflet," Jenn said, her heart heavy. She hadn't known the flood had taken so many small ones. Her dragon's choice, to keep the news from her till now, and while she understood why, she'd have to talk to him, soon, about the importance of knowing the truth.

Bannan shaded his eyes, looking over the field. "Will they let us help?"

The idea surprised her. From the sudden cessation of grumbling in the hedges, it surprised the efflet as well.

Wisp sent a breeze. "It is not the efflet, but the terst turn-born you should ask. The kaliia is their doing."

Jenn nodded.

There was no ford to wade at the river, for there wasn't a river at all. She came to a stop where chill spring water should have lapped at her knees, wrapping her arms around the ache in her middle. "Ancestors Wit—" Her voice stopped in her throat.

Bannan touched her elbow. "You couldn't have known."

Jenn heard the hollowness to his voice. He thought—*how could he not?*—that she'd done this not for Marrowdell or its people, but to find him.

Ignorance, Aunt Sybb said, might be forgiven. It was never an excuse.

"I have to fix it," she said quietly. "Before they come home, I must."

If only she knew where to start. Last year's reeds lining the shore were flattened under hardened mud, the riverbed choked with trees, with dead neyet, their branches and roots intertwined. Upstream, downstream, it didn't matter where she looked.

Silence cut to the bone.

She'd done marvels before. While Bannan didn't doubt Jenn Nalynn's magic and trusted her heart, this wasn't a problem like waalum hunters or a trapped god. This was nature. Water flowed where water chose. Now, with the head of the valley plugged between the Fingers of the Bone Hills, water chose to avoid Marrowdell altogether.

Ancestors Bewildered and Beset, help tend the kaliia? Without water, it would wither and die, along with the apple orchard and forests. The turn-born wells, on his farm and the village, would sustain people for a time, but who'd want to live here?

And if Marrowdell was uninhabitable, what then of those who couldn't leave? Even should Jenn take him and Delfinn to another part of the edge, it would be the end of the village. Her heart would break.

As it might now, the truthseer thought, standing with his love in the empty river, unable to offer comfort.

A breeze, hot and brusque, found his ear. "You're in the way."

Bannan whirled around to find Scourge behind them on shore.

The kruar wasn't alone.

At first, Jenn couldn't believe what she was seeing. The tinkers and their laden wagons, Scourge in the lead, coming down their road as if it were harvesttime and everything normal. Which it wasn't, in any sense.

Except the kruar pulling the wagons rolled their eyes and snapped at one another as they passed, being their nature, and Mistress Sand stepped away from the caravan to take her in a hug, as was hers, so she had to believe.

If not yet understand. "I was to meet you," Jenn blurted.

"That you were, Sweetling. Yon beast coming instead was a surprise, na?" Sand chuckled, even though she stood where a river used to be. "Clever truthseer."

Bannan, who'd know that wasn't wholly a compliment, not from a turn-born, gave his graceful bow and smiled. "We're glad of the help."

"Help, na? That's what you think we are, na?" But Sand chuckled again and even Master Riverstone waved. In fact, now that Jenn paid attention, all of the turn-born appeared unusually jolly as they crossed to the village, wagons clanking and clattering over the ruts.

Delfinn, Jenn thought suddenly. They'd feared her unchecked power so much, the prospect of a second turn-born in Marrowdell made them—

Friends again, she told herself firmly, glad to her core. She hadn't appreciated how unhappy she'd been, knowing her existence upset such powerful beings to the point where some had felt forced to oppose her.

Agreement wrapped around her and Jenn smiled, hugging Sand again. "Help indeed," she said. "I've sent a message of my own to bring the people back, but I want—" Lost for words, she waved a hand somewhat desperately around them, winding up pointing at the great oak, almost hidden by the corpses of unfortunate neyet.

"Let us set up and together we'll decide what's needful and first," Mistress Sand said comfortably. Then glanced up at the clear sky with the beginnings of a frown. "You've a dragon too many."

The silly youngling, Jenn thought, understanding Wisp's exasperation. "It's Marrowdell's," she stated, relieved when Sand gave a nod, accepting.

After that, it was to the commons to put up the tinkers' tents and plan.

"Welcome back, idiot beast." Bannan leaned well over to rub Scourge's great neck, feeling barely a twinge from his injuries. Among the gifts of the terst turn-born was healing, something Jenn insisted be first.

He'd no argument, glad to be able to do what came second, namely to ride to the Northward Road and offer all aid he could to whomever he found.

They set off at an easy lope, the truthseer determined not to risk the result by pushing too hard at the start. "It wasn't a flesh wound, by the way. Tagey thought I was mauled by a bear."

Scourge huffed. "Proud of yourself, are you?"

Bannan grinned. "I am, actually." His messages hadn't quite gone where he'd planned, and the outcomes had been unexpected, but all in all?

Yes, he was proud. They'd defeated the toad queen and—much as he needed to touch the boy to know in his heart—rescued brave Werfol. He'd found his love and she'd found him, though to be fair they'd dragons to thank for it.

And much else. "Our Wisp has a young protégé. Have you heard?"

An ear aimed back and Bannan grinned.

~Great Lord of Dragons! I saw the turn-born! I saw ALL of them at once!~

The house toad dared give Wisp a sympathetic look. Being the girl's and peculiar, he chose not to take offense.

Curious as he remained about those little cousins in the palace— Werfol's hidden army in truth—

Wisp chose not to inquire, having the youngling, again, to school. ~If you saw them, they saw you.~

Its eyes widened comically.

Wisp regarded a clawtip, waiting.

A few ragged breaths, then, in a rush, ~That means they approve of me, Great Lord of Dragons! I'm famous and—erp!~

The same clawtip effortlessly pinned the youngling's snout to the ground. ~I will tell you what your continued existence after such foolish trespass means, youngling.~ Wisp offered generously, then paused. Waited.

An eye moved wildly, searching every direction before meeting his glare. ~I would like to know, lord.~

Finally. ~Jenn Nalynn interceded to save you. This time.~

A faint, deeply concerned, ~Why?~

The youngling had proved of some use, but that wasn't why, of course. The girl's good heart would never allow the other turn-born to cause harm and they couldn't act against her will in Marrowdell, Wisp thought with great satisfaction.

Not that he'd say so.

~She hasn't given you a name. When she does?~

He lifted his clawtip, then drove it deep into the ground.

Lessons could be entertaining.

TWENTY-EIGHT

*O*N BEING INVITED to what she presumed an official meeting of turn-born—her first—to discuss and, hopefully, agree on those particular expectations required to heal Marrowdell, Jenn wasn't sure how she felt to be handed a mug of beer and sent to sit on a wide blanket beside Sand's small white dog, Kaj, spread in the open as if on a picnic, while the rest of the turn-born emptied the wagons into their big yellow tents.

Tents they'd badly needed a few days ago, and Jenn resolved to ask the trick of opening the trunks and for permission, in case they did again.

Master Clay dropped down to sit beside her, a mug in his hand. "An occasion, Sweetling." His face, its mask, featured big bushy eyebrows and a strong nose overshadowing a rare but winsome little smile, framed by huge dimples. He tapped his mug to hers. "Why so glum, na?"

She took a polite sip, startled anew by how the taste sang to her. "There's so much to do, it's daunting," she said, determined to be forthright. "For one thing, there's my—Melusine's roses. How do we bring them back?" For they must, she believed it. Without them, the village had a stark, barren feel.

He looked over her head toward the Nalynn home and its empty wall, then shrugged, returning his attention to the beer. "I can't say. Those are your family's. They've nothing to do with us."

Oh dear. That wasn't promising. Still, there was, Jenn reminded herself, the rest of the valley. "When is the meeting?"

"Meeting, na?" Clay looked surprised, then understanding dawned. "We're meeting now, Sweetling. Waiting on you. Don't you feel it, na?"

Jenn felt her mouth open and closed it hastily.

Now? With Mistress Sand and Flint and Tooth busy spreading beds, and Master Riverstone with the kruar, while Chalk and Field-stone sorted bundles—

Though come to think of it, there was a pressure at the back of her mind. Building like a headache but more like bubbles.

A moth flew by, dipped to taste her beer, then flew off, its wing-beats slower and slower until it stopped—

Jenn felt herself grow larger and larger, though she didn't at all, but that was the feeling, when, all at once, she grasped what was happening.

Expectations. New ones. Huge ones, some of them, waiting all around her like the strings of a harp ready to be played. Because what the turn-born *said* to one another was more like music than argument; each proposed a note, the whole to decide which and when and, very possibly, how loud or soft.

Where did she fit in it?

Her mug tumbled from her hands. She sensed Clay catch it, though didn't see.

Being too busy. Much too busy.

Here was a note about springs underground and others to call them forth and gird them in stone.

There a note to call down lightning to tear apart the dam she'd built from the ridge and others to keep it from buildings.

Weaving beneath and through, a melody well underway without need of her, for the turn-born cared most for the kaliia and would see it restored. Their expectation brought efflet from the Verge, flying down the Tinker's Road, already digging through the fields. A suffi-ciency, soon, to clear the fields and tend them.

Wisp, she knew, would be especially pleased.

What was that note? Faint, tremulous.

Hers.

It posed a question: *What if we ask the sei to move?*

DISAGREEMENT!

Jenn winced, though really, she shouldn't have expected them to like that one. She wasn't sure she did, the Spine altered already and being used to the Bone Hills where they were, with no knowing what a sei moving another part of itself in the edge might do to the rest of it.

She thought harder, aware of the turn-borns' patience, wishing for more of her own. It was hard, seeing what she saw everywhere, with people hopefully on their way.

You couldn't rush a pie, Peggs would say. Pies taking preparation and time to bake.

She didn't have to bake the valley, it was already.

Prepare it?

Jenn sculpted a wish, no, a series of wishes, aware of *attention* and *interest*. They let her continue—would stop her, she'd certainty and every hope—were she to make a mistake.

There. The other notes vanished, hers strong and ready. Supported, she realized, as never before.

They left it to her, to make them real.

Jenn Nalynn sat on a blanket, unconsciously lifting her hands as if to play a harp.

And Marrowdell answered.

First, the riverbed shook itself clean, stones and gravel rising up through the silt.

Next, small rain showers moistened the dried mud, dissolving it, washing it from reedstalks and sandbars.

The trees choking the river, the corpses of neyet, rotted in place and fell away, though the greatest logs did not. Through no expectation of hers, those split and shattered, becoming trimmed lumber and logs at rest on shore, and Jenn may have wondered but had no time or reason to object.

For under the rockfall water niggled and nudged, receiving her invitation but needing to make its own way. Water chewed and chipped, poked and pushed, a ripple here, a burst there—

Others heard the water and knew what Jenn wished. They put their many small feet to the work, their will and joy to do so, and Jenn was grateful yet again to Marrowdell's toads.

It didn't, in the end, take much at all, the water eager to return and ever so much happier going downhill.

Where it belonged.

Wishes made, Jenn went with her mug to stand in the empty river, watched by the other turn-born, who hadn't interfered but agreed.

To wait.

The first person Bannan Larmensu saw heading toward Marrowdell up the Northward Road was Tir Half-face, and his heart soared.

Best of all, his friend drove a fine carriage, pulled by four matched bays, the carriage and horses belonging to Lady Sybb Mahavar of Avyo, and that most dignified lady actually leaned out a window to wave her creamy 'kerchief at the truthseer. "We're coming," she called gaily. "We're all here!"

And it was, he saw, the truth.

Behind her carriage came Davi's big wagon, pulled by Battle and Brawl. Cheffy and Alyssa sat cross-legged on the draught horses, waving as well.

There were not one but three more wagons, some carrying piglets, and horses, all of Marrowdell's including Wainn's Old Pony and others, followed by cows and lumbering pigs, every one healthy, happy, and with the scent of home in their noses.

And people. On foot, on horseback, on wagons. Not just Marrowdell's absent families, but Palma and Allyn from Endshere, and Great Gran with three young women he recognized as her great nieces.

Bannan began to wonder where to put them all.

Not that he could bring himself to worry. They'd the turn-born's help, and Jenn Nalynn—and if the river was gone, well, they'd seen that for themselves before leaving, and if its flood downstream had been a concern, there appeared no sign of harm here.

Though there would, he knew, be tales to tell.

Kydd rode right up to Scourge, who behaved for once, Wainn holding on behind him. "I told you he'd be back," crowed the younger Uhthoff happily.

"That I am. And Jenn."

Kydd's keen eyes searched his face. Whatever he saw made him let out a contented sigh. "And we're safe. Aunt Sybb said so, but—"

"And so did I," Wainn reminded his uncle.

Kydd smiled. "So you did."

By this point they'd been passed by all but Satin and Filigree, plodding along. "I should catch up to the carriage," Bannan said apologetically. "Prepare Aunt Sybb."

If he could. Marrowdell wouldn't be as she remembered.

Scourge needed no urging, disliking intensely being last to anything, but even as they started past the rest, the kruar came to a snorting halt, then plunged into the brush and old snow beside the road, careening down the slope like a crazed goat.

Bannan managed to shout, "IDIOT BEAST! What are—" before Scourge stopped.

Hock-deep in water.

Water filling the river from here to the far shore, including the rapids from which they'd pulled Wisp, then a man, to safety.

The place where he'd first laid eyes on Jenn Nalynn and fallen in love.

She'd done it!

Like the river, life came back to Marrowdell in a sparkling torrent—slow at first, there being only so much room through the gate and Aunt Sybb's magnificent carriage taking precedence—then faster and faster until the road and paths between houses were full of people and animals, sorting themselves out with laughter and exclamations.

Jenn Nalynn found herself on the Nalynn porch, her heart too full to let her move, feasting on the sight. Ancestors Beholden and Utterly Blissful, if she wanted to be helpful, she'd be inside, starting tea and a fire to warm Aunt Sybb's bones, guaranteed to find the northern spring chill.

But she couldn't bring herself not to watch, to be sure all was real.

So the porch was where Peggs found her. "You're home!" her sister cried, and they fell in each other's arms; though Peggs was much rounder than Jenn remembered, so she had to stretch.

And nothing would do then but Jenn pull her sister around the side of the house before their father and Aunt Sybb could see their mother's missing roses, to discuss how to soften the blow, Peggs being wiser about such things.

Only to find their father already there, on his knees.

"Oh, Poppa," Jenn said gently, going to kneel beside him. Peggs did the same, using her shoulder to help.

They put their arms around one another, grieving over the empty ground.

"What's this, now?" Aunt Sybb came around the house, Tir hovering beside her, Bannan right behind.

And there was Kydd. And more came, until everyone stood looking at where Melusine's roses used to be and her daughters and their father knelt.

"I can't wish them back," Jenn admitted quietly. "I've tried."

Hands on his shoulder, Aunt Sybb kissed her brother's bent head. "Roses aren't wishes, Dear Hearts," the wise lady told them. "They're a promise. One your mother made to you, with love. You've only to remember that."

Jenn met her father's eyes. Her sister's. Gave a nod.

This was, after all, Marrowdell.

"Think of them," she urged. "How they were and should be." Closing her eyes, she did the same.

Strong stalks in winter, dead leaves rustling against their window, old nests and hips and thorns, oh yes.

Spring's first swollen bud, Radd always the first to spot it, but then their father checked the roses every morning and night.

Summer's wealth, of green and cool shade and oh, Melusine's roses, deepest red and huge, though never so heavy as to break off.

Unless asked nicely.

The fragrance—

Of roses! Jenn opened her eyes, a rose bloom tickling her nose as stems surged from the ground, in full leaf, in magnificent late-summer flower, growing and growing until they reached the eaves then spread to the sides to encase the house.

Everyone cheered.

"Ancestors Blessed, that's more like it," Aunt Sybb announced with satisfaction. "Who would like tea?"

"That's how it happened, sir. Honest truth. A moth."

The *sir* was a habit, the gleam in the eyes above the leather half mask a promise of mischief, and Bannan sat back, glass in hand, to toast his old friend. "'A moth.'"

"A right unseasonable beast, but, seeing's how you're familiar with such occurrences, perhaps not."

Kydd gave him a wry look. Bannan chuckled. "I'm not sure 'familiar' is the word I'd use, but you're right. I'm not surprised." Jenn's magic, reaching beyond the edge to inspire the Lady Mahavar to insist all was safe and they were to go to Marrowdell at once, sweeping up not only the refugees they'd met up and shared camp with, but those already with her from Endshere.

There being cargo.

And a surprise. "You found the hives."

"Great Gran did," Tir corrected, shaking his head. "You don't argue with that one. And then Allyn had to bring the supplies he bought for Marrowdell last fair—and Palma to come with her manuscript to show Master Jupp." He grimaced, holding out his glass. "Bloody cavalcade and us with only my axes. A wonder we made it."

No, it had been Jenn Nalynn—and very possibly the presence of those two potent ladies. "I counted six. What of the seventh?" Kydd leaned forward. "Any sign of it?"

Something dark slid behind Tir's eyes. "We kept watch for corpses in the flood, not bees."

There was a pause, the four of them, for Sennic had joined their fire as well, likely thinking it might have gone the other way.

If not for dragons, Bannan thought peacefully.

"Those were dragon wounds we healed your man of, Sweetling, most of them. You sure you want it here, na?"

Jenn stood beside Sand at the rail, watching the livestock drink at the river, Tadd and his brother riding bareback to keep things orderly. There were troughs filled with grain and bales of hay, and none of it had to do with dragons.

Yet did. "I'm sure. The sei asked Wisp to teach it. We don't know why, but it's been helpful."

Though inclined, her dragon warned, to more of Wainn's blood which it wasn't, she'd been firm, to have.

"Many have." Sand nodded to the fires behind them. If the air this night was warmer than usual for early spring, the turn-born hadn't argued. "Some think to stay."

Jenn thought of the lumber. "You're agreeable?"

"Our Devins is lonely," Sand said, which was true in general if not at the moment, the tall young man surrounded by Palma's cousins. "And families need room to grow, na?"

They did. Zehr was already planning cradles—

~Elder sister. It's time.~

Jenn looked down at the house toad and nodded. "Wen's coming."

Sand clapped her hands. "Good, good. We've the birthing day gifts."

How had she forgotten?

But first. Jenn collected herself. "Mistress Sand, I've a request for you and the others to consider."

A cluck of the tongue. "Sounds serious. Ask away, Sweetling. I make no promises, mind."

"I know." Turn-born must consider consequence and there'd be some, from this. But Jenn was determined. "Bannan needs to see his family. Werfol will need his uncle's help, as he grows into his gift." She paused.

Sand waited, eyes hooded.

"I seek your permission. I'll accept without argument if you refuse. I want you to believe that."

A hand waved her past it. Trust, that was.

"This is what I would wish." And Jenn told her.

The girl warmed the night, something Wisp appreciated from his perch atop the Treffs' barn. There were too many feet of every sort in the village tonight—

He'd no interest in having one land on his tail.

~I don't have a name yet, Great Lord of Dragons.~

~Stating the obvious won't get you one.~

~Yes, lord.~

There'd been a tedious number of such exchanges, the youngling dour and uncertain tonight. Pondering its future, Wisp concluded.

He'd have told it not to think so much, if he'd thought it would work.

~Count nyphrit. To yourself,~ before it could annoy him further.

A peaceful moment. Someone played a flute. Wisp felt content—

~Someone comes, lord!~

~An expected visit,~ he replied loftily.

Though he, like the girl, hadn't been sure Wen Treff would come, Marrowdell being unexpectedly full.

With too many feet.

TWENTY-NINE

*L*ANTERNS HUNG FROM branches and everyone helped arrange benches and bring out chairs, creating a great circle. The occasion of birthing gifts was a joy of itself, but to know these had come from the tinkers, who traveled far and wide, put a glow to Hettie's cheeks and had Peggs clinging to Kydd's arm as if fearing they'd inspire a birth on the spot.

Jenn kept looking around.

"I haven't seen her," Bannan whispered. "Are you sure—?"

"She's coming," Jenn assured him.

"I'm here," said Wen Treff, who hadn't been a heartbeat ago.

But was now, looking normal and a little anxious, so Jenn took her hand. "Where's Delfinn?"

"Here," said Wainn, startling them anew, if not Wen, who smiled. And why not? The young father glowed with happiness, his awkward hold on the wee bundle in his arms so tender Jenn swallowed the lump in her throat.

Bannan made a gentle herding motion. "It's time to join the others. We saved you seats."

Between the cluster of Treffs, who looked less happy than most, and Dusom, sitting with Aunt Sybb, Great Gran, and Radd Nalynn, with Master Jupp nearby with his trumpet to ear.

Reluctance, in the hand she held gently, and Jenn gave it a little squeeze. "I'm told this is all about the baby," she whispered.

Though it would be, of course, about Wen as well and what was to happen next.

Wen gave a nod. Reclaiming her hand, she held it out to Wainn, and together they walked to the waiting circle.

Jenn took Bannan's, holding on so tight he glanced down at her. "It'll be all right, Dearest Heart."

Would it?

Ancestors Fraught and Frustrating, there was no saying, when it came to Lorra Treff.

But in that, Jenn was mistaken, for the first person to spot the couple and baby arriving was Great Gran.

And the first thing she did was shout, "It's a girl!"

Which, if not an outright guess, was good enough to bring Lorra to her feet to see for herself, and then Davi, then the rest of the Treffs, all surrounding Wainn and Wen.

Somewhat to Jenn's surprise, and possibly his, Master Dusom was the first to hold Delfinn, his granddaughter, and walk around showing her. There wasn't a dry eye in the village, everyone remembering how he'd lost his own baby girl, Ponicce, and her mother, Larell, then taken such good care of Wainn.

"The gifts, na?"

The crowd stilled in anticipation, sorting itself out. By now, Delfinn was cradled in Lorra Treff's arms and, by that lady's look, not going elsewhere. Davi had his big arm around Wen, who would, Jenn knew, soon be.

Gifts, she thought happily, first.

"Hettie's waited the longest," Mistress Sand proclaimed. Flint and Sand carried between them an enormous wooden crate.

Jenn didn't think Hettie's eyes had ever been so wide. Tadd, holding Elainn and Torre, beamed from ear to ear.

Frankly, in Marrowdell, the crate alone was treasure, but inside was more.

Clay did the honors with a hammer and chisel.

The sides fell away with a bang.

Inside was a mass of straw, which was, Jenn thought, a bit of a letdown except for its hint of something breakable inside, which might not be the wisest choice in that household, but she trusted Mistress Sand and waited eagerly with the rest.

"C'mon, Hettie."

Encouraged, Hettie rushed forward. After an instant's anticipation, she grabbed huge handfuls of straw, tossing it aside.

Until she uncovered a pony.

It stood no taller than her knee, was covered in sparkly blue and red dots, and wore a golden saddle and bridle. The mane stuck up, ending in white fluff, and Jenn supposed it was a charming statue of some sort.

Until the pony blinked and stretched its head.

Everyone gasped.

Hettie went to her knees in front of it, enchanted. "What are you?"

"It's a babysit-on," Sand told her. "Call it out. The name's—" she looked to Riverstone.

"Crackers."

"'Crackers'," Sand repeated triumphantly.

Hettie coughed, looking at Tadd, who shrugged. "Come out, Crackers," she called gently.

The little pony tiptoed neatly from the rest of the straw, then stood waiting. It had, Jenn noticed, sparkles on its hooves as well as appealing brown eyes.

"It's an artifice," Bannan told her in a low voice. "From the Shadow Market in Channen, I'd say."

Though they could no longer be sure of that, Jenn knew, Bannan having told her of the mimrol hidden beneath the ruins of his home, and she telling him of Nonny's bottles and Urcet.

"Put a baby on it," Riverstone said eagerly. "It can tell what it needs."

Tadd, juggling two with some difficulty, came forward without hesitation and passed the squirmiest to his wife, who held the swaddled infant and stared at the pony, quite at a loss.

Sand clucked her tongue. "Like this." She took the fussing baby, and held whoever it was over the highly inappropriate saddle.

The pony turned its head to take a look, then gave a delicate shake.

The saddle neatly transformed itself into a high-sided sloped seat, the hooves developed rockers, and the pony's eyes half closed, as if ready to sleep.

Hettie clapped her hands.

Sand tucked the now-crying baby, swaddle and all, into the seat. The pony began to rock, very gently, back and forth.

The crying stopped.

Became a slightly smug coo.

Hettie grinned. "You didn't bring another, by chance?"

"They can share," Tadd said firmly, bowing to the turn-born and taking hold of his very happy wife.

There was, in short order, a second crate produced, larger than the first. Inside was a magnificent new stove—larger than Bannan's by half—and while Kydd looked crestfallen, clearly preferring a magical pony, Peggs gave a squeal of delight and declared herself ready to cook that instant.

But first things, first.

"Wen Treff," Sand summoned, producing a tiny velvet bag from her belt. As Wen came forward, the turn-born held up her free hand. "There is nothing we can give, you won't find for yourself. This is for Delfinn." Her voice became solemn. "It can only come from you."

Wainn joined Wen, their daughter in his arms.

Suddenly Jenn felt all of Marrowdell watching, not just the people, but the ground, the air, the river—everything within the valley.

And possibly some from beyond.

Mistress Sand shook out the contents of the bag and lifted a delicate chain. Hanging from it was a small silver disc. "This is a compass of the heart. If ever you wish your daughter to find you, Wen, this will be her truest guide."

Wen took the disc, closed her eyes, and pressed her lips to it. "I so wish."

It bound them, Jenn sensed. Through the edge, through the Verge, and she judged it eased Wen's heart, however little, by how she smiled as she returned it to Sand, who put it over Delfinn's sleeping head.

The turn-born looked for Jenn, finding her, and raised an eyebrow in question. *How did we do?* that was.

Perfect. The gifts were perfect and Jenn smiled to say so, from her heart.

Then Wainn, who'd been silent till now, stepped with his daughter, away from Wen and Sand, turning to face their families.

Yet his eyes met and held Jenn's.

And when he spoke, what she heard was different from everyone else that night.

"Thank you for this gift," they heard. "Delfinn and I will need everyone. Especially Hettie, at first, because she has extra milk."

That drew a laugh, and Hettie nodded vigorously.

"Be happy for Wen. She does what is right." The baby made a tiny sound, loud in the slightly concerned silence following those words.

They hadn't seen her leave, Jenn thought, who had, for Wen had looked at her last and longest, her eyes filled with the light of the Verge.

Wainn glanced down at the baby, wrinkled his nose, then looked up with distress.

"I think I need help now."

More laughter. Others came to him, Hettie first but all the rest were there, to embrace the newest to Marrowdell and give her their love.

As they had, Jenn Nalynn knew, to her.

Seeing his chance, Bannan took Jenn's hand and pulled her aside. He didn't stop pulling until they'd gone right around the Treffs' barn and out of the lanternlight, and if they kissed then and long, he'd no complaint at all.

But, Ancestors Dazzled and Dazed, he'd questions, so when they came up for air, he put Jenn, reluctantly, at arm's length. "Wen's gone for good, isn't she?"

"Yes. I don't think, in the end, she could bear a proper farewell."

Something unexpected in her voice made him try to see her face, outlined by starlight. "You aren't sad."

"I can't be. Marrowdell—Wainn—told me where she's gone. She's not alone. She's with the little cousins."

"In their secret paths." Sensing her surprise, he chuckled. "I haven't told you of those yet, have I? Scourge and I met Wen within them. She helped us, in her way."

Which had never been obvious, Bannan thought, thinking back, but always, in hindsight, wise.

Something rustled in the hedge. He paid it no mind.

Then a chill breeze found his ear. "Beware. Nyphrit are emboldened."

Jenn heard as well. Looked up at the roof, having a better sense than he where to find dragons. "Why?"

Scourge slid from a shadow, looming and protective. Scraped at the turf and snarled at the hedge, now filled with red eyes. "All the little cousins went with Wen. They've left Marrowdell."

Ancestors Abandoned and Alone. He shouldn't, Bannan told himself as he ran with Jenn back to warn those gathered to move inside and lock their doors, feel that way, but how could he not?

The house toads had guarded Marrowdell all these years, faithful and true.

Who'd guard it now?

~Hunt.~

Loosed, the excited youngling launched itself from the rooftop, snapping up the first nyphrit that dared leave the protection of the hedges.

A protection the vile things were about to lose.

The efflet brought by the turn-born roused in their multitudes, infuriated by nyphrit near their crops. Smaller, yes, but with wicked claws of their own and numbers.

Yling took flight, darting down to spear those nyphrit approaching the people, who now scattered for shelter.

Such as it was.

Wisp stretched a wing. He supposed he should take part. Would, if necessary.

Once done. He aimed an eye at the house toad within his claws, the girl's, impressed by its calm. It had thought to leave with the others, vanishing like mist.

Not quickly enough.

~Elder brother, I matter to Marrowdell. Just this——~

Wisp tightened his claws the slightest degree.

~Elder brother, you must let me go.~

He *must*, the dragon thought grimly, do no such thing. ~Why do you desert Jenn Nalynn and her people?~ Including the baby of special interest to Marrowdell's other denizens.

~All must make the offering.~

As he'd feared. ~This is about Wen.~

No response.

The little cousins were up to something, that was plain. Something they either considered private or reprehensible, but what could be so important they'd neglect their duty?

Beyond a dragon to fathom.

Wisp eased open his claws. ~Go. Abandon us to the nyphrit.~

The house toad canted its body. Was that *reproach*? ~We will be back, elder brother.~

~Hope there's a Marrowdell when you do,~ Wisp grumbled.

CHIRCY

"ANCESTORS BESET AND Beleaguered, I told them it was safe to come home." Jenn sat by Mistress Sand, seeking the turnborn's help while Bannan squeezed people into houses and barns. "What can we do?"

In the Verge, she'd wished nyphrit into rabbits. Not, Jenn sighed to herself, a wise approach here.

Seemingly unconcerned, Sand patted her knee. "Nyphrit are a nuisance, Sweetling, nothing more."

A nuisance with teeth and claws and appetite, not that any turnborn had to worry. Jenn stiffened. "They have to be stopped before they hurt anyone." Or anything, the piglets the right size for a snack and the horses thoroughly upset and ready to bolt back up the road.

"I see you must do something." Sand clucked her tongue to her teeth, studying Jenn's face. "Remember how you put everyone to sleep, na? Convenient, to do it now."

A trick she'd played before knowing what she was or understanding the harm, her younger self eager to be in her meadow with Wisp. A small and unplanned magic, in hindsight, to hope those already comfortable and asleep would stay so a while longer—

"I won't wish *at* people." And certainly not when they'd be helpless—

"Why would you, na?" A hand caught at air, fingers rounded in a trap.

"The nyphrit? Put them to sleep?" Jenn stared at the turn-born. "How?"

Sand shrugged. "That's your magic, Sweetling, none of ours."

"To have one," offered Master Riverstone, silent till now, "might be of use."

"To know it, na? A good notion. Go catch one, Sweetling."

A nyphrit? Jenn swallowed her objection. She'd no better idea.

Sand looked to Riverstone, both to her. The turn-born, she realized, weren't done.

"What is it?"

"With everyone safe, you can give your Bannan his surprise, na?" At her astonished, grateful look, Mistress Sand ducked her head as if hiding a smile.

Jumping up, Jenn hugged Mistress Sand. Then hugged Riverstone, and nothing would do but she hug each and every turn-born, who laughed and hugged her back.

Before leaving the tent to find a nyphrit to put to sleep, Jenn Nalynn faced the seven who wore the seeming of tinkers over bodies of glass, who loved her the best they could, lacking practice, and trusted her now. They'd packed, she'd noticed, needing to leave and soon. A strain, to linger here, after crossing with burdens and doing so much.

For her. For Marrowdell.

Jenn curled her fingers over her full heart. "Hearts of my Ancestors, hear my heart's plea. However far we are apart, Keep Us Close."

And though terst and turn-born, they responded as one. "'Keep Us Close'."

"I've already told Wisp." Jenn Nalynn shook her finger under Scourge's nose. "You aren't to take advantage. It's not fair."

The kruar gave her, then Bannan, an appalled and pleading look. "You're sure?" he murmured to his love, feeling much the same.

Thanks to Jenn Nalynn, there were piles of sleeping nyphrit up against buildings. Piles under hedges. Even a pile beside the village well, and the sight would have given any villager nightmares had they dared venture out.

He felt queasy himself, seeing their number.

"I'm sure." Jenn chewed her lower lip. "Though I suppose it wouldn't hurt to—" a gesture toward the Spine and its forest, "—take them away."

Before Bannan could ask how she thought that might be accomplished, unconscious nyphrit began to rise into the air, limbs dangling. To his true sight, each was being lifted by a pair of grim little efflet.

If Jenn believed they'd simply carry off their blood enemy to leave safe and sound and able to attack them again, he'd be the last to dissuade her.

Especially when he could tell she'd something else on her mind.

Sure enough, Jenn tucked her small hand in his elbow, dismissing the matter of nyphrit with a brisk, "If you're not too tired, Dearest Heart, there's something else we need to do."

"Tired?" He swept her up in his arms and nuzzled her neck until she made a happy little sound. Why then, it was necessary to nuzzle further—

She wriggled free, dancing back. "Follow me!"

Bannan having his own idea of what was happening proved most distracting. Which helped her avoid watching nyphrit fly through the air like hundreds of comatose bats, but he insisted on carrying her across the river—collecting kisses all the way so they almost fell in twice—then thought to carry her to the farm despite his recently healed injuries.

Putting her foot down, literally, Jenn darted ahead, hearing him chase behind. While it was a delicious game, she was impatient for something else.

So she shortened the road until their next steps fell on the path to Night's Edge.

Bannan came up beside her, winded and rather perplexed. "Jenn?"

"Come with me."

They weren't alone. A warm breeze tickled her bangs and something crashed through branches. The dragons were curious.

Or concerned, at least hers. She took heart. The turn-born hadn't objected.

A moth appeared. Flew ahead. *Curious?*

Or prepared to stop her. What the sei would or wouldn't do being beyond her knowing, Jenn kept walking, Bannan's breath soft on her neck.

Till they arrived in Night's Edge.

In the distance, the river sparkled, flowing between flat, even fields. The Bone Hills, in this instance, felt a little close for comfort.

"What's this about?" Bannan asked very quietly, perhaps feeling the same.

"I have to show you." Jenn walked around the meadow, not quite sure why or what she sought, only that it would be here.

And was. Her feet landed where there'd been a round of ash and destruction, now dried grass—admittedly trampled by livestock, but alive and healthy. The place she'd made her first fateful wish.

"Dear Heart?" a breeze, soft and puzzled.

Standing there, Jenn let herself become glass and pearl and light. But mostly pearl, the tears of a sei, the part of her linked to both edge and Verge, aware of everywhere and all of it, of wherever she wanted to be.

And how.

A crossing like no other, a single, careful stitch—a deep and thought-filled wish—to draw here to—

There.

Jenn blinked, flesh again and relieved to see nothing had changed.

A moth landed on her dress, peacefully tidying its wings. The sei, offering an opinion?

Or having none.

She looked for Bannan. Held out her hand. He took it willingly, head angled in question.

"Come with me."

And took a step.

He'd watched with his deeper sight and been blinded by whatever magic Jenn Nalynn wove in her meadow. His eyes, Bannan thought, knuckling them, weren't right yet.

Because they showed him a forest beyond a slope of white stones, and the rise of a mountain topped with snow against a sky filled with stars and it wasn't possible—how could it be?

"BANNAN!"

He whirled around, arms up in time to catch his sister, who hugged him with all her great strength.

Over her head, he saw Jenn Nalynn, standing a little apart, and oh, the joy of her smile.

"Two dragons! There's TWO! What do you mean, you can't see them?" Semyn moving slower than a tortoise, Werfol grabbed his sleeve and pulled. "This is the edge. You have to see them!"

His brother freed his arm with a jerk. "It's not the turn, Weed. I can't see anything unless they let me."

With a world of wistfulness in that, so Werfol looked right at the strange dragon, his eyes molten gold. "Show yourself to my brother. Please?"

The dragon gave a great start that sent it partly into the air, and hit the boys with a gale-force bellow. "YOU CAN SEE ME?"

Werfol covered his ears. "DON'T SHOUT AT US!"

A breeze, soft and warm, found his ear. "I apologize for the youngling."

And there was Wisp, magnificent Wisp, shaped from light and as real as rock. Semyn cheered and Werfol grinned, but didn't move. Eager as he was to run to his friend and throw his arms as far around the deadly neck as he could—and while *almost* sure Wisp would tolerate such a display, at least for a little—the presence of a strange dragon meant this wasn't the time.

Dignity mattering to dragons.

Still, he could bounce from foot to foot, and did.

"Youngling, show yourself."

The other dragon landed. While Werfol could see all of it, it seemed to have trouble coming into view, as if not good at the technique—

—or maybe shy. Which was a different sort of idea about a dragon, and Werfol grew even more interested in it.

There. Done, the strange dragon—the youngling, Wisp called it—endured Semyn's wide-eyed stare.

Smaller than Wisp, it was, with a hide covered in white palm-sized scales edged in shimmering orange except on its head, where the scales were more like Wisp's and tightly packed. The wings were shiny as if new or hardly used, and its tail lacked spines, but it was the eyes that caught Werfol's attention. Wisp's were a deep wild violet.

The youngling's eyes were pale orange, with flares of red at their heart, and, at this moment, studying him with equal interest.

"Is it a girl or boy?" Semyn asked, which was rude, the youngling right there.

But a fascinating question, and Werfol looked at Wisp when the youngling didn't speak up.

Perhaps afraid to be too loud again.

"Our genders reveal themselves in the mating flight, young Westietas, a once-in-a-lifetime event. For this one?" Wisp knew how to shrug with a wing. "Not within yours."

The youngling looked disappointed, Semyn ready to ask another question.

Werfol jumped in, giving a quick little bow. "I'm Werfol Westi-etas and this is my brother Semyn. What's your name?"

Its head lowered. "I DON't have ONE yet."

"That was much better," Semyn praised, guessing, as did Werfol, the youngling tried its best.

A brighter look.

"Weed! Semyn!"

Werfol rolled his eyes, mouthing 'found us' to his brother, who shrugged it off and waved at the approaching guard. Sending Dutton was *unnecessary*. They weren't hiding so much as they'd 'absented themselves from proceedings,' as Momma would say, and while he'd been glad to see Uncle Bannan and amazed to see Jenn Nalynn?

Neither were as fun as dragons.

Who'd vanished again, rather than be discovered, but were still here, Werfol saw.

Before they could leave, he just had to ask.

"Wisp, can I keep it?"

The boys weren't the only ones to flee the confines of the tent. The girl stood watching, shadow in shadow, unusually still and quiet. He felt her amusement at Werfol's brash question. Shared it.

The youngling, on the other hand, quivered with stress. ~What is the truthseer's intention, Great Lord of Dragons? Does he mean to kill me? Do the kruar?~

Legitimate fears—if not of Werfol, clearly entranced by the possibility of his very own dragon, nor of the two patrolling the forest edge—as the guard arrived, weapons rattling and in no good temper, posing the appearance, at least, of threat.

Prudence dictated they not find out. ~Hide yourself, youngling.~

The boys left and Jenn came close. "That was kind of you both. Thank you."

~Leave us,~ he ordered the youngling. When it didn't move, he sighed and gave it a task. ~Follow the young truthseer, but stay within the edge. Hear what he has to say of you.~

Spying caught the youngling's fancy. *He'd thought it might.*

Once the other dragon rose and veered away, once they were alone, Wisp showed himself. "This was reckless."

A small smile. Her hand waved. "Bringing us here? Did you not want to see Werfol?"

The dragon ignored the question; he had and she well knew it. "You made what has never been, a crossing not to the Verge but from edge to edge. You broke the rules of the sei." How, a question he wouldn't ask. *Why?*

That, he feared, he knew.

Ah, but it pleased her to answer, for Jenn's glad smile widened and she spread her hands, then brought them together, palms touching. "I didn't. Not really. Wisp, you know how I can shorten distance between where I am and where I want to be. I've simply done that from—yes, a new crossing in Marrowdell—to the one already here. When we cross, we still pass through the Verge, just—very quickly. Without all the—" A hand waved in the air, encompassing the dangers of that other realm.

Much as it pained him to admit, it was a clever use of one of her more disconcerting abilities. "Still reckless," he growled.

"I asked the turn-born. They approved." Her voice held wonder. "The sei allowed it. I wasn't sure they would."

Lost for words, he scratched at the ground. What weren't rocks hastily rolled and bumped out of reach.

"Ah," she said, as if he'd answered, and sat, as if in their meadow.

And not in what wasn't.

"I'm sorry. I should have asked you first of all. Dearest Heart." A sigh. "Everything was happening so fast, from Delfinn to the turn-born. Suddenly, I had my family back and more, while Bannan couldn't be sure if Werfol and his sister made it home. I couldn't bear it. I had to try."

Her great, good heart would be, the dragon suspected, the death of him as well as best thing in his life. "What's done is done," he said

at last, not ready to forgive but resigned. Jenn Nalynn was who and
what she was.

"I gave it rules," she said, as if coaxing him to play.

"'Rules?'" he echoed numbly.

"They're like rules," she qualified unhelpfully. She lifted a hand,
counting on her fingers. First finger. "It's hidden. Bannan's crossing
can't be found without me."

Wisp felt a perilous curiosity. "Does he know you've named it
for him?"

"Not yet. Once I take someone through with me—" a second finger rose, "—they can find it again." A third. "If they've that magic—
or I've granted it—they can use it without me. Like you," this with
satisfaction.

Wisp grumbled. "And the youngling."

Her face fell, having not thought of that, but only for an instant.
A fourth finger shot up. "Bannan's crossing can't be used by those of
ill intent. Even me, if I'm angry or meaning harm to anyone."

A situation impossible to imagine.

Her hand dropped to her knee. "And it's really small," she admitted, as if a failure. "I'm quite sure a wagon won't fit."

A dragon could but try to keep up. "Slightly less reckless than I
feared," he told her at last. "Promise to consult me before altering the
universe again, Dear Heart."

A dimple. "I swear by the bones of my Ancestors. Now, what's
this about Werfol and Imp?"

She'd named the youngling. Wisp tried the word. "'Imp.'"

"It's what Aunt Sybb would call us when we did something we
shouldn't and the outcome made her laugh. A small creature of magic
who tends to make funny mistakes."

That suited.

"An imp is also," Jenn Nalynn added softly, "a sprout taken from
a special tree, that you very much want to grow strong and healthy."

"We won't tell the youngling that," the dragon decided.

Though pleased, very much, by the thought.

CHIRTY-ONE

THE SUN WAS rising when Jenn and Bannan took their leave of the Westietas, the boys gone to their beds and adults in need of their own. They'd declined offers of goods to take back, to keep their visit secret.

However tempting. Jenn had thought to bring a small bag of Bannan's favorite tea and maybe a bar of the soap she admired; items easily explained, she'd proposed, if anyone asked, as come in the mailbags brought from Endshere by Aunt Sybb.

Bannan had warned the smallest lie was a seed for trouble. Lila had nodded agreement, though her eyes were hooded, as if to hide thoughts of her own.

Best, Jenn decided, not to know.

She waited in the edge while Bannan made his farewells to those in the house. When he returned, he took her in his arms and buried his face in her hair for a long moment. "Are you all right?" she asked, feeling him tremble.

"Ancestors Blessed," he whispered hoarsely. "More than all right, Dearest Heart. Overwhelmed. Grateful. Exhausted by joy. I'd not thought to see them again so soon. To have the chance, after all we've gone through—I'm forever grateful. I've memories to warm the years to come. And letters to write," with a grin. "The distance between us doesn't feel as vast anymore."

She smiled herself, that being truer than he knew.

They walked to the crossing and she was surprised to find it marked, in a sense, the small ones called scree gathered nearby, as if curious—or alarmed.

Jenn wasn't surprised to see two cloaked figures standing together at the limit of the edge, Lila and Emon there to catch a final glimpse of them.

Believing this was.

Jenn took Bannan's hand but, before taking the step back to Marrowdell, turned to face him. "There is no more distance between you and your family, Bannan Larmensu, than a step."

He saw it was the truth but not how.

She traced his dear face with her fingers, resting them on his lips. "I didn't make a crossing, Dearest Heart. I built you a door. One to use whenever you wish, with or without me."

"I can come back tomorrow."

"You can." She tried not to smile, but wild hope lit his eyes, and she'd been right, Jenn knew it, to do this. "And be home for tea." Reading his quick look to where Lila and Emon stood, she grew serious. "It only seems to bypass the Verge. It won't be safe for those who suffer there."

A wider world, for one who could, and despite her dragon's fussing, Jenn had no regrets.

Bannan held out his arm, his eyes golden. "Let's go home."

They took the step together.

Dragons having gone ahead.

A sunbeam woke him from what, Bannan thought fuzzily, had been the most wonderful dream. A dream where he'd walked from the meadow to Lila in a heartbeat. Received back his key, if not the scarf, and given a promise.

A dream where he'd a door connecting those he loved most—

"Ooof!"

The house toad, having landed on his stomach, gave him a look as if to say he'd stayed abed far too long and were there biscuits?

"You're back!" He restrained the urge to hug it, little cousins not in favor, settling for a wide grin. "Welcome home."

A dignified blink.

As well expect answers from the sun, Bannan thought cheerfully. "Jenn's in the kitchen," he guessed, his love not beside him.

The toad opened its wide mouth, a strip of paper on its tongue.

This was new. Warily, Bannan reached in to retrieve it.

A note, in her handwriting, and he read it with abrupt haste. "She's gone to see Wen," he told the toad.

Who didn't look surprised.

Jenn went with Wisp, the invitation including him, crossing at the Spine and becoming turn-born to hang from his leg. She could, she thought, get used to flying like this—

—except it was a burden to her dragon, who'd not complain, and nothing wrong with her feet.

But the invitation felt imperative. As if something held breath to wait for her and she mustn't delay.

They flew over the mountain of sei, under deep valleys lined with rivers of mimrol, accompanied by dragons who kept a respectful distance.

And one that did not.

Green, the dragon who flew too close and made Wisp snarl, bizarre in shape with glittering eyes. Jenn paid it no attention. If the sei joined them, it was in honor of the one waiting.

Here.

The palace where they'd seen the last of the toad queen, once a lifeless home for ghosts. No longer.

When Jenn later tried to describe it to Bannan, words failed her. The Verge seemed to have exploded with magic. Towers aimed in every direction, each now uniquely different, with doorways and openings suited to whoever approached. There was kaliia, here growing larger than neyet, filled with efflet who giggled. Silk threads of every color wove a tapestry before her eyes larger than the sky and they passed through it—

—became part of it—

—were set loose from it to land on the floor.

A floor now carpeted in soft moss, with eyes that blinked cheerfully where it wasn't crowded with house toads, only these were brown, with dainty gold filigree around their huge black eyes. They looked, not at the dragon or turn-born, but to the throne at the center of the cavernous room.

~Made of white pebbles,~ Wisp observed, trying not to sound impressed.

But was, of course. How could he not be?

As thrones went, Jenn thought, familiar only with illustrations and those very old, it was surprisingly like a couch, wide and with comfortable cushions. The toads moved aside to make an aisle for them to approach, so they did. The woman who reclined on it, a bare foot on an armrest, waved a greeting.

Wen Treff.

More house toads sat with her on the throne, and there was, still, a toad on her shoulder. She wore light and air, but her face and form remained her own, and her smile warm and sincere.

And happy. "Welcome to my new home." Lowering her foot, Wen gestured to Jenn to sit on a cushion beside her.

Wisp settled on the floor. House toads inched closer and closer until he rumbled a warning.

"It looks different," Jenn told her. "Better. Much better."

Wen at peace, in her rightful place as Nonny would say, was different too. Smiling easily, her long fingers expressive as she drew them through the air. "I'm to say it will grow, but not over what's here. A well-behaved palace." With a twinkle in her eye, she went on, "You can ask, you know."

"Why you?"

A chuckle. "I'm a good listener. It turns out the little cousins desired someone who'd also speak for them. Other," a nod to Wisp, "than you, dragon lord, though we thank you for all you've done."

A chorus filled the world. ~WE THANK YOU.~

Wisp lowered his head in acceptance.

"A queen," Jenn whispered, her eyes wide. "What will your mother say?"

"That I should be there." A flicker of sadness. "She doesn't realize how long ago I left."

Jenn held out her hand. Wen took it and they sat in silence a moment.

Then Wen's lips quirked up. "Though, Ancestors Witness, Mother's tactics for resolving squabbles in Ayvo's pottery guild—which she'd lecture us about endlessly—might come in handy here. But queen? The little cousins held the title in hope in their hearts a very long time and I couldn't refuse." Her face changed, grew stern. Regal, in the best way. "I will redeem it."

Suddenly Jenn noticed a small box on the couch. "That's not—"

"The wizard? No, we left him in Marrowdell. But it is a prison."

~A PRISON!~ Now a cry of victory.

Wisp ROARED in answer.

Jenn wasn't so sure. The toad's vanquished queen, all that spite and power, in a box? "Is it secure?"

"A drop of blood from every toad who lives went to make it."

Explaining the desertion of Marrowdell's, Jenn thought queasily.

Wen's voice changed, deepened, held the Verge as it had once Marrowdell, and everything stopped to listen. "MY—LIFE—SEALS—IT."

With a little shake, she was Wen Treff again, and smiling. "Thank you for coming, Jenn Nalynn, and you, dragon lord. It's good to have friends." A wink. "If you'd like to come again, send word by toad. We welcome guests."

~GUESTS! GUESTS!~ The toads' cheerful chorus followed them from the palace.

And to the crossing home.

"I'm not used to it yet," Peggs said, eyeing her new stove. "You'll tell me if the pastry's tough."

Jenn, sitting on the ladder with her mouth full of perfect pie, nodded vigorously. As did their father, Radd, perched on a bucket. Roses bobbed outside the windows, shut for now, the weather cooler with a promise of rain.

But it was spring, after all, and rain important.

And the neyet's legacy of great value. Bannan and Kydd were helping Zehr build a second room on Hettie and Tadd's house, while Davi and Anten measured for an expansion to Devins', and the Uhthoffs would soon have a nursery. The entire village bustled, inside and out, moving with the season.

At sunset, there'd be a common pot of stew for all in the mill and a cask of Palma's famed cider to share. It wouldn't be the last, for those from Endshere would be back in hopes of a summer wedding.

If not sooner.

The curtain between kitchen and parlor—now again Aunt Sybb's bedroom—pulled back. The Lady Mahavar entered, her waistcoat impeccable and topped with a fashionable lace collar. There was, Jenn noticed, more gray in her hair this year, but more sparkle in her eyes as well. "I hear there's already a pie, Dear Hearts?"

Radd jumped to his feet, bringing a chair with cushions to put by the table. "And tea, Sybbie."

She settled, her shoes, gleaming with polish, together. Gave Jenn's bare toes a wink, Peggs' roundness a smile, then Aunt Sybb told her family what she hadn't, till now, had time to say.

"A change of place does wonders for the heart, doesn't it?"

~I have a name!~

Already regretting the impulse to tell the youngling, Wisp

snarled from his nest under Bannan's stove. ~Take it and give me peace.~

The youngling, Imp, had graduated to a rafter, though Bannan's house toad kept a wary eye out for transgressions.

A dragon could hope.

Imp dangled its head to better look at Wisp. ~You have a name, Great Lord of Dragons. I have a name. Can I have a house of my own now?~

Where had that—Wisp glared at the toad, who gave every appearance of innocence.

Then who'd planted that notion? ~No.~

~Can I have my own turn-born now?~

~NO!~

~Can I——~

Wisp lunged up, taking the foolish youngling by the throat, the pair of them hanging from the rafters and shaking down dust and cobwebs, much to the little cousin's distress. ~You have a name. Be careful you don't lose it.~

Something heavy thumped into the door. A deep, familiar voice rumbled, ~When you're finished playing, there's a bear.~

Struck by a dreadful possibility, Wisp tightened his grip. ~Imp, have you been listening to that old fool?~

The youngling gave a noncommittal croak.

Bah. ~Stay here.~

Letting go, Wisp flew up and through the roof, circling over the kruar. ~Have you nothing better to do?~ he taunted.

~A bear,~ Scourge repeated, lips curled back, prancing in place. ~Came sniffing after the wagons. Might be two.~

He'd prefer three. The big winter bears that put up a fight—

The youngling burst through a wall. ~Can I come?~

Make that four.

Concerning the Denizens of Marrowdell

Alyssa Ropp, child, daughter of Mimm and Anten, sister of Hettie and Cheffy, stepdaughter to Cynd, stepsister to Roche and Devins. Born in Marrowdell. Helps in dairy.

Anten Ropp, brother of Cynd, father (with Mimm) of Hettie, Cheffy, and Alyssa. Widowed then married Covie. Stepfather of Roche and Devins. Tends the dairy.

Aunt Sybb (the Lady Sybb Mahavar, nee Nalynn), sister of Radd, aunt to Peggs and Jenn. Lives in Avyo with husband Hane Mahavar where they own several of the better riverside inns. Spends summers in Marrowdell.

Bannan Marerrym Larmensu, son of Maggin and Gyllen, brother of Lila, rider of Scourge. Former Vorkoun border guard who went by the name of "Captain Ash." Truthseer and, in Marrowdell, farmer. Beloved of Jenn Nalynn.

Battle and Brawl, Davi Treff's team of draft horses.

Cheffy Ropp, child, son of Mimm and Anten, brother of Hettie and Alyssa, stepson of Covie, stepbrother of Roche and Devins. Born in Marrowdell. Helps in dairy.

Covie Ropp, mother (with Riedd Morrill) of Roche and Devins, stepmother to Hettie, Cheffy, and Alyssa. Widowed then married Anten. A baroness in Avyo. Tends the dairy. Village healer.

Crumlin Tralee (the Lost One), once resident of Marrowdell. Disappeared under magical circumstances. Currently in a box guarded by house toads.

Cynd Treff (nee Ropp), sister of Anten, wife of Davi, aunt to Hettie, Cheffy, and Alyssa, aunt to Delfinn. Gardener and seamstress.

Davi Treff, son of Lorra, brother of Wen, husband of Cynd, uncle to Hettie, Cheffy, and Alyssa, uncle to Delfinn. Village smith.

Delfinn Uhthoff, baby, daughter of Wen and Wainn, granddaughter of Dusom and Lorra, great-niece of Kydd and Peggs.

Devins Morrill, son of Covie and Riedd, brother of Roche. Stepbrother of Hettie, Cheffy, and Alyssa. Stepson of Anten. Came to Marrowdell as a boy. Tends the dairy.

Dusom Uhthoff (Master Dusom), father of Wainn and Ponicce, husband of Larell (widowed), brother of Kydd, grandfather to Delfinn. Formerly professor at Avyo's Sersise University. Village teacher and helps tend the orchard.

Elainn Emms, baby, daughter of Hettie and Tadd, twin of Torre.

Frann Nall, former business rival and later friend of Lorra Treff. In Avyo, holdings included riverfront warehouses. Village weaver and quilter. Died of natural causes.

Gallie Emms, mother of twins, Tadd and Allin, and baby Loee, wife of Zehr. Author (pen name Elag M. Brock) and sausage maker.

Good'n'Nuf, Ropps' bull.

Hettie Emms (nee Ropp), daughter of Mimm and Anten, sister of Cheffy and Alyssa, stepdaughter of Covie, stepsister of Roche and Devins, wife to Tadd, mother of twins Elainn and Torre. Came to Marrowdell as a child. Village cheese maker.

Himself, boar.

Imp, youngling dragon Wisp has been ordered by the sei to teach.

Jenn Nalynn, daughter of Melusine and Radd, sister of Peggs, sister by marriage to Kydd. Born in Marrowdell under magical circumstances. Turn-born. Beloved of Bannan Larmensu.

Kydd Uhthoff, brother of Dusom, uncle of Wainn and Ponicce, husband of Peggs, father of her baby-to-be, great-uncle of Delfinn. Came to Marrowdell as a young man. Formerly a student at

Sersise University. Tends apple orchard. Village beekeeper and artist.

Larell Uhthoff, mother of Wainn and Ponicce, wife of Dusom. Died by misadventure on the Northward Road.

Loee Emms, toddler, daughter of Gallie and Zehr, sister of Tadd and Allin. Born in Marrowdell.

Lorra Treff, mother of Davi and Wen, great-aunt to Hettie, Cheffy, and Alyssa, grandmother to Delfinn. Formerly head of Avyo's influential Potter's Guild. Village potter.

Melusine (Melly) Nalynn (nee Semanaryas), mother of Peggs and Jenn, wife of Radd. Died by misadventure.

Mimm Ropp, mother of Hettie, Cheffy, and Alyssa, first wife of Anten. Died by misadventure.

Peggs Uhthoff (nee Nalynn), daughter of Melusine and Radd, elder sister of Jenn, wife of Kydd, expecting his baby, great-aunt of Delfinn. Came to Marrowdell as a toddler. Village's best baker and cook.

Ponicce Uhthoff, baby, daughter of Dusom and Larell, sister of Wainn, niece of Kydd. Died by misadventure on the Northward Road.

Radd Nalynn, father of Peggs and Jenn, husband of Melusine, brother of Sybb. In Avyo, owned mills and a tannery. Village miller.

Riedd Morrill, father of Roche and Devins, husband of Covie, cousin of Riss, great-nephew of Wagler Jupp. In Avyo, was a baron and served in the House of Keys. Died by misadventure.

Riss Nahamm, cousin of Riedd, great-niece of Old Jupp, wife of Sennic. Came to Marrowdell as a young woman. Creates tapestries and cares for her great-uncle.

Satin and Filigree, sows.

Scourge, the Larmensu war horse. In Marrowdell, his true nature is revealed.

Sennic Nahamm (nee Horst), former soldier, husband of Riss. Took the name of Horst from baby Jenn, who continues to call him Uncle Horst. Hunter and village protector.

Tadd Emms, son of Zehr and Gallie, brother of Loee, twin of Allin, husband of Hettie, father to twins Elainn and Torre. Came to Marrowdell as a babe. Miller's apprentice.

Tir Half-face (Tirsan Dimelecor), former Vorkoun border guard. Bannan's friend and companion. Has taken service with the Lady Mahavar in Avyo.

Torre Emms, baby, son of Hettie and Tadd, twin of Elainn.

Wagler Jupp (Old Jupp, Master Jupp), great-uncle of Riedd and Riss, great-great-uncle to Devins and Roche. Former Secretary of the House of Keys in Avyo. Currently writing his memoirs.

Wainn Uhthoff, son of Dusom and Larell, brother of Ponicce, nephew of Kydd, father (with Wen) of Delfinn. Came to Marrowdell as a young boy. Injured by misadventure on the Northward Road. Communes with edge.

Wainn's Old Pony.

Wen Treff, daughter of Lorra, sister of Davi, mother (with Wainn) of Delfinn. Came to Marrowdell as a young woman. Prefers to talk to toads, but recently has been known to talk to people. Communes with Verge.

Wisp the dragon, once Wyll the man, Jenn Nalynn's dearest friend and protector.

Zehr Emms, father of the twins, Tadd and Allin, and baby Loee, husband of Gallie. A fine furniture maker in Avyo. Village carpenter.

Concerning the Denizens of Endshere

Allin Anan (nee Emms), son of Gallie and Zehr, brother of Loee, twin brother of Tadd, husband to Palma Anan. Came to Marrowdell as a babe. Now lives in Endshere as barkeep in Palma's inn.

Bliss, not a nice person.

Cammi, postmistress.

Dinorwic, thief and smuggler.

Great Gran (Caryn Anan), great grandmother of the family. Former resident of Marrowdell.

Hager Comber, son of Harty, village smith.

Harty Comber, father of Hager, village smith.

Larah Anan, young boy, Palma's brother. Clears tables in the inn.

Palma Anan, sister of Larah, wife of Allin. Born and raised in Endshere. Owns and operates The Good Night's Sleep inn. Author.

Shedden, village healer.

Upsala, unscrupulous trader who sold Bannan his ox.

Concerning the Denizens of the Bay of Shades, Eldad

Dawizards (dire-ones), dedicated sect who come to the Bay of Shades hunting for magic to contain and destroy.

Flesie, child, lives in Shadesport. Communes with edge.

Granny Bunac, lives in Shadesport. Best cook.

Heathe, lives in Shadesport. Waalum hunter.

Lenzi, lives in Shadesport. Waalum hunter.

Marni, lives in Shadesport. Waalum hunter.

Nonny (Noemi), lives alone on her boat, the *Good Igrini*. Originally from the deep south of Eldad. Dives for mimrol. Friend to Urcet.

Symyd, lives in Shadesport. Waalum hunter and finder of magical things.

Urcy (Urcet a Hac Sa Od y Dom, Urcy Shade's Ass), former scholar and author exiled to Shadesport after visiting Marrowdell with Dema Qimirpik. Friend to Nonny.

Concerning the Denizens of Ansnor

Author's Note: Names marked with an * first appear in my Night's Edge novella, "A Pearl from the Dark." Those with a + first appear in my Night's Edge enovella, "A Dragon for William." Both of these stories take place between *A Play of Shadow* and *A Change of Place*. All other names come from the novels themselves.

+Araben Sethe, engineer consulting with Emon.

*Calym Lapec, resident of Loudit, lensmaster. Token smuggler exposed by Roche Morrill.

Dema Qimirpik, visited Marrowdell with Urcet the Eld. Resident of temple near Loudit.

*Deter Elenyas, former Ansnan soldier released from prison. Traveled with Edis and Jon. Betrayed Edis.

*Disel, resident of Loudit, smith's apprentice. Friend of Roche, Flam, and Lenert. Received scholarship to attend Vorkoun's Riversbend University.

*Edis Donovar, former Ansnan soldier released from prison. Traveled with Deter and Jon until being betrayed. Befriended by Roche and saved by the magic of the edge. Now a magical creature.

*Flam, resident of Loudit, musician, friend of Roche, Disel, and Lenert. Received scholarship to attend Vorkoun's Riversbend University.

*Jon Palyenor, former Ansnan soldier released from prison. Traveled with Edis and Deter. Betrayed Edis.

Kanajuq, servant to the dema, resident of temple near Loudit. Came to Marrowdell.

*Lenert, resident of Loudit, miller's apprentice. Friend of Roche, Disel, and Flam.

*Noabi Lapec, resident of Loudit, runs post office.

Panilaq, servant to the dema, resident of temple near Loudit. Came to Marrowdell.

Roche Morrill, son of Covie and Riedd, elder brother of Devins. Former resident of Marrowdell, lately of Loudit. Received scholarship to attend Vorkoun's Riversbend University. Dreadful dreamer. And truthteller, by the wish of Jenn Nalynn.

*Wibler the Great (Master Wibler), resident of Loudit, senior glassmaker.

Concerning the Denizens of Vorkoun

Author's Note: Names marked with an * were first mentioned in my Night's Edge novella, "A Pearl from the Dark." Those with a + were first mentioned in my Night's Edge e-novella, "A Dragon for William." Both take place between *A Play of Shadow* and *A Change of Place.* All other names occur first in the novels.

Adrianna Morven, former nurse of Lila and Bannan, related to their mother.

+Aunt Kinsel, Emon's father's sister, great-aunt to Semyn and Werfol.

Bish Fingal, one of Emon's trusted companions. Betrayed him in Mellynne and was killed by Dutton.

+Breeta, new Westietas smithy.

+Chancellor Rober Milne, chief administrator of Vorkoun.

Cheek, one of Emon's trained crows.

Dauntless, kruar who came from the Verge to carry Bannan to Marrowdell. Now lives on Westietas estate to be close to Werfol.

Dutton Omemee, Emon's senior guard, assigned as companion to Werfol and guard to Semyn.

Emon Westietas, father of Semyn and Werfol, husband of Lila. Baron, holding the seat for Vorkoun in the House of Keys. Currently in disfavor and exiled by Prince Ordo.

+Fullarton, head of Vorkoun's Potter's Guild.

+Gore, administrator of waterworks in Vorkoun.

Gyllen Marerrym Larmensu, wife of Maggin, mother of Lila and Bannan. Died in landslide.

Jarratt, aide to Gyllen Larmensu. Died in landslide.

Herer, one of Emon's trusted companions.

Ignace, aide to Maggin Larmensu. Died in landslide.

+Ioana Tagey, sister to Nam, former cook at Marerrym estate. Escaped landslide and now head cook for the Westietas.

+Issan, Semyn and Werfol's former tutor.

Kimm Larmensu, uncle of Maggin, great-uncle to Bannan and Lila. First to ride Scourge in battle.

+Lady Estaire, member of a Vorkoun noble house.

Lila Westietas (nee Larmensu), daughter of Maggin and Gyllen, sister of Bannan, mother of Semyn and Werfol, wife of Emon. Baroness. Truedreamer.

Maggin Larmensu, husband of Gyllen, father of Lila and Bannan. Truthseer and rider of Scourge. Died in landslide.

Nam Tagey (Tagey), brother to Ioana, former groundskeeper at the Marerrym estate, friend to Bannan. Escaped landslide and works for Lila in Vorkoun.

+Namron Setac (Master Setac), tutor Lila hires for Semyn and Werfol. Member of a secret society concerned with preventing another catastrophe in the edge.

Nimly, scullery boy at Westietas estate. Mute.

+Revis, Westietas housekeeper and only original house staff left.

Rowe Jonn, soldier in Lila's personal guard. Killed protecting her sons on the Northward Road.

Ruthh, former seamstress to the Larmensu. Lila had her sew Bannan into his bedroll for a prank.

Ryll Aronom, seniormost of Lila's personal guard.

Seel Aucoin, soldier in Lila's personal guard. Killed protecting her sons on the Northward Road.

Scatterwit, one of Emon's crows.

Semyn Westietas, young boy, elder son of Lila and Emon, brother of Werfol, nephew of Bannan. Heir to the barony.

+Sendrick, Westietas' new seniormost servant.

Spirit, kruar who came from the Verge to carry Lila to Marrowdell. Now lives on Westietas estate to be close to Werfol.

+Tess, twin to Tixel. New staff. The pair referred to by Werfol as "Liar Twins."

+Tixel, twin to Tess. New staff. The pair referred to by Werfol as "Liar Twins."

Werfol (Weed) Westietas, young boy, younger son of Lila and Emon, brother of Semyn, nephew of Bannan. Truthseer and truedreamer.

The Making of Shadesport

Growing up in Nova Scotia, I learned to love the smell of the sea and to know water as huge and ever-moving. Moving to the shore of Lake Ontario—which in the mid 1960s didn't smell so great, and while huge, often doesn't move much at all—proved a shock. I came to appreciate and love it, eventually, but missed tides and those shoreline seawater pools brimming with life.

Thus I relish any chance to write about the edge of the sea. To include tidal pools and drifting seaweed. To bring back what's never far from my memory: the ceaseless crash and mumble of waves, the tang of fresh-caught fish and exposed shells, the daily courage of the people who make their living there. The Bay of Shades and Shadesport, its village of fisher folk, feel like a home-coming. So much so, I had to watch I didn't overindulge in my beloved seascapes, though I did allow myself to name Flesie after my best friend growing up there, Florence Giles, or Flossie-Mae as I called her.

Tides? The Bay of Fundy was where we'd take visitors to witness the profound impact of tides and informed this story—including how Nonny's boat rose and fell with them. That's a real thing, trust me. While any cove along the Atlantic shore would have done, and Shadesport's buildings owe their shape and colour to those in villages like Quidi Vidi, Newfoundland, we spent many a summer climbing the rocks at Peggy's Cove (before it grew into such an attraction those same rocks had to be roped off or tourists be lost to the sea). So you'll find some of that wonderful place in these pages.

Preliminary sketches of Nonny's boat and Shadesport.

The Bay of Shades lies within the edge, a place of wild magic and unusual creatures. In *A Play of Shadow*, I based the nyim on terrapins, a brackish water turtle. For *A Change of Place*, I wanted something much larger for Jenn to encounter. A powerful creature at home in the water, but unlike a fish. I went with the dugong of Australia's western coast (*Dugong dugon*), a relative of the manatee; an amazing, unexpected sort of mammal. As with my nyim and house toads, my outward changes from the real thing were few. Enlarged eyes. A small change to the visible teeth—if not so much in diet, for waalum, as I called these new and wonderful creatures, like dugong, are grazers. The moment I'd the name and shape, it was off to the writing races!

The sea butterflies? Those, dear reader, are quite real. They are free-swimming snails called Thecosomata and remarkably beautiful. A quick search will turn up videos of them "flying" in the ocean. Isn't nature grand?

We Can Help With That

While I felt confident writing about the Bay of Shades, there was an aspect of Eldad (the southern domain of my world) where I needed help. Trains. Specifically steam engines and everything about them. Roger's brother, Tony Czerneda, is an expert on trains, especially model railroads, but he loves the real sort as well. When I asked, the dear man brought me a stack of very helpful books on his last visit. (Some of which I've returned. The rest are on my shelf because I'm not done with Eldad or trains quite yet.) Tony graciously answered my follow-up questions, hopefully unaware they've only just begun—but what's family for? Thank you, brother!

I elected to have the Marerrym estate, Bannan and Lila's ill-fated childhood home, be a vineyard, because that gave it a plausible income stream plus a necessary reason to ship crates hither and yon. Also, I like wine. Meaning I needed to know about running a vineyard in the early 1800s, that being the era roughly informing the technology of my stories. Lanterns and candles. Coal stoves and steam engines. Fortunately, I'd been reading and enjoying the work of Angelina M. Lopez, who grew up on a vineyard. When I reached out to her, she immediately answered my questions and gave me tidbits I couldn't have guessed. Or googled. Real people know the stuff. Thank you, Angelina! Any mistakes are mine.

At a convention pre-COVID, that being the go-to mark for so

much, Ed Greenwood used the term "DAW wizards" to describe my wonderful publisher. I immediately asked his permission to use it someday, not that I knew when. Fast-forwarding to post-COVID, I knew it had to be in my next Night's Edge novel. Why? Because Ed was the first to read and love *A Turn of Light*. I reread his email about it every so often, not that I don't remember every kind word. Thank you, dear friend.

Put Me in the Story!

A veritable host of dear and familiar folk have wound up in Marrowdell and other settings in Night's Edge. Some generously bid on a character name in support of charity, for which I thank you, most recently through the SFWA charity auction, where Blaine Fleming gave me the name of his niece, Noemi Hope, to use. Others are here as part of a tribute to my now-ended and beloved sff.net newsgroup (which lives on as the Grey Stone Tower on Facebook, if you've missed the company). The rest of the namings were special gifts, from me to you, including the names of Hettie's twins.

To all, I'm privileged to be trusted with your names, or variation thereof, and thank you for any character details you provided. I hope you enjoy the result. (The usual proviso applies, in that I make stuff up to serve the story first and foremost, so it's most likely you won't recognize yourselves. Hence the following list. However, any resemblance you do spot? Please take it as the compliment I intend.)

Here's the full list to date because I'm so happy to share it. Some are characters who are mentioned, but don't appear in the story. Others walked in and took over the place. A few wound up on a map. Again, thank you to all, and I hope you enjoy!

Marrowdell:

Alyssa Ropp—Alyssa Donovan
Elainn Emms—in remembrance of Elaine Lones, from Lance Lones
Hettie Emms (nee Ropp)—Henri Reed
Torre Emms—from Henri Reed
Treff (friend) Frann Nall—Fran Quesnel
Treff, Cynd—Cindy Hodge
Treff, Davi—David Trefor James
Treff, Lorra—Lorraine Vivian James
Treff, Wen—Gwen Veronica James

Outside Marrowdell:

Bish, Emon's companion—Anne Bishop
Caryn Anan (Great Gran)—Caryn Cameron
Clairr River—Claire Eamer
Dawnn Blysse, artisan—Dawn Bliss
Edis Donovar—Edith Starink
Flesie—Florence Giles (Flossie-Mae)
Heathe—Heather Dryer
Herer, Emon's companion—Robert Herrera
Jym Garnden, astronomer in Avyo—James Alan Gardner
Kimm Larmensu, Bannan's great uncle—Kimm Antell
Koevoets and Moniq, fair goers—Monique Koevoets
Kotor and Mila Rivers—Janet, Willem, Leo, and Mila Chase
Larah Anan, Palma's little brother—Lara Herrera
Lehman, infamous author—Susan Lehman
Lenzi—Julie Lenzi
Leott, artisan—Elliot James Godfrey
Lianna, wife of Stevynn—Liana K
Loiss, Bannan's former friend—Lois Gresh
Lornn Heatt, Lila's assumed identity—Lorne and Heather Kates
Marni—Marni Cooper
Palma Anan—Shannan Palma
Renee, Bannan's former friend—Renee E. Babcock

Rhonnda Taff, artisan—Rhonda Donley
Rowe Jonn, Lila's guardsman—Jonathan Crowe
Ruthh, infamous seamstress—Ruth Stuart
Sarra River—Sarah Jane Elliott
Seel Aucoin, Lila's guardsman—Jennifer Seely
Stevynn, artisan—Steven Kerzner
Thomm, artisan—Thomas Czurgai

Thank you all!

We'd Like to Invite You . . .

Bear with me, please, for this section's going to be longer than usual. Why? Because I need to thank my hosts not only from the year past, but for the wonderful events surrounding the release of *To Each This World* and *Imaginings* in 2022. I'm incredibly grateful to all involved.

Like most of my peers, I continued to do virtual events, because we all have the tech now and it's cool. The very best part—other than a fancy top with shorts—is the opportunity to meet folks from far and wide. Not to mention attend events I might not otherwise.

Foremost of those in 2022 was CanVention, where I'd the extraordinary honor to be inducted into the Canadian Science Fiction and Fantasy Hall of Fame. My sincere thanks to this organization and its members, especially Clifford Samuels and Clint Budd.

I conducted workshops, again via Zoom, for Clarion West (my thanks to Rashida Smith) and Fyrecon 6 (thank you, Jenna Eatough). I wish every success to the talented and earnest participants of each. I'm grateful to Ed Willett, Jason DeHart, and Marty Kurylowicz for featuring me in their excellent podcasts.

It was my great privilege to be a guest panelist or speaker for several groups, including the fabulous Ephemera Reading Series (my thanks to KT Bryski); Ashland Public Library's Women in Sci-Fi panel with Lena Nguyen, K. Eason, and Mur Lafferty; Strong Women Strong Worlds (my thanks to Terri Bruce and company); Pro Writing

(Michelle Adams) hosted Dan Hanks, Chris Panatier, and me as we talked about being writerly colleagues across continents; my thanks to Ted Presler and Lillian Galloway of The Southwest Word Festival; and I very much enjoyed being part of DAW Books' virtual Library Fantasy Book Buzz with fellow DAW author Bradley Beaulieu and DAW editors Katie Hoffman and Navah Wolfe. Librarians rock!

Throughout, I'd a most able team on my side. Thank you Sara Megibow, Leah Spann, Kayleigh Webb, Jessica Plummer, and especially Sarah Christensen Fu for your enthusiastic help with events virtual and in person, in some cases lining them up for me, in all cases cheering me on and giving me your tangible and highly appreciated support. One example? Roger had made fabulous trading cards for *Each*—and Sarah arranged for those to be preorder treats. Wow! I felt like royalty.

A special shout-out to Mysterious Galaxy Books. I've wanted to visit you for always but with this pesky continent between us, it was hard to imagine. Then, for *To Each this World*, you found a way, hosting a virtual launch from my kitchen by my dear friend and colleague Marie Bilodeau. Yay!

At last it was time to go in the world, to see you, dear readers and friends. (There were hugs.) Thank you Can*Con 2022 for bringing Becca and Chris from Bakka-Phoenix from Toronto to Ottawa in time for *Imaginings* to launch. I signed so many books! For *Each*, we arranged drop-in signings at every Chapters and Indigo Roger and I could reach, with the generous help of staff there, finishing up with a mind-blowing flashmob signing at Ancaster Chapters (thank you Scott and Vanessa!). And, for the first time since the pandemic, we walked *into* Bakka-Phoenix. A store full of you. My heart was full indeed.

My thanks to Sophie Mathewson and Emily Wolst of Lakehead University, Orillia, for inviting me to speak as part of their TALL series on science fiction and our future in space—with a bonus visit to Manticore Books. Thanks, Michael! I was privileged to be a panelist for the Merrill Library's Women in Speculative Fiction event, with Michelle Sagara and Chinelo Onwualu. My thanks to Ames Geddes,

Isabel Fine, and Kimberly Hull (and to Bakka-Phoenix for the book table).

Roger and I returned to Alfred University at the kind behest of Dr. David DeGraff—astronomer, author, and friend—and we had a wonderful time, especially on telescope night. Our thanks! The trip let us stop at several Barnes and Nobles enroute to sign books and yes, we'll be back!

A highlight of 2023 for me was being a Guest of Honor at the 15th NASFiC, the National Science Fiction Convention (held when the Worldcon isn't in North America). Pemmi-Con was held in Winnipeg, Manitoba. Special thanks to Jannie Shea and Robbie Bourget, as well as all the concom, from my family as well. Your kindness won't be forgotten. A big shout-out to John Toews of McNally-Robinson for efforts above and beyond to get my books to Winnipeg in time, and to my cousin Sue for her gifts of new boa and Esen top! As a bonus? Roger and I saw a great deal of Toastmaster-Extraordinaire Tanya Huff (whom we adore and received a boa as well). Hurray!

Then came Can-Con 2023, in Ottawa, in person. My thanks to the concom, especially Marie Bilodeau and Brandon (I'll catch you yet) Crilly. Sara Megibow was the Agent Guest of Honor and, though I tried not to be selfish because she was there for you, as it worked out we'd a wonderful amount of time together. And she met Roger! (Which, as you know, means he's now her favorite. Happens Every Time.)

It's impossible to fit all the names here of those who've been helpful, gracious, wildly supportive, and made everything better for me and my work these past years. Know I'll remember (I keep lists, in fact) and thank you from the bottom of my writerly heart.

The More Usual Acknowledgments

The summer of 2022 marked monumental changes in my publishing family. My editor-dear and long-time friend, Sheila E. Gilbert, retired. Our collaboration officially began December 1996, but we'd chatted for many years ahead of that. Our last book together would be *To Each This World*, my twenty-third novel with DAW Books. Wow, time seems to have flown. Thank you, Sheila, for your support, your enthusiasm for everything I've tossed your way, your uncountable kindnesses to me, my family, and friends, and for being you. I may be taller (inside joke) but I'll always look up to you.

Another change was the sale of DAW Books to Astra Publishing House. My first book under this new partnership was *To Each This World*, and I can't thank the Astra publicity team enough for how they embraced my book and all they did to promote it during what had to be a complex overlap. (Ask me about the Great ISBN Hiccup next time we're together.) I've been overjoyed by their support—and to have Sarah Christensen Fu now part of the DAW family! I'd also like to take this opportunity to add my warm welcome to the fold to Navah Wolfe, Madeline Goldberg, and Laura Fitzgerald.

To Each This World marked another milestone in my career, being my first title in the able hands of my agent Sara Megibow, of KT Literary. Thank you, Sara, for that and so much more. You've guided me through galaxies of tumult and transition like the fabulous starship captain you are, and I couldn't be more grateful.

Sara also inspired Roger and me to put together my twenty-fifth-anniversary collection, *Imaginings*. A pure joy collaborating with my other half, as I'm sure you can imagine, since he's my favorite, too. Roger's artistic prowess, graphic experience, and skill set produced a wonderful book. (And making decisions shoulder to shoulder whilst sipping wine? Spectacular!)

Ah, but now we come to this book, *A Change of Place*. My first to be edited by long-time DAW editor and terrific person Katie Hoffman. Thank you, Katie!! It's been reassuring having you at the helm—a role I know wasn't easy, given the decade since my last Night's Edge novel, not to mention all you had to do as DAW Books blossomed into its new self. Congratulations and respect!

As for that decade—continuity is hard to come by, yet readers Will Notice, so I'm deeply grateful to DAW Books for bringing Matthew Stawicki back to do this cover, a task he undertook just as beautifully as for the previous novels. The waalum! The bridge! You are a joy to work with, sir. Thank you, Janet Chase, for taking a look at the early draft of this book and pronouncing it phenomenal. Nice word, that. Cyn Wise and Starr Leydic-Burnett took on the task of rereading the earlier books, then combing through this one for continuity. I can't say how reassuring that was! Thank you both. And thanks to Sarah Beth Durst who read it flying to World Fantasy—in raw draft form—and gave the first blurb. Most appreciated. As always, my thanks to Managing Editor Joshua Starr, who stood ever ready to answer the oddest author question. You rock!

This look back wouldn't be complete without expressing my sincere thanks and appreciation to Arley Sorg and Tim Pratt of Locus Magazine, for featuring me in the December 2022 issue. A fantastic experience from interview, to photo shoot, to crying over my copy. Arley also suggested I turn to Natalka Roshak for her wise and generous advice on how to sell a stubborn short story. Thanks, Natalka. We did it!

Boxes packed with homemade treats arrived on our doorstep as wonderful surprises. Thank you, Julie Lenzi and Janet Chase, for sharing your delicious creations. Made our winters considerably brighter.

As it happened, Channing Whitaker and I shared our final deadlines, May 31st: mine for the proofread of this book, his to submit his MFA thesis, a terrific science fiction novel. Channing, it's been my privilege and joy to be your mentor through this process and to accept your completed work. Congratulations, fellow scribe!

Last and never least. To my friends. To my family. I can't write those words without tears coming to my eyes, so I'll leave you with this.

However far we are apart,
Keep Us Close.

Photo by Roger Czerneda

An unabashed romantic and optimist, **Julie E. Czerneda** finds something remarkable wherever she looks. Dragons and magic—and house toads—hold a special place in her heart—and in the heart of her Night's Edge series. As a former biologist, her studies of the natural world heavily influence the imaginative landscapes in these books. *A Turn of Light* and *A Play of Shadow*—the first two books set in Julie's magical world of Marrowdell—won international Aurora Prix Awards for Best SF/F novels. Shortly thereafter, she was awarded membership in the prestigious Canadian Science Fiction and Fantasy Hall of Fame.

Julie always wishes to send her earnest thanks to you, her dedicated and kind readers, as well as to the tireless and passionate team at DAW Books who have shepherded both her fantasy and science fiction novels into bookstores for over twenty years. She is represented by Sara Megibow of kt literary and can be found wilderness camping, gardening, or online at czerneda.com

Julie is thrilled to share that *A Change of Place* will be the first of at least three more Marrowdell books coming soon—in print, ebook and audiobook.